P9-DXT-260

I WENT TO THE BOX AND LOOKED IN.

It was a man, dead, as far as I could tell. At least, I hoped so. He had long, sharp claws where his fingers and toes should have been, and his teeth were long and jagged and looked razor sharp. His expression was a contortion of fury and hatred.

"He looks like the man I killed. Right before I killed him, I mean."

"They all look like that," Martini said quietly.

"What are they? And don't say mutants," I added.

"Superbeings is what we call them," White replied. "Roswell's history is somewhat true. Aliens did crash-land here in the late nineteen-forties. However, when we opened the ship, the aliens were all dead. Our scientists studied them, of course. Different body structures, but they were more like humans than not. There were what we took to be books with them, and those were in a language so different from ours that it took decades to decipher."

"What did the books say?" I asked, wanting to stop looking at the dead superbeing in front of me and not being able to.

"Turned out the aliens were on a mission of mercy," White said. "They weren't the only ones sent out, just the only ones sent to Earth. Their planet had been invaded by a parasitic race. They'd learned how to fight against the parasites, but they knew this would only make other planets targets. So they sent emissaries out to warn the other populated planets of the threat."

"What do the parasites do?"

"Guess," Martini said softly.

When White didn't counter that, I gave what I was in some way hoping was the wrong answer. "The parasite attaches to someone and alters them into a superbeing, capable of great destruction. They're attracted to rage and fear, or whatever pheromones are given off from those emotions. That's how they pick their new host."

DAW Books Presents GINI KOCH's
Alien Novels:

TOUCHED BY AN ALIEN

ALIEN TANGO
(*Available December 2010*)

TOUCHED BY AN
ALIEN
GINI KOCH

MAIN LIBRARY
Champaign Public Library
200 West Green Street
Champaign, Illinois 61820-5193

DAW BOOKS, INC.
DONALD A. WOLLHEIM, FOUNDER
375 Hudson Street, New York, NY 10014

**ELIZABETH R. WOLLHEIM
SHEILA E. GILBERT
PUBLISHERS**
http://www.dawbooks.com

Copyright © 2010 by Jeanne Cook.

All Rights Reserved.

Cover art by Daniel Dos Santos.

DAW Book Collectors No. 1506.

DAW Books are distributed by Penguin Group (USA) Inc.

All characters and events in this book are fictitious.
Any resemblance to persons living or dead is strictly coincidental.

If you purchase this book without a cover you should be aware that this book
may have been stolen property and reported as "unsold and destroyed" to the
publisher. In such case neither the author nor the publisher has received any
payment for this "stripped book."

The scanning, uploading and distribution of this book via the Internet or via any
other means without the permission of the publisher is illegal, and punishable by
law. Please purchase only authorized electronic editions, and do not participate
in or encourage the electronic piracy of copyrighted materials. Your support of
the author's rights is appreciated.

Nearly all the designs and trade names in this book are registered trademarks.
All that are still in commercial use are protected by United States and international trademark law.

First Printing, April 2010
1 2 3 4 5 6 7 8 9

DAW TRADEMARK REGISTERED
U.S. PAT. AND TM. OFF. AND FOREIGN COUNTRIES
—MARCA REGISTRADA
HECHO EN U.S.A.

PRINTED IN THE U.S.A.

To Steve and Veronica,
for being mine and, in your own ways,
always being ready to "bring it."

.

ACKNOWLEDGMENTS:

They say writing is a solitary pursuit, but not the way I do it. Unsurprisingly, therefore, I have a lot of people I want to thank for a variety of reasons.

First off, a huge thank you to my agent, Cherry Weiner, for taking me on even though she had a full list, and for also being the best agent, and friend, any writer could hope to have.

To Sheila Gilbert, my awesome editor, thanks so much for taking a chance on a new author and making the entire publishing and editing process a joy—I'm spoiled by having the best the first time out of the gate.

Special thanks to Lisa Dovichi, critique partner extraordinaire, BBFF and barometer. Could not, literally, have done it without you.

And now, the really long roll call. Thanks to: Phyllis, for saying "of course you can write" way back when and never taking it back; Mary, for being the best and most dedicated beta reader in the world, and Sal, for not complaining about the reams of paper used in the pursuit of this dream; Kay, for always believing in me, even those few times when I didn't; all the girls (and guys) at Innerlooks Salon, for biweekly support and cheerleading; Dixie, for pushing for me to "write funny" for years; Pauline, for always being excited about my writing career and getting everyone around her excited about it, too; Kenne, Joe, Amy, James, Michelle, Keith, and Peggy, for always making even my most minor literary accomplishments sound like I was taking the world by storm; Willie, for speed beta reading and the English Professor eye; Mom, Dad, and Danny for being excited and supportive before they even understood that writing was going to consume my life; Jeanne, Michelle, Melba, Carol, Barbara, Cathy, and Marlene for being there when I had to scream about real life and then reminding me that writing was my real life; all the wonderful women and brave men in Desert Rose—you set a fabulous example of success and made it easy to duplicate; Danielle, Sean and Hilary, for long-distance European atta girls; Josh, partner in crime; Nick, for emotional support and soul cleansing at any time of day, from any and every part of the world; the Big Dawg Pack, for moral as well as writing support; Absolute Write Water Cooler, for education, support and motivation; Brittany, Kathie, Kathy, Norma, Ellen, Evelyn, Amy, Suzella, Jo, Carole, Mike, Christine, Akiko, John, Jill, Miranda, John, Mike, Michelle, Tom, Talene, and everyone else who helped along the way—you know who you are.

Most importantly, love and thanks to my most demanding critics: Veronica, for being supportive, excited, helpful and understanding of her mother's obsession; and Steve, for being the most patient, supportive and understanding husband any writer could hope for, especially after I burned out the fifth PC in a row and all you said was, "Let's go get you a better one."

WHAT GETS ME IS THAT IN ALL THE COMIC BOOKS and movies and even novels, whenever someone gets superpowers, there's at least an eighty percent likelihood they'll use said powers for good.

It's always some man or woman of science looking for a cure for the world's ills who gets hit with the gamma rays, or an outcast kid who happens to have a wise oldster around to show him the right ropes as soon as the mutation hits. The few bad guys who turn superpowered always have some fatal flaw that renders them easy pickings for the good guys, who also manage to outnumber the baddies every time it matters.

In real life, of course, it never works that way. At all.

In real life, there are no superheroes.

Of course, this doesn't mean there are no superpowered beings.

But never fear—I'm on it.

Yeah, it doesn't sound all that comforting to me, either.

CHAPTER 1

MY FIRST SUPERBEING WAS AN ACCIDENT. Literally and figuratively.

I was walking from the courthouse to the parking garage. Jury duty was over, I'd been released early, right after the lunch break, so I was free to go back to work and try to catch up on my missed half a day.

The parking garage was across the street, so I had to wait for the light. As I stood there hoping I wouldn't sunburn, I witnessed a small fender bender. One slow-moving car rear-ended another right in front of the courthouse, about fifty feet away from me.

The drivers got out—man from the front car, woman from the rear—and he started yelling at her immediately. At first I figured he was raging because he'd been hit and the start of summer in Arizona always makes everyone here a little crazy, but I could hear him, and it dawned on me that this was his wife.

She was apologizing, but he wasn't having any of it, so she got mad, too. Their fight escalated into shouting in a matter of moments. This was a full-on domestic dispute, the kind the cops rightly want nothing to do with.

The light changed, and I wondered if I should just head across the street to avoid getting involved with these two when it happened. The man's rage went supernova, and all of a sudden he sprouted wings out of his back.

I'm not talking little wings, either. They were huge, easily six and a half feet high and I guessed the span as double. They had feathers, but they were odd looking, which, I know, you'd figure would be a given in the first place. But they didn't look like bird feathers—they gleamed, and not with blood. There was a viscous substance on them, and as I watched, the man turned toward his horrified, screaming wife and shot blades out of the feathers that lined the wings' edges.

She was cut to ribbons in a matter of seconds, and he turned toward the courthouse and let more blades fly. The main Pueblo Caliente courthouse, a nine-story building with mostly glass walls, was built a few years ago and was really very modern and attractive, doing its best to pretend the city hadn't once been a pioneer cow town.

I flinched as the projectiles hit. Glass shattered and flew everywhere—the courthouse went from sleek to rubble in a matter of moments. I could hear screams—the people coming out of the courthouse, those near the windows in the first few floors, anyone in his path, maybe more—were all being cut down, possibly murdered by this man. I couldn't guess how far the projectiles went; for all I knew, they were going deep into the building.

I don't know why I didn't try to run or hide. In hindsight, I could say maybe I just knew it would be futile. But at the time, that wasn't what I was thinking. I was scared, but more, I was angry, and I just wanted to stop him. He wasn't slowing the attack at all, and I realized he was enjoying it, enjoying the power, the fear, the death.

His back was still to me, and I could see a spot, right between where his shoulder blades had been and wings now were. Something was there, pulsing, almost like a human heart, but it didn't look like a heart. It resembled a small jellyfish, really.

I tried to think of what I could use to stop this monster—it wasn't as though they equipped marketing managers with Uzis. I didn't take my eyes off the pulsing thing on the man's back as I dug through my purse and my fingers found my weapon—my heavy, expensive Mont Blanc pen. It had been a gift from my father when I'd gotten a promotion at work. I doubted this was what he'd hoped I'd use it for, but I wasn't holding any other options.

I dropped my purse, kicked off my heels, and ran, straight for his back. He was moving closer to the courthouse but was still less than a hundred feet away from me, and back in school I'd been on the track team. I was a sprinter and a hurdler, and some things don't leave you, even if you haven't done them for a while.

Because he was a little taller than me, I knew I needed to be airborne when I hit him. I judged it and leaped at the last possible moment. My pen slammed into that jellyfish-like thing on his back just as he started to turn. I could see his eyes—they were wide, glowed red, and no longer looked human.

As I drove the pen into his back, his mouth opened, but he didn't make a sound. His eyes, however, went back to human, and they glazed as I watched them die. Then his body fell forward and mine with it. I scrambled to my feet, covered with ooze from his wings and the exploded jellyfish thing.

The police arrived. After all, many of them had been inside the courthouse. The scene was chaos—people screaming, glass and blood everywhere, sirens in the distance—but as I stared down at the dead body, all I could think about was whether I should retrieve my pen or not.

A man appeared out of nowhere. He was over six feet, big and broad. I didn't register much else, other than his suit, which I was pretty sure was Armani and looked excellent on him, meaning he probably wasn't with the police. My eyes were drawn back to my pen, still sticking out of the dead man's back.

"How did you know what to do?" he asked, without any opening formalities.

"It just seemed . . . right," I answered, winning the Lame Reply Award of the hour. "Can I take my pen out?"

He squatted down and examined the body. He pulled the pen out slowly. I got the impression he was ready to ram it back in if the body gave the slightest indication of coming back to life.

"I saw his eyes. They weren't normal, and then, as I killed him, they went back to human again. And I saw him die," I added. I wondered if I was going to have hysterics and realized I wasn't. I was somewhat relieved.

The man looked up at me. I registered his face now—rather broad features, strong chin, light-brown eyes, dark, wavy hair. Handsome, definitely. I hated myself for it, but I looked immediately to his left hand. No ring. I looked right back at his face, but he'd noticed and grinned. "Jeff Martini. Single. No current girlfriend. And you are?"

"Wondering if I'm going to be arrested." I noted several of Pueblo Caliente's finest bearing down on us with a determined attitude.

Martini stood up. "I don't think so." He turned around. "Our agency will handle it, gentlemen. Please perform crowd control."

The cops all stopped and did what he said, no arguments, no issues. I felt nervous now, much more than I had before.

He turned back to me. "Let's go." As he said this, a large gray limo with tinted windows pulled up across the street. Martini took my arm and led me over.

"I need to get my car," I protested. "And my shoes." I hopped from foot to foot. I contemplated standing on top of Martini's shoes, then figured the brevity of our relationship probably meant I shouldn't.

"Give me the keys," he said.

"I don't think so." I pulled my arm out of his grasp and managed to find a tiny patch of shade to stand in. "What the hell is going on?"

An older man got out of the back of the limo. He was built like Martini but was at least two decades older. They didn't look related, but I was pretty sure they were in the same line of work—whatever that was.

He gave me a long look. "Give Jeffrey your car keys, please. You're wasting time, ours and yours."

"Then I get to sleep with the fishes?" I asked with as much sarcasm as I could muster.

He laughed. "We're not the Mob, we're an authorized world-government agency. You can stay here and be questioned by the police about the death of that unfortunate, or you can come with us."

"You'll tell me what happened? I mean, what really happened?"

"Yes." He moved aside and indicated the car's interior.

"We'll also help you get cleaned up and keep you out of the papers."

"Why?" I didn't move toward the limo or to get my purse.

He sighed. "We need agents. Ours is a dangerous job. And it's a rare thing when a civilian not only has the courage to do what's needed but also the natural instinct to know where and how to kill a superbeing."

I felt a nudge, and as I looked around, Martini handed me my purse. He had my shoes as well. "Pickpocketing part of the trade?" I asked as he tossed my car keys to another man who'd appeared out of pretty much nowhere. Same Armani-clad look, maybe a bit smaller in build, but still obviously one of the crew. "I don't think I fit the agency's look," I added as I grabbed my shoes and put them back on.

Martini grinned again. He had great teeth and a great smile. I was already disgusted with myself for looking for a wedding ring and more now that I was paying attention to his looks while I was possibly teetering on the edge of life or death.

"We can use some female intuition," Martini said. "That's what it was, right? You didn't know what was going on, but you knew what to do."

I shrugged. "I have no idea. Can I have my pen back?"

Martini laughed. "Only if you get into the car with us." He leaned down. "And only if you tell me your name," he whispered in my ear.

My knees went weak then. Somehow, this made it all real, not something I'd wake up from in a moment. I felt myself blacking out, felt Martini catch me and lift me into his arms, and then . . . nothing.

CHAPTER 2

I WOKE UP INSIDE THE CAR. I was sitting up, leaning against someone who had his arm around me. Even the confusion of waking up from fainting didn't cause me to wonder whose arm it was. That I didn't mind made me want to turn myself over to Gloria Steinem as a real failure as a modern woman.

"...think she'll be willing to be an agent?" It was a man's voice, but not Martini's and not the older man's, either. I kept my eyes closed and tried not to change my breathing too much.

"Hope so." This was Martini. "Be nice to have someone easy on the eyes around."

"Jeffrey, this isn't a dating service." This was the older man. "You'd better hope she doesn't slam that pen of hers into your groin when she comes to."

"I didn't give it back to her yet," Martini said with a laugh. I could feel him move a bit. "Can't wait to find out why she used this."

"It was all I had." I opened my eyes to see him holding my pen out to the others in the car. I snatched it out of his hand. It was still covered with slime.

"I'm more interested in how you knew where to stick it." The third man's voice. I looked around and realized Martini and I were facing the back of the car, Martini across from the older man, me across from this one. He was built along the same lines as Martini and the older man—big, handsome, and Armani-clad. He was also bald, and his skin was the kind of black that looks almost ebony.

"All the men handsome in this agency?" I asked the older man. "Because, if so, trust me when I say I can help you recruit all the women you want."

He laughed. "I'm Mr. White."

"Right. And he's Mr. Black?" I said, indicating the man across from me.

"Great sense of humor," the black man said dryly. "No, I'm Paul Gower. But thanks for the compliment. His name really is White. Richard White. Don't call him Dick."

"Unless he acts like one?"

"Not even then," Gower said with a small smile. "Now, you going to impress us with your manners and tell us your name?"

"No. I'm sure you all went through my purse while I was out." I looked up at Martini who contrived to look innocent. "Right. So, you know who I am."

"Actually, you woke up before I could find your wallet," Martini admitted. "I don't know how you found that pen; your purse is like a black hole."

"I prefer to think of it as Mary Poppins' carpetbag. Okay, okay," I added to the looks I was getting from both White and Gower. "I'm Katherine Katt, k-a-t-t, and yes, before you ask the obvious, my parents call me Kitty."

"I like it," Martini said with a sly grin.

"What do your friends call you?" Gower asked.

I gave him a long look. "You're not my friends yet."

White chuckled. "Fair enough, Miss Katt."

"Oh, let's call her Miss Kitty," Martini pleaded.

I wiped the slime on my pen off on his pants. "I'm not gracing that with a response."

"My God, I think I'm in love," Martini said with a laugh. But he didn't take his arm from around my shoulders.

"I'll bet you say that to every girl who stabs some weirdo with a pen." I tried not to think about the fact I liked his arm around me. There was more going on, and I had to stop acting as though we were at a singles bar.

"Only the sexy ones," Martini replied, pretty much wrecking my not-a-singles-bar mind-set.

"I'd have gone with beautiful," Gower said. "Women tend to prefer that compliment."

"But we want her because she's smart and resourceful," White said, and I could hear something in his tone that sounded like my father's when he'd finally had enough and wanted us focused on business.

Martini and Gower heard it too, because they stopped bantering and both looked more serious. Me, I didn't care about White's wants. Yet.

My phone beeped and I pulled it out. I'd missed a lot of calls. "Thanks for not letting me know people were trying to reach me."

"We could hear the phone," Martini said. "Just couldn't find it in that thing."

I took a look at my missed calls list. "Mr. Brill, Caroline, Chuckie, Janet. Normally I'm not so popular at this time of day."

"Maybe they're lonely," Martini said. "Who's Chuckie?"

"A friend, why?" One of my oldest friends, actually, but I didn't see any reason to share this with Martini.

"He the one who has the 'My Best Friend' ringtone?"

"Yes, what of it?"

"Just like to identify the competition early," Martini said with a grin.

"There is no competition, because we are not an item." There, I was back on firm, feminist footing. Besides, Chuckie and I weren't dating, and one fling a few years ago didn't count. "However, I really need to call these people back, particularly my boss, who I'm sure would like to know why I'm not back at the office yet."

White shook his head. "No, we can't allow that, I'm sorry."

My phone rang again. It was Sheila. Martini snatched the phone from me before I could answer it. "Look, that's one of my other oldest friends. I need to answer." The phone stopped ringing, but started right up again.

Martini looked at it. "Amy. Don't tell me, let me guess . . . another old friend?"

"Yeah. Sheila and Amy are my best girlfriends, Chuckie's my best guy friend. I've known them since ninth grade. I really think I need to answer my damn phone."

It stopped ringing again and I snatched it out of Martini's hand.

"So, why does only this Chuckie guy get the special ring-tone?" Martini asked.

"I'm not gracing that question with a response." I looked at my phone. Text messages were pouring in.

"I have to insist that you not contact anyone yet," White said, before I could type a response of any kind. "I assure you, we'll let you return calls in a short while."

I had the feeling White would suggest that Martini crush my phone in his hand if I argued, and Martini looked strong enough to do it. I gave up and shoved my phone back into my purse. "So, what's this actually all about? I mean, I don't think that was a movie set, so how did that man sprout wings?"

White sighed. "I'll tell you about it when we get to headquarters."

"Just where is headquarters? As I mentioned and my missed-call log shows, I'm supposed to be back at work."

"If you join us, you won't be going back there anyway," White said.

"Great health and dental," Martini offered. "Mental health benefits are the best going."

"What about vacation?" I asked as sarcastically as possible.

"I was thinking Cabo, maybe Hawaii. You must look great in a bathing suit, even if you do sunburn," Martini replied without missing a beat. "I'll make sure to put sun-screen all over you, though, I promise."

White gave another sigh, of defeat this time. "We'll ex-plain it to you as soon as we can pry you away from Jeffrey here."

"Not gonna happen," Martini said cheerfully. "She's looking, I'm looking, no rules about intercompany rela-tionships, so get used to us as a couple."

"Geez, you sure are confident I'm going to throw myself at you." I wondered if this really was his usual way with women, or if he was going to turn out to be some insanely desperate, smothering, clingy man who proposed on the first date and then stalked his exes after they ran screaming into the street to escape him.

"Nope. You just think we're all hot, and I know how to stake a claim early." Martini nodded to Gower. "Make sure you spread it around—she's mine."

Gower shook his head. "He'll propose on the first date, but don't let it panic you. He's not as mentally unstable as he seems, as unflattering as that last comment might be taken by you. Jeff here just knows what he wants quicker than most of us."

"Great." I looked back over to White, who seemed both amused and frustrated. "Where, exactly, is this headquarters? I'm asking because I live around here, and I know the fastest routes to the airport at any given time, and we are clearly heading to the airport."

White smiled. "You are just what I've been hoping for."

CHAPTER 3

IT TURNED OUT HEADQUARTERS was in New Mexico, of all places. Several miles outside of Roswell, New Mexico, to be exact.

It was a short plane flight from Saguaro International. Of course, they had a private jet, gray and mostly unmarked. The limo driver was also the pilot, and he fit the mold, though like whoever had my car, he was smaller than Martini.

During the flight I made several *Men in Black* jokes that weren't met with a great deal of real or even forced laughter, and Martini continued to use his considerable charm to make me unsure whether I should start picking out china patterns or consider plastic surgery in addition to going into my own version of the witness protection program in order to make sure he'd never be able to track me.

On the plane I got a chance to take a look at myself, and I figured Martini was just playing around, because I was a disaster. Barring this group having the best dry cleaners in the world on staff, my suit was ruined. My hair was a mess, and my face was dirty. My shoes and purse were about all that had survived relatively unscathed. I decided not to care and felt I could maybe read the Feminist Manifesto again without total shame.

Against all commercial air flight rules, I was allowed to send text messages to those who had called or sent texts to me, mostly because the list kept on growing and Martini wouldn't let me actually speak to anyone. He also insisted on reading my texts over my shoulder, which he said was for security reasons but seemed more so he could lean over me and breathe in my ear.

Everyone other than Chuckie seemed to take "I'm okay but with the police and don't know when I'll be free" in stride. It didn't surprise me that his response was to let him know immediately if I was actually in trouble. He'd been given the nickname Conspiracy Chuck in high school, and, much as I hated to admit it, it was apt. Of course, all things considered, this seemed conspiratorial in some way, so maybe Chuckie wasn't that far off.

The trip from the lonely airstrip where we landed to our destination was fast, made in a large, gray SUV. I made a Men in Gray joke that also fell flat. Apparently these guys were not fans of humorous science fiction.

We reached what I assumed was headquarters, possibly the most unexciting building I'd seen in a long time. Corrugated steel, which I figured made the place like an oven inside, painted in good old Navaho White, the most boring of paint choices. It was trimmed in taupe. Nothing could have said "industrial boredom" better.

"Wow. If a building's importance is directly proportional to how dull, dingy, and unassuming it looks, you guys must work for the most important agency in the world."

"We do," White said quietly as he opened the thick metal door marked "Employees."

He ushered me inside, and I was treated to a spectacle of—not very much. Boxes and crates of all different sizes, mostly. It was a warehouse, and I had guessed the interior temperatures correctly.

"Color me totally unimpressed. What is this, prank week at the mental institution? Or is this the Armani outlet, and you're just letting me in on some super deals early?"

"She can tell the designer," Martini said under his breath. "Amazing."

"Focus, man, focus," Gower said in the same tone. "Pull it damn together, Jeff. You're freaking her out. And me, too."

"I think she likes it," Martini replied with a grin.

"So, the real thing's underground, right?" I asked White, doing my best to ignore the other two for right now. "Or are you going to push a button and then everything will flip around and become all impressive?"

"Neither," White answered. He went over to one of the crates, nodded to Gower and Martini, and the two of them pried the lid off. "Take a look," White said. It was an order, not a suggestion.

I decided I was dead if they wanted to kill me anyway, so it wasn't as though giving them the opportunity to push me into a big box was being more foolhardy than anything else I'd done all day. I went to the box and looked in.

"Oh." I wasn't screaming, and I was really proud of myself. Martini moved next to me, and I knew without asking that he was ready to catch me if I fainted again. I found this comforting because what I was looking at wasn't comforting at all.

It was a man, dead, as far as I could tell. At least, I hoped so. He had long, sharp claws where his fingers and toes should have been, and his teeth were long and jagged and looked razor sharp. His expression was a contortion of fury and hatred.

"He looks like the man I killed. Right before I killed him, I mean."

"They all look like that," Martini said quietly. "The faces are different, some men, some women, but they all end up looking at humans like this."

"What are they? And don't say mutants," I added.

"Superbeings is what we call them," White replied. "It's not a perfect description but it's good enough."

"How?"

"Roswell's history is somewhat true," White said. "In that aliens did crash-land here in the late nineteen-forties. However, when we opened the ship, the aliens were all dead. Our scientists studied them, of course, but they didn't find anything of much interest. Different body structures, but they were more like humans than not. There were what we took to be books with them, and those were in a language so different from ours that it took decades to decipher."

"It took a supercomputer," Gower interjected. "No one made any decent strides until the eighties."

"What did the books say?" I asked, wanting to stop

looking at the dead superbeing in front of me but not being able to. This creature would never protect the weak and helpless, you could see it in every part of him.

"Turned out the aliens were on a mission of mercy," White said. "They weren't the only ones sent out, just the only ones sent to Earth." He let that one sink in for a bit before he continued. "Their planet had been invaded by a parasitic race. They'd learned how to fight against the parasites, but they knew this would only make other planets targets. So they sent emissaries out to warn the other populated planets of the threat."

"What do the parasites do?"

"Guess," Martini said softly.

When White didn't counter that, I gave what I was in some way hoping was the wrong answer. "The parasite attaches to someone and alters him or her into a superbeing, capable of great destruction. They're attracted to rage and fear, or whatever pheromones are given off from those emotions, and that's how they pick their new hosts."

"I say it again, she's mine," Martini said.

"And," Gower added, "because the parasite amps up everything, the emotions are enhanced to the point where the host isn't able to think rationally."

"Under most circumstances," White corrected. "There have been some who were able to control it."

"Good guys?" I managed to pull my gaze away from the clawed beast in the box.

White shook his head. "There are no good ones, not that we've ever run across. There have just been some who have been able to control their reactions to the parasite and successfully survive. Until we find and stop them."

"How does anyone survive being like . . . that?" I pointed to the thing in the box.

"Those few who can control the parasite in some way are able to revert to human form. We aren't sure if they're aware of the parasite or not." White looked sad for a moment.

This struck me as odd. "Why not?" No one answered but they all looked uncomfortable and a little embarrassed. "So, you aren't sure because you've never caught any of them, right?"

"No," Gower said. "We've caught them. But only in their superbeing form."

"No," Martini corrected. "We've killed them in their superbeing forms."

"You've got this monster in a box. Why not box up these other ones?"

"They're a lot harder to kill, the in-control ones," Martini added. "Hard to follow them back to their lair or whatever when you're dead or injured. And so far we've only been able to stop them by destroying them. Not a lot of pieces left kind of destruction."

"The longer a superbeing can remain in control, the stronger it grows," Gower added. "We have a few we know of that have survived for years. They stay dormant, in whatever their human form is, until something triggers them. We haven't been able to determine who they are in human form." He looked just a little uncomfortable—I had a feeling he wasn't telling me everything. However, I wasn't in a position to push it.

"Nice. How long have they been around?"

"The first ones showed up right about the time we'd made a little headway in the translations," White said. "So, call it the late sixties, early seventies. We'd gotten enough to know the aliens were warning us about something, so when the first superbeings appeared, it wasn't a complete shock."

I thought about it. "They showed up in Vietnam, didn't they? The rage from both sides would have drawn them, right?"

"Oh, yes," White said quietly. "The unrest that war caused undoubtedly drew the parasites here. But both sides were able to destroy them. The superbeings become somewhat invulnerable, but when you're using machine guns and tanks, you can destroy them nine times out of ten."

"What if you kill the human part but not the parasite part?"

"You can't kill the host unless the parasite wants it dead. The parasites can move, but it's iffy. It's not just the strong emotions—there has to be some connection between parasite and host for the pairing to take."

"If you hadn't killed it first try, it might have moved to you," Martini offered.

"Thanks a lot. So, I'm being recruited because I'm homicidal maniac material?"

"No," he said with a touch of impatience. "They like strong people, but not just physically strong. They like bravery, intelligence, compassion."

"They're looking for a love connection?" I was back to hoping I'd wake up soon.

"In a way," Martini said with a shrug. "They want to live, they have to live with the host, why not have it be someone they like?"

"If they like all that, why do they turn their hosts into these . . . horrible things?"

"They aren't horrible things to *them*," Gower answered.

I thought about it again. "They don't belong here, so what they adapt their hosts to don't belong here, either. On the right world, they'd be a benefit. But on the wrong ones, they're a plague."

"Yes," White said. "But from what the aliens' books told us, the right world for these parasites died when its sun went supernova. Instead of destroying the parasites, it sent them into the far reaches of space, searching for hosts so they could fully live again."

"It would be sad if they weren't turning humans into horrifying, murderous creatures." I shook myself. "But they are. So, what's in the rest of the boxes? More of them?"

"Yep," Martini said. "Your little friend'll be here soon. Just have to preserve, box, and ship him on over."

"In my car?"

"Hardly. But don't worry, I'll take you wherever you need to go."

"I feel so lucky. Why save them all, especially if they're not leading you to the scarier ones?" I directed this question to White.

"We need the proof. We also have scientists who do tests on the bodies, to see if we can spot similarities so we can predict the people more likely to be potential hosts."

"You do all this here?" I looked around. "I don't buy that for a minute."

"No," White said with a chuckle. "This is just the first stop."

Something wasn't adding up right, many things, really,

but I decided not to argue or point out my concerns yet. "Show me more of them."

As we went around the room on my personal horror tour, more agents arrived, two of whom were carting in a new box. Extra large. One of the agents was the guy who'd taken my car keys. The other with him was great looking, just like the rest of them.

It was hot and I was sweating, yet none of the bodies in the containers were decomposed or even smelly. I put my hand inside some of the boxes, with White's permission. Just as hot in there.

A few more agents came in and out, some carting boxes with dead superbeings, some just milling about. All of them were male, and while there were standard variations in body types, facial structures, coloration and the like, all of them would be classified as handsome by the majority of the population. Lots of hunky agents were here—and none of them other than the set with me had come through the only door. I wasn't sure how they'd gotten in, but however it was, it wasn't via normal means.

There was nothing else in this warehouse, but I was outnumbered by a lot. Not that I thought I'd have a chance against White without help, let alone any of the others.

I leaned up against the large box that held my personal superbeing, crossed my arms, and gave it my best shot at not sounding scared and freaked out. "What's really going on?"

CHAPTER 4

"WHAT DO YOU MEAN?" White asked in a very calm tone. But I wasn't looking at him. I was looking at Martini and Gower, and both of them looked guilty.

"I mean that some things don't add up." Martini wasn't looking at me, and I was pretty sure it was because he was trying not to give anything away.

"Like what?" White asked pleasantly.

"Like all of you, for starters." I looked around. "You're all too good-looking. I'll bet when I meet some scientists, they'll all be hunks, too. While it's a great fantasy, there's no way this many great-looking men would all be working in one agency, unless it's a modeling agency."

"That's all? You're worried about our looks?" White seemed amused.

"No, it's just the start. This isn't a headquarters, so you brought me here to show me the bodies. I guess it makes sense as an initiation ritual. But it's too damn hot in here. On Earth we keep dead things we want to preserve very cold, not very hot. Everything in here is roasting, me included, but I'm pretty much the only one breaking a sweat. Everyone else and everything in these boxes is just fine. That's not normal, for this world at least."

"What else?" White still seemed calm and unconcerned. Of course, he had backup and I didn't.

"You all seem to move too fast. You appear out of nowhere, no one tries to stop you, the cops do what you tell them without argument. That's not normal, either. And you claimed there was nothing of interest in an alien spaceship other than some manuals. Sorry, but that doesn't ring true no matter what. The metal, the components, everything that made the thing fly, all of that would be of huge scientific importance. NASA would have an interest, even if no other government agency did. Aliens that are more like humans than not would be hugely interesting, just as interesting as if they were nothing like us. Every single thing in that spaceship, starting with its mere existence, would be fascinating to anyone with at least a normal IQ."

"What do you think this all means?" White asked me. He seemed interested in my answer but not worried.

"You come from Planet Hunk, sent to Earth to protect and serve. And make the ladies happy."

Martini started to laugh, which was sort of a relief. He finally looked at me again, and I was interested to see that his expression hadn't changed much from what I was getting used to. He looked confident and interested and intelligent, but like White, he didn't look worried.

Gower shook his head. "You gotta give it to her, boss. She's a smart one."

"It's a little more complicated than that," White said.

"Well, gee, I have the time."

White shook his head. "Not here."

"No, *right* here. I'm tired of the game, whatever it is. You tell me what's going on or you take me home and leave me the hell alone for the rest of my life. And that would include you," I directed to Martini. He just grinned.

"No. It's easier to explain if you can see it," White countered.

"See what?"

"The crash site. Our Science Center in Dulce, New Mexico. And Home Base."

"The UFO Tour," Martini added cheerfully. "There are a lot of folks who'd pay good money for this."

"All of them considered crackpots." One of them being one of my best friends, too, but that wasn't important right now. "Of course, since they're apparently right, I guess we should call them intuitive government whistle-blowers."

White shrugged. "There are reasons to lie. I'm sure you

can guess most of them. But that's not the point. Yes, we brought you here as a test. You needed to see that there were more of them, many more, than just the one you'd experienced yourself."

"What else?" I asked. "I mean, there has to be more to why you brought me here, first, than just to give me a private tour of the Museum of the Grotesque."

"I wanted to see you sweat," Martini said. "I think it's sexy. You do it really well, too."

"You could have done that back home and saved a fortune in jet fuel."

"It's worth the cost. Not every day we recruit a hottie from Hot Town." Martini was grinning as though he thought this was the first time someone had tried that one on me. Every female in Pueblo Caliente had heard a variation on that line by the time she was twelve.

Gower rolled his eyes. "This may explain why we don't have a lot of female operatives."

"Because of Mr. Horndog here?" It was a toss-up between that or Cliché Man, and I went for the more obvious trait.

"I'm not a horndog," Martini protested. "I just like you. The rest of them, pah, they're nothing."

"Not buying it. Not buying any of it." I looked around again. There were more men in here now, all of them clearly agents like Martini, White, and Gower. All of them were watching me and only me.

A loud ringing started, which caused me and several of the men to jump. I recovered first and dug my cell phone out of my purse.

"Don't answer that," Martini told me.

"I thought you took that away from her on the plane," I heard White say to Martini.

"I would have, but she hid it back in her bag on the plane," Martini replied. "Finding her keys was the only easy thing about that purse. You feel free to search through it for anything. Maybe the contents only respond to their owner or something, but it's a nightmare in there."

"She's a woman," Gower chimed in.

I checked who was calling and flipped the phone open. "Hi, Dad," I said as loudly as possible.

"Jeez, Kitty, stop screaming. Your mother is freaking out and wanted me to call."

"What's wrong with Mom?"

"She says she saw you tackle a terrorist at our court-house on the news, while she was in the airport waiting for her plane."

"Dad? Can you hold on a second, please?" I covered the mouthpiece and looked over at White. "Just when was that 'we'll keep you out of the papers' thing supposed to happen?" As I asked, it dawned on me that Amy was in France, Sheila lived on the East Coast, and Chuckie was most likely in Australia, which meant my little escapade had made not only the Pueblo Caliente news, but the news of the world.

"Why?" he asked, looking worried.

"Because I wasn't too upset by my boss, half of my coworkers, my best male friend, some of my sorority sisters, my two best girlfriends, the guy at Blockbuster, and my landlord checking in on me earlier, but apparently my mother, who is on a business trip in New York, saw her only child tackle a terrorist on the six o'clock news, and she's a little freaked."

White looked at the man I recognized as the one who'd been the recipient of my car keys. "What the hell happened, Christopher?"

Christopher shrugged. "I keep telling you, handheld electronics make our jobs a lot harder. Someone got the entire thing on their video cell phone and streamed it on the Net. We were able to alter the superbeing to look like he was carrying a load of explosives and semiautomatic weapons. No time for anything else, including editing out the princess here."

I decided to hate him. "Just where is my car?"

Christopher gave me a lazy grin. "It's parked somewhere safe. But not at your apartment. I fed your fish, though."

"Aren't you Mr. Thoughtful."

"Better than being the Horndog."

White interrupted this exchange of wit. "So the entire world has seen her, not just the local news?"

Christopher shrugged. "Sounds like it."

I went back to the phone. "Dad, I'm with Homeland Security. Everything's okay. I used the pen you gave me to stop the lunatic. I didn't get hurt, and I'm not in trouble, just taking care of debriefs and that sort of stuff."

"So, you did tackle a terrorist?" I could hear pride and fear warring for dominance. "I didn't see it, I've been with my grad students all day, prepping for finals and summer session." In other words, a typical day in early May for my dad. At least one of us had the comfort of a routine going on.

"I didn't know he was a terrorist, Dad. I just sort of . . . reacted. One of those once-in-a-lifetime hero things. Nothing to worry about."

"Right." He sighed. "Well, your mother will be relieved to know you're okay, and probably more thrilled about this than I am. You sure the Homeland Security people aren't going to ship you off to Guantánamo Bay?"

"Dad, would they have let me keep my cell if they were doing that?" Of course, the reality was they just hadn't found it or snatched it away from me, but for some reason, I felt that I had to protect them. White, for one, was looking particularly grateful.

"I suppose. I'll call you every couple of hours, just in case. If you don't answer, I'm calling the police. Where are you, now? Still in town?"

"Not exactly." I thought like mad. "They took me to Vegas. Apparently there's some big Homeland Security facility there."

"In Vegas?" he asked, clearly incredulous. "We have a Federal building downtown and they took you to Sin City?"

"Perfect cover. Who would suspect?" I was amazed at how easily making this crap up was coming to me. Martini looked particularly impressed, and even Christopher seemed to be sneering at me a little less.

"Makes sense. Did they give you the pen back?"

"Yes, Dad. They took all the samples they needed, cleaned it, and it's back in my possession." That was my father in a nutshell—do you still have the expensive gift I got you? Not that he was materialistic, it's just that spending large sums made him nervous, so it was a real occasion when he did.

"Good. Okay, check your watch, let's make sure we're on the same time."

"Dad, for God's sake."

"Fine, fine. I'll set the alarm so I'll wake up in the night, too."

This was going to be hell, but then again, how did I know they weren't going to do something to me? "Okay, Dad. But if, like at four in the morning, I tell you to not call again, you'll understand, right?"

"Sure, Kitty. I know you're a grump when you wake up, just like your mother. Maybe we'll take the calling in shifts."

"Dad, Mom's going to have jet lag. Let her sleep."

"Her daughter just stopped a terrorist. I think she'll be wired."

"Great, then yeah, let her call, too. Maybe the rest of the family can go round robin with it."

"Great idea! I'll make some calls between now and the next two hours."

"Dad . . . joke. Really, a joke. Please don't call anyone else. I think the Department is worried I'll become a target for attack. Let's not give them any reason to be right." I was good at this. I'd almost never lied to my parents in my entire life, and now I was lying to my father like a natural.

"Okay." I could hear the disappointment. "Not even your uncle?"

"Definitely not Uncle Mort." Uncle Mort was a career Marine heading into his fourth decade with the Corps and the last person I wanted advised. Unless, of course, I was in danger. Then I wanted Uncle Mort to rally the troops and come save me. However, Uncle Mort would be likely to know there was no Homeland Security facility in Las Vegas. "I don't want him to feel like he has to come or something. I'd like to do this on my own."

"Okay, kitten. I understand. I'll only call Uncle Mort if you don't answer the phone."

That I could get behind. "Sounds good. But, Dad, remember, in the wee hours, try calling more than once. If I'm safe and asleep, I may not hear the phone even if I have it right by me."

"Three times, that's it. You don't answer, I call in the Marines."

"Great, perfect plan. I'll talk to you, well, every two hours for a while. So, love you, gotta go now."

"Love you, too. Be good, and don't let them push you around. You're a hero, and heroes deserve respect."

"Will do." I closed the phone and looked back to White. "My father will be calling me every two hours from now until I'm released by Homeland Security. He has an extensive network of friends and family, and despite my telling him not to, I'll bet he calls a few of them anyway. Your move." I looked at Christopher. "Oh, and nothing had better happen to my parents, either."

Christopher shrugged. "I'm image control, not eliminations."

"Great." I turned back to White. "So?"

"So," he sighed, "we have two hours to convince you to tell your father that all's well."

"Give or take. He's willing to call regularly for days. This is probably fun for him."

"I guess we'll have to time things out," Martini said. "Don't want him calling at an inopportune moment. Could ruin the mood. Though I'm used to waking up at odd hours."

"So far, I see it as a nonissue," I told him. He just grinned again.

"We need to go," White said.

"Nope. I want some answers. Start with the boys here," I indicated the rest of the crew with my cell phone, right before I dropped it back in my purse. "I'd like to know if I'm dealing with aliens or just weirdos."

"Both," Martini interjected before White could open his mouth. "I'm the only normal one."

"I weep for our species. Mr. White? I'd really like some honesty. And I'd like it now."

CHAPTER 5

WHITE HEAVED A SIGH. "It's complicated. Can we compromise, and I tell you about it while we travel to the crash site?"

I decided it might be a good idea to acquiesce, particularly since Christopher and some of the guys near him looked as though they'd be willing to just beat me over the head and solve the issue that way. "Fine. Start while we're walking to the car."

He nodded, and Martini and Gower moved and flanked me. "Don't mind Christopher," Gower said in a low voice. "He's upset that he screwed up. Your picture out there creates huge issues to fix."

"He's gay," Martini added.

"No, I'm not," Christopher said from right behind me. I managed not to jump. "But the princess here isn't my type."

"I'm crushed."

"Don't be. I like 'em stupid." Christopher walked around us and headed to the door to the parking lot, which he held open. Apparently he was now part of my entourage. Accordingly, I took a closer look. He was at least six inches shorter than Martini, but still taller than me by at least a few, so I called him about five-ten. Straight brown hair, green eyes, slender but clearly well muscled. Handsome, of course. There were, I had to admit, worse ways to go than surrounded by this much drool-worthy manflesh. Thing was, I didn't want to go.

"So, I'm not hearing an explanation," I said to White, who was now next to Gower.

"This building we're leaving is the holding facility. You're right, it's hot. When the superbeings create, they alter so much that they aren't human at all, not really of this world any longer. Therefore, they preserve in the heat. We have a high heating bill in the winter."

"So their world was close to the sun that went supernova?"

"We assume." White sounded impressed. "You're very bright."

"Which is why Christopher there isn't ready to settle down with me, like Martini is. We've established that. I'm sort of the open book in this library, let's not forget. No cracks," I said, quickly, looking up at Martini. "I really want some answers."

He nodded with fake solemnity, and White went on. "You're right, there was plenty in the spaceship beyond books, and yes, we've been studying everything since the crash itself."

There was something about the way he said the word "we" that made me stop. "You aren't really with the American government, are you?"

"Well," White said, as Martini gently but firmly took my arm and started me moving again, "we do have some American government people involved and in the know. But I told you already, we're a world organization."

"Which world?"

I could see I was right by the way White's eyes shifted, just a bit. "In the car," was all he said, though. The car was another gray limo; I decided they must be standard issue. It wasn't the same one I'd been in before, which was a relief.

Christopher held the door to the back seats open for me, and I climbed in, humming the *Men in Black* theme song. I made sure I was in the forward-facing seat, so I could see the driver as well as the other passengers.

"They're fictional," Martini said. He got in and settled himself right next to me. "I'm real," he added as he put his arm around my shoulders.

"Real annoying," Christopher said as he closed the door after White and Gower, then climbed into the front passenger seat. I wasn't sure I disagreed, though I didn't protest about the arm or the fact that Martini had pulled me closer. I felt safer next to him for some reason, illogical or not.

Our usual driver and pilot took the wheel. "Care to tell me who this is?" I asked White.

"James Reader," White answered, somewhat reluctantly I thought.

"I'm a human, like you," Reader said, turning around and flashing me a toothy grin. "I actually *was* a male model, if you want an autograph."

I felt my jaw drop. "Oh, my God, I recognize you! You did the big Calvin Klein spread a few years ago that raised so much controversy."

"Which one was *that*?" Gower asked. "Isn't controversial pretty much the definition of a Calvin Klein ad campaign?"

Reader grinned again. It was an awesome grin, making Martini's seem just ordinary. "Mine had the *most* controversy. Then I retired at the height of my fame to pursue my passions. Which was the cover story for joining up with this crew." He winked at me. "Don't worry, babe. They're okay. Odd in their way, but okay. I'll look out for you, even keep the horndog here at bay if you want me to."

"He really is gay," Martini said.

"Yeah, but that doesn't mean I'm gonna let anyone hassle my homegirl here," Reader said as he turned around. "We humans have to watch each other's backs, or you aliens are gonna take all the credit for saving the world." Reader started the car, and we drove off.

I looked out the windows—there were several gray SUVs moving out with us. "All the boys coming along?"

"All the ones here, yes," White said. "We have to make sure you're protected."

"Um, why?"

"You were identified as stopping a terrorist, who the media have decided was part of the Al Dejahl terrorist organization," Christopher answered in a clipped tone. I got the feeling Gower was right—he wasn't happy about this screw up. "That'll alert any superbeings who might be in control to the fact you're a threat."

"Great. So, what planet are you from?"

Gower was the one who answered, which I found interesting. "We can't pronounce our native language here— humans can't understand it."

"Worse than Yiddish," Martini added.

Gower rolled his eyes. "Jeff, shut up. We're from the Alpha Centauri system. You call our suns Alpha Centauri A and B. We call them, well, the big sun and the little sun. And our world, the world. In our own language, of course. People are more alike than you'd realize, even people from different planets."

"So, you're saying you're humans?" I was taking this very well and was rather proud of myself.

"No, only Earth has humans. There are real differences, significant ones."

"We're better in bed," Martini whispered to me.

"Jeff!" Gower looked as fed up as he sounded. "Give it a rest for the whole five minutes it'll take me to explain this."

"Fine," Martini sighed. He slid down in the seat a bit. "I'll behave."

Gower gave him a look that said he didn't believe a word of it, then went on. "We were one of the planets the original aliens warned, just like Earth. We call the aliens Ancients, because their race was much older than ours. The ship that arrived at our planet didn't crash, but the crew couldn't survive in our atmosphere. The ones who landed here would have died as well. Their world, we've figured out, was a lot closer, spacewise, to the one the parasites came from than ours or yours, and it made them very different from our two races."

"They reached our world a hundred years before yours," White added. "We didn't have good enough space travel to reach any other inhabited world for decades after they landed, though."

Gower nodded. "We got most of what we needed from the Ancients' spaceship. Just as Earth scientists did and are still doing today. But we've had more time than you."

"Earth did a better job with translation," Christopher added.

"True," Gower agreed. "We were clear a menace was coming, and we could figure out that more worlds than ours were warned. They had a star map, and we used it to determine which worlds were the ones presumed in danger."

"We came to Earth to help," White added. "You needed us. You still do."

"So these brilliant Ancients set out to warn all the worlds, and they don't wear space suits? How stupid is that?" I felt bad for asking, but it had to be said.

"You go, girl," Reader called from the driver's seat. "That was my first question, too. You'll love the answer."

"They thought they could adapt," Gower said in a resigned tone. "They were shapeshifters from all we can tell, and they'd been able to do it before. But their planet was closer to the galactic core than ours are, and things are different there than out here."

"So how many planets is it safe to assume they couldn't adapt to?" I felt a pang of pity for these Ancients, doing their best to save the galaxy and in a way failing before they could even begin.

"Most of them," Gower said with a sigh. "Most of the inhabited planets are far from the core, not near it. We don't know why. We've been too busy fighting to keep this threat at bay to do any form of exploration."

"They might be figuring it out back home," Martini added. "But we don't know. Radio waves take forever to get through, so communications is pretty poor. None of us are going back, but we knew that coming here." For the first time since I'd started this journey he didn't look confident or happy—he looked lonely and sad.

"You leave a lot of family back there?" I asked quietly—it wasn't a raucous moment.

"Not a lot. No wife," he added with his normal smile.

"Oh, thank goodness." Glad to see that moment of personal exposure wasn't going to last longer than a nanosecond. Not that I could blame him. They might be aliens, but they were also clearly men.

"Most of us don't have immediate family back on our home world," Gower said. "Our families are here."

"What do you mean, here?" This was getting weirder by the moment.

"We perfected a transference system, where we don't

need spaceships to get here," White replied. "It works very well to send us from our home world to Earth."

"But we can't go back," Christopher added. "Our world's core is different from Earth's; the magnetic pull here won't allow the system to work in reverse. So, for some, it was better to send the whole clan out."

"Why so? That seems odd, really."

"It's how they are," Reader said. "Think of them like a huge extended Italian family and you'll be on the right track."

"You're all related?" I looked around. "That would explain the hunkiness, but not your skin tone," I said to Gower.

He shrugged. "My father married an African-American woman. Earth genes dominate over A-C ones, at least the ones that deal with physical appearance."

"So you're an alien-human hybrid?"

"Yep. Jeff's a pure alien, though," Gower added with a chuckle.

"My parents both came as operatives," Martini said. "I'm Earth-born but full A-C blood. Same with Christopher and most of our younger agents."

"So, you're U.S. citizens?"

"Yep, with all the rights therein," Martini confirmed. "We're also considered political refugees, almost like the Indian Nations."

"We have various areas assigned to us," Gower added. "All over the world but centered here in the U.S. Super-beings can and do form anywhere and everywhere, but for whatever reason, they seem to land in the U.S. about twenty times more often than elsewhere."

"Go U.S.A. What about you?" I asked White. "When did you arrive?"

"I came as a young man," he said. "Those of us who weren't born here are naturalized citizens. It's important that we show loyalty to the country that accepted us."

"So you're a native from Alpha Centauri?"

"Yes, I was born on A-C, though I now consider myself an American. My wife came with me. She felt the same."

I thought about it. Christopher's surliness was suddenly even more understandable. "Your son favors his mother, I see. Must be hard, screwing up in front of your dad."

Christopher turned around, and he looked furious. But I could really see it now—the same eyes, nose, and mouth as White. "Better than lying to my father," he spat out.

"But not as useful *or* fun." I looked up at Martini. "So, where do you fit into the family?"

He grinned. "I call him *Uncle* Mr. White. And that's Cousin Paul," he added with a nod toward Gower. "His father is my mother's sister's husband's brother."

"I can't wait to see how you all handle Christmas. So, your father is Uncle Mr. White's brother?"

"Nope, my mother is his sister. Keep the last names straight." He looked over at Gower. "She's starting to slip. Christopher might get interested after all."

"Not likely," he snapped.

I gave up trying to keep the family relationships straight. I figured I'd ask Dad to map them into his family tree software program once I knew if I was making it out of this alive or not. "So, how many Alpha Centaurites are there here on Earth?"

"Alpha Centaurions," Christopher corrected in a snippy tone.

"We call ourselves A-Cs," Gower said quickly. "Trust me, it's easier. And, there are several thousand of us. Not all are working as agents, of course."

"Not all are amazingly hot looking men? Wow, crushing news. Of course, I don't have any really moronic girlfriends to fix Christopher there up with anyway." He didn't reply, but I could see his neck turning red. I wondered if I'd ever see my car again, then decided that was the least of my worries. "So, what do all the female A-Cs do for fun and profit?"

Reader was the one who answered, as we pulled up to an area enclosed by a high, nasty-looking chain-link fence topped with barbed wire that meant business. "They're the scientists."

CHAPTER 6

THE GATE SWUNG OPEN, but there was no indication of an electronic eye or any kind of mechanism. There were also no people around.

"How does it do that?" I asked Martini.

"Well, there's these things called hinges, they move and let the part we call a gate open up, and—" I elbowed him in the ribs, hard, before he could finish.

"I have the beeper," Reader told me. "It's just a garage door opener, really."

This was a letdown, but, oh, well. I looked out the windows. There wasn't much around, but the fencing seemed to go on for miles. "Where are we?"

"The ranch where the Ancients' ship crashed," Gower answered.

"This is the real one," Reader added. "There's a fake the government runs that tourists and UFO theorists think is the real crash site."

"Why? I mean, why show me a crash site? Wasn't it picked clean years ago?" The wisdom of hiding a real UFO crash site wasn't something I needed explained.

"As far as the fake site and the general public knows, yes." Gower gave me a friendly smile. "Relax, we're not taking you out here to kill you and bury your body off the beaten track."

"It's just stop two on the UFO Tour," Martini added.

"You'll love it. Most women want to marry the first alien they've met after seeing the crash site."

"I killed the first alien I met," I reminded him.

"Nope, that was a superbeing," Martini corrected cheerfully. "None of us from A-C are superbeings, other than in the sack."

"I'm sure. Just in case, though, I have great cell phone reception, and I'm sure my dad can get a call through."

"You worry too much," Martini said. "Want a Coke?"

"You have that?"

"It's a limo," Reader reminded me. "We have more than Coke."

"But since your fridge was only stocked with Coke products and frozen dinners, we thought we'd be nice," Christopher said. He looked over his shoulder at Martini. "Nothing but junk food. Good luck ever seeing a home-cooked meal from that one."

"I'll manage. I'm all about the nice restaurant experience," Martini said as he produced an iced glass bottle of Coca-Cola from the inside of the door next to him, popped the cap off, and handed it to me. "Straw?"

"Thanks." I decided not to question why they had bottles and not cans, nor how they were keeping them frosty in the heat. I had a feeling it wouldn't be an answer designed to inform or comfort.

We bumped along, me sipping my Coke and wondering just how thoroughly Christopher had searched my apartment and why. I looked behind us—all the SUVs seemed to be following. "We're sort of a conspicuous parade, if you were wanting to stay under the radar," I mentioned to White.

"Never complain about having too much backup," he said.

"Cryptic. How refreshing."

"We're here," Reader said as he stopped the car.

I looked around. "Not much different here than there."

Christopher got out and opened the rear door on Martini's side. "We go the rest of the way on foot, princess."

"Nice that we have you as our official doorman," I said. Martini and White got out, Gower indicated I should go before him. Martini and Christopher both offered me their hands to help me out. I avoided both. Martini gave me a hurt look. "Big girl, not impressing anyone, clothes already ruined. When I'm dressed up, feel free to help me out. Like this, why bother?"

Christopher snorted. "That should be a treat. You wear a tiara when you go out, princess?"

I gave him what I hoped was an icy stare. "I'm not really sure where you've gotten the 'princess' idea from, but stow it, manservant."

White looked pained. "Christopher, manners would be appreciated."

"Yeah, why ask her for any," Christopher muttered as he turned away.

"What *is* his problem with me?" I asked Martini under my breath as we started trudging toward what looked like more of the nothing that was around us. Christopher had stalked on ahead, Gower and White were in front of us, Reader behind. The rest of the boys in the band seemed to be staying with their cars.

Martini actually seemed to give this some thought. "I don't know," he said finally. I was fairly sure he did know but didn't want to tell me.

"I think he likes her," Reader said, coming up on my other side. "And he doesn't like that he does."

"Great," Martini muttered. "You know you're mine, right?"

I rolled my eyes. "Insofar as it matters, if it meant having to choose between you, Christopher, and marrying a tree, you're number one."

"I'll take it. I plan to grow on you."

"Like fungus?"

"I was thinking more like a vine," Reader said.

"Not a clinging one," Martini said. "More like a jungle vine you can enjoy swinging from."

"Sounds better than having to lower my intelligence level to please Mr. Personality up there."

I pondered this as we went along. It was odd. Martini I could understand. He'd seen me check him out. But I'd had almost no interaction with Christopher before he started being a jerk. If Reader was right, then Christopher had made his decisions about me based on, what? My car? My apartment? How would he get "princess" out of my fabulous housekeeping skills? Or my stuff?

I decided not to care. Martini was enough to deal with on top of everything else. I'd worry about Christopher if and when he became a real issue. Besides, Reader was gay, so maybe he just thought Christopher was interested in me because he wasn't interested in him. After all, in my experience most guys expressed interest more along Martini's lines, not by snarling and snarking at me.

There was another ringing noise. This time, since more than twenty aliens weren't staring me down, I didn't jump, just dug my phone out of my purse. "Mom, what's up?"

"Kitty, are you all right? Your father said that really was you I saw."

"Yeah, it was me, with Homeland Security now, blah, blah, blah. I'm sure Dad told you. I thought you were on a plane."

"I was. We sat on the runway for what seemed like hours but was probably only thirty minutes. Then they took us off the plane. Apparently I'm stuck in New York for the foreseeable future. Due to the terrorist attack you stopped they've shut down all air travel, in case it wasn't a lone incident."

"Oh, are you kidding me? Hang on." I covered the mouthpiece. "Hey, Christopher! My mother is stranded in New York because of the recent terrorist activity. Any chance in the world you can stop opening doors and, call me crazy, get this taken care of so people can return to their lives?"

He spun around. "Look, you have no idea of what you're dealing with," he snarled. "It's not that easy, and—"

His father cut him off. "Enough." He said it quietly, but White's voice carried authority when he wanted it to. He walked back over to me. "Please tell your mother to gather her belongings, go to a taxi stand, and one of our people will pick her up."

"Oh, *hell* no. You are *not* kidnapping my mother."

White heaved a sigh. "If you want her home, we have to pick her up."

"Lots to do in New York. Why's she in a rush?" Martini asked.

"She likes sleeping in her own bed with her own husband. Why should I have my mother go with any of you?"

"Safest place for her," Reader said quietly. "Superbeings come in different varieties. We know we have some that are in control. If one of them makes the connection between your mother and you . . ." He let it hang, but I got the point.

I went back to the phone. "Mom? Homeland Security's going to pick you up."

"Why? Oh, God, things aren't safe, are they?"

"Well, let's just say it'll be safer for you to be with them." I hoped. "Get your stuff, go to the nearest taxi stand, wait for a gray SUV or limo. Don't get in unless the men are really drop-dead gorgeous."

There was a pregnant pause. "Come again?"

"Work with me on this one. Just make sure they're good-looking."

"There's a whole lot you didn't tell your father, isn't there?"

I remembered why I'd never bothered to learn to lie to my parents. My mother never, ever fell for it. "Yes, Mom, there is."

"Are you safe and will I be safe? And is your father safe?" I heard the worry, there more when she was asking about Dad than for me or her.

"Dad's fine," I said, giving White a meaningful look. He nodded his head, and so did Gower. "They're watching the house." More nods. "But they're not watching you, yet, so they want you under protection." Nods again. "They'll meet you at the taxi stand. Just remember, gray, not black, great looking, not average or ugly."

"Not really for us to say, but thanks," Martini said quietly, with his usual grin.

"Which taxi stand?" Mom asked. I heard her telling someone to let her have her checked bags.

"It won't matter, they'll find you."

She groaned. "They won't release my bags."

"They're holding her bags," I told White.

His reaction wasn't what I was expecting. He spun to Christopher. "Get her and her things, now!"

Christopher nodded, and then he was gone. Literally. One second there, the next, empty air.

My stomach clenched. "Uh, Mom? Stay around people, stay away from anyone acting weird, and someone'll be there, really, really fast."

"Okay. Hmmm."

"What?"

"You know, I think I just spotted weird. Kitten, I'm going to go. Hopefully your new friends will find me quickly." With that, the phone went dead.

I tried to calm my stomach, but it was hard. "My mom's in trouble. Someone weird was there, I think they're after her."

"We'll take care of it," White said.

Martini put his arm around my shoulders. "It'll be okay."

"How? And how the hell did Christopher just up and disappear?" I felt like crying, and that always made me mad. I pulled away from Martini, and I saw that two of the SUVs were gone.

"We're at the crash site," Gower said. "It allows us to do certain things more . . . easily."

"What kinds of things? Time travel?"

"Not in the conventional sense." Gower sighed. "Look, try to calm down. I promise you your mother will be fine. And, yes, we have your father under protection now."

I was scared, but I knew I wasn't going to be able to help my mother in a dead panic. "What, I ask again, is going on?"

CHAPTER 7

GOWER POINTED. "Look there."

I did. There was nothing, just flat earth with the occasional desert scrub brush on it, and I said as much.

"No, there's actually a huge depression," he said with a small smile. "You can't see it because it's camouflaged."

"Okay. So? How does this help my mother?"

"Who do you take after?" Martini asked.

"What? Why is that a relevant question now?" I wanted to kick him but managed to refrain.

"Just answer me. Who do you take after?" He didn't seem like he was playing around.

"My mother, mostly. At least so everyone says."

"Then she'll be fine." He smiled at the expression I knew was on my face. "If you take after her, then there's more risk of another woman in your family killing another 'terrorist' than of your mother getting hurt."

I wanted to believe him, but it wasn't easy. "Maybe."

"What's your mother do for a living?" Gower asked, in a very soothing tone.

"She's a consultant."

"Consultant for what?" Gower prodded.

Reader started to laugh. I turned, and he was holding a folder. He hadn't had it before. "Acorn here did not fall far from the tree."

"Where did you get that from? And what does it say?" I tried to read it, but he moved it away from me.

"Nope, you have to calm down and pay attention to what Paul's trying to show you. Then, maybe I'll let you see the file on your mother." Reader winked. "It's all good, you'll be proud."

"*If* I can have your attention," Gower said.

"Fine." I was starting to hate all of them, not just Christopher.

Gower reached out and pulled me next to him. "Put your hand on top of mine," he instructed. I did, and then he moved our hands just a bit—and they disappeared. I pulled my hand back involuntarily, and there it was, still attached.

He brought his hand out, too. "It's an optical illusion. We have equipment hidden here. The residue from the Ancients' crash boosts the power."

I thought about what they'd said in the car. "You have a transference machine here?"

"Several," White answered. "As Christopher told you, they don't work for us to go back to A-C, but . . ."

"They work just great to get you to, say, JFK Airport in New York?"

"Exactly."

"There were some in the warehouse, too, weren't there?"

"Marry me," Martini said.

"Yes," Gower answered. "It's how we transport the dead superbeings back without issue."

"Okay, but how big are these things? Because I don't think you had one at the courthouse."

"We all have personal models," Gower said. But he wasn't meeting my eyes.

I looked at Martini. "I want the truth."

He grinned. "Say you'll marry me first."

"I'll marry you before any tree on Earth."

"Good enough for a start. We're aliens, remember? Anyone with A-C blood has the ability to travel at what you'd call hyperspeed."

"So you're like the Flash?"

"No," Gower sounded pained. "That's a comic book character."

"Actually," Reader interjected, "it's a good comparison. Look, you know how the Flash had to eat a ton because he burned so much fuel?"

"Yeah." I hated having to admit, right here, under these circumstances, that I was a total comics geek-girl, but I didn't have much choice. "But he also made sonic booms, and I haven't heard those."

"Right. Because they don't work like the Flash. Flash could go fast if he had enough fuel. They can go as fast as they need, but only for what they could do not moving fast."

"And it was starting to sound so clear." I looked to Gower. "Your turn."

"Let's say I can run five miles and not be dead tired," Gower said. I nodded. "I can move those five miles as fast as I need to, blink of an eye kind of thing. But, if I can't, say, run ten miles and not be exhausted, then I can't run ten miles in the blink of an eye, either. I can only do whatever I'm physically in shape to do, nothing else. It's why we all have to stay physically fit."

"As an example, I can make love for twelve hours straight," Martini offered. "However, I've never tried to make it go faster, so maybe that's not a good example."

"But, so far, your most winning argument." I looked back to Reader. "So, back to the Flash. He also made the wind whoosh around you, blew newspapers, that sort of thing. They don't."

"Right, 'cause they're real. Think of it as them stopping time and moving through everything in a way that doesn't create disturbance. They don't stop time, but the way they move can't be seen by human eyes. They also move faster than film, video, or digital can catch. But in such a way that they don't create any more disturbance than if they were just strolling."

"Okay, I'll buy that. So, how did you show up where I was?" I asked Martini.

"We monitor any unusual activity. To you, it seemed like just a few seconds, maybe a minute or so, from the point the fender bender happened until you killed the superbeing. But that was enough time for me to spot the change in his body chemistry, get to a transference machine, get to the airport in your town, and get to you in time to save the day."

I let the last comment pass. "So you've got a transference machine in, what, every major airport?"

"Every airport around the world," Reader said. "It's pretty impressive."

"Where are they hidden?"

"Restrooms, mostly," Martini answered. "You'd be amazed at how easy it is to just appear in a stall and go out. No one ever notices."

"You probably land in the women's restroom."

He grinned. "Only when you're in there."

I thought about this again. "How many miles can you run?"

"Fifty, without breaking a sweat." I realized he was serious.

"You all like that?"

"All field operatives have to be able to do twenty-five miles without a problem," White answered.

I looked at him. "You too?"

"I can do fifty, just like Jeffrey and Christopher." I got the feeling I'd insulted him. I decided he could live with that.

"I can do two," I offered. I mean, I had to show I wasn't totally without skills.

"Your mother can do twenty," Reader said. "Damn, you're slipping, girlfriend."

"My mother cannot do twenty miles." Could she? We'd never talked about it much. She'd been thrilled I'd gone out for track, just as she had. Well, maybe when she was younger she'd done twenty miles.

"Can, did, and does regularly," Reader said, sounding impressed. "Geez, it took me months to get up to ten miles. I can do twenty-five now," he added.

"Mr. Meets-Minimum, I see."

Reader shrugged. "Beating your two, girlfriend. Besides, I'm the driver. They don't drive or fly real well, as a rule."

"Really?"

"Yep," Martini confirmed. "Our reflexes are actually too fast. Every driver we have is a human operative. Even Paul has too much A-C blood to be able to drive or fly."

"But fast reflexes are good for flying," I protested. "My uncle says so."

"Fast reflexes for a human are what you and James have," White explained. "And all your machinery is made for humans. Believe us when we tell you that our reflexes are fast enough to destroy the machines, not handle them better."

"Oh, my God. Christopher took my car!" I loved that car. I took better care of it than of my apartment.

"He took your keys. Someone else drove it," Martini said reassuringly. "We roll with drivers at all times."

"He sounds so 'street' when he says that," Reader said with a laugh.

"Yeah, you're all keepin' it gangsta, really." I shook my head. "Okay, so you can move fast. How do the human operatives make time, though?"

"If we're touching you, you move as fast as we do," Gower said. "You wouldn't notice it, either, even if we're going at hyperspeed."

"You'd be too busy blacking out," Reader said. "Trust me, I still do."

"Is that why I fainted before?"

"Nope," Martini said. "That was because you were overcome by my lips being so close to yours."

"Good to know. So, other than making my hand disappear, why are we here, exactly?"

"Well, we were going to use the transference machine here to go to Dulce," White answered. "But I'd prefer to wait until we know the situation with your mother is handled."

"Christopher won't take her here or the Science Center, though," Gower said. "Standard procedure is to take her to Home Base."

"True," White sighed. "Okay, off to the Box, then."

"No. I want to see this crash site, since we're here." I was worried about Mom, but if I believed them, the A-Cs were taking care of her. I wanted to see the crash site as a distraction, so I could focus on it instead of on what I couldn't do. Mom's training, as I thought about it.

"Fine, as long as you're up to it," White said.

"Hold onto me," Martini said, offering his hand.

I decided not to argue. He had a good grip—it was clear he was holding my hand firmly but not so that he'd crush it. I had to admit, I felt better with him touching me.

We walked forward, and then, right there, where nothing had been before, was a huge, rounded ditch. I could see where something big and heavy had landed and then skidded for a good, long way, ending up right in front of where we stood.

I looked back. I could still see the limo and the other SUVs. "Can they still see us?"

"Lift your top. If they react, the answer's yes."

"You're so suave. Can I let go of your hand now?"

"It'd be better if you didn't, and not just because I like holding your hand." He led me around the outside of the ditch. "If you were to slip and fall, you'd get hurt, and if you fell through an open door, you'd get sent to whichever transport point you hit. Not pretty and not safe, especially under the circumstances."

"I don't see anything but the ditch. I mean, at least I can see that now. But I don't see any machinery, let alone a door, open or not."

"It's cloaked."

"Like in the movies?"

"Only real, yes." Martini was fiddling with something. He seemed to be spinning a dial in the air.

"What are you doing?"

As I asked, he stopped fiddling with the air and then pushed at something I also couldn't see. There was a hissing sound, like an air lock opening, and then Martini stepped onto thin air. At least, that's what it looked like. "We call it 'opening the door.' Come on in," he said, pulling me with him.

As I stumbled over, I saw we were now in a dome made of glass and metal. Inside it were what looked like the metal detectors at the airport—doorways that go nowhere. There were dozens of them, and two particularly large ones, at the edges of the dome, opposite each other. I could also see more men who looked like the rest of the boys from Alpha Centauri in there. They were bigger and more imposing than Martini or Gower, and I got the distinct impression they were security.

One near us nodded to Martini. "You taking a trip?"

"Probably. Giving a tour."

"Enjoy." His tone made it clear this was unlikely.

We wandered through, with Martini nodding or speaking to most of the men there, all of whom seemed bored but completely alert at the same time. "Security checkpoint?" was all I could think of to ask.

"Yep. This site is still active."

"What do you mean, active? Like radioactive?" I started to worry that I'd never have children.

"Well, in a way, but it's not dangerous. Residue from the Ancients' fuel source is still here—its half-life makes your nukes seem like kiddie toys. That residue helps power our transference gates. The Ancients had a lot of technology that was far beyond ours, which means much more than yours. That's not an insult to Earth," he added quickly. "You're just a younger civilization than we are. And we're babies compared to the Ancients."

I felt small and very insignificant all of a sudden. "How many inhabited worlds are there?"

"Plenty, but out our way? Not too many. We live in the boondocks, spacewise. You're even more in the middle of nowhere than Alpha Centauri is. But we're your closest neighbor."

"And like a good neighbor, Alpha Centauri is there."

"If the slogan fits." He looked down at me. "It's always hard, the first time you find out it's true, that you're really not alone in the universe."

"Why?" I wanted to cry again, but this time it wasn't making me mad, it was making me feel like a little girl.

Martini seemed to pick this up. He moved us into an area without a doorway to nowhere or a security guard nearby and pulled me into his arms. I didn't protest. "It's okay. It passes," he said, patting my back. "It's hard for us, too. We're taught we're different as soon as we're old enough to understand it, but we don't get the full details until we're teenagers. It's a shock, and we have a whole extended family to help us through it."

"I don't want anything bad to happen to my parents. I don't understand half of what's happened, but I know everything's changed."

"They'll be fine. I promise." He rocked me for a bit, and I tried to relax. "I could get used to this," he said quietly. "But I think we need to get moving."

He let me go but still held my hand. "I think I like you

better like this," I said as we moved back into the main part of what I was coming to think of as a terminal.

He grinned. "I'll keep it in mind."

"So, where can we go from here?"

"Anywhere we need to." Martini pointed to the big doorways. "We take the vehicles through them."

"How? Aren't we in a dome or something that's like a building?"

"Yes. There are entry points all over the dome, though. We just open the big doors for the cars."

"Does each doorway thing correspond to an airport?"

"We call them gates, and no. We have gates programmed to go straight to Home Base and our Science Center, but otherwise, we calibrate for each trip. A superbeing can show up anywhere in the world, at any time, so we need the flexibility."

"Makes sense." I looked around. "This place seems pretty quiet."

"That's because the grid's quiet," Gower's voice came from behind us. I jumped and probably would have fallen if Martini weren't still holding my hand. "Nice to see you two getting cozy," Gower added with a grin.

"Just keeping her from leaping through a gate to who knows where," Martini laughed.

"Ready to go to the next stop?" Gower asked Martini.

"I think so. She's seen everything here."

"I don't understand it all," I interjected. "Like how this can all be hidden not only from the American government but from all the other countries who monitor what we do?"

Gower shrugged. "Our technology's more advanced, and some of this is the Ancients' technology, too. And the cloaking technology hides more than just the physical presence. I could spend a couple of hours and give you a lecture in advanced alien science, but time's wasting. We need to get to Home Base."

CHAPTER 8

TURNED OUT THE TWO BIG GATES were the ones calibrated for the Science Center and Home Base at all times. Gower went to have the dome opened for the vehicles with us to go through, while Martini and I waited.

"If we weren't detouring to, hopefully, meet up with my mother, where would the next stop have been?"

"Science Center. It's okay, we have gates at Home Base to Dulce. You'll still get to see it." He sighed. "This always takes forever."

"What?" Everything seemed to be moving fast to me.

"Loading the cars through. They're harder to send, especially with someone in them. Calibrations take longer, everyone goes slowly, just in case, that sort of thing."

"Do we have to go in them?" I didn't like going through a drive-thru carwash. I had no desire to be in a drive-thru transporter.

"Nah, I'll take you through a regular one." Martini looked down at me and cocked his head. "You need anything before we see your mother?"

I thought about it. I knew I looked awful, and it didn't take much imagination to come up with how my mother would react. "Yeah. A change of clothes would be great."

He nodded. "Stay right here." Letting go of my hand, he walked over to where Gower was. I couldn't hear them, but it was pretty clear they were arguing. Martini seemed to win, because he came back grinning as usual. "We're all set. You and I are making a quick stop at your apartment before we meet the others back at Home Base."

This seemed awfully easy, considering the load of men who'd been with us so far. "What does Paul over there think we're doing?"

Martini shrugged. "Going to Home Base first. We'll still probably beat the limo, let alone the rest of the cars."

He had a point. The gates were still being calibrated, and while I could see the cars, they weren't moving. Reader wasn't even in the limo; he was leaning against the door, still reading the file on my mother he'd somehow acquired.

"Will we be safe?"

"Sure. I'll be with you." He flashed me his largest grin. "You worried about not being able to control yourself once we're alone?"

"Hardly. I want to be sure all those superbeings you've been warning me about aren't going to get me while we take an unauthorized side trip. Besides, I know who'll get the brunt of the complaints if we do."

"Me, so what are you worried about?" He sighed. "Look, we can go ahead to Home Base and you can see your mother looking like we've spent the last hour or so having a wild time in the dirt, or we can get you changed. Your choice."

I was somewhat suspicious of his motives and what I was getting into, but in addition to changing clothes, I really wanted to know what Christopher had done during his time in my apartment. "Okay, let's go."

"That's my girl!" Martini grabbed my hand again and trotted us off to a gate at the opposite end of the dome from where the cars were. He shooed the security guard away, and I was interested to note there was no protest given.

"Your security details always this lax?"

"Nope. I'm just a popular guy. Now, hush, I need to pay attention while I do the calibrations." He fiddled around with some knobs and buttons on the sides of the gate. His hands were a blur, and I had to stop watching. "Okay, all set," he said less than a minute later.

"I thought you said your reflexes were too fast for driving."

"These aren't human-created." He cocked his head. "You okay? That was a dumb question, for you."

"I think it's all starting to blur into total insanity," I admitted. "I feel like Alice, but you're one weird white rabbit."

"I'm more like the Cheshire cat." Martini laughed. "It's natural. Let's get you home and changed. You'll feel better." With that he moved us right in front of the opening. "It's going to be tight, but I want us going through together. So, don't take this the wrong way, but I'm going to have to hold you as we go through."

"I suddenly see why you suggested this." I was going to protest but he picked me up before I had the chance.

"Arms around my neck, just because I like it." I did as he asked because it was more comfortable and, truth be told, I was scared about going through the gate. He shifted me a bit, then walked through.

I was instantly glad he was holding me, because the transference wasn't like walking through the invisibility shield around the dome. We seemed to be standing still while the world rushed by us, just like in the movies when they speed up the film to show how fast time's passing. Only it was ten times faster and totally nauseating.

I buried my face in Martini's neck. He held me a little tighter, and the nausea subsided. "Almost there," he said softly. I felt a slight jolt. "It's okay," he said in a very low voice. "We're here. Don't talk."

As I drew my head up, I remembered where he'd said the transference devices were stationed. "I'm in the men's restroom?" I hissed in his ear.

"Yes," he said, still quietly. "Now, hush."

He kept me in his arms, and neither one of us spoke. I heard the unmistakable sounds of liquid hitting porcelain, which was both gross and proof we weren't alone.

Saguaro International is a busy airport, and it occurred to me that Martini and I could be stuck in this stall for long enough that we'd be late getting to Home Base. He must have thought the same, because he opened the stall door, just a crack. I was impressed that he could hold me with just one arm, but I decided now wasn't the time to mention it.

He watched while I listened. The splattering sound stopped, I heard a zipper, then fading footsteps. Martini put me down and opened the stall door more. This wasn't the most spacious stall in the world, and I was squished. He walked out and I could breathe again, not that I wanted to.

I heard him walking quickly; then he came back, grabbed me, and we headed toward the exit. As we did so, several men came in, all with rolling suitcases or garment bags. They seemed to spot me at the same time, and all stopped dead in their tracks.

"Oh, my gosh, I'm so sorry!" I said to Martini. "My contacts both slipped out during the flight, thank goodness you stopped me before I got all the way in here! Excuse me, sorry, sorry, can't see a thing anyway!" I said to the men who were gaping at me. I shoved through them and got out.

Martini came after me. I heard him saying something about ditzy women that was greeted with some chuckles. He shook his head when he was out of the bathroom. "You really can think on your feet."

"You know that's a crime I can be jailed for in this state? Being the wrong sex in the bathroom?"

"Humans have weird laws. Now, let's get going." He took my hand again. "This is probably going to be really unpleasant."

Before I could ask him how unpleasant, he started moving and I was going right along with him. It was different from the transference, but not by too much. We moved around the people as if they were frozen. There were a couple of times I was sure we went through walls, but it was just that Martini moved us around obstacles more quickly than I could see them.

We were out of the airport, racing through the streets and on the freeway, flying past cars I knew were going at least sixty-five as if they, too, were standing still. Then, off at my exit, through the streets of my neighborhood, shortcutting through the park, going up the back way, and into my apartment.

We stopped inside. My stomach was roiling, but it had been more exhilarating than the transference process. "How'd we get inside?" I managed to ask.

Martini held my house keys in his hand. "I searched your purse. That thing is worse than I'd thought. Slowed us down a bit."

"I'll make a note to buy something with more compartments when I feel like making it easy for you. I'm glad I'm not passing out like Reader said I would."

"I went slowly." I got the impression he wasn't lying.

"That was slowly?"

"Yes. Now, you going to change or what?"

"You're not watching, that's what."

He grinned. "I know. I'm going to check out your fridge. Just to see if I like your frozen dinner selection." He sauntered off like he owned the place.

I decided to do what we'd come for. As I walked through my living room to the bedroom, I noted that nothing seemed amiss.

My bedroom was the best part of the apartment—double doors leading to the living room, which were now closed to keep Martini out, huge window with a great view of the mountain preserve, a large walk-in closet, a vanity area with good lighting, and a full bathroom. The bedroom was why I'd taken this place—put together, the living room, dining room, kitchen and tiny utility area were about the same square footage as my bedroom.

My bed was still a mess—I didn't live by the make your bed every day rule. I had stuff all over the place, but it was my stuff, and it was pretty much where I'd left it. I dumped my suit in the bag I used for dry cleaning, hope managing to spring eternal. I washed my face, gave it a couple moments of thought, then pulled on my most comfortable pair of jeans. They were sort of clean, too. I had a feeling we'd be spending a lot of time in the heat, so I figured I should wear a T-shirt. Which one was a difficult choice, though. I didn't want to wear something I loved, because the chances of it ending up like my suit were high. But I also didn't want to wear something I hated, or something that didn't look good on me, for a variety of reasons, all of them related to vanity.

I finally settled on one of my Aerosmith T-shirts. I had several; this one was well-worn, and I'd feel better with Steven, Joe, and the rest of my boys backing me up, so to speak. I grabbed a hoodie, just in case, added socks and sneakers, and I was finally all set.

I looked around. If Christopher had searched for something, he sure hadn't disturbed anything.

Except, I realized as I started to brush my hair, in one area. I didn't use the vanity as intended, I'm not much for wearing makeup. I used it as a place to do my hair and display pictures. And they'd been moved.

I put my hair into a ponytail, tossed my brush, a headband, a couple of extra scrunchies, and my spare hairspray into my purse. Then I examined the pictures.

He'd moved them all, not much, but enough for me to notice, because I never dust. I could see fingerprints in the dust on the frames, as well as smudges in the dust on the counter, showing where a picture had been and now wasn't quite on the spot any more.

The pictures here were the ones that mattered most to me—my parent's wedding picture, my senior picture from high school, my sorority composite picture, me and my parents with my car when it was brand new, a multi-picture collection of my closest friends from school, college, and work, another multi-picture set of our relatives and pets through my lifetime.

But the ones that had the most dust removed from them were from my sixteenth birthday. Chuckie had been into photography at that point, and while he pretty much refused to have his picture taken, he'd gotten some awesome snaps of others. In one I was wearing a tiara and holding my cats, Oingo and Boingo, with my parents and Sheila and Amy around me, all of us grinning like idiots. In the other I was still in the tiara, but I was with my then-boyfriend, Brian. He and I were pretending to do the tango, we were both laughing, and he had me dipped, so that I was upside down in the shot with one leg up in the air.

So that explained the princess and tiara comments. Prick.

There was a knock on my bedroom doors. "Are you dressed yet or can I come in?"

"Oh, come in." I'd deal with Christopher's invasion of my privacy later.

Martini came in and gave me an appraising up and

down. "You clean up nice. A little casual, but that's okay. However, you should know I like the Stones better."

"Proof you're an idiot, just as I suspected." I grabbed my purse. "Do I need anything else?"

He shook his head. "Nope. Just do me a favor and claim you were worried about twisting your ankle in your heels."

"You don't want to get bawled out by Uncle Mr. White in front of the whole Home Base crew? And I was all ready to be impressed."

"If you admit that you wanted to come here so I could ravage you, I wouldn't get in trouble."

"Dream on."

"Bed's right there. Though, looking at it, maybe we'll have our first romantic moment at my place. I actually understand the concept of cleaning and straightening."

"I'm thrilled. If you can cook, too, we might begin to have an understanding."

"I'm a great cook." He took my hand again. "You tell me what you like, I'll make it for you."

"Your second strong argument. I'll try to focus on your strengths while you race us back to the freaking men's room at the airport." I made sure everything was off and locked.

"We could go to the one in the ladies'. Saguaro International actually does have a ladies' room gate, and I don't mind at all," he said with his widest grin yet.

"You really aren't clear on the concept of quitting while you're ahead, are you?" We left the apartment, and I locked the door. I wondered when I'd see it again.

"Hey, I fed your fish."

"So, supposedly, did Christopher. They'll probably die from overfeeding now."

"I'll help you through your bereavement."

"You're a prince."

Martini opened his mouth, then slammed it shut. He seemed to be listening, but I couldn't hear anything.

"What is it?"

"One of the people who checked on you earlier was your landlord?"

"Yes. Nice people. Paranoid, but nice."

"That's it. What apartment are they in?"

"Why?"

"We're right here. Let's have you go reassure them you're okay."

"Suddenly you're all about the caring of what my friends, family, and extended circle think?"

"That's me. Let's go visit your landlord. You'll be glad we did, trust me."

"Not yet, but maybe I will in a few years." We walked downstairs, and I knocked on the landlord's door.

It opened a crack. "Katherine?"

"Hi, Mr. Nareema. Just wanted to let you know I was okay."

"I saw you on the news. You were very brave." At least Christopher hadn't made me look like a dork, insofar as Mr. Nareema was concerned anyway.

"Thanks, it was sort of instinctual, not planned."

"I understand. There have been people in your apartment. Men. In matching suits." Mr. Nareema sounded frightened. Then again, he always sounded frightened.

"I know. They were from the government."

He gasped. "Do we need to flee?"

"No, no," I reassured quickly. The Nareema family had had to flee their homeland and still weren't over it. I'd never gotten the full why out of them, mostly because it was hard to talk to any one of them for more than five minutes without feeling like a total paranoid yourself. "They're good government. Protecting us. They wanted to make sure everything was safe here."

"It is," Martini said, with, I had to admit, a very charming smile.

"Good." Mr. Nareema didn't sound convinced. "Take care, Katherine. Call if you . . . need help."

"Thanks, I will." We backed up a step, and the door closed. Several locks were turned. Martini and I walked down the hall. "That was fun."

"He sounds like he feels a little better," Martini said. "Apparently I reassured him."

"*You* did? Really? You're a prince to all, aren't you?"

"Let's see if you still think that in a minute," he said. He took my hand, took a step, and then we were moving. This time I could tell it was faster, much faster. As we flew along, everything was going by so quickly I couldn't take it in, couldn't figure out where we were, and my brain politely asked to shut down.

Just as things were going black, we stopped. Martini pulled me into his arms, and I leaned my head against his chest. "Just breathe slowly," he said quietly, while he massaged the back of my neck.

"What're you doing?" I mumbled. It felt good, and my stomach and head were clearing.

"A little trick I know for keeping beautiful agents from passing out on me again."

"I'm not an agent."

"Yet." He rubbed a little more, and I felt normal again. "All better?"

"Yeah." I pulled away from him a bit. "How is it you know what I'm feeling?"

"I'd like to say it's because I'm so in tune with you." He sighed. "Actually, it *is* because I'm so in tune with you. I'm empathic. It's a great trait in a field operative. I'm probably the best empath we have. It's one of the reasons I got to you first."

I considered this. A part of me really felt manipulated. The other part, however, was relieved to not be fainting or throwing up. "So, that's why you wanted to visit Mr. Nareema?"

"Yeah. I picked up anxiety, focused toward your apartment and extending toward you. Paranoia really broadcasts well, emotionally speaking. And I wasn't kidding—he felt better seeing you, but even more so seeing me."

"Knowing them, that doesn't really ring true. You look official."

"And I left after telling him everything checked out okay. Trust me, his anxiety dropped enough to fall off my main radar."

Nauseated or not, this was interesting. "So, you get emotions from everyone? Doesn't that get overwhelming fast?"

"It can." I raised my eyebrow and he grinned. "Okay, yes, it does. A lot. We have blocks—mental, emotional, and drug-related—that all empaths use to keep the emotional chatter down to a minimum."

"But then, how are you useful if your powers are muted?"

He shrugged. "Our jobs are to spot where a superbeing is likely to form. They don't attract to low-stress situations for whatever reason. So we only need to monitor high-level emotions. The closer we are to someone, the easier it is to pick up their emotions as well."

"So, what if someone's fighting next door when you're trying to sleep?"

He grinned. "Don't worry. I won't lose focus when we're intimate."

"Believe me, last thought on my mind." I had another thought that was well ahead of wondering how Martini stayed in the moment while doing the deed. "Is that why you could control the police at the courthouse?"

Martini shook his head. "Nope. That's technology. Ours, not the Ancients'."

"You have mind-control technology?" This was disturbing, much more so than discovering that Martini probably already knew I was freaked out by this news.

"Yes, but it's not what you think. You'll get to see how it works either at Home Base or the Science Center. But we need to move it."

"Lead on to the bathroom," I said with a sigh, resigned to another ditz performance.

CHAPTER 9

GETTING INTO THE MEN'S ROOM wasn't as tricky as getting out. Martini went in first and waited until the other men left. I found a sign that said the bathroom was temporarily closed for cleaning, which meant no one else was going in. We went to the stall, Martini made some movements in the air, and we were whooshing off again.

This time I didn't even attempt to watch or enjoy it. He held me again and I put my face in his neck and tried to pretend I was on a tilt-a-whirl. Of course, I hate the tilt-a-whirl.

I felt the jolt that meant we were at our destination and opened my eyes as Martini put me down. We were in a doorway of, as I looked around, a small shed that said "Explosives" on it. But the only thing inside the shed was a gate. I looked outside the doorway—lots of buildings looking both dull and oppressive, lots of jeeps, lots of men in uniform, lots of jets.

"We're at an air base?"

"I mean it, marry me. Yes, we're at the Groom Lake U.S. Air Base. Or, as we call it, Home Base."

"Or, as the rest of the world calls it, Area Fifty-One." I was a comics geek-girl, and, hey, I could recognize the names if not the faces, as it were. After all, Chuckie had been one of my best friends since ninth grade, and anyone nicknamed Conspiracy Chuck clearly lived for UFO stuff. Area 51 had a lot of names, and I knew them all.

"I think our kids are going to be fantastic," Martini said, as he started off toward one of the bigger and more oppressive-looking buildings about a quarter mile away. "How many do you want?"

"I want to know why I could see the gate here and at the crash site but not in the bathrooms."

"They're cloaked. Duh."

"Uh-huh. So how can *you* see them?"

He looked over his shoulder. "Keep up. And, yeah, okay, the cloaking doesn't actually work on anyone with A-C blood. We can see the cloak but we can also see through it, because the light waves aren't moving too fast for us. They're too fast for any human or human-made device. And, before you ask, the parasites and the superbeings don't have A-C blood, so they can't see through the cloaking, either."

I wasn't sure if I believed him, but I got the impression he wasn't lying. "So you're saying that there are no A-C-based parasites?"

"Not that we know of." Martini sounded sincere, but I wasn't as sure about the lying this time, particularly since he pointedly wasn't making eye contact. But this brought up a question all the excitement had washed away. "What happened on your planet when the parasites arrived?"

Martini didn't answer me. Him not talking was shocking in and of itself, but this was pretty damning. I caught up to him and grabbed his arm. "Tell me what happened when they got to your planet."

He stopped walking and turned to face me. Martini's expression was unusual—solemn and tense. "They never came to Alpha Centauri."

I decided to take this news calmly. I ran through all the questions this statement brought up and decided to go with the bottom line. "Why not?"

"We aren't sure. Once the Ancients arrived, it was the 'there are other inhabited worlds' wake-up call for us. It might just have been that our ozone shield worked to keep the parasites out."

"Ozone shield?" I wondered if Al Gore knew about this, and I figured he didn't or we'd already have a documentary about how much better the Alpha Centaurions were at protecting their precious resources.

"Same issue as Earth has right now. We just figured out how to create a world shield that keeps the good stuff in and filters the bad stuff out. It's similar to the cloaking technology."

"Why hasn't someone shared this with Earth?"

He sighed. "You don't have the right raw materials to make it work. We have some elements on A-C that don't exist on Earth. Maybe because of the double suns, maybe just because of how our world evolved. Like our ability to travel at hyperspeed. There are some things we can do that a human will never be able to."

"Could you export the materials to us?"

"Possibly, but the parasitic threat is much more real and much more serious. A few superbeings could destroy the world tomorrow. And these days hundreds can show up in the course of a week."

"These days?"

"The number of parasites reaching Earth is increasing each year. In the sixties, it was a few, almost like a military advance team. Now? Now it's all we can do to keep up with them." He let that sit on the air for a few moments, then continued. "We got the shield up on Alpha Centauri a few years after the Ancients arrived. We've never had a parasite sighting. We do get messages from home, three to five years after they were sent. Those your governments do intercept, but they're in our native language."

"And we're too slow to understand it, right?"

"Slow only in the physical sense."

This begged another question. "Then how did you know what was going on? Why did you come here?"

He started walking again, quickly, and I had to trot to keep up. "We told you. You needed us."

I thought about this as we raced to the building that was marked "Administration."

"The parasites couldn't get through the shield, but I'll bet you saw them knock on the door. We're farther out from the galactic core than you are. They couldn't get in at your place, so they headed to ours."

Martini held the door for me. "You're taking this very well. I'll be sure to tell the kids about it all the time."

"So, why your family group? I mean, if you all are really related?"

We entered the building. It looked like every military headquarters I'd ever seen on TV or in the movies—lots of terminals, screens of all sizes, desks with papers, much hustle and bustle from the many people moving about with purpose. Only the vast majority of the personnel were really great-looking men. There were some ordinary guys mingled in, all wearing Air Force uniforms. These I took to be humans.

The building was quite large and had a big gate at the end opposite from where Martini and I were. The last SUV was arriving as we walked in. I could see the other cars and the limo parked in a formation that made it seem they were ready to race off at any moment. There was a huge sliding door in front of the cars, which I assumed was how our little motor pool would exit the building gracefully.

"Dammit," Martini said under his breath.

White had spotted us and was striding toward us, looking furious. "Where the hell have you two been?" he snarled as he got within earshot.

"I almost broke an ankle in that dome thing," I said before Martini could answer. "Plus I didn't want my mother to see me looking like I'd been hit by a bus. I blackmailed Martini into taking me home first."

"Blackmailed? What, you offered to let him kiss you?" White asked, not seeming convinced or appeased.

"No, but that's a good one I'll save for later. I told him I'd have my father send the Marines over to the real crash site."

"You have no idea of the risks you just took," White sputtered.

"I think I do. There are a few superbeings in control of the human to superbeing and back again merry-go-round, and they want to take over. I'm identified as able to stop them, so they want to kill me. However, unless being an in-control superbeing means you become an utter moron, which I doubt, they know damn well I'm with you all now. Which means they have less than no interest in my apartment, since it's hard to hold a couple of guppies and a Siamese fighting fish hostage. Besides," I added as White seemed to be calming down, "I think I can run and fight a lot better dressed like this. I might be less cranky this way, too."

"I doubt it," White muttered.

"Where's my mother?" I looked around but didn't see her. Didn't see any women other than me, actually. White didn't answer. This crew had a real issue with lying effectively or even believably. Good to know. They might be fast, but humanity still had the edge in con artistry. "Well?"

"They aren't back yet," White admitted.

I managed to remind myself that his son was, presumably, the other part of the "they" who weren't back along with my mother. I wasn't reassured. "Where are they?"

"We believe they're still in New York." White looked uncomfortable.

"What do you mean, you *believe*?" I tried, but I couldn't keep the anger out of my voice.

"It means they got into trouble," Martini said softly. "We're going, right now," he said to White. "Her, me, James, and Paul. You stay here in case the others get back before we do."

White didn't argue. Martini grabbed my hand, and we started to run to the limo, but at human speed. "Who's actually in charge around here?" I gasped out.

"We have a situation, so that would be me," Martini said in a clipped tone. "Moving out, Alpha Team, now!" he shouted at Gower and Reader, both of whom were standing by the limo.

Reader and Gower ran toward a smaller gate I could now see was near the carport area. "Not taking the limo?" I asked as we followed them. I could see Gower making calibrations.

"No time. We'll get a car when we're there." Martini, still running, swung me up into his arms. Reader went through the gate, then the two of us. As I was flinging my face into Martini's neck, I saw Gower moving behind us.

Then the horrible whooshing feeling followed by the jolt of arrival. Martini opened the stall door and put me down. We were indeed in the men's room at what I assumed was JFK, and it was full.

Reader was there, looking as though he was trying not to laugh. Gower stepped out of the stall we'd just vacated. "Great," I heard him mutter behind me.

The men's room occupants who weren't part of our little

team were, to a man, staring at us with a mixture of horror, embarrassment, and fear on their faces. I reminded myself that Martini and Gower couldn't lie, and Reader was too busy trying not to crack up. It was up to me. Again.

"Gentlemen, thank you so much!" I started to applaud. "You've helped us get a great scene for the new reality series, Life With A Former Male Model," I pointed to Reader. "Our production assistants will be here in a couple of minutes with release forms. If all goes well, you'll see yourselves on television in a few months! And, we will allow you to review footage to make sure that if any of you don't want certain, ah, portions of the film with you in it shown, we can remove it before airing." I looked at Gower, Martini, and Reader, all of whom were managing to keep their mouths shut. "Gentlemen, we need to move. We're due in the women's restroom in fifteen. Sorry, folks," I said, as I grabbed Reader and moved him along, "no autographs right now, we're on a tight schedule."

We scrambled out of the bathroom, and Martini headed off. The rest of us followed. He was still moving at human speed levels, so Reader and I were okay. "When do you think they'll realize we weren't holding any cameras?" Reader asked me as we raced along.

"About the same time they realize no one's coming in with release forms. Or when they go to the information desk to ask why the release forms aren't coming. How does he know he's going in the right direction?"

"I don't know if he's told you, but . . ." Reader seemed uncomfortable.

"Oh, right, he's an empath. Who's he tracking?"

"Whoever's the most terrified. Didn't freak you out?"

"Did, but I was too busy being glad he'd realized I was going to barf and pass out and was fixing that to care."

"You could do a lot worse," Reader added as we rounded a corner.

We headed toward the runways, not baggage claim or the arrivals and departures area. It was already night here, which, as I thought about it, made sense. At least the time zones were working normally.

"Thanks for sharing. I'm more worried about my

mother than whether or not Martini and I have that special spark."

"They make great mates," Reader said. "I mean, really great."

Yes, we were indeed heading toward the planes, which meant that, shortly, we were going to have to deal with security. I wasn't looking forward to that. Martini slowed, nodded to Gower, then Martini grabbed my hand and Gower grabbed Reader's. They now moved us at hyperspeed, though at the slower pace, so we were less likely to barf or pass out when we stopped. We raced past security, through the terminal, and out the gate that seemed the farthest exit point in this entire airport.

We hit the tarmac and slowed down to human speed. I noted that Gower and Reader didn't seem at all uncomfortable holding hands. "What speed?" Gower asked Martini.

"Human. Need to conserve energy." There was nothing at all in his demeanor to suggest humor or frivolity. He let go of my hand, and Gower did the same with Reader's, and then we started off again, Martini in the lead.

"You and Paul?" I asked Reader as we brought up the rear.

"Yep. You caught that one a little late."

"Not really. I thought you'd joined up because you were recruited, not because you'd, well, married in."

"Actually, I was recruited. Like you. Superbeing created at a photo shoot. Everyone else freaked, I killed it. The gang showed up, I got the tour and was in. We didn't have this much excitement when I joined up, though."

"Lucky you." We were running under airplanes. I'd been in a lot of them, but it's a daunting thing to look up and see the belly of the plane and realize you don't have to duck to get under it. "So, when did you two hook up?"

"Oh, a while after I'd been an agent. Just started working together, found out we liked the same things, started hanging out, realized we both wanted to be more than friends, that sort of thing. A-C's don't have the same hangups about homosexuality that humans do. It's refreshing."

"They do seem, well, nicer than us."

"This group, yeah." He was quiet while we dodged several baggage carts and were yelled at by a lot of airport workers. "When we're through this situation, ask Jeff about why they came here. I mean, them, in particular, not in general."

"I don't think he wants to tell me."

"He probably doesn't, but he will if you ask him."

I would have pursued this, but we weren't alone on the tarmac anymore. There were several men running toward us, all looking terrified. From what I could see, they'd been driving baggage carts. The tarmac was fairly well lit, and the moon was out. As I looked farther in the distance I could see what looked like a big monster out of a Ray Harryhausen film up ahead of us.

"Take a cart," I called to Reader.

"Why?" he asked as he jumped into one of the two nearest us. "We can run faster than these things move."

I got into the other one. Thankfully, they worked like golf carts. "Maybe we can ram it or something."

"You're insane," Reader said with a laugh. "I think you and Jeff might be the perfect couple."

"Maybe. What do you all use for weapons against these things?" We were driving side by side, and while the speed of the carts wasn't all that fast, we had to shout.

"Can't use tanks and artillery here, so nothing."

"Nothing?? What kills these things, besides my pen?"

"Depends. This one's in control, so it's hard to say."

We got closer, and Reader braked, hard. I followed his lead but ended up ahead of him. "What's wrong?"

Reader looked pale. "It's Mephistopheles."

CHAPTER 10

"WHO'S MEPHISTOPHELES? You mean like Faust's devil?"

Reader nodded and pointed to the superbeing who was stomping around the tarmac. We were close enough to see that he was trying to stomp on people—and two of those people were Christopher and my mother.

I took a closer look. We were near what looked like the air freight section, and there were floodlights all over the place, so seeing was easy. The superbeing was big, easily twelve feet tall, which made me wonder how he got around New York without tanks and artillery showing up on a daily basis. He resembled a huge faun, with a goat body for the lower half and a human torso and head. His arms looked human, but his fingers ended in claws, similar to those of the dead superbeing I'd seen at the warehouse. He had huge bat wings and they, like the rest of him, were blood red. The hair covering his lower body was also this color. Curling horns came out of his forehead, and his face wasn't all that pleasant to look at—not ugly, but so far from human and contorted with so much hatred your eyes just wanted to look away.

"So, you know this thing?"

"Yeah. He's the strongest of the in-control superbeings." Reader sounded totally freaked out. "We need some weapons."

"Which we don't have, unless they're invisible." I started

to wonder if pacifists ran this operation. Maybe we were supposed to talk the monster out of killing my mother.

Martini and Gower were there now. As near as I could tell, this just meant Mr. Mephistopheles was getting a chance to stomp more people I knew, because I didn't see them producing a gun or any other kind of weapon. They were just running around the thing, like Christopher and the other guys in Armani who were there. I counted seven, not including Martini and Gower.

"Ram the legs with the carts." I started mine up again and headed toward the monster. This was, I admitted as I "raced" along at about fifteen miles per hour, not the greatest plan. But it seemed better than running around aimlessly.

I checked over my shoulder, Reader was right behind me. Good. He might be scared but he was willing to do something.

I hooked my purse over my neck so I wouldn't lose it. As we got closer, I could hear the monster—he was talking.

At least, I thought it was language. It wasn't something I understood, though I got the impression the A-C crew did because they seemed to be reacting to whatever it was Mephistopheles snarled at them.

My mother spotted me. She and Christopher were together; he had hold of her hand, and they were dodging the hooves. But when she saw me, she stopped, pulled away from Christopher, and stood still. Then she started shouting at the monster. "Hey! Ugly! Over here!"

I thought she was insane, until I realized that she'd figured out what Reader and I were trying to do and was working as a distraction, so the monster wouldn't turn around.

She got Mephistopheles' attention. I had a feeling he was after her more than any of the A-C crew anyway. She backed away, but he was coming for her. As she moved I saw she still had her purse, too, over her neck just like me. She reached inside it and pulled out a gun.

Reader and I were close to the hooves now, and we both put the pedal down. For these carts, it meant we might have hit seventeen miles an hour now. Whoo hoo. But it couldn't hurt and might help.

I hit the right hoof first, and Reader hit the left a couple of seconds later. It didn't knock Mephistopheles down, but it did shove him off-balance. He started teetering. I decided getting out might be a good idea, and Reader seemed to agree. We both jumped at the same time.

This left the carts on their own. They stopped, which turned out to be a good thing. Mephistopheles was off balance and he stepped back, right onto the cart I'd been in. But it wasn't solid, and it caused him to go down, butt first, right onto the entire baggage cart Reader had been driving.

Reader was next to me now. "How do we kill this thing?" I asked while we moved around the rest of the baggage cart I'd been driving.

"No idea. Newly formed ones like you and I took out are easy. Aim for the parasite."

"The jellyfish thing."

"Right. But if they manage to remain in control, the jellyfish moves inside the body, and it could be anywhere."

"Okay. Then how do we all get away alive?" I was willing to retreat. I had no ego attached to dying nobly.

"We run like hell. But everyone's tired. Only Paul probably has any energy left, since you and Jeff took a side trip."

"How'd you know about that?"

"I know Jeff, and you've changed clothes. You aren't the only smart one around, you know."

"Oh, duh. Okay, so no one's got any hyperspeed left. The carts are smooshed, and we walk faster. Um, any ideas?"

"Pray someone has a gun in their bags," Reader offered.

I looked at the bags. Most people packed their checked bags as I did—as if they were going on a year-long trip and had to cram everything they owned inside in order to survive. They were likely to weigh a ton each. It was crazy, but no crazier than using a pen to kill one of these things.

"Grab the bags and start heaving them at him." I tried to follow my own advice, but these things were heavy as lead.

Reader didn't argue. He just grabbed the other end of the bag I was trying to move. We swung it back and forth and then launched it, just as Mephistopheles tried to stand up.

Score! Hit his knee, and it caused him some problems. We grabbed the next bag and did the same.

Some of the A-C crew saw what we were doing and came over. I didn't know any of them, but I did get to remind myself that if I died right now, I'd be surrounded by five hunks and so could possibly go happy.

Mephistopheles caught on to what we were doing and started to bat at the flying luggage. This caused us to have to dodge hurtling suitcases, but it also meant he was focused on us, not my mother.

I would have been happy about this, only Mom wasn't cooperating. Instead of running away, she headed toward him. She waited until she was in close, then started firing.

The bullets hit, but they didn't penetrate. She used the entire clip, popped it out, reached back, pulled another clip from somewhere, put it in, and fired again. This time, instead of aiming for his torso, she went for the head.

Better results, but still, it was more of a distraction than a deterrent. And he paid more attention to her than to our assault with the Luggage of Doom.

Christopher, Martini, and Gower were by my mother now. I got the impression they were trying to get her off the offensive and into run away mode. It was certainly what I'd be suggesting right now. But she wasn't having any of it.

Mephistopheles got to his knees and swiped at my mother. I got scared I'd see him kill her. Fear, like tears, made me angry. I didn't think about it, I just ran toward him. "Get away from my mother, you freak of nature!"

Freak of nature is not necessarily the biggest insult one could hurl, but it sure seemed to offend Mephistopheles. He spun toward me, snarling. I still couldn't understand him, but his expression said it clearly—he didn't care for me.

He reached out and grabbed me. His grip wasn't pleasant, but he wasn't crushing me, either. He had my lower body, so my arms were free. I risked a look around as he stood up. Gower and Christopher each had one of my mother's arms and were dragging her away. Reader was moving the other agents away. And Martini was headed right for us.

I had no idea what he thought he was going to do, but

I didn't have a lot of time to ponder, as Mephistopheles brought me up to face level. His eyes were horrible, but as he stared at me I saw them change and look more human. "You are trouble," he said, and it was in English.

"Your breath stinks. What's your point?" Twelve feet of scary fugly, and this was the best statement he could come up with?

His eyes narrowed. "You won't be trouble much longer." He opened his mouth, and I got the distinct impression he was going to try to bite my head off.

The hell with that. I fumbled in my purse and my hand hit my hairspray. Why not? It hurt if I got it in my own eyes. Besides, I didn't have any mace. I pulled it out, flipped off the cap, and sprayed, right into his mouth and eyes.

"GAAHHHH!" he screamed as he let go.

I didn't have time to scream as I fell. But I didn't have to. I didn't hit pavement, I hit Martini.

"Can we go now?" he asked, as he turned and ran.

"How do we stop that thing?" I watched Mephistopheles stomp around, gagging and rubbing his eyes.

"We have no idea, though no one but you has ever tried hairspray." We reached the others, who were all together.

Martini set me down and Mom grabbed me. "What did you think you were doing?" She hugged me tight.

"Could ask you the same thing. Mom, I can't breathe. You're squeezing tighter than our monster friend."

"Dammit," Gower said. I pulled away from Mom and looked in the same direction he was. Mephistopheles was shrinking.

"Isn't this good? He's getting smaller."

"He's going back to human form," Martini said, his voice clipped.

"Great. Let's stop him while he's our size." I wasn't seeing the problem.

"No, let's get out of here," my mother said, with a lot of authority. How had she been put in charge?

The men agreed, and we all started moving. I kept turning around. Mephistopheles was smaller, only about nine feet now, and shrinking all the time. The wings were gone, the horns, too.

"Why are we running away? Why aren't we killing that?"

Martini grabbed my hand, presumably to keep me from racing back. "He's invulnerable in his human form, too."

"And he's the head of the Al Dejahl terrorist organization," my mother added angrily.

"Who?" Second time today the same group I'd never heard of was mentioned, but then, I wasn't a big follower of international politics. "Isn't the, ah, terrorist I stopped supposed to be from that same place?"

"Yes," Christopher snapped. "They're the easiest terrorists to blame anything on, because they're thrilled to take the credit."

"Isn't that making them more powerful, though?"

"We're fighting a war, princess."

"Badly, from all I can tell. So, who are these Al people?"

"Al Dejahl," Mom said in a pained tone. "It's a worldwide terrorist organization. They make the news regularly."

"And not just from altered footage like today," Gower added.

"Yes, I guessed. What's their deal? 'Go their god' or something?"

"Why am I at all surprised you don't know? They weren't in a comic book, they don't make rock CDs, and they aren't known for their swimsuit calendars. Of course you don't know who they are." Mom's sarcasm knob was turned to full. I figured I was one smart mouthed comment away from being grounded, even if I did live on my own.

"Sorry, kind of overwhelmed here. And also wondering, still, who these guys are." And why one of them was an in-control superbeing, but I figured I'd stick with one big question at a time.

"They've got cells in, as near as we can tell, every country in the world," she finally explained. "Some are single operatives, some are cells of twenty or thirty. Very mobile, very hard to catch. They aren't religiously motivated, they just want the world in a state of chaos."

"Their leader is Ronaldo Al Dejahl. He's one of the richest men in the world," Christopher added. "You'd know him as Ronald Yates."

"So? Why can't we kill him, especially because of all those things?" I didn't see the downside to getting rid of a man who'd made his fortune in the porn industry and then gone legitimate by becoming the head of one of the biggest media empires around.

"Killing a public figure's sort of bad for the image," Martini said. "There's more to it, but can we please just get to safety?"

I looked over my shoulder. I could see a man, now, not a monster. "He's back looking human. Well, as human as he can be." You couldn't miss pictures of Yates. He was in his seventies but looked as if he were pushing ninety. He claimed to never drink, smoke, or indulge in any kinds of narcotics, but he constantly dated twenty year olds, making Hugh Hefner look like the poster boy for morality. However, he owned the media outlets, so they showed pictures of him all the time.

"Wonderful job," Martini muttered. "How the hell did this escalate?" he asked Christopher.

"He was after her," Christopher said, nodding toward my mother.

Mom shrugged. "I wasn't going to stand there and be an easy target." She looked at me. "Nice new friends you've picked up. Homeland Security my ass."

"Nice gun you've picked up. Consultant my ass," I shot back. Okay, so I decided to risk the smart mouth. I *did* live on my own, after all.

She grinned. "I *am* a consultant."

"She just consults on counterterrorism," Christopher added. He sounded impressed.

We were back at the terminal, and I could see a lot of men in uniforms heading toward us. They weren't universally handsome, which meant, I was pretty sure, we were in trouble. They all drew weapons.

"How do we get out of this?"

"You all shut up and let me handle it," my mother snapped. "Put your hands up and stop running, now."

We did as she said as she stalked out to meet the oncoming throng, all of whom were pointing their guns right at us.

"Federal officer!" my mother shouted, holding up something that looked like a thin wallet.

"Federal officer?" I said under my breath. When had this happened?

Reader was on my other side. "I told you it was an impressive file," he whispered.

Whoever was in charge came to my mother. None of their guns were down. "What's going on?" he asked her.

"I'm a federal officer, and if you don't put those goddamned guns down right now, I'm going to make sure you all end up working night security at a Taco Bell." My mother sounded both furious and completely in charge.

The man shot a look at what she was holding up, nodded, and then lowered his gun. The rest of them did the same.

"Holster your weapons!" Mom shouted. They all complied. I was impressed. Normally, I only saw her order me and my friends around like this.

"What's going on?" the man asked her again.

"I'd love you to tell me," Mom snarled. "We're attacked and pursued by a terrorist faction, in the middle of JFK, after the government issued a level-red security threat, no less, and it takes you, what, thirty minutes to get your act together and come out to support? I want names, job histories, and excuses, in writing, on my desk tomorrow morning. You and your so-called team there might also want to spend some time praying you have good answers as to why your response time was so slow."

She jerked her head forward. "My team, roll out. We're needed back at Headquarters. Remember," she snapped at the leader of airport security, "on my desk by oh-nine-hundred tomorrow, or you're all fired, without review."

With that, she stalked off, marching right through the guards, all of whom let her pass. The rest of us scurried after her. I hoped we looked official, but Mom's little rant had apparently done the trick. We weren't held up.

We got inside the airport again, marching through as though we had somewhere very important to go. I wondered just how much of a letdown "destination bathroom" was going to be after all this.

Christopher caught up with my mother, but we didn't go to any of the restrooms. Instead, we headed outside, to a taxi stand. I noted that one of the agents I didn't know was carrying luggage, my mother's if memory served.

We waited about three seconds, and then two gray limos pulled up. The agent put Mom's bags in the trunk of the first one, Christopher did his doorman thing, and Mom got in, followed by me, Martini and Gower. I made sure to be in the back facing front again, and Martini made sure he was next to me. Reader kicked the driver out of his seat, and Christopher took shotgun. We were rolling within thirty seconds. I looked behind us—the rest of the crew were in the second limo, following us.

"Well, that was fun," I said. "Now, who wants to go first and tell me what the hell is going on . . . Mom?"

CHAPTER 11

MOM LEANED BACK IN THE SEAT. "This thing equipped with anything to drink?" she asked Gower.

He nodded, and Martini pulled out a bottle of Coke. "Straw?"

"Sure, thanks," Mom said. "I was hoping for something stronger, of course."

"Not safe yet, no need to be impaired," Gower said.

"I want some answers," I said again. "Like right now. Mom, what is this, welcome to my secret life?"

She sighed. "I didn't want you to know until you were old enough."

"I'm twenty-seven. When did you think I'd be old enough, when I was forty?"

"Maybe." She smiled. "Your father doesn't really know, either."

"You haven't told Dad?" I was shocked to my core. As far as I knew, my parents had no secrets from each other. And now, here was my mother, Mrs. Rambo, and Dad had no idea.

Martini leaned forward and offered his hand. "Jeff Martini. I plan to marry your daughter."

Mom laughed as she shook his hand. "Angela Katt. I want the write up of your full financial portfolio and family tree."

Martini grinned. "No worries, have it all ready." He looked at me. "See? Your mother likes me."

"My mother's apparently trained to take on the Terminator. Right now, her liking you doesn't carry the same weight it usually does."

Mom rolled her eyes. "Kitty, stop being so dramatic. All parents have secrets from their children."

"You're packing heat! And you're a federal officer! I don't call those secrets, I call those lies."

"I can give her the *Reader's Digest* version if you want," Reader called out. "I read your whole file."

"Go for it," Mom said. "I don't find looking back all that interesting."

Reader laughed. "Fine. Okay, at sixteen, your mother was on a school trip to Washington, D.C. During an excursion, she heard another girl being attacked, so your mom went and saved this girl from being raped."

Mom shook her head. "No one else, men included, were doing anything. It was the middle of the day, and she was screaming for help. It wasn't a hard choice."

"This girl turned out to be the daughter of a senator," Reader went on. "Needless to say, the whole family was grateful, the senator to the point that he took a fatherly interest in your mother's career. He sent her to college, provided training, was her patron, really."

"He was a great man," Mom said fondly. "I still miss him."

Recognition hit. "Are you talking about Grandpa Roger?"

Mom smiled. "One and the same. He was like a second father to me, and it meant so much to him that you considered him family."

"So Aunt Emily is the daughter you saved?"

She nodded. "Why do you think she always wanted you to take self-defense classes?"

I had to let this sink in. I'd known Grandpa Roger, Aunt Emily, and the rest of their family weren't really blood relations. But Emily was my mother's best friend, even though they lived across the country from each other, and never once had anyone shared that Grandpa Roger had been in politics. They'd never really talked about how they met, either, and I'd never seen them all that often growing up, though they'd always sent great presents at my birthday. The why for all of this was a real revelation, though.

Reader went on. "In addition to other pursuits, your mother is possibly the only non-Israeli, non-Jew who's been a member of the Mossad."

"You're in the Mossad?" I managed not to scream this question out. My mother was in the Israeli Intelligence Agency? How had *that* happened?

"Was. How do you think I met your father?"

"Dad was in the Mossad!?" This seemed completely impossible.

"Oh, no," Mom laughed. "He was on a trip to Israel, though, when we met."

This story I knew. They'd met at a café in Tel Aviv. Dad had been impressed that someone who wasn't Jewish was living in Israel, Mom had thought Dad was really handsome, the rest was history. But I wanted the details now.

"So, how'd you meet him, really?"

"At the café, just as we've told you. Only, I was following him for his protection. He was there with a college group that was marked for attack by one of the many terrorist factions in the Middle East. Jewish-American graduate students, it was like waving a red flag in front of bulls."

"And he didn't know?"

"Well, he figured it out when the bullets started flying," Mom said casually, as if this were a normal courtship tale. "He thought it was sexy," she added with the smile she always had whenever she was thinking about Dad in a romantic way.

"Ugh. I think it's unreal. So then what?"

"Then she supposedly retired and started work as a consultant," Reader supplied. "Only, retired applied to being an active agent for the Mossad. In reality, she went to work for the American government in an antiterrorist organization."

"You work for the C.I.A.?" I wondered whether there was anything I actually knew about my mother.

She laughed again. "No. It's a smaller organization, reporting directly to the White House. We work independently of the other federal agencies. Besides," she said, patting my knee, "I really am a consultant."

"Yeah, in the past twenty-eight years, she's mostly consulted with international and multinational corporations, teaching them how to protect against terrorist attacks, how to get their people out of hostage situations, things like that."

"So you got pregnant and had to slow down?" I asked a bit more sarcastically than I'd intended.

Mom shook her head. "You make sacrifices for your child, and all she can do is be resentful."

"So, how long have you known about the aliens?"

Mom looked completely shocked. "What aliens?"

Martini coughed, loudly. "Uh, maybe we should cover that back at headquarters."

"She doesn't know?" I was shouting, but I'd had about all I could take.

Christopher turned around. "What's the matter, princess? Want to turn all the work over to Mommy?"

I lunged at him. I would have gotten him, too, even though he jerked away toward the windshield, if Martini hadn't grabbed me by the waist. "Listen, you little weasel, let's go, right here." I clawed at him, I'd had enough.

"Katherine Katt!" Mom's tone was one I'd heard all my life: I was in trouble.

"He started it!"

"And I'm finishing it." Mom pushed on my shoulders, gently, and I let Martini pull me back next to him. She turned around. "Christopher, I rather like you, but if you insult my daughter again in my presence, I'll break your neck. And trust me, I can do it." She turned back. "That goes for the rest of you, too."

There was dead silence in the limo. Gower and Martini were exchanging meaningful looks. I got the impression they were trying to make escape plans in case Mom or I totally lost it. Christopher was glowering and looked embarrassed. Reader was driving in the intent way people do when they do not want to engage the rest of the car's occupants at all. And I was seething at Christopher and still trying to readjust my entire life's history into what I'd learned in the last few minutes.

On cue, my cell phone rang. Everyone jumped, and I

dug through my purse for it. It took a little longer to find than usual—the run in with Mephistopheles had jumbled stuff up more than normal. I got my phone opened on the sixth ring. "Hi, Dad!"

"Kitty, sorry I'm calling a little late, couldn't get off the phone with your Aunt Karen. So, how goes it?"

Wow. Now there was a question I had no idea how to answer. "Um . . . pretty good." Well, we were all alive, right? That was on the good end of the spectrum.

"You sound funny. Are you really okay?"

No, but I didn't think telling him that was a good idea. "I'm pretty good. Kind of tired. Lots of running around."

"Are you in Guantánamo?" he asked sharply.

I managed a strangled laugh. "No, Dad, I'm in a limo."

"Oh, nice. Hero treatment? Good. So, everything else okay? Do I need to call Uncle Mort?"

"No, no Uncle Mort right now." I looked at Mom, in case she disagreed. She nodded.

"You know, I can't reach your mother," he said. "Maybe she's back on the plane."

"Um, I don't know why you can't reach Mom," I said, giving her the "what now" look.

She sighed and held out her hand. I put the phone in it. "Hi, honey," she said. There was a pause while I figured Dad reassessed the situation. "Yes, I'm with Kitty." Pause. "Noooo, we're not in Vegas." She gave me the "what the hell" look. I did the universal "fake it" response.

"No, in New York." Pause. "Yes, Kitty's new friends in . . ." Martini, Gower, and I all mouthed, "Homeland Security," ". . . Homeland Security came and picked me up."

Pause, eye roll. "Yes, they have fast jets." Pause, closed eyes. "We're fine. Really." Sigh, eyes open. "Yes, it's related to my job." Annoyed face. "No, I did not ask them to pull Kitty in. You shouldn't even have to ask that." Really annoyed face. "No, you are not calling Mort. If I want backup, I will call for backup. I do not want backup, we do not need backup, and Kitty is an adult and is doing just fine, thank you."

Longer pause while I guessed Dad was ranting. Mom had a very resigned, heard it all before look on her face.

"Honey? I love you, Kitty loves you, and we are in the middle of helping Homeland Security with a major situation, so, please, stop worrying."

Stop worrying? She tells him that and he's supposed to *not* worry? I started questioning Mom's ability to handle a situation that didn't involve guns.

Mom sighed again. "Honey, look, everything's fine." Narrowed eyes. "No, I don't know there are several gray cars parked around the house." I made violent movements, pointing at Martini, Gower, the limo, and the car behind us. Mom nodded. "They're probably Homeland Security vehicles."

Ah, her "duh" look. "Yes, guarding you." Double duh. "Yes, to keep you safe." Rolling eyes again. "No, frankly, I think spending our tax dollars on your protection *is* a good use of funds. I couldn't care less about some stupid owls in Oregon, okay?" Ah, their old argument. Dad was far more ecologically minded than Mom. I knew where this conversation was headed.

I cleared my throat. Mom looked over. "I'll take it from here," I suggested as I put my hand out.

"Love you, honey, here's Kitty back," Mom said hurriedly. She flung my phone back to me.

"Dad, let's keep it down to just a family level, okay?" I said, as I heard him start in on his usual eco-friendly rant.

"Fine," he said, clearly still upset. "What is really going on?"

"Pretty much what I told you. When they discovered I was related to Mom, they pulled her in. Nice of the two of you to share what she really did for a living."

Guilt trips always worked on my father. He went instantly into contrition mode. "Kitten, I'm sorry. We didn't want you to worry. Your mother knows what she's doing, and she hasn't done fieldwork since before you were born." This I felt was a whopping lie, but I also had a feeling Dad might not know it was a lie.

"Okay, whatever. Look, Dad, I'll deal with it. We're okay, but we really need to get back to work. Don't let anyone in who isn't really drop-dead handsome, okay?"

Long pause. "I don't really know what you or your

mother consider handsome," Dad shared, sounding embarrassed and a little grossed out.

"Dad, if a woman or a man comes to the door who is less good-looking than Brad Pitt or Angelina Jolie, do not open the door."

"Angelina Jolie might be by?" Dad suddenly sounded perky. Great, this was information I hadn't wanted.

"Not likely, but who knows? However, anyone not as good-looking as those two should not be allowed inside, got it?"

"Sure. You sure you're with Homeland Security and not some Hollywood producer?"

I found myself wishing I'd gone with the Hollywood lie in the first place. Too late to use it now. "No, we're not about to star in a major motion picture. Dad, just relax. I think you can stop calling every two hours, though." Mom nodded emphatically. "Mom agrees," I added.

"I'm sure she does," he huffed. "Well, I want regular reports from you two, then."

"Dad!"

"Well, when you can. I'm on the edge of my seat here, wondering if my girls are safe or not."

He had a real point. "Okay, Dad, I promise one of us will call you the next break we get. We're perfectly safe, though," I lied.

"Okay, kitten. Well, love to you and your mother. Tell her I'm not upset any more."

"Will do, Dad. Love you." I hung up. "He's not mad at you any more."

Mom snorted. "So he claims."

"I'd take it," Martini suggested.

"Right now, I just want to take a nap," I said.

"No sleep 'til Home Base," Gower stated.

"I'd rather go for no sleep 'til Brooklyn." Everyone gave me a blank stare.

Reader laughed. "Don't think we have time to take in a Beastie Boys concert, girlfriend." At least there was one person in the car who I could relate to. That I had the most in common with a former international male model was an irony I was too tired to marvel over.

"Pity. I could use the rest. Yes, okay," I said to Gower's angry look, "no sleeping until we're back. So, where are we going now?"

"Safe transference point," Martini answered.

I thought about it. "Heading to LaGuardia are we?"

He grinned. "I'd like a lot of kids," he said to Mom. "But we're still discussing it."

She sighed. "Ask her how often she has to get new fish before you make a final decision."

CHAPTER 12

THE TRIP TO LA GUARDIA WAS QUIET. And slow. We were stuck in rush hour traffic, which in New York is impressive.

Everyone was tired, so we didn't talk much. I was okay with that. It gave me more time to plot how to run Christopher over with a truck.

A little whining from Martini got Gower to reverse the no napping mandate, and pretty soon everyone but Reader and me seemed out.

Martini shifted in his sleep, put his arm around me, and pulled me next to him. I wondered whether he was really asleep, but I figured he wouldn't have let his head bob against the seat and the window if he was awake. I shoved my purse between his head and the window and he snuggled into it.

Christopher was slouched into the corner of the front seat, Gower was sleeping in the same way across from Martini, and Mom had curled into a ball, using her purse as a pillow. For some reason, all of them sleeping made me more alert.

I saw Reader look at me in the rearview mirror. "You can snooze too, if you want," he offered. "I'm fine."

I shook my head. "I'd like to, but someone else has to be conscious." Even though I was bone tired, I was also totally wired and wide awake.

He grinned. "Yeah, we have to watch over our brothers from another planet."

"True enough." I considered everything that had happened today and was very proud that I was more interested in getting some answers than in freaking out. "So, they have all these things like gates and we sit in traffic?"

"That's the way it goes, girlfriend."

"Why?"

He was quiet for a moment. "Some because it helps keep a lower profile. Some because our enemies might not expect it. And some because they want to fit in."

This seemed possible if they were hanging with a lot of other male models. Not so likely if they were wandering around with the rest of us. "Does it actually work? The fitting in, I mean."

"Somewhat. Jeff's the best at it, by a long shot."

"You just trying to make me like him?"

Reader chuckled. "No. But of all of them, he's the most adaptable. Always has been, at least since he was a teenager."

I thought about Chuckie for some reason. He was adaptable, too. He'd had to be—the smartest guy in the room tends to draw a lot of unwanted attention from big, mean jerks. Chuckie had grown up into a really awesome adult, which made me wonder if Martini had been similar in childhood. Then again, call it loyalty, call it stubbornness, but it was going to be hard for anyone to prove to me that they were a match for Chuckie's brainpower.

The urge to send a text to Chuckie telling him what was really going on was almost overpowering. I mean, even Professor X and Brainiac liked to hear they were right now and again. I glanced at Martini. He was still clearly asleep. And I was plotting to share his existence with someone not in the know, and he wasn't reacting to it. "How can Martini be napping?"

"Um, he's tired?"

"No, I mean, he's an empath. He said he was really powerful."

"He is. Jeff's the most powerful empath on the planet."

"Impressive. But he's asleep."

"I'm not following you, girlfriend."

I tried to figure out how to explain what I meant without sharing that I wanted to let Chuckie in on the Big Secret. Well, per the confusing explanation of A-C hyperspeed ability, Reader was also a comics fan. "Daredevil has to sleep in that whole immersion chamber thing in order to drown out all the sound."

"Oh! Gotcha. Well, it's a little different for the empaths. They have blocks."

I sighed. "Really, Martini told me that much already. I don't understand what they are or how they work. And, is it like in the X-Men, where the mutant powers usually show up during puberty?"

"I don't fully understand it all, either, since Paul's not an empath, but I'll give it a shot. A-C talents can show up any time before adulthood, which for them is similar to us—around twenty-one. The stronger the talent, the earlier it shows. The average is, like for the X-Men, somewhere around puberty."

"So, what happens when the acne coincides with the ability to know how mad your mother really is with your crashing her car?"

"I'm not going to ask why you used that example, girl-friend. The A-Cs test all their kids when they're young to spot talent inclination. It's only an issue for some of their talents. I mean, scientific aptitude doesn't mean you have to shut anything off."

I thought about the fun Chuckie had had prior to college. "Other than maybe your brain."

Reader chuckled. "Yeah. So, the empathic-likely get trained in how to block off emotions. It becomes not quite as automatic as breathing but about as automatic as blocking a punch if you've trained in a fighting form long enough."

"Okay. Martini mentioned drugs."

"Yeah. They shoot a variety of drugs into the empaths. None of them are harmful to their metabolisms—it's not like they're addicts. The drugs enhance the blocks and blocking ability and strengthen their empathic synapses."

"How often do they wear off?"

"Depends on the empath and what he's doing. The more activity, physical and emotional in particular, or the more onslaught of emotions hitting the empath, the sooner they burn out."

"So, getting into a fight with your mother would burn you out?"

"Depends on the fight. But a fight like we just had with Mephistopheles, where people you care about are in danger and you're also physically fighting? That can wear you down fast."

"Is that why he's sleeping?"

"Probably. And he's learned to put what they call sleep blocks up automatically. From what Paul's told me, Jeff can and does sleep like a rock, unless someone nearby is in real danger, because their emotions have to be off the charts and they have to be the negative ones—fear, hatred, and the like—or he's trained to ignore them."

"So you and Paul can be romantic next door and Martini's not going to know?"

Reader laughed. "He might know, but he's not going to wake up and rate our performances. He'll ignore it, because that's part of what the blocks do—help them ignore all the emotions around them. Like Daredevil's chamber but without the being locked away and submerged in water parts."

I considered this as we sat there, not moving much, if at all. "So, when did the strongest empath on the planet's talent surface?"

Reader cleared his throat. "Birth."

"Um, you're kidding, right?"

"No, I'm not. Jeff's parents aren't empathic, they aren't talented in any way. So from what I've gotten, it was hard on them."

"Had to have been harder on him."

"Yeah. Jeff had to be in isolation a lot as a child. And as for what that's like, you'll have to ask him—I've never spent any time in or around the isolation chambers."

"Why not?"

"They creep me out. They make Daredevil's chamber look like a tanning bed. But Jeff insists they're not that bad. Christopher won't give me his opinion about them, though."

"Does he go into isolation?" And could we put him there right away?

"No, not that I've ever heard of." He looked to his right. "But as a child, Christopher wasn't all that much better off."

"He's an empath?" I found that hard to believe.

"No, different talent. But his surfaced at birth, too. It's why they're a team—no one else can keep up with them, in that sense."

"And yet the image of me killing a 'terrorist' made the international news. You know, there's a part of me that's really unimpressed."

Reader laughed again. "They're only human, if you know what I mean. Everyone makes mistakes, girlfriend, even you."

"Point out what mistakes I've made today, other than agreeing to get into the limo in front of the courthouse."

"Too busy driving to think about it." Reader looked over his shoulder and flashed the cover-boy grin. "But give me a little time and I'm sure I can come up with something."

"I'll bet." I closed my eyes and tried to rest. Couldn't. Opened my eyes. "What happens when they run down? The empaths, I mean."

"Again, it depends on the empath. Usually they just need to sleep. If they're not doing well, they need to sleep in isolation. They do almost a system flush, to clear out toxins that build up from the exposure to negative emotions. Then they put the good stuff back in. I don't really know much more about it."

"Because you haven't asked?"

"Because no one wants to talk about it. A-C talents seem physically connected as much as mentally, at least to me. It's hard to get a straight answer."

"They don't want us knowing their weaknesses."

"Can you blame them?"

I thought about it. "Honestly? No. So what happens to Martini when he gets drained?" Reader was quiet. "Ah, James? Are we being followed or something?"

"No."

"Then why are you suddenly Mr. Silent Night?"

He sighed. "The stronger the empathic talent, the longer they can last, so the more they can push themselves." He didn't say anything else.

Of course, it wasn't hard to figure out the obvious conclusion. "And, therefore, the harder they crash."

"Right."

I looked at Martini. "He sure seems healthy."

"He is. And hale and hearty and whatever other descriptions you might want to apply. At least until his blocks wear down. Then he becomes, first, almost like a regular human—can't pick up much, it's like the talent mutes."

"You said at first. What happens at second? Or third?"

"The muting goes away, and it's a barrage of emotions. Hard to handle."

"Like putting a chameleon on plaid?"

"Yeah, pretty much. Then it starts to affect him physically and mentally. The reactions are similar to anyone who might have pushed themselves too far physically and mentally, only they hit faster and, from all I've seen, a lot harder. After that, if he doesn't get care in time, and in time means really fast . . ."

"The dramatic pause is great, only it's lacking that certain something. Like actual information."

Reader looked over his shoulder again, only this time he wasn't smiling. "If he doesn't get care in time, Jeff will die."

CHAPTER 13

THAT CHEERFUL STATEMENT SAT ON THE AIR for a while. I resisted the urge to wish it were Christopher instead of Martini who was the walking death time bomb, then reminded myself I wasn't attached to any of them, least of all Martini, and decided I could worry about something else.

"So, would this evening's entertainment mean Martini's at death's door?" Okay, I could almost worry about something else.

"Nope. Believe me, when Jeff's that bad, you'll know."

"Can't wait." Since imminent death wasn't on the docket, unless we were trapped in the never-ending traffic jam and were going to die from old age, still sitting in this limo, I chose to relax.

I watched the cars as we all inched forward. Which was so very soothing that my mind raced to the next set of questions it wanted answered while we snailed along. "Why can't we kill Yates?"

"We have to kill him when he's Mephistopheles."

"Why?"

Reader sighed. "It's complicated, but I'll give it a try." He was really pushing the complicated. I wondered if there was a hidden message Reader was trying to get across to me, but if so, I wasn't picking it up.

"Didn't you ask these questions when you joined up?"

"Yeah, I did. But the scientists handle most of this, and

they don't share all that much information with one of the human drivers, even if I am a part of Alpha Team."

"Seems unfair."

"I deal with it. You still interested in all the superbeing stuff, or do you want to head to office politics?"

"I think I'm more at risk from a superbeing, so let's deal with that."

"And you say you work in marketing? Anyway, when the parasite hits, it takes over. That's why the superbeings mutate immediately." I'd seen that in action, so no argument there. "But in the rare cases where the human-parasite combination doesn't go berserk, the parasite internalizes." He'd told me as much already, so, fine. "In those cases, the human brain seems split. So when they're in human form, they don't really know they have a parasite inside them. As far as we can tell, it's only when the parasite senses a threat that it converts back into a superbeing."

This was news. "So in the cases where the combination is, what—stable?—the parasite is smart enough to hang out as a human unless threatened?"

"Seems that way, yeah."

"Does the parasite remember it *is* a parasite?"

Reader sighed. "We don't know. There are only a few in-control superbeings, thankfully. But because there are a limited number, and we can't find them, we don't have a lot of intelligence about them. Most of what we know is conjecture."

"No Cerebro-type thing for finding parasites or superbeings, huh?"

"No. I know a lot of this sounds like the comics, but reality means we're stuck with certain things we can't get around. Or haven't gotten to yet. Honestly, I think one of the scientific teams *is* working on something similar to a mutant finder like Cerebro, but they're a long way away from it working, at least as far as any field agents are aware."

"Okay, so, I still don't understand why we can't kill them while they're in human form."

"Politically, it's a bad thing. We'd come off like terrorists murdering an innocent person."

"But they aren't people any more."

"Yes, well, the thing is, if the parasite isn't active, or,

rather, if you can't see them as a superbeing, then when they die, you still can't. And," he added, "the parasite can escape and reestablish itself with someone else. The parasite has to be killed, and it can only be killed while the entity is in superbeing form or if it's separated from any host."

I thought about this for a bit. "But you all told me the human forms could be killed only if the parasite allowed it."

"Yes. But let's use Yates as an example. He turns back into a human, is totally confused about why he's standing in the middle of the tarmac. You go to kill him. Maybe the parasite decides it would rather join with you—Yates is old, you seem more compatible, Yates is able to come back to human too well, whatever the reason. So the parasite does let you kill Yates. And then it moves to you."

"So you'd kill me and the parasite, too." I didn't like this plan, but it seemed logical.

"Right. Only, do you really think we could?"

I considered this. I knew he wasn't asking if I thought they were capable. "I don't know."

"I don't think we could. We *know* you."

"Well, yes, but I could see someone, say, Christopher, managing to get past that and do me in anyway. And," I had to admit, "it would be the right thing to do."

"Maybe. I don't want to be in the position to have to find out—with you or anyone else we work with. Besides, we need the bodies in their superbeing forms, for study, for proof. If we kill Yates, we're murdering terrorists. If we kill Mephistopheles, we're heroes."

"Fine line. And hard to do if he's invulnerable no matter what."

"He's vulnerable, we just have to figure out where the parasite is inside him. It's harder than you'd think."

"Not in the torso or head."

"Could be, though. You have to hit the spot exactly. It's why tanks and heavy artillery work well—they have a more likely chance of hitting the area when they're hitting the entire being."

"So why didn't anyone call in the military? I mean, there was a huge monster stomping around JFK. I can't understand why the entire police force wasn't called in."

Reader sighed. "We monitor all of this kind of activity from the Science Center and from our other bases. The moment we can spot the superbeing showing up, we alter all media. No one sees it, so no one reacts to it."

"How many bases are there?"

"We have them dotted all over the world. The most active one outside of those in the U.S is Euro Base, located in Paris, but there are several on each continent. We have a lot of bases spread over the U.S. Gate technology lets us get around, and, of course, there are gates in every airport the world over, even the tiny, obscure ones."

"That's fine, but speaking of that, what about the people there, in the airport? What do they think happened?"

Reader seemed uncomfortable all of a sudden. "Well, that's complicated."

Again with the complicated. "Because it's the mind-control thing Martini mentioned to me, right?"

"Yeah," Reader sounded relieved. "It's complicated to explain, though," he reiterated, in case I'd missed it the first time. I wanted to ask if "complicated" was Reader's code word for "I'd rather not say," but I wasn't sure what I'd do if he replied that the answer to that would again be complicated.

Decided to find out. "James, what's with all the complicated? It's like your code word."

"You're good." He sounded impressed. "Complicated means classified. As in, civilians don't get to know this."

"So, why are you telling me? Or, conversely, why don't you want to tell me?"

"I have no problem giving you what I have, girlfriend. I'm just not sure I'm supposed to. Besides, the mind stuff really is complicated as well as classified."

"So Martini told me, at least the complicated part. Feel free to take a stab at it. Who could I tell that would believe any of this anyway?" Other than Chuckie, though I didn't say that for a variety of reasons, not wanting them to snatch him and do God knew what to him being one of the stronger ones.

I felt Martini's arm tighten around me. "I'll do it," he said drowsily. "Just cuddle up here."

"My mother is snoozing right across from us," I pointed out.

"She seems cool with it," Reader offered.

"You're not helping."

Martini pulled a little harder, and I gave in. Snuggling up against him really wasn't all that bad. "Okay, I'm cuddled. So talk."

"Naps are good for you," Martini said, sounding a bit more awake.

"Information's better. Spill it."

He gave a good-natured grumble but opened his eyes a crack. "Oh, okay, fine. The mind-control device is for large crowds, only. It doesn't work on one person. It's not even mind control, really. More like creating a group hallucination."

"How does it work?"

Martini yawned and stretched. He looked like a big cat. Then he settled back and moved me a little closer. "Odorless gas that affects the brain's receptors. Human brains only, because we don't need to fool any A-Cs and we don't care about fooling any of the superbeings."

"How is this gas dispensed?"

"It's in the air all the time," he said, as if this was just a minor thing.

"You have gases in the air that give humans mass hallucinations? All the time?" I was outraged, but kept my voice down. People were sleeping, after all.

"They're natural to Earth," Martini said patiently. "We just know how to use them."

"Just how do you use them?"

He sighed. "We can see the gases, and all agents know how to manipulate them. Basically, we create what we want the human crowd to see and project it. Alien technology, remember? We've all got devices implanted into our brains, sort of like radio transmitters, only really tiny and set up to handle these kinds of things." He yawned again. "That's why no one was asking what happened with the superbeing you took out. I altered what everyone saw. Christopher's side of the house handles the media. Normally they can get to the cameras and the like and alter them before any human notices."

I pondered this for a bit. "I saw the man sprout wings and start killing people."

"You were intimately involved in the action, so you weren't affected by the mass hallucination."

"That seems convenient."

He groaned. "Nothing's easy with you, is it? It's not convenient, it's adrenaline and the fight-or-flight syndrome all humans have. When the adrenaline starts pumping, it either helps or hinders the hallucination. If a person's reaction to danger is flight, then they see the hallucination. If it's fight, then they see reality. And, before you can ask, in the case of law enforcement or military personnel, all those trained to fight no matter what, and all those who are fighters by nature, if they aren't intimately involved in the action, they're affected by the hallucination."

"The guys who were driving the baggage carts didn't think they saw a monster," Reader added. "They saw whatever Christopher wanted them to see. Your mother, on the other hand, was intimately involved and saw what the rest of us saw."

"You and I weren't intimately involved when it started." Reader and Martini both were quiet. I looked up at Martini. "What does that mean? I assume I won't like it." I didn't expect an answer from Reader—besides, I had a feeling his reply would be that this was complicated.

Martini looked uncomfortable, but I stared him down. "It means I gave you a shot when you passed out the first time. It protects you against the hallucinations. You can't see what we project any more."

I considered this. "You made it so you can't fool me like the general populace?" He nodded. "How long will this last?"

"I gave you enough for a week. If you end up becoming an official agent, you'll get regular injections monthly."

"They don't hurt," Reader threw out. "They use some special alien shot-giver thing, much nicer than a hypodermic."

"I'm thrilled." I wasn't that upset. They'd made me less susceptible to them, not more. If I could believe them. Then again, fast or not, Martini hadn't been there when the man had sprouted his killer wings. If he'd wanted me to see something else, it hadn't worked. And if I believed he wanted me to at least go to bed with him, he certainly wasn't doing himself any favors by making me less adaptable to his will. I decided to let this one slide.

He picked it up and looked relieved. "Thanks," he said quietly. "I'd really rather not have a fight with you right now."

We were still sitting in traffic—I was fairly sure we'd gone about a whopping ten miles in forty-five minutes—and I got sleepy all of a sudden. "You making me tired?"

"Nope," Martini said with a chuckle. "It's just been a big day."

"O-kay," I said through a yawn. His chest was right there and rather inviting. I leaned my head against it, and I didn't have to be an empath to determine he liked it. He pulled me closer, and I was so tired that I decided to ask about the double heartbeat I was hearing when I woke up.

CHAPTER 14

I AWOKE WITH A START. "It's in his throat!"

"What? Kitty, are you all right?" My mother put her hand to my forehead. "You might be a little feverish."

"I'm not feverish. Where are we?" I looked around. Still in the limo, but it looked like we were at the airport. "Where's Martini or Gower?"

"They all went inside to make sure we'll be safe in there."

"So they left us alone in the car? Like this is some sort of shield?"

Mom coughed. "They explained that it is. Their cars are, um, special."

It figured. "Okay, so we're all safe and sound in the vehicle?"

"Supposedly. What were you screaming about when you woke up?"

It was fuzzy, but I could still see it. "When Mephistopheles had me up to his face, when it looked like he was going to bite my head," I said slowly. "Remember?"

"Vividly. I'm glad your father won't have the memory."

"Well, didn't it strike you as odd, that he was going to eat me, versus stomp or crush me?"

"Kitten, I was watching some monster try to eat my baby. I wasn't giving the oddity of the situation a lot of thought."

"Me either. I was focused on his bad breath and getting my hairspray out." I could just see it, in the back of his throat. "Martini said it would move to me. Oh, I am so grossed and freaked out. Where the hell is he, anyway?" It was a shock to realize I wanted Martini next to me, right now, more than anything in the world. Because I was finally really and truly terrified.

"He's inside the terminal. Kitty, what are you trying to tell me?"

I was about to answer when the car door was flung open and Martini's head appeared. I managed not to shriek. "What's wrong?" he asked, clearly frightened.

I was about to ask *him* what was wrong and why he'd tried to give me a heart attack when my brain kicked in. Empath, remember? Empath who liked me. Duh. It was nice to know that if I was scared, he'd be right there. "I'm sorry, we're okay," I said as reassuringly as I could. "I just realized something."

"To the point where your entire being was terrified and screaming for me?" he asked. He looked shaken.

I pulled him into the car and kept hold of his hand. "I'm sorry. It's okay. I was, well, am, scared, but the threat isn't immediate." I hoped.

He didn't look convinced, but he did settle down in the seat. "What *is* the threat?"

"The parasite is in Mephistopheles' throat, hanging back there like a third tonsil. He was trying to eat me, not to kill me, but so the parasite could move to me. The hairspray must have hit the parasite and just made it go haywire for whatever reason. It *was* extra hold."

Martini went back to looking concerned. "Dammit, I knew you were too tempting."

"As flattering as that could be but probably isn't, why so?"

He heaved a sigh. "Anyone capable of being a human agent is also very tempting to the parasites. For all we know, the parasite you killed was actually heading for you when the man near you got enraged and it shifted its focus to him."

This was not comforting news. I was homicidal-maniac-parasite bait. Not exactly what I'd always hoped to attract.

Gower, Reader, and Christopher showed up now, all

looking worried. Apparently Martini had run to me at hyperspeed without telling them where he was going or why. I was rather touched even while I reminded myself this was a power to be used wisely.

Martini brought the others up to speed on what I'd told him. To a man they looked disturbed. "We have to get her to the Science Center," Gower said finally.

"No argument," Martini agreed. "But now I'm worried about the trip from here to there."

"Why? I mean, we've been trotting all over the place. Why worry now?"

Christopher gave me a withering look. "Because now the most powerful in-control superbeing knows exactly who you are and is undoubtedly looking for you."

"You all said the superbeings don't remember what they are when they're back in human form," I protested. "That their brain is split."

"True," Martini said. "But the superbeing portion will remember this incident. And if it manifests again tonight, it's going to be hunting you down."

"It has more power as Yates," I argued. It was feeble, and I knew it. But it was worth a shot.

"You're younger and healthier," Christopher snapped. "And, from all I can tell, nastier."

"That's enough," Mom said quietly. "We're all upset. This is not the time for little games." She gave Christopher a long look, and I saw him back himself down. Interesting. Mom looked to Gower. "I'm now very concerned about Kitty's father, as well as the rest of our extended family."

Gower shook his head. "They're all under protection. We have them mapped and agents covering all of them, pets included."

"Not that I object, but why the pets, too?" This was a new one, at least in my admittedly limited experience.

"If you love it, it's got potential as a hostage," Martini answered.

"My fish are safe."

"They might be the only things that are," Mom said dryly. "I'd like my husband with us."

Gower shook his head. "He's safer at your home. At least for right now."

Mom gave Gower a look that could freeze water in the Bahamas. "Young man, ensure that I don't have to say this more than once. I don't care what planet you're from or what powers you have or what you think you can do better than humans. I've been protecting that man since I was nineteen, and if you think I'm going to trust his safety to any of you right now, you're insane. I want my husband with me, where I know he'll be safe, and I want him with me now, or I will show you that Mossad training is the best on any planet."

Gower actually looked as though he was going to argue, but Martini spoke up. "Do it. Now." It wasn't a request, it was an order. Gower didn't fight it, just nodded and left the car, presumably to make the arrangements. Interesting again. Christopher followed him. Both of them were on their phones.

Martini was concentrating. "I'll be right back." He got out of the car, too, joining Gower and Christopher. They were off their phones and clearly arguing.

Reader sighed. "Let me see if I can get them to calm down."

"Why are they so upset?"

Reader shrugged as he got out of the car. "Mephistopheles does that to them."

I was happy we were inside the car with the doors shut while the menfolk argued. Mom looked worried. "I'm not clear on all this alien parasite business yet. Christopher had time to give me only a few details while we were running for our lives, and honestly, I was so distracted I didn't even realize they were aliens until you said something—I was thinking experimental weapons and technology. You really got under his skin fast," she added.

"Yeah, but I think Martini makes fast decisions because he's an empath."

"Probably, but I'm not talking about Jeff. I'm talking about Christopher."

"The jerk? I have no idea why he hates me, and I couldn't care less right about now."

Mom gave me an odd look. "Why do you think he hates you?"

I snorted. "You mean aside from everything you've already seen? Calling me princess, asking about my tiara. He went through my stuff at home, pawed my pictures all up. I barely know any of these guys, but Christopher and I haven't stopped fighting pretty much since we met. If my trying to strangle him earlier wasn't a clear enough clue that we don't exactly get along, let me clarify that for you right now."

Mom still had that odd look going. "Ah. Okay. Well." She straightened her skirt.

"What?"

"Nothing," she said, not looking at me. "We'll talk about it later."

Whatever the argument was, Reader seemed to have gotten the situation calmed down. At least it looked as though everyone was playing nicely together again. Martini opened the door and stuck his head in. "We're just about set. I want you two ready to move, okay?"

"Sure. So, now what?"

"Now we go to the bathroom. Quickly."

"I don't actually need to go," Mom said dryly.

"Yes, you do. You explain it to her," Martini said to me as Gower called to him. He shut the car door and went back to the other men.

While I explained the traveling system, Martini, Reader, and Christopher milled about outside the car. I couldn't tell what they were doing, though Gower seemed to be getting Mom's luggage out of the trunk.

"The bathroom," Mom said finally. "Unreal."

"But effective. We're going to use the men's, I'm sure. I don't think Martini wants us separated."

"That's clear. But, you know, choose your husband carefully."

"Mom."

"Mom, this isn't the time or the place. Besides, I meant he wouldn't want us splitting up because it'd leave the two of us exposed." I thought about what she'd just said. "What's wrong with him?"

"Other than the fact that he's known you less than a day and wants to marry you? And is, from what they've said, an alien? Oh, gee, nothing."

"He's an empath. I think that makes him more emotionally committed." I had no idea why I was defending

Martini all of a sudden. "And Reader says they make great mates."

"James and Paul may have a wonderful relationship, but that doesn't mean you'll have the same."

"How'd you know about them?" I'd been with them for hours and it took seeing them holding hands for me to catch on. Mom's with them an hour and knows their life story.

She shrugged. "You get trained to spot things like this."

"In the Mossad?"

"Among other places, yes. Let's get past that, shall we?"

"I guess. He's really handsome. And he's funny."

"No argument. They're all handsome. Looks aren't everything. Your father was the best looking man I'd ever seen when we met, but I didn't marry him because he was a hunk. I married him because of the kind of man he was, because of how he treated me and cared for and about me."

"Fine. Well, Martini's doing a lot of caring."

"Just don't make a decision based on how someone acts for one stressful day."

There was more to it, I could tell, but I decided not to argue with her. "Fine, no final mating decisions will be made tonight."

"Good."

"So, Dad really doesn't know what you do?"

She sighed. "He knows, to a certain extent. What he understands is that much of my work is classified, and information filters on a need to know basis. He doesn't need to know, so he doesn't ask. He knows I'll tell him when he *does* need to know. He's fine with that." She gave me the hairy eyeball. "I expect you to be fine with that, too."

"I suppose." At the moment, what choice did I have, anyway? "I'm sure it's all complicated."

"True enough." Mom looked around. "What's taking them so long?"

"I have no idea."

Martini stuck his head into the car. "We're making sure we've got the airport cleared, just in case." He grinned at our shocked looks. "Empath, remember? I can pick up the mutual impatience." He looked straight at Mom. "And I care about her a lot more than you think I do." Then he went back to the other men.

"Well, it'd be hard to fool him, I'll say that," Mom said quietly.

"Unlike Dad?"

She rolled her eyes at me. "As I said, Dad knows more than you think he does."

"But not everything."

She gave me a slow smile. "No man should know everything about his wife. There's no mystery then. And mystery is good for a long-lasting relationship."

Words of wisdom from The Mossad Mother. I guessed I'd just accept it and argue with her later. Martini was too close by to deal with all this now.

"I think they have two hearts," I said to fill the silence.

Mom looked thoughtful. "I guess that would explain the speed."

"Did you get the whiz tour with Christopher?"

"Yes, to get outside onto the tarmac. It was interesting."

"Did you black out?"

She smiled. "No, he said he went slowly."

"Yeah, Martini did that with me the first time, too. Regular speed for them is pretty hard to take."

"I'll bet it is. Alpha Centauri, huh?" She still looked thoughtful, not freaked out.

"Is this just another day at work for you?"

"In a way. You get used to having your world turned upside down in my line of work." Mom sighed. "I keep on planning to retire, but then something happens, and you realize it's not just your family you have to protect. Sometimes you really do have to save the whole world."

I could relate to this, far too well after today's events. "The supposed terrorist I killed sprouted wings and shot knives or something worse out of them. It was horrible."

"And you stopped him." I could hear the pride in her voice.

"Guess it's in the genes."

"It's always nice to know your child will do the right thing, the brave thing, when it matters. No one knows what they'll do until they're tested. Not everybody is a protector." She looked straight at me, and I realized she had tears in her eyes.

I leaned across and hugged her, this time just as tightly as she hugged me. "I love you, Mom." She kissed my head, and I felt that maybe this whole day had been worth it after all.

We finally pulled apart, and Martini stuck his head back in the car. I knew without asking he'd waited for our mother-daughter moment to be over. "Time to go, ladies."

CHAPTER 15

MARTINI TOOK MY HAND, and Christopher took Mom's. I wasn't wild about it, but it wasn't as though I wanted to hold his hand instead, so I didn't say anything.

Gower and Reader were in the lead, then Mom and Christopher, with me and Martini bringing up the rear. The other agents with us were flanking in formation, one in front of the other, with three on either side of us. Two of these had Mom's luggage split between them. We looked very official. I was the only person not in a suit, and I felt underdressed.

Not that it mattered. Because there were no people in the airport. At all. "Where is everyone?" I asked Martini.

"Evacuated."

"I didn't see anyone run out in a panic."

"Because we know how to evacuate."

I thought about it. "You used some mass hallucination thing, didn't you?"

He smiled. "You think? Yeah, we moved everyone to the baggage claim area."

"Will they be safe there if something happens?"

"Hope so. Hope nothing's going to happen, though." He was looking around. It wasn't obvious, but looking at him, I could see his eyes darting everywhere.

"But you're still worried."

"We don't know if the in-control superbeings can or do communicate with each other. Mephistopheles is well known to us, but the others, not so much."

"Whether they're well known to Mephistopheles is what you're worried about."

Martini nodded. "I just want to get everyone back safely to one of our strongholds. We can sort everything else out then."

"Think you'll manage to explain more then, too?"

"Maybe." He grinned. "I'm always willing to explain things to you in private."

"I'll bet." I tried not to admit that the idea of being alone with Martini was starting to sound appealing.

We reached a men's restroom, and Gower and Reader went in first—cautiously. This wasn't reassuring. "I thought you cleared everyone out."

"Everyone we know about or can affect." Martini was still on the alert, and so was Christopher when I glanced his way. He caught me looking at him, gave me an angry glare, then looked away. Charming as always.

Gower came back out. "Calibrated for single entry only. I know you're worried about them," he added as Martini opened his mouth, to protest, I assumed. "They're going to have to go through alone. This is an older gate, we've taken too long already, and they're both capable women, not little girls."

"Fine," Martini said, sounding exasperated. "Let's get moving."

We went in, and I noted the men's room at LaGuardia was no nicer than the ones at JFK or Saguaro International. "Why didn't we use the ladies' this time? If no one was around?"

"Because Mephistopheles is after two women," Christopher snapped.

"Who are with ten men," I snapped right back.

"Children," Mom said tiredly, "stop it. Please."

The two agents who had Mom's luggage went first, one at a time. Martini wanted Mom flanked, just in case, so Reader went next, then Gower, then Mom. She didn't seem flustered at all. In fact, she seemed interested and excited. She did exactly what Martini said, and I watched her step into the stall and disappear. It was unsettling.

Christopher was going next. "Don't let the princess hold things up," he said to Martini.

"Oh, I think I can manage her. Better than you, at least," Martini said casually, keeping a very firm hold on my hand.

"Yeah, enjoy that," Christopher muttered as he gave me one last glare, stepped into the stall and, happily, disappeared from view.

Martini looked at the four agents left. "You all get back to the cars and get them back to East Base."

The four of them looked uncomfortable. "Christopher told us to wait until the two of you were through the gate," one finally admitted.

"And Christopher's in charge of image control. Who, do you happen to remember, is in charge of active situations?" Martini's voice was clipped and filled with authority. I found it interesting to see which of them got huffy when.

The agent who'd spoken up dropped his eyes. "You are, Jeff. But Christopher thought it was important for us to watch your back."

"Right. I know exactly what he wanted watched. You and the rest of our crack image control team get out of here, now. Get back to East Base and, as an idea, try to monitor if we have Mephistopheles or one of his cronies heading out of their respective states. You know, if you think you can handle it."

Admittedly I'd only known them less than a day, but in all that time I hadn't seen Martini be anything but genial. Even when he was all business, he wasn't rude or nasty. This was sort of a shock, and an unpleasant one.

The other agents seemed confused as well, but they left, albeit reluctantly. Martini watched them leave. Then he turned back to me. "Ready to go?"

"Sort of. You want to share why you were just Jerk of the Year to those guys?"

"No."

"What's going on between you and Christopher?"

I'd hit the target. Martini's eyes narrowed. "Nothing."

"You know, none of you can actually lie, not even Paul."

"Time to go through the gate." He shoved me, gently, toward the bathroom stall.

I refused to budge. "No. I want some answers. Christopher being a jerk seems like his natural state of being, but you're not acting like what I'd call normal. For you, I mean."

"Look, I don't want to talk about this here. We just spent a lot of time and energy so we could get you and your mother out of here safely. Let's not have all that go to waste, okay?"

"No. The last time I asked you a question you didn't want to answer, we ended up in New York. I want the answer to this question before we end up God knows where. Now, what's going on that's making you act like this?"

He wasn't lying, I could tell—but the answer was a bit of a surprise. "You. Now, let's get moving."

"You're mad at me?" I didn't know what I'd done differently that would have caused him to be this upset.

Martini gave a growl of exasperation. "No, I'm not mad at you! I'm crazy about you! Yes, I know, less than a day. Empath, remember? Gives you certain insights into people. Now, can we please go?"

I let him move me to the stall while I digested this. "So Christopher doesn't want you with me, does he?"

Martini snorted. "That's for sure."

"Well, who cares what he wants? But that's no reason to be nasty to those other agents."

"Fine. I'll send them all a fruit basket once we're out of here. Now, step through, please. So I can step through, and we can get to safety."

He seemed so stressed out and upset, and he was leaning over me, trying to get me fully into the stall and through the gate. I didn't think about it, I just leaned up and kissed him on the cheek. "Okay, I'll be good."

Martini gave me a slow smile. "Nah, I like you just like you are." Then he bent down and kissed me back, but not on my cheek. And I forgot about where we were, evil things trying to kill me, or anything else.

CHAPTER 16

THE ONLY SEMI-COHERENT THOUGHT I could muster was, if his kiss was any indication, Martini wasn't lying when he said he was great in bed. Because I was ready to find out, right then and there.

His mouth covered mine—soft pillowy lips you could fall into and a tongue that knew just how to twine with mine to make my knees go weak. His arms went around me, pulling me away from the stall and turning me so my body was fully against his. My arms went around his neck, and I kissed him back as deeply as he was kissing me. He had one hand behind my head and the other at the small of my back; we were pressed so tightly together I almost couldn't breathe, but I didn't want to pull away. I was perfectly willing to stay like this for the next several hours.

Finally, he ended our kiss—gradually and sensuously. As we drew apart, I slowly opened my eyes to see his smoldering back at me. "I'd be happy to continue this conversation somewhere else, when I know nothing's going to show up to try to kill us," he said with a small smile.

I managed to stop myself from suggesting we not worry about anything but getting out of our clothes as quickly as possible. I may have just had the most mind-blowing kiss of my life, but it hadn't turned off my brain completely.

I didn't say anything, just nodded. He gently turned me around and moved me back to the stall.

"Jeff, what do I do?"

"Wow, one kiss and you're finally calling me Jeff? I've still got it." He bent down and nuzzled my ear. I had to stop my eyes from rolling back—maybe I really had fainted the first time because his lips were so close to mine. "You just walk through. I'll be right behind you, so don't dawdle." He kissed the side of my head, and I stifled a moan of pleasure.

He stroked my arms and let go. On my own. Forced to walk into a men's toilet stall all by myself. I took a deep breath and stepped in. Just before I hit the toilet, a totally unappealing idea based on its cleanliness level, the bathroom disappeared and the horrible whooshing feeling started right up.

For me, nothing wipes out the happy glow of intimacy faster than feeling nauseated. I was still moving, I could tell I was, but I felt as if I were standing still and the world was moving past me. My foot seemed to be moving in slow motion. When it finally hit the ground and the destination jolt hit me, it was just in time. I didn't want to exit the gate barfing, and it had been a close call.

I finished stepping through, and Martini came out seconds after me. Clearly, the journey didn't take as long as it had felt like.

"You okay?" He put his hand on my lower back.

"Sort of." I figured he was picking up the nausea.

I looked around to see Christopher glaring at me, his arms crossed over his chest. "Took you long enough."

"I had to send your boys off," Martini said before I could think up a suitable reply.

"They were supposed to wait." Christopher sounded furious.

"I didn't want them to," Martini said with a shrug, while he moved us away from the gate.

"I'll bet you didn't," Christopher snarled. "You aren't authorized to give them direction."

Martini stopped and walked over to his cousin, until he was right in Christopher's face. "I know what this is about," he said in a low growl. "You want to play games, fine. This isn't a game to me."

"They're all games to you." Christopher was matching Martini's tone and facial expression. The anger was rolling off both of them, I didn't have to be an empath to feel it, and I wondered whether they were going to start a cage fight without the cage.

I heard a woman clear her throat. "Kitty, could you come help me with something for a minute?"

I looked over my shoulder to see Mom standing there. She had that funny look on her face again, and I decided it might be wise not to be nearby if Martini and Christopher started to really go at each other.

Mom grabbed my arm and dragged me off. I looked back to see both men watching us. Christopher still looked angry, but Martini looked upset.

We got out of sight of them, and I noticed we were in what seemed like a huge cavern, loaded with more computers, desks, and screens than I'd seen at Home Base, or ever, really. "Did we land in the Bat Cave?"

Mom made her exasperated mother sound. "No. This is the Dulce Science Center for Extraterrestrial Studies."

"Or, next stop on the UFO Tour, whichever you can say three times faster."

Mom shook her head. "You're really a joy to work with." She stopped dragging me along. "Look, you need to stop baiting Christopher."

"I beg your pardon? What are you talking about? There's nothing I'm doing on purpose to piss him off. He's just a jerk, to me and about me."

Mom rubbed her forehead. "God, are you dense."

I was about to demand an explanation for this insult when I heard someone call my name. "Kitty, over here!"

I looked around and saw Reader waving at me from across the room. He was gesturing, and it was clear he wanted me over there. I sighed. "Mom, duty calls. You can explain my density later."

"Trust me," I heard Mom mutter as I headed for Reader.

Unlike Home Base, this place was loaded with women. I was glad I'd changed now—I felt dowdy enough next to most of them in the relatively clean clothes I had on. In my bedraggled suit I might not have been able to make it to Reader without self-destructing from embarrassment.

I could tell they weren't human, though. Not that they

had antlers or something growing out of their heads, but they all seemed genuinely nice. I was stopped by many of them as I walked across the large room, and every one asked if I was okay, told me my mother was the greatest, said I was a really brave young woman, or gave me some other atta-girl sentiment. It was as if I'd fallen onto the Planet of the Honestly Nice Cheerleaders. I didn't fit in, but, boy, was I glad they didn't seem to notice.

When I finally made it to Reader, I wondered why Martini would even know I was alive, let alone be interested in kissing me. He had more gorgeous women around him in this room alone than there were in the entire American Southwest.

Reader gave me a commiserating grin. "Now you know how I felt when I first joined up."

"But you were a top male model—*the* top for a long time."

He shrugged. "You've taken a look. It's one thing to be attractive when other people around you are ordinary. When everyone's gorgeous, you have to figure you're not that great."

The idea that Reader would have had any kind of self-consciousness or felt unworthy lookswise with this group had never occurred to me. "Paul doesn't seem to mind," was all I could come up with that wasn't going to make me sound both stupid and unobservant.

"Yeah." He gave me a big smile. "And he had a lot of gorgeous to compare me to."

"Oh, my feelings of total inadequacy in the looks department were showing?"

"Just a little. Trust me, they're both really into you for yourself. Including how you look. Which is great, take it from the gay man."

"Both?" I was going to ask him who he was talking about when White came over.

"Finally. Miss Katt, I'd like to have you debrief us on your experiences with both the superbeing you eliminated and Mephistopheles."

"Nice to see you again, too. I'm fine thanks, how are you?" He didn't crack a smile. Oh, well. No sense of humor in the son, why was I expecting one in the father? "What's to debrief? Your agents were around for both, and I've already told you pretty much all that happened."

"Yes," White said with a show of forced patience. "But I'd like you to debrief our lead scientific team." He gestured behind him at several women who would have made Raquel Welch green with envy. The only saving grace was some of them looked about Raquel's age, so I could tell myself Mom should be the one feeling inferior, not me. Of course, I knew my mother and doubted she'd feel inadequate against anyone.

"Are you Angela's girl?" one of them asked me.

Angela? She'd been here no more than five minutes longer than me and she was already on a first name basis with the beauty queens?

"Yep, that's me." I remembered Reader had said all the female A-Cs were scientists. Great, so they were better looking *and* smarter than me. For this I'd gotten up this morning?

"Your mother is just the most amazing woman," another one offered. "We're totally in awe of her."

"Me, too." I mean, I'd spent most of this day in total awe, over just about everything, including my mother.

"Now, now," I heard Mom's voice behind me. She was chuckling in that way people do when they're being complimented and want to pretend they don't actually want to hear it. "This is really Kitty's time."

Oh, great. This was my initiation into the Kick-Ass Females Club, wasn't it? I mean, every one of the A-C women looked as though they could easily run as far and as fast, if not faster, than any of the men. There were some I could say looked downright Amazonian. All of them were stunning, and they ran the gamut to ensure that no man would ever be short of his "type."

And then there was me. I wasn't Mossad trained. I wasn't from Planet Dazzling. I was just a marketing manager from Pueblo Caliente, Arizona, who could wield a mean pen.

I caught Reader's eye. He grinned. "Welcome, fully, to my world."

CHAPTER 17

WHITE LED US INTO A GOOD-SIZED CONFERENCE room. Martini and Christopher were already in there, sitting at opposite ends of the long, oval table, glaring at each other. What a fun meeting this was going to be.

The conference table gleamed in an odd way, and I assumed it was alien made or at least influenced. The chairs were all black and looked reasonably comfortable. There was no phone, screen, or whiteboard, though. Just glass panes on each side, so meeting in here would be like meeting in a fishbowl. I couldn't wait.

I pointedly sat next to Martini, who was at the far end of the room, earning another glare from Christopher. I glared right back and then turned to watch White usher everyone else in.

Several of the Dazzling Sisters filed by and took seats around the table, then Mom, Gower, and Reader came in as well. Mom leaned down and said something privately to Christopher, who nodded, and looked away from me and Martini. Then she came and sat next to me.

"Please try to remain civil," she said as my personal aside.

I wasn't thrilled with her choosing to side with my enemy. "Sure, no worries," I muttered back. "I'm used to him being a total jerk. So, is he the son you've always secretly wanted or what?"

"Boy, do we need to talk," Mom said with a sigh.

More women came in and a few more male agents as well.

The conference room was packed. Gower and Reader were across from each other in the middle of the table, but standing with their backs against the glass walls, as were the other male agents. In fact, the only men sitting were Christopher, Martini, and White. I found this yet another interesting tidbit to file away in hopes of it meaning something more later.

"We'll dispense with the introductions," White said by way of calling the meeting to order. "Miss Katt's had a long day, and I don't want to lose any of her information to delay or fatigue."

Martini made some motion on the table, and suddenly it was a movie screen, albeit a weird one. It appeared to be showing only one picture, but as I looked down in front of me, I could see the images closer up, as if the screen had adapted just for me. I looked out of the corners of my eyes and could see it was the same for Mom and Martini.

We watched the news report of what had happened. "You know, I'm never buying linen again," I said to Mom. "I look like I've slept in that suit."

"It's you. I just figured you had." My mother, the standup comic.

"Do I really run like that?"

"Yep," Martini confirmed. "Don't worry, I think it's sexy."

"Thank God. I think I look like a cheetah on drugs." I looked over to White. "Why are we watching this? This is the fake."

He nodded. "I wanted you to see what the news media's shown. It may matter later on."

"Like when Mephistopheles or one of his pals comes to try to kill me or ask me to join their exclusive club?"

He had the grace to look unhappy. "Yes."

"Fine. Seen it. It was more exciting in real life."

White nodded, and the picture changed. This time, it was the real thing. I watched the man sprout wings again, saw the carnage. Only it was worse this way. In real life I'd only seen him kill his wife, and I'd stopped watching that to focus on how to stop *him*. Now, I knew he was stopped, and I was able to see what he'd done. It was sickening, in all the worst ways.

Martini reached under the table, took my hand, and gave it a little squeeze. I squeezed back, harder, and didn't let go. The benefits of being with an empathic man were starting to look pretty good.

"What can you tell us that we can't already see?" White asked me.

"I have no idea," I had to admit, as I scanned everything I hadn't seen before, which was a lot. "Your cameras really caught everything, more than I saw at the time."

"Not our cameras," Christopher corrected. "This is a compilation we made from the variety of amateur shots taken." He glanced at his father. "At least a dozen different camera phones and a couple of video cameras caught some or all of this. We had to alter them all and then make sure they matched each other." White didn't seem impressed one way or the other.

However, in the interest of remaining civil, I decided to be Suzy Supportive. "Nice job. Very smooth, not choppy at all."

"I'll let my team know you appreciate their work," Christopher said, snarl and glare both set to low.

"Panoramic, even." In fact, I had to figure at least one of the photographers had been there doing something else, because there was a lot of detail far away from the main action. "Someone was really focused on the top of the building, weren't they?" As I said this, I noticed a movement in the upper level of the courthouse and a flash of color that didn't fit. "Um, can we do a rewind?"

"Sure," Martini said and made some different hand motions. "Tell me what you're looking for."

As the picture rewound, I saw it again. "There, stop, go forward . . . right there."

Martini froze the picture, and I pointed to the ninth story. There was something familiar there. "Can this zoom in?" No sooner asked than done. We were now all staring at a window on the ninth floor of the courthouse. There were some people standing at the window, watching the carnage below. Two of them were very close to the glass. And one was wearing a suit that looked very familiar.

We all stared at this image for a few long moments. "What's the big deal about this window?" Mom asked finally. I assumed she was speaking for the entire room.

Nothing that had happened all day surprised me more than who spoke up. "I see it," Christopher said, and for the first time all day he didn't sound angry or nasty—he sounded freaked out. "How can Kitty be down on the street, killing a superbeing, if she's up in that window, watching the action?"

"Get a load of who 'I'm' with," I added, as I tried not to panic and failed utterly, if Martini's hand squeeze was any indication. The picture zoomed in even more. Now it was easy to see "me" and the man next to me, even though the picture was fuzzy.

"Ronald Yates." Mom's voice was like lead.

In a room full of humans, I figured pandemonium would be breaking out right about now. In a room full of aliens, not so much. Everyone was staring at the pictures, studying them. What I found a particular relief was that no one was asking me how I'd managed to be in two places at once.

Christopher spoke again. "Jeff, this'll take both of us."

Martini let go of my hand and stood up. "Right." He walked over to the middle of the table and so did Christopher. They were on the same side as Gower was, so on my right. The women who were sitting in this area got up and moved out of the way. No one was speaking.

The image went back to singular—no longer an image per person, just the entire table filled with this shot of the ninth-story window, with "me" and my buddy, Ronald Yates, framed within it. He had his arm around "my" waist, and I wanted to barf.

Christopher put his hand on my image, palm flat against it. Martini put his on top of Christopher's. It looked as if they were doing a two-man "go team" move, only their hands stayed in place.

After what seemed like the longest minute of my life, they took their hands away and looked at each other. "It's not her," Christopher said.

"Nope. It's not human, either," Martini added.

"What the hell is going on?" Mom asked, echoing my thoughts this time.

"And, not that I'm arguing, but how could you tell it wasn't me?"

Gower was the one to answer. "We've each got different talents, things on A-C that aren't odd or even special, but things that are amazing on Earth. Jeff's our strongest empath. Christopher's our strongest imageer."

"Come again?"

Gower managed a grin. "Someone who can touch a real image and know the person whose image is being touched. Our imageers can manipulate images, too, live or after the image is captured. It's a common trait on our home planet."

"The Earth tribes who think pictures take a part of their soul are right, to a degree," Christopher explained. "The pictures copy the image of the souls and the minds, just as they copy the image of the body."

"Yeah, if we were still on A-C, Christopher would be an artist," Martini added.

"It's an artistic trait?" Mom sounded suspicious.

Christopher shrugged. "On Alpha Centauri. Here it's a useful trait for what we do."

"Like wiretapping only different," I suggested.

He shook his head. "Your mind is amazing. The way it does and doesn't work, I mean."

Mom, put her hand on my arm before I could offer up a suitable retort. "Yes, but you're saying that's not Kitty's mind in that image."

"Right," Martini said quickly, presumably to prevent me from lunging for Christopher's throat again. "I can feel the person through Christopher. That's not a human woman. It's not an A-C woman, either. I have no idea what that thing is, but it's not Kitty."

"I think it's a machine," Christopher said. "It doesn't have a human mind at all. Close, but very different at the same time."

"And he complains when I say the same thing," I muttered to Mom.

"Later, please think about this," Mom whispered back. "I mean, really think about it." She spoke in a louder tone. "But the big question is, why?"

Everyone was silent. I decided to do some thinking right then, but not about Christopher. "What about the man with whatever is supposed to be me? Is that really Yates?"

"Good question," Christopher said. I almost fainted. He and Martini did their hand thing again. But this time it was fast. "Oh, yeah, that's him," Christopher said, as they snatched their hands away. He sounded repulsed.

"He's gross?"

"All the superbeings are . . . unpleasant for us," Gower answered, as I watched women near both Christopher and Martini hand them some sort of hand wipes, which the two of them used as if they were germaphobes who'd just shaken hands with a leper.

"How'd he get from Arizona to New York in time to attack my mother?"

"Private jet would do it," Reader said. "He wouldn't even have to use any powers, just get in the Yates private SST and you're there. He had several hours between the two attacks, after all."

"SST?" Oh, good, something else I didn't know.

"Supersonic transport," Mom translated. "Okay, no argument, he's got more than one. But again, why?"

Silence. It was nice to think with the aliens—they seemed to think with their minds, not their mouths. Of course, I was a human. But the two other humans in the room were keeping their traps shut, and I decided to follow suit.

Which worked for a while. Problem was, sitting in silence for me means I am no longer thinking about whatever it is I'm supposed to. My mind wandered before the first half a minute, thinking about the entire day, kissing Martini, how I'd discovered my mother was not who I'd thought she was, kissing Martini, how it was sort of shocking the person I had the most relatability to right now was a former top male fashion model, kissing Martini, wondering if Reader and Gower went to clubs or just stayed in, kissing Martini, and wondering if Dad was going to show up soon. None of this got me any closer to anything other than possibly falling into bed with Martini.

I forced myself to think some more. Why me? Really, why me? I wasn't anything special. Oh, sure, I had a mother who was apparently the queen of antiterrorism, but I wasn't involved with any of that.

Something inside my brain kicked, very hard. What had Mom said, the *first* thing she'd said, about Yates? Not that he was a monster, not that he was a tycoon, not that he was disgusting. She'd said he was the head of a terrorist organization I'd never heard of. But Mom had heard of it.

So maybe that meant Yates had heard of Mom.

CHAPTER 18

"UM, WHEN IS MY FATHER GETTING HERE?"
   I got a lot of "looks" from around the table, but
Gower recovered the quickest. "He'll be here shortly. He's
with four agents, and they've reported in regularly."

"They're not taking a gate?"

"No, why?" Gower gave me a penetrating stare. "You
want to share what you're worried about?"

"My family, the safety of the nation and the free world,
stuff like that. I'll explain it all, but we need our entire extended family under a heavier watch than you've done so
far. And make sure it *is* our family, when you go to take
them away to whatever hollow mountain in their general
neighborhoods you feel is safe."

"No argument," Gower said slowly. "But why?"

"Because this isn't about me." I looked over at Mom,
who had a suspicious but confused look on her face. "It's
about you. You're outed, Mom, in whatever ways that
means in your line of work. Yates isn't after me for me; he's
after me to stop you and whatever it is you're doing to his
terrorist operation."

I looked back to Christopher and Martini for some sort
of confirmation. "You both felt it—that's not a real person
next to Yates. But it's something that looks just like me,
down to the choice of suit. I was released from jury duty
early, but I'd been on the ninth floor. Either their timing
didn't work out or—"

"Or the men who tried to stop us from getting your car were sent to kill you," Christopher finished.

"Say what?" Mom and I shouted in unison.

He sighed. "I didn't mention it because I thought they were there because of us. There *are* Earth agencies trying to stop us, you know. It's why we didn't take your car to your apartment—we didn't want someone following it and attacking you because you were associated with us. But with this . . ." He shrugged again. "I think you're right."

Another reason to faint, but I let it pass. "So, you think the superbeing I took out was part of Yates' plan?"

"No, I think it saved your life," Martini said. He looked to Christopher, who nodded, and then looked back at me. He was trying to hide it, but I could see a lot of worry, and fear, in his eyes. "If it hadn't formed, you'd have gone to get your car and been murdered. We don't monitor those. I mean, I feel them, all our empaths do, but we've managed to learn how to ignore them, because we've had no choice. You learn to block and filter emotions or you go insane. So you'd have been killed. They'd have replaced you with whatever that is, and no one would have noticed."

"I'd have noticed," Mom said dryly. "It might look like my daughter, but a couple of words in and it would have been clear."

"It's a robot, Mom. A couple of words in, once it was in the house, and then it goes boom, and you and Dad are dead. They aren't trying to stop you. They're trying to kill you." I looked back to Christopher and Martini. "That's why Yates attacked Mom at the airport. Because his first plan got wrecked and everyone saw me on national television, alive and well. You screwing that up was probably a really good thing."

"Thanks, I think," Christopher said with a grimace that, if I chose to be charitable, was probably more of a smile.

"Yates owns a lot of media," Reader added. "But he's also got his fingers in other industries, and robotics is one of them."

"So he raced back to New York, because he'd know early that the airports were being shut down due to fear of more terrorist attacks. Speaking of which, how was he allowed to land, and what the hell were you doing on a commercial flight?"

"Money and power have their privileges," Mom said.

Reader nodded. "You'd be amazed at how the rules don't apply to the truly wealthy, influential people of the world."

"And I was on a commercial flight because this trip wasn't a job for the government. I was doing some consulting for a large international conglomerate whose name you don't need to know. They made the travel arrangements. First class," Mom added. "Not as good as the private jet, but, you know, better for their bottom line."

My mother's life was so much more interesting than I'd ever guessed. I wanted to review every year of my life and figure out which of my memories and beliefs were based on reality and which were not, but now wasn't the time. "I think we can assume Yates knew your travel plans. You couldn't come home, so he went to you."

Mom nodded slowly. "It makes sense. We're close to proving he's the head of Al Dejahl."

"And you're in charge of that operation, aren't you?"

"Yes. But I'm not the only one involved." She looked at Gower. "We need the rest of my terrorism unit under protection, too."

"Come with me. We'll get that taken care of right now."

Mom and Gower raced out of the room. Everyone else looked around at each other. Finally one of the Dazzlers spoke up. I thought she resembled a young Sophia Loren. "So, is this a superbeing issue or an American government issue?"

"Does it matter?" I wondered if they were going to consider just letting my family be slaughtered.

"Yes and no," White answered. "Superbeings are involved, so it's us. But the threat is to American counterterrorism. We have certain responsibilities in that case."

"You have to let those agencies know it's time to work together?"

"We have to let them know to stay the hell out of our way," Christopher replied. His father didn't argue.

Reader pushed off his glass wall. "I'll take care of it." Sophia's look-alike and the one who really looked like

Raquel Welch when she was in that fur bikini went with him. I hated myself for not being sorry to see them go. I also felt bad I had no interest in getting to know any of the females. I had been a lot happier surrounded by all the males. I wondered if Reader preferred hanging with the Dazzlers or if, by now, he was comfortable merely being one of the boys. It might be different for him, since he was gay and drop-dead gorgeous, but I had a feeling it wasn't.

Turned out, the other females wanted to get to know me, however. "Maybe now's a good time for those introductions. I'm Lorraine." This was from one who looked younger than me, had a figure to die for, and blonde hair I was pretty sure wasn't dyed. She was beautiful. "I'm a junior member of the Exoskeleton team."

"We work on trying to figure out why and how the parasites turn a human into a superbeing without killing the human," another added. "Oh, and I'm Claudia." She had long, flowing brown hair, big brown eyes, and, just like Lorraine, a killer figure. She was about my age. I found myself hoping she was Martini's sister so that maybe I could not hate her. "Oh, and that was my mother, Emily, and Lorraine's mother, Melanie, who went out with James," she added. "They're part of the Liaison team, working with Earth scientists and government agencies on mutually beneficial projects."

It certainly ran in families. "It must be nice to get to work so closely with your mothers," was all I could think of as an insightful comment.

Both of them nodded, but where the older women in the room couldn't see, Lorraine rolled her eyes and Claudia mouthed "not really." I started to like them.

They went around the table, giving first name introductions and highlighting which scientific team they were on. Apparently, this meeting had been invitation only, and each team had sent one or two representatives to get the information and report back.

"How many people work here?" I asked once the round robin had stopped. I'd given up trying to learn any more names. I figured I'd deal with it as I went along.

"Several thousand at any one time, more during a state of emergency," Lorraine answered. "Earth agencies have the top three levels. We have the bottom ten. There are two levels in between that we share."

"This place goes down fifteen stories?" Suddenly I felt claustrophobic.

Claudia nodded. "It's safer that way. For more reasons than the alien parasitic threat."

One of the other women, who I thought was called Bernice, or Bethany, or something that started with a B, began explaining why it was great to be buried in the ground, what they did on each floor, and how some of the floors were just given over to living quarters. While a bed sounded great, B-girl didn't have the most engaging speaking voice. This thrilled me for all of thirty seconds. Then I started to get bored. Then sleepy. Then very sleepy.

I managed to look at Lorraine and Claudia. Claudia was resting with her head on one hand, looking totally bored. Lorraine had leaned back in her chair and, if I was any judge, was fast asleep. I decided I liked them a lot.

B-girl finished droning on, and there was silence. It dawned on me she'd asked me a question as her closing line. But I couldn't bring up what it was.

Amazingly, Christopher was the one who saved this situation. "I'm sure Kitty wants to get some sleep," he said. "I think we can leave the rest of the debriefing for tomorrow. We've identified the real threat, and she's not as integral to it as we'd first assumed."

I wanted to mention that I knew Mephistopheles' parasite wanted to move west into my body, but I yawned instead. Widely. I couldn't help it, I could barely keep my eyes open.

"I'll get her settled in," Martini said.

Christopher looked as if he were going argue, but White nodded. "Do. We need to ensure we're monitoring the right things anyway."

The meeting broke up. I saw Claudia nudge Lorraine awake. The two of them hung back and left the meeting with me and Martini. "Sorry about Beverly," Claudia said as we walked out. "She's very enthusiastic."

"And dull as dust," Lorraine said with a yawn. "I don't know how you stayed conscious."

"She had me to look at," Martini offered.

Both of them laughed. "Yeah, right, like that'd keep a girl up," Claudia said, nudging him in the ribs.

Martini managed a chuckle, but he looked embarrassed, and not in a good way.

"Um, just asking, you know, but which one of the guys do you think is the cutest?" I felt like an idiot, but I had to figure out if they were serious or not.

Claudia shrugged. "We don't really go that much for external looks. I know, it's a big Earth thing, we get it. And we don't judge. I mean, it's the way your entire planet's been raised. But, well, A-C women really like brains."

"Martini's not all that dumb," I said, wondering why I was even trying to make them think he was hot. I mean, I kind of wanted him for me, so this was not smart.

Lorraine snorted. "No, he's not. But, um, gee, how do I say this?"

"You mean with me standing right here?" Martini asked, and I could tell he was working to keep his tone light. "Just tell her the truth. I don't have the right IQ level."

"But we love you anyway," Claudia said, patting his cheek.

"So, um, who does have the right IQ level?" I was fascinated.

"It's not IQ so much as aptitude," Lorraine corrected. "I mean, your Bill Gates, Stephen Hawking, men like that, they're geniuses, yes."

"And so dreamy," Claudia said. She was serious. I managed to keep my jaw closed, but it took effort.

"Yeah, but then they're guys who just have aptitudes for science and stuff. Physicists, man, your good physicists are just so amazing." Lorraine's chest was heaving. I noted that Martini wasn't looking at it. He wasn't looking at me, either. He was looking up, and a quick glance told me it wasn't at a threat. He was just trying to pretend he wasn't here.

"Don't forget the rocket scientists. Or the engineers who work on all the advanced projects," Claudia reminded her. "Some of your astronauts are dreamy, too." She was big on dreamy. I'd never considered using that word to apply to any of the people they were listing, though. Martini, Gower, Reader, even Christopher, sure, dreamy to the max. But not the Nerd Army. Somewhere, somehow, I was going to have to get a text to Chuckie—he deserved a cut of this action, and if they got hot for Bill Gates, they might die over someone smarter, younger, and a whole lot better looking.

"I mean, sex is great, don't get me wrong," Lorraine said as we headed toward what looked like a bank of elevators. "But without the mental connection, well . . ." She gave me a grin. "I'm sure you understand."

"Uh, yeah. Totally." None of the A-C men I'd met seemed like morons, so, truthfully, I didn't actually understand, and I wondered if I ever would. It was as if I'd fallen into an episode of "Beauty and the Geek." I wondered if I'd see Ashton Kutcher anywhere around. He'd be hard to pick out based solely on looks, but maybe he had the right kind of mind, and Claudia and Lorraine would be mooning over him.

"Well, we're going to our floor," Claudia told me. "You and Jeff'll be heading to the transient section, so we'll see you tomorrow." She gave me a hug, Lorraine did, too, and then they got into what I hoped was an elevator. They waved as the doors closed. At me, not at Martini.

We stood there for a few moments in silence. "They seem nice," I said finally, avoiding what I really wanted to ask.

"If you like being emasculated every minute of every day, yeah, they're great."

"I think you're smart." It wasn't worth a lot, but maybe it was worth something.

"I think you're the most insightful woman in the galaxy," he said with a weak smile. "Now, let's check on your parents and then get you settled into a room."

CHAPTER 19

WE FOUND MOM WITH GOWER, at a large screen that looked like something out of a futuristic movie—clear glass with lights and writing moving on it seemingly without outside assistance. I decided to ignore it, and maybe it would go away.

"Where's Dad?"

"On his way. He refused to go through the gate." Mom sounded tired and exasperated.

"Why?"

I heard barking and hissing. I looked around Gower to see the four agents I assumed had been sent to escort my father being dragged by four big dogs. All the dogs were bearing down on us, as only excited dogs can. And they were all headed for me.

"He wouldn't let us take them through the gate," one of the agents gasped to Gower as he lost his grip on the leash he was holding.

One dog free meant the other three would just have to work harder. Within a second the others had yanked out of the other agents' hands.

Dudley, our Great Dane, hit me first. He knocked me into Martini, who thankfully kept both his and my balance. Dotty, the Dalmatian, was next, jumping and howling. Duke, the black Lab, joined the dog pile, followed last but in no way least by our pit bull, Duchess. Yes, my parents had given all the dogs D names. They were adorable that way.

"They haven't seen you in a while," Dad called, huffing a bit, because he was dragging a huge rolling suitcase and carting our three-cat carrier at the same time.

"I see we're moving in," Mom said to Gower.

"What, no birds?" Martini asked me. I tried to answer, but Duchess was trying to lick me, and I didn't want to kiss my dog in the same way I'd kissed Martini.

"They said I had to bring the pets," Dad said by way of hello to Mom.

"Yes, Sol, good plan." Mom sighed. "Could you put the cats down?"

"They're scared, and with good reason," Dad huffed.

"I'd like to get a hug," Mom said wryly. Gower relieved Dad of the cat carrier, and Mom was finally able to give Dad a squeeze.

"Kitten, are you okay?" Dad asked, free arm still around Mom, while he gave Martini his standard look for any man near me—the Father Glare.

"Just fine, Dad. Covered in slobber now, but fine otherwise." I'd finally gotten the dogs off me by shoving them at Martini, who was now trying to pet four dogs with two hands. That he was doing pretty well impressed me and, as I looked at my father's face, told Dad that Martini was evil and to be kept far away from me.

"Who's the octopus?" Dad asked, confirming my intuitive guess about his reactions, based on my entire life's history.

"This is Jeff Martini," Mom said. "He's been instrumental in keeping me and Kitty alive. Paul Gower," she went on. "Also one of our protectors."

Protectors? I thought Mom and I had been doing a good portion of that work, but I decided to shut up. I had no idea how much Dad really knew about Mom's exciting secret life, after all.

"Pleased to meet you," Dad said with a smile for Gower. He grunted at Martini.

"I see I'm doing well with your entire family," Martini said to me, as Dudley grabbed his arm with his jaws.

"Just swat his nose. He's playing, and that's how we tell him to stop."

"I miss your fish." Martini got out of Dudley's clutches

only to have Duchess decide she liked him a lot. Pit bulls can really lick, and she was going at it full steam.

"Nice menagerie." Christopher's voice came from behind me.

I managed to keep my fists from clenching. "You said all our pets were in danger," I reminded him as I turned around.

"Normally they go into the kennels."

I was going to protest, but Dad beat me to it. "There is no way I am putting my animals into some jail! They are part of our family, and they are staying with us." Dad was glaring at Christopher in the same way he had glared at Martini.

"Yes, they're staying with you," Christopher said, sounding amused. "Angela, we have you in a large suite. Your luggage is already in there." Angela? He was on a first-name basis with my mother, too? I wanted to scream.

Mom gave Christopher a beaming smile. "Thanks, you're a doll. I'd like to get in there and try to relax. As hard as that's going to be."

She and Christopher shared a chuckle. I tried not to gag.

"Chop, chop," Dad said to the four agents who I assumed he now thought were his personal porters. "Stop yanking at the dogs' leashes this time. They respond just fine to a gentle hand and a firm tone."

Yes, from one of the three of us. Our dogs were well-trained, but they also knew they could get away with murder if my father wasn't in the mood to discipline them. And Dad was almost never in that mood.

The agents dragged the dogs off, Dad and Mom followed, Dad still pulling his huge suitcase. Christopher took the cat carrier from Gower. "I'll take them to their room." He looked over at me. "Want to say hello to the felines before they go off to rip the room to shreds?"

"They're scared," I said, as I went over to the carrier.

"That's because they're smart," he said quietly.

I looked up at him. He didn't look as though he was mocking me. "Yes, they are."

"How're you doing?" Christopher asked in the same soft tone.

I resisted the urge to be nasty, hard as it was. "Really tired. Fairly overwhelmed."

"Cuddle one of your cats. You'll feel better."

I wanted to pet them, and though they seemed to be quieting down, they were still so worked up I knew it wasn't safe to try through the carrier's slots—at least, not if I wanted to stay unshredded myself. And opening the carrier in a room this large with this many hiding places was beyond a stupid idea. "I'll visit them once they've settled down."

"Fine with me." He pulled the carrier away like I'd insulted him. So much for my bothering to be pleasant. "You'll get the princess settled?" he shot over his shoulder to Martini.

"Yep. As soon as I wash my hands and face," Martini added to me, as Christopher strode off. "You need us for anything else?" he asked Gower as I stifled a yawn.

"Nope, just get her settled in, get some rest, and we'll regroup tomorrow. We have every Base on high alert; we should be okay. Good night, Kitty," Gower said. "If I get to call you that now."

"Sure, sure, you're all my friends," I said through a yawn I couldn't stop. "Even Mister Pissy."

Martini put his arm around me. "Let's get moving and get you tucked in."

We went to the elevator bank where we'd left Claudia and Lorraine. I could tell my parents had gone this way too—there was fur and slobber in abundance.

"What floor are we going to?" My head started to bob of its own accord. I leaned against Martini as much to stop giving myself whiplash as to snuggle. Our kiss seemed like a very long time ago.

We got into the elevator, and the moment the doors closed, he shifted and scooped me up in his arms. "We're going to the transient floor, which is the eighth."

"From the top or the bottom?" I asked as I snuggled my face into his neck. Nice neck, comfy to sleep against.

"Uh, it's the middle, either way you look at it. You're wiped, that's proof."

"Mmm huh," I managed. I wasn't asleep, but I was close.

I felt the elevator stop but had no interest in looking around. Martini carried me down what I assumed was a hall, but it could have been through a disco, I wasn't paying any attention. He stopped after a bit, I heard a soft whooshing sound, we moved again, and he put me down.

"Here's your room. I'll show you where things are tomorrow." He took my hand and led me through what looked like a sitting room into the bedroom. There was a chest of drawers, and he opened the one on the top right. "Standard issue white T-shirt and blue pajama bottoms in here. They'll fit you; room's been furnished for your needs. In there," he pointed to a door opposite the chest, "is the bathroom. I figure you don't care about anything else right now."

Martini leaned down and kissed my forehead. "Can you get undressed by yourself?"

He wasn't asking in a romantic way at all. I got the feeling that if I said no, he'd take my clothes off, put the nightclothes on, tuck me in, and trot off. It was comforting, but I also had a feeling him doing that would cause me to wake right up. "Yeah, I think so."

"Okay, I'm down the hall a few doors if you need me." He kissed my forehead again. "Get to bed, my Miss Kitty."

"O-kay," I said, yawning through each syllable.

Martini left the room and I managed to crawl out of my clothes and into the nightclothes provided. I pulled the covers back, fell into bed, snuggled into the pillows, and managed to pull the covers over me.

Just before I was out, my mind flashed back to the pictures on my vanity at my apartment. There was something about Christopher pawing them my subconscious wanted me to pay attention to, but exhaustion took over before I could consider, let alone grasp, what that might be.

CHAPTER 20

I WAS HAVING A NIGHTMARE. It was one of those dreams where you know you're asleep, but you can't wake up, no matter how much you want to. And I really wanted to.

Mephistopheles was the center of it, huge and ugly, stomping around trying to destroy everything and everyone who mattered to me. He had me in his hand, and I couldn't get away this time. I had to watch while he stomped my parents and our pets, all my extended family, all my friends, everyone I worked with, anyone I knew, and then all the A-C people I'd met. Everyone was smashed, destroyed, crumpled and broken. They looked like bloody paper dolls.

Martini and Christopher were the only ones left alive. Then Mephistopheles put me into his mouth, and the parasite moved to me. I felt it join with me, and it turned me into something horrible, much worse than Mephistopheles could ever be. But my body didn't change, I still looked the same.

Mephistopheles dropped me on the ground, but he didn't die or disappear, he stood there, urging me on. Both Martini and Christopher had guns out, and they were aimed at me. But they didn't shoot. I reached out and took their guns, crumbled them like dust in my hands. Mephistopheles laughed.

I grabbed Martini and Christopher both by their necks. Even though they were bigger than me, I could lift them easily off the ground. Mephistopheles laughed and clapped, as if this were a funny game.

I squeezed their necks, cutting off their air, killing them slowly.

Martini just looked at me sadly. He didn't even try to stop me.

Christopher managed to speak. "Where's the fight in you when we need it?"

Then I snapped both their necks, and Mephistopheles said, "We have won."

I woke up sobbing. I wanted to be sick but couldn't remember if I'd had anything to eat since yesterday morning, when the world was normal. It wasn't even twenty-four hours ago, but it felt like forever. There was only bile in my stomach, and though it churned, it didn't try to come up, preferring to sit there and cause pain.

I grabbed one of the pillows and screamed into it. I was too frightened and horrified to even try to leave the bed. I didn't know where I was, couldn't find anyone's room even if I had the courage to get up. I didn't want to look and discover some jellyfish thing was on me, turning me into what Mephistopheles wanted. I wanted my mother and father, someone who could hold me and tell me everything was all right, but they were somewhere else in this vast complex, maybe next door, maybe miles away. And I was as afraid of the dark as I had been as a little girl.

There was urgent knocking at my door, but I was crying too hard to say anything. Part of me was afraid it was a monster, Mephistopheles or something like him, but I managed to remind myself that monsters didn't knock.

I staggered out of bed and banged into the dresser, the wall, and the doorway. I could hardly move normally, and I couldn't stop crying.

Before I could make it there, the door opened and Martini ran inside. He didn't say anything, just picked me up and held me. I wrapped my arms around him and cried even more.

"It's okay, baby," he said softly. "I'm here, it's okay."

I tried to tell him what was wrong, but I couldn't talk. He carried me into the bedroom, pulled the coverlet off the bed, then went back to the living room area, murmuring comfortingly the whole time. There was a lounger in there, and he settled us in it, with me curled up in his lap. He wrapped the coverlet around us.

"You don't have to tell me right now," he said in a low tone. "I have a good idea of what's wrong."

I shook my head. "It was horrible."

"I know, I could feel what you were going through." He kissed my forehead. "Cry as much as you need to, then calm down. No rush." He tilted the lounger back, so we were pretty much lying down.

He stroked my head and hair the whole time, kissing my forehead gently from time to time. He was wearing the standard issue nightclothes, and his T-shirt was soaked from my tears by the time I cried myself out.

"I feel like a stupid, scared little girl," I admitted through my last few tears.

"You're scared, and size-wise you're a little girl," Martini said with a chuckle. "But stupid? No, you're not stupid. At all."

"It was a dream, but it felt real."

"Most dreams do. We'll have Paul interpret it tomorrow."

"Is that what his special skill is?" It was so nice to talk about Paul rather than my nightmare.

"Yep." Martini kissed my forehead again. "So if you don't want to talk about it until then, that's fine."

I took a deep breath. "I think I can interpret it without him." I told Martini everything about the dream I could remember, including what Christopher had said right before I killed the two of them.

Martini was quiet for a minute or so after I finished. "What's your interpretation?"

"You mean other than I'm a lot more scared than I thought I was?"

"Yes. Being scared isn't stupid, Kitty. It's smart. This is scary stuff we're dealing with. World-ending kinds of things. Only idiots or the insane feel no fear in these sorts of situations, and you're neither."

"I think . . ." My voice trailed off while I tried to form what I felt into words. "I think my subconscious is trying to warn me about something."

"Seems pretty clear." He shifted a bit. "Don't take this the wrong way, but do you mind if I take my shirt off? It's kind of wet."

I managed a laugh. "Go ahead."

He moved me around a little and stripped the T-shirt off. A glow from the hall came through the bottom of the entry door—I could see his muscles ripple. He was totally ripped, but not overly muscled like a body builder. He tossed the shirt aside and pulled me back next to him.

I slid between his legs, resting my head on his chest. I wrapped one arm around his waist and held onto his shoulder with the other hand.

"That's nice," he said. "Now, why don't you tell me what you feel up to about what you think your dream means."

I snuggled closer. He felt so warm and strong, it made me feel safe and secure. I heaved a sigh and started to actually relax. Martini tucked the coverlet back around us.

My eyes closed of their own volition. I tried to think, but his heartbeats were lulling me back to sleep. "Just scared," I got out finally. "Tired."

"Okay, baby. You just go back to sleep, then."

"What time's it?"

He kissed my head. "Around midnight. Plenty of time for more sleep."

"Yep." I heaved another sigh and let the exhaustion win.

CHAPTER 21

I WOKE UP AGAIN, BUT THIS TIME it wasn't because of a dream. I'd tried to move, but something had prevented it. It was still dark, but the glow from under the entry door illuminated things enough to remember where I was and whom I was sleeping on top of.

Martini was asleep, I could tell by his breathing. He had both arms wrapped around me, and due to the position I'd gone to sleep in, I couldn't move.

My face was buried in the hollow of his chest, between his impressive pecs. This was, frankly, a nice place to be. He had hair on his chest, not so much that it was a rug but enough to look manly. It was soft, and I rubbed my face against it, figuring it would relax me and I'd go back to sleep.

It did relax me, but it didn't put me in the mood to sleep. It also caused Martini to start waking up. He growled sleepily, so it sounded more like a purr, and his arms tightened around me. I tried to move and he shifted, so we were both on our sides in the lounger.

It was nice to change positions, but now I could move even less. "Jeff," I whispered. "Jeff, I'm stuck."

"Mmmm?" He released his hold a bit so I could move enough to look at his face and see his eyes open slowly. "This is nice." He smiled and his voice was still drowsy.

"Yes, but can we move?"

He blinked. "Huh? Oh." He came fully awake. "Did you have another nightmare?"

"No, I'm just sort of stiff lying here."

A different smile crept across his face. "I know what you mean."

My sex drive woke right up and shoved my pelvis forward. Yep, he was *fully* awake. I considered pulling away, but he moved and kissed me. I stopped thinking about the fact that I'd known him for about a day and focused on how this kiss was just as great as the first one. Possibly better, since he wasn't wearing a shirt and the rest of the clothes we were in were pretty thin.

He wrapped one leg around me and pulled my body closer to his, while his hands stroked my back. My arms were still around him, and as our kiss got deeper and more passionate, I held him more tightly. Soon we were entwined around each other, in the hottest make-out session I'd ever been a part of. Martini's lips and tongue owned mine, and this aroused me more than anyone else's entire range of moves ever had.

The man could kiss, and his hands weren't slackers, either. He stroked the small of my back in such a way that I was squirming, trying to get his hand lower or him inside of me, preferably both at the same time.

His other hand roamed my side, coming close to but not touching anything I desperately wanted touched. It was erotic and tormenting at the same time. Our bodies rubbed against each other, and all I wanted was to get out of this chair and our nightclothes and into the bed, as fast as possible.

Martini moved his mouth from mine so his tongue and teeth could toy with my neck and ear. This left me free to moan and gasp, about all I could contribute when he was doing this, other than my body continuing to thrust wildly against his in the hopes he'd take the hint and move past foreplay before I self-destructed.

I felt him smile against my skin. "I told you, I take my time with this." His tongue slid up my neck to tickle my ear. "How badly do you want to get out of this chair?" As he asked, he slid one hand under my T-shirt. He stroked my stomach while I tried to remember how to form words.

My inarticulate moan of pleasure and desire must have been comprehensible in alien-speak, because he moved away from me. This was not what I wanted, but the separation didn't last long. He got out of the chair and picked me up, stripping my T-shirt off at the same time.

I wrapped my legs around his waist while he displayed as much skill with my breasts as he had with everything else so far. His tongue twirled around my nipples, making them harder than they'd ever been before, including in the snow, while I ran my hands over his head, my fingers through his hair, and ground my pelvis against his rock-hard abs. As his teeth gently toyed with me, my head fell back and my body shook as pleasure coursed through me, fast and hard. I'd never had an orgasm at second base before, and I hoped the rooms were soundproof, because I was yowling like a cat in heat, and for the same reasons.

Martini spun us around, deposited me on the bed, and slammed the bedroom door shut. It wasn't all that dark—I realized there was a night-light somewhere in the room. I could see him looking at me. He slowly ran his eyes up and down my body as he moved onto the bed on his hands and knees, between my legs.

"You are so damned sexy," he growled.

I tried to share that he wasn't a slouch in this department himself, but my brain and mouth couldn't get their act together. I just reached for him and managed to make a sort of mewling sound.

He grinned and slid on top of me. "Is this what you wanted, baby?" I arched against him, loving the feel of his skin against mine, and he grinned again. "Me too."

He grasped my wrists and moved my arms out and then down, holding me captive. Then his tongue slammed into my mouth and caused me to writhe against him as if we were in an earthquake. His body held mine in place while he rubbed himself against me, so close to entry but prevented by two thin pieces of cotton.

This kiss went on until the final aftershocks of my orgasm passed. Then he pulled away and sat up on his knees. He slid my pajama pants off slowly, oh, so slowly, until they were at my knees. He moved to my side, his lips and tongue traced my stomach, as he pulled the pajamas the rest of the way off.

He was in a position where I could reach him, and I

decided I should take a more active part in this experience. I traced him through the pajama bottoms he was still wearing. He was incredibly well-proportioned—the phrase "hung like a horse" came to mind.

He liked it, if his thrusting toward my hand was any indication. I stroked him through the thin cotton, controlling myself from trying to shred the pajamas off him in order to feel his skin against my hand.

Martini gave a low growl of pleasure, and then his mouth moved downward. This time I couldn't stop my eyes from rolling back in my head. As his tongue moved over me, my hand tightened around him instinctively—it had no intention of letting go right now, possibly ever. The other one managed to find his head. My fingers twined through his hair and moved against his scalp in time with his tongue's movements.

He growled again and increased his ministrations until I was almost out of my mind, causing wave after wave of pleasure to course through my body. I'd had multiple orgasms before, well, a couple of times, but never this fast or intense.

I managed to form words. "Jeff . . . oh my God . . . *Jeff* . . . please . . ." Okay, they weren't the most coherent words, but they were clear, and if not clear, at least I wasn't screaming too loudly.

He took pity on me and moved slowly up my body, stopping to say hello to my breasts again and find out if they'd missed him. They had, but the rest of me wanted him, too. He moved, and despite my one hand's best efforts, pulled out of my grasp. I moaned my distress at this turn of events, but then his mouth was back at my neck, and I was moaning because I couldn't help it.

People have different erogenous zones, and one of my least obvious but most effective areas was my neck. Anywhere, but in particular the sides and back. Martini proved he could find each individual spot on my neck to make me moan and gasp out an orgasmic symphony.

My hands were clawing at his back while I wrapped my legs around his torso. If he wasn't going to come inside, I was going to do my best to force him.

He chuckled and moved up on his forearms. "Do you want something, baby?" His tone was erotically teasing, and it made me want him even more, which I wouldn't have thought possible by now.

I wrapped one hand around the back of his neck while the other tried to rip his pajamas off. I also finally got a clear sentence out. "Make love to me, right now, or I'm going to go insane, or kill you, or both."

Martini flashed his killer grin. "I was just waiting for you to ask nicely." He slid his pants off, managing to keep my body under his control. This might have been due to him kissing me, of course.

Then his body was fully on top of mine, our skin rubbing together. He was close, but not inside, just stroking me lightly while I moaned and whimpered and tried to move enough to get him past the threshold. He leaned up on his forearms again, but he wasn't grinning—he looked as out of control with desire as I was.

His eyes locked with mine, and he thrust inside me. I tried to keep eye contact, but I couldn't. My back arched, and I leaned my head back as his full length entered my body. He was hard as steel, but it didn't hurt, he felt perfect, as I'd always fantasized someone would. His movement created erotic friction, and each thrust moved me closer to another climax.

His tongue ran over my neck, and his breath was hot in my ear. One hand slid into my hair while the other roamed my torso and teased my breast. Each moan of pleasure from me earned another nip, lick, or stroke, to the point where I was almost out of my mind from the feelings he was creating in me.

I wrapped my legs around his and he moved up onto his hands, his thrusts increasing in intensity. I stroked his chest and arms, feeling his muscles, his hair, and the heat of his body, enjoying every sensation.

I was able to look at his face again. Martini was watching me, his expression a combination of desire and conquest. As our eyes met, he changed the rhythm, moving faster and harder. My body responded to his, and we slammed against each other, each hit making me cry out with pleasure.

I was at the edge of orgasm, and I could tell he was finally ready to join me. We were both panting, our bodies in perfect time. My hands tightened on his upper arms as the

explosion of pure ecstasy started. I could tell I triggered
him as my body contracted around his. He exploded inside
of me—the hot liquid pumped out as his body pulsed inside
mine and made my orgasm spike each time. This time it was
his head thrown back as he groaned from the release.

Our bodies finally stopped throbbing, and he lowered
himself back on top of me. I wrapped my arms around his
upper body as my legs relaxed and unwound from his. He
buried his face in my neck. He kissed me and murmured
I was his and he was never letting me go against my skin.
Finally he claimed my mouth again, this kiss still erotic, but
also tender and soft.

He rolled off and pulled me next to him. I draped my
body onto him, my leg hooked over his, and he wrapped his
arm around me while I leaned my head on his chest, keeping hold of his shoulder. Somehow Martini found the sheet
and pulled it over us.

He stroked my arm and kissed my forehead, and I snuggled closer to him, enjoying the way his naked body felt
against mine and reveling in the afterglow.

"You're mine, you know," he said quietly.

I kissed his chest. "Only if we do that again. A lot."

"You drive a hard bargain, but I think it's a fair price."

I heaved a sigh. "Good. Nice to know I negotiate well."

Martini chuckled. "You do everything well."

"Flattery's nice. Especially coming from the alien sex
god."

"You say the nicest things."

"You *do* the nicest things."

He moved my head and kissed me, another tender kiss.
"I'll do whatever you want, whenever you want it."

I had a somewhat evil thought, but this statement *had*
sounded like a firm commitment. "How about making love
to me again, right now?"

Martini grinned as he shifted me completely on top of
him. "Have I had time to mention that our double hearts
give us a great deal of stamina and rejuvenation capability
not common to Earth men?"

I was right on top of him, and it was clear he wasn't
lying. "Suddenly, I can see you weren't bragging—once you
go alien, you really do never go back."

CHAPTER 22

I HEARD AN ANNOYING BEEPING. I recognized it as some sort of alarm clock. I didn't want to pay any attention, but it wouldn't shut off.

I was on my side with Martini wrapped around me, my back against his chest. We'd finally fallen asleep some hours after we'd left the lounger, exhausted from physical activity and sexual fulfillment. I had no desire to leave this position or the bed, but the damned alarm wouldn't stop.

I opened my eyes, but there was no clock on the nightstand next to my side of the bed. However, the night-light, or whatever had been dimly on last night, was now turned to high. It was as bright in the room as if we were above ground and had a window without any curtains to keep the sun out.

I felt Martini stirring next to me. "Jeff, can you shut off the clock?"

He yawned. "Nope." He kissed the back of my head. "Alarms are room-based. Until we get out of bed, it'll just keep going."

Great, I was housing with the Extreme Morning Militants. What a joy. "Why do we have to get up now?"

"Time to get ready to go to work." He moved me around so we were facing each other, kissed me until every part of my body was wide awake and rarin' to go, and then he rolled over and got up. The alarm didn't stop. "You have to get up, too. It's set for all occupants." He went into the bathroom.

"So it's going off in your room?" I dragged myself to the edge of the bed and sat up. Not good enough for the Alarm from Hell.

"Nope. There's no one in my room to be awakened." He stuck his head out of the bathroom door. "But it's nice to see you still think I'm hiding a wife somewhere."

I managed to stand, and the alarm shut off. What a relief. I sat back down and it started again. "I hate that thing." I stood and leaned against the wall, and the sounds of silence greeted me. At last.

"It's effective."

"So's a snooze alarm."

"We don't do snooze alarms."

"I guessed." A thought occurred. "Um, Jeff? How are you going to get dressed? Without anyone knowing you spent the night with me?" By anyone I specifically meant my parents. I didn't care about anyone else's opinion, but the thought of my father catching us worked like an ice bath—I was wide awake now.

"No idea. I figured I'd just walk down the hall and get my clothes."

"Just like that?"

He looked back out. "Yes. Just like that." His expression changed, and I realized he looked hurt. "You don't want anyone to know, do you?"

"What do you mean?"

"You feel guilty and ashamed, and you want to hide."

"What makes you say that?"

He gave me the "duh" look. "I'm an empath. Remember?"

"Oh, right. But it's not what you think, or feel, or whatever." I moved into the bathroom and put my arms around him. "All of those feelings are because my mom and dad are down the hall. I don't want my *parents* to know, just yet anyway. I've known you for about a day, Jeff. Maybe this is normal for you guys, but my parents aren't going to be thrilled to discover I learned exciting new sexual positions with a guy I just met."

"Let alone an alien guy you just met."

"I don't think Mom cares about that. Dad probably won't, either, once he gets to know you all. But, um, they don't really want to know their daughter's a slut." There, I'd said it.

Martini put his hands on my shoulders and moved me away. I looked up at him, and his expression was shocked and confused. "You're not a slut. Why would you even say that? Is it just because it was with me?" There it was, the hurt and disappointment in his eyes again.

I remembered the conversation with Claudia and Lorraine, and it occurred to me that the impression of overwhelming confidence Martini projected might be, at least in some ways, an act.

"No," I said as gently as I could. "Jeff, I think you're gorgeous. You're smart and you're funny. You're the best kisser on, I'd guess, two planets. And, just to clear things up, I've never been with anyone who had the potential to perpetrate death by orgasm on me before. I'm not ashamed that, I guess, we're a couple. But it's different for women than men."

He looked a little less hurt, but still confused. Another thought crept in. Two in one morning, possibly my personal best.

"How many Earth women have you dated?"

He shrugged. "Not too many." But he wasn't making eye contact.

I moved his head so he had to look at me again. "How many is not too many?"

"Counting you?" I nodded. "A handful. Less than ten."

I managed to keep my jaw from dropping just in time. I'd dated a lot more guys than this. I *was* a slut. "How about A-C women?"

"Well, growing up, sure, plenty. I mean, over ten." He swallowed. "But, you know, as they get older, they want something different."

"Something smarter yet far less attractive?" I couldn't help it, it was impossible to comprehend choosing Geek of the Year over Martini, unless we were only talking about earning potential. And even if he'd dated over twenty women total, I was still ahead of him. I was the winner of Slut of the Month club, at least in this room.

"I guess, if that's how you put it." He still looked miserable.

"Well, it's how *I* put it. Jeff, it's different for women, at least in how Earth folk think of it. A man can date a lot, sleep with someone on their first date, and he's a stud. A woman who does that is considered loose or a slut, or worse."

"Oh, one of the Earth double standards." He sounded both relieved and as though it was old hat. "Like all the other prejudices, based on one rule for some and a different rule for others."

They must have taught them this in A-C schools. He sounded as though he was discussing a concept, not something he'd ever experienced himself. "So, A-Cs don't have a gender double standard?"

"Nope. We also don't have sexual preference issues or skin color issues." He was looking as though he didn't want to tell me something again.

"What issues *do* you have?" Reader's suggestion to ask why they'd been the ones chosen to come to Earth popped into my head. "Why was your family, or whoever were sent here, the ones selected to come to help Earth?"

"We need to shower and get dressed." Bingo. He obviously didn't want to answer this, and it was clear it was connected to our prior discussion.

Great sex must have helped my mental synapses—my mind was working as though I'd been up for hours and already had a full pot of coffee. "What prejudice *does* Alpha Centauri have, and how does it relate to all of you here on Earth? Oh, and I'm not showering or dressing until you answer me, and I think I'm satiated enough that even if you try kissing me, it won't work as a distraction from this."

"Damn." He heaved a sigh and turned away from me, fiddling around with the shower. "Religion," he said shortly, his back to me.

"How so?" He was tense, I could see it in the way his back muscles were bulging. I rubbed his shoulders, stroked his back, and I felt him relax.

"There's only one official religion on Alpha Centauri."

"But you're all a part of the unofficial one?"

"Right." He felt the water and stepped into the shower, seemed to consider something, then pulled me in with him.

This was fine, and I allowed him to stall a bit longer by making out with me under the flowing water. Okay, I allowed him to stall a lot longer by making love to me in the shower. Mind-blowing, just like every other time. I really found myself again hoping the room was soundproof, especially because I really got the echo reverberating when he had me against the side of the shower with my legs wrapped around his body during my second of four orgasms. It was a long shower, but I had no complaints about water waste. We even managed to clean off in there somewhere.

We were out and toweling off and I decided to pick the conversation back up, now that I could speak coherently again. "So, the religion thing. It's rampant here, so I don't understand why you're avoiding telling me about it. Are you guys devil worshipers or something?"

He winced. "No. That's part of the problem, though." Martini got really busy toweling off.

I nudged him. "Jeff, c'mon. Just tell me. It'll be okay. You're from a different planet. You have two hearts. You run fifty miles in the blink of an eye. And you're a sex god. I think I'm prepared for a difference in religious backgrounds."

He sighed. "That's just it. There's not that much difference."

This was intriguing. "I want an explanation. With more words than you've gotten out so far."

Martini rolled his eyes. "Okay, fine. It was great while it lasted. The world-sanctioned religion is similar to most of the religions on Earth. One ruling God-being created us all, good people go to Heaven, bad people go to Hell."

"Okay, so what's the problem?" I realized I only had the clothes I'd arrived here in to put on. Great.

"You have clean clothes in the drawers," Martini said. "They should be sized for you, but we'll get some stuff from your apartment later, just in case."

"How—"

"Empath. Your worry level spiked as you looked at the dresser. Try to keep up."

"Smart ass." I pulled open a drawer—underwear, bras included. And they fit. Score another one for alien technology. "Okay, fine. Back to religion."

"If we must. The world religion doesn't believe in re-demption. Basically, if you commit murder, you're going to Hell. You can be as sorry as you want to be, but you can't atone, there's nothing you can do to save your soul."

"Nasty. Does it keep violent crime down?"

"From what I've been told, yes, for the most part. But . . . we don't believe that."

I could hear the fear in his voice. Religious persecution was a galaxy-wide trait, who'd have figured? "What do you believe?"

"We don't believe in Hell as a specific place. We believe a soul can be redeemed, that mistakes can be atoned for. We think a person should do right because it's right, not because their soul will be in eternal jeopardy if they don't toe the line. And," this sounded dragged out of him, "we don't believe we just showed up one day on the planet. We believe in evolution."

I let this all sink in for a bit. "How much science is there on Alpha Centauri? A lot? I mean, you built an ozone shield, right?"

"*My* people built the ozone shield. Scientific aptitude is stronger in us than in the rest of the world."

"Is that why you came to Earth, because you had the better scientific aptitude?"

Martini looked right at me, and his face was like stone. "No. We were sent to Earth because it was a convenient way to get us off the planet. We were the ones saying we had to help, we were the ones who realized the ozone shield had protected our world but would just send the parasites all the faster to yours. It was the perfect political solution—exile our entire population to another planet, help that planet at the same time, double win for everyone."

"Except for those of you who will never see your real home world, and who are always going to be different, no matter what you do."

He nodded. "If one of our people had married into a standard family, then they had the choice to stay on our home world. In some cases, they did, in others their imme-diate families came with us to Earth. But there wasn't a lot of intermarriage, for a variety of reasons, so that percent-age of our population here is pretty small."

"So, your religion, is it something someone chooses?"

"No. We're born into it. We aren't pretending—we may not all look alike, but we're all related by blood somewhere, traceable back to about twenty or so original family units from centuries ago."

There it was. I thought this had sounded vaguely familiar. I hugged him tightly. "It's okay, Jeff. I'm not horrified or turned off or even mildly shocked. After all, we Chosen People from different planets have to stick together."

CHAPTER 23

THE CLOTHES IN THE DRAWER for me were what I'd seen most of the other women wearing—a black slim skirt and white oxford-type shirt. I hadn't known Armani made this stuff for women, but I doubted the A-Cs were into faking designer labels. "Is this the official garb of your scientific facility, or does everyone double as a waitress?" Sadly, there were no attractive shoes. I was stuck with my sneakers. Fortunately, they were black and white Converse, so I could pretend I was just dressing for semi-stylish comfort.

"Yep. We like to keep things simple." Martini was back in his nightclothes. His T-shirt was still a bit damp.

"Okay, you're going straight to your room, right? Not going anywhere near my parents?"

He rolled his eyes. "They're farther down the hall. And, yes, I'll run. God forbid anyone should know I was here. Got it."

"It's not like that. Come on, you're the empath. What are you feeling from me?"

"Anxiety."

"And that's *all*?" I knew I had more going on than anxiety. Lust had to be in there somewhere—he looked hot in the official nightclothes.

"You're kind of making me go a little . . . haywire." He grinned. "Has to do with romantic involvement. It's an empathic thing."

"Well, I guess that's flattering." We went to the door, and I grabbed and kissed him. "I mean it, I'm not ashamed to be with you. I just don't want to deal with my parents about it right now."

He gave me a crooked smile. "Okay, I'll trust you on it. For now."

I opened the door with the intention of checking to see if the coast was clear and just avoided my father's fist slamming into my face.

"Hey!" I jumped back, right into Martini.

"Wow, amazing," Dad said. "I was just about to knock." He stepped in and noticed Martini. Dad went from genial to furious in less than one second. "What is he doing here at this time of the morning?"

I thought very fast. "He knew I didn't know there were clothes here for me and came to give me a head's up."

"In his sleepwear?" Dad's voice was sounding more like a bear's growl.

"I'll just let you two chat," Martini said as he slipped around and out, using, I was pretty sure, a little boost of hyperspeed. He mouthed, "Sorry," at the door, and then he ran down the hall, for sure using hyperspeed. Nice. He was out of the situation, and I was stuck alone with my father about to go all Cotton Mather on me.

"Dad, it's not what you think."

"Oh, I'm sure it's not. I'm sure it's worse. You know they're aliens? From another planet? What are you thinking, Katherine?" This was bad. Dad only called me Katherine when he was beyond furious.

"Daddy, really, you're overreacting." And these days I only called him Daddy when I was in total panic.

Dad was about to explode when a throat cleared. We both looked at the door and saw Mom standing there. "Sol, I think you need to calm down." Mom was on my side in this? I was ready to sob with relief.

"Do you know who was in here with her, in his pajamas?" Dad sputtered.

"I'd guess it was Jeff," Mom said, giving me a "we'll talk about this later" look.

"Exactly! And as much as I'd like to believe otherwise, I'm sure he spent the night here!"

"Only part of the night," I admitted. "Because I'd had a nightmare, and he came in to take care of me."

Dad was about to rant on when Mom put her hand up. "Jeff came in because your nightmare woke him up?" I nodded. "What kind of nightmare?"

I sat down on the sofa. "The horrible kind." I told them both about my dream. It wasn't any less vivid even after all the great sex and religious revelations.

Mom was quiet when I finished, but Dad spoke. "Kitten, why didn't you come to us?"

I shook my head. "Dad, I couldn't get out of bed, and I had no idea where you were. It was so awful . . ." I felt tears start to come, and I stopped talking. I'd cried enough last night.

"Sol, Jeff's an empath, a very powerful one from what Paul and Christopher told me. And he's very interested in Kitty romantically. When she woke up from a nap in New York, she panicked, and he came running. I think it's understandable he'd do the same thing last night."

"But he was still here this morning," Dad snapped.

Mom heaved a sigh. "Sol? Do you remember the day we met?"

Dad got a nostalgic look on his face, but his smile was very cat-satisfied. "Yes. Exciting day."

"Very," Mom said dryly. "And, if you'd care to recall, I spent the night with you. For your protection."

My jaw dropped. "You and Dad slept together the first day you'd known each other?" Sluttiness ran in the family. I didn't know whether to be relieved or grossed out.

Mom rolled her eyes. "Shockingly, yes. We had sex in order to conceive you, too. Hope you can deal with the surprise that you weren't a virgin birth."

"But that was *us*," Dad protested.

At this, Mom and I both laughed. My father was many things, but a hypocrite wasn't one of them. He realized what he'd said and laughed, too.

"She's twenty-seven years old, Sol," Mom managed to gasp through her laughter. "And, to shatter another ridiculous illusion of yours, Jeff wouldn't be the first."

Dad sighed. "Yeah, I know. I had to figure at least one boyfriend in college managed to break her resolve down."

I managed to keep a reasonably innocent look on my face. I figured this wasn't the time or the place to share that I'd lost my resolve earlier than college.

Mom chose not to shatter this little fantasy of my father's either. "Right. So enough with the huffy father routine. We have a matter of national and global security at hand, as well as at least two entities trying to kill us, or worse. We need to work as a team, not spend our energies bickering about natural human and, apparently, alien drives."

"And yet you're okay with her becoming intimate with a space alien?" Dad was going to take one last shot at the righteous parental indignation.

"They're religious exiles from their world," I blurted out.

"How so?" Dad asked.

I related what Martini had told me. "So," I finished, "they've been persecuted for their religious beliefs, and since they're born into those beliefs, really it's persecution based on who they are."

"That's too bad, but still . . ." Dad seemed sympathetic but unconvinced.

"Sort of like they're the . . . the Jews of space," I tossed out in desperation. I saw Mom put her head in her hands at this.

But it worked. Dad's eyes widened. "You think they keep kosher?"

"Sol!"

"Just asking."

"Sol, *we* don't keep kosher, for God's sake!"

"Is he circumcised?" This to me, with total scientific interest beaming from every pore.

"Dad!"

"Well, is he?"

"Yeah, because it helps us fit in as humans," Martini said. I looked up to see him leaning against the doorway. He was back in the standard issue Armani suit. But now I knew what was under the clothes. He looked great in them, but I wanted to rip them off. Only, not in front of my parents. "So, anything you want to ask me about my relationship with your daughter? I've already shared my intentions with your lovely wife."

"And what might those be?" Dad asked. I winced in anticipation of Martini's answer and Dad's reaction to it.

"I want to marry her and have a lot of kids. Oh, and I knew that within the first hour I'd known her."

Dad looked pleased, and I wondered if there was something in the water around here. "Oh, then, that's fine. You go to temple?"

Martini shook his head. "Not like yours. But, yeah, we all practice our religion here. It doesn't involve anything a normal Judeo-Christian religion would find appalling," he added quickly.

"We can get into the intricacies later," Mom interjected. "I think Kitty's dream is more pressing."

"I agree," Martini said. "Ready to get something to eat and find Paul?"

I leaped up. "Absolutely."

"Oh, I need Kitty for just a minute," Mom said. "Why don't you take Sol to the dining room, Jeff? Christopher's already shown me the way, so I'll get Kitty there."

Martini gave her a suspicious look, but he nodded. "Sounds fine. See you in a couple minutes," he said to me as he and Dad left the room. I could tell he was worried. So was I, so we were in sync.

Mom closed the door as they left, then turned around and crossed her arms over her chest. "You want to explain why you didn't listen to me?"

I sat back down. We weren't going anywhere fast. "I haven't said I'd marry him. Martini just told Dad what he told you."

Mom sighed. "You take any time to think about what's going on between you and Christopher?"

"No. Look, we can't say two sentences to each other without snarling. I'm glad you think he's wonderful, but, looks aside, I think he's ninety-nine percent jerk with one percent usefulness thrown in."

Mom sat down next to me. "Okay, I'm not going to push this, because I was serious—that dream of yours has me freaked out. I think your subconscious picked up something we're all missing, so I agree you need to tell the others about it so we can figure out what's really going on. I'm sure our lives depend on it."

She put her arm around my shoulders. "I know you think I don't like Jeff, but I do believe there's more depth to him than he lets show. Am I right?"

I nodded. "He came in to take care of me, Mom. I was so terrified . . . ." I had to stop and swallow. Thinking about the nightmare was still affecting me. "And, you know, I was attracted to him from the moment I saw him."

"Who wouldn't be?" Mom asked with a laugh.

"Well, apparently all your new best girlfriends forever." I told her about Claudia and Lorraine. "It's weird. I think the A-Cs might be better off here. There's not a human man or woman who wouldn't consider them the hottest things on two legs, their women want our smart men regardless of looks, and their men probably just want anyone who doesn't make them feel like attractive morons."

"They have fairly strict rules about human-alien marriage," Mom said quietly. "Christopher told me about it. It's one of the reasons he's upset with Jeff—the likelihood the two of you would be allowed to marry is slim."

CHAPTER 24

I **HADN'T SERIOUSLY CONSIDERED MARRYING** Martini until Mom said no one would let us. Then the rebellious part of me that had me reading Betty Freidan and putting up Susan B. Anthony posters in my room two decades past the height of the Women's Movement kicked in.

"It's not their choice, it's ours."

"Your little Jews in Space line is more on the mark than you realize," Mom said patiently. "Orthodox Jews from Space might be more accurate, though."

"I know you and Dad had issues in getting married—"

"And only the fact I was in the Mossad and had saved his life allowed his parents to manage to accept me. Your father and his siblings rebelled against their parents' strict outlook, but they had the rest of the world to support them. The A-C clan doesn't. For example, Jeff has no options for health care other than from another A-C being, unless he's excited about becoming a human experimental toy. You couldn't have your children at any hospital at home, for the same reason. They'll look human on the outside, but on the inside, the A-C genes are dominant."

I took a deep breath. "I'm not ready to get married, so this is sort of a silly conversation."

"You need to know what you're getting into. I didn't think I was going to marry your father, either. It just sort of happened, falling in love, real love, not lust."

"I do lust Martini," I admitted. "I don't know if I love

him." I thought about the flashes of pain I'd witnessed and the way he'd looked lost and lonely talking about the home world he'd never seen and never would see. "I care about him, though."

"It's clear he cares about you, as well. Just be aware—he's not the only one." Mom stood. "We'd better go. I'm sure you're hungry after getting a lot of, ah, exercise last night."

"Says who?" I stood too, hoping I looked righteously innocent.

"Says the supremely satisfied glow and relaxed body language. I'm your mother, let's please remember. Lost your virginity in college my ass," she added as we went to the door.

"Oh, let him keep his illusions."

"I will. He's hard enough to live with when he's got them intact. Every shattered illusion takes weeks to get him over."

"Sorry."

"It's okay. I'm used to it. Besides, he makes up for it in other ways."

"Too much information! I don't want to hear another word about your sex life. We've already covered more of mine than I wanted to share."

"That's fine, we can talk about your shoes instead. Starting with, why?"

We wandered down unfamiliar corridors, but Mom was striding along as if she'd lived here all her life. "All I had, thanks so much. You were packed for a trip, and Dad got to bring whatever he wanted. I was lucky Martini broke a rule and took me back to my apartment to change out of my suit. Besides, they're comfortable."

"You look as though you're trying to bring the eighties' suit and tennis shoes look back. Comfy, yes. Attractive, not so much."

"What are you, the Terrorism Fashionista?"

"Just get a more appropriate pair of shoes before we have to go anywhere."

We hit the dining area just in time. It was a sea of black and white Armani. I saw Martini waving, but I'd have found them without the help—Dad's yellow polo shirt stood out like a beacon. "Why don't you do something about *his* wardrobe?" I asked as we made our way to them.

"He's married, you're single."

"I thought we were avoiding that train of thought."

"Only for now."

The dining room was filled with long tables and typical industrial-type chairs. It gave me the feeling of being in a military unit that just happened to wear designer fatigues. Dad and Martini were at the end of one table; Gower, Reader, Christopher, and White were with them. There was an empty chair between Martini and Reader and one between Dad and Christopher. I knew where I was sitting. We reached the table, and Martini pulled out the chair for me. Christopher beat Dad to Mom's chair. I saw Dad give him a glare similar to the one he'd shown Martini earlier. Good, at least one of them wasn't ready to adopt Christopher into the family just yet.

There was no menu. Food was served family style, with a wide variety of options. This was a relief—hearing Dad's complaint about pig products being the only breakfast option was never fun, and I'd learned it by heart before I was five.

Mom and I filled our plates and started eating, while Martini gave the others a very high-level and abbreviated version of last night. He left out any form of innuendo, but I had a good view of Christopher's expression, and it was clear from the glaring he'd made the same assumptions as my parents. Either that or the room wasn't soundproof, and the whole compound was aware that Martini had introduced me to the Alpha Centaurion Love Knot.

Gower waited until Martini finished. Then he leaned forward so I could see his face clearly. "I'd like the full details from you. But it'll be easier if I'm touching your head. Are you all right with that?"

"Sure." I didn't have makeup on and my hair was in a ponytail, so no big deal.

Gower got up and moved behind me. He put both palms flat against the sides of my head. "Go on. Tell us about it, but I'd like you to try to see it in your mind as well."

"No worries." I couldn't get the images *out* of my head any time I thought about them. I went through the whole dream again, and it was just as horrible as reliving it for my parents had been. I ended up closing my eyes because that way I had a better chance of not crying.

I repeated everything, including what Christopher said before I killed him and Mephistopheles' closing line. Then I stopped and tried to clear my mind so Gower would get the hint.

He took his hands away slowly, massaging my temples as he did so. Some of the horror dissipated. "Rub her neck," he said quietly to Martini. "Base of the skull in particular."

Martini's hand slid up my back to my neck. I managed not to arch into him, but it required effort. His ministrations relaxed me, and I was able to open my eyes safely.

To see Christopher looking at me with a mixture of anger and hurt in his expression. It was different from being glared at, but still unsettling.

"I don't actually want to kill you," I told him. Mostly, I added to myself to remain somewhat truthful.

"Paul, what do you think?" White asked.

Gower sat down. "I'd like to hear what Kitty thinks, first." He sounded guarded.

"I've got nothing, other than I'm scared by Mephistopheles. A lot."

"But it's Yates you should be afraid of," Reader said thoughtfully. "He's the one who tried to replace you with a robot."

"Maybe she's not afraid of him because she didn't interact with him," Mom suggested.

I felt something tickling inside my brain, but not enough to form an idea yet.

"Or it could be she just figures her mother will handle it," Dad said with some pride. I noted his arm was around the back of Mom's chair. Not unusual, but rare for them in a group situation. I got the impression he was jealous of Christopher.

"Maybe it's just a nightmare," White suggested. "People do get them."

Gower shook his head. "Come on, Richard. All dreams mean something, you know that."

"James, what do you think?" I asked. The tickling in my brain got more intense.

"Why?"

"I don't know. I just want to hear what you think about all this. You were the only human besides me who was there. Mom doesn't count because she was unaware of the aliens or superbeings before the incident at JFK." My conscious mind wasn't where this was coming from.

"Okay. I don't think Yates is real to you because you've never met him."

"But I have, in a sense. He's as much a part of Mephistopheles as Mephistopheles is of Yates." Almost there.

"But Yates doesn't know he's a part of Mephistopheles," Christopher said, sounding exasperated. "We told you that last night."

And there it was, another epiphany. Alien sex was great for my mental processes. "That's it. I think there are two plans."

"Well, we know Yates has a plan." Mom said patiently. "It would make sense that Mephistopheles would be a part of it."

"No, I mean two different plans, planned by two different beings who don't know their plans intersect. As Christopher mentioned, you all told me an in-control superbeing's brain is split, and the human brain doesn't know it's part of an alien hybrid. Well, maybe the parasitic brain doesn't know, either. Yates has his plan, and it's terrorism-based. That's why he wants to kill my mother. But Mephistopheles has a different plan."

"What plan would that be?" White asked carefully.

I closed my eyes and thought about it. "In my dream, Mephistopheles' parasite moved to me, but he stayed the same. I didn't change outside, but I could feel the change inside. I wasn't me any more, I couldn't stop doing what Mephistopheles wanted."

"Oh, my God," Gower said. "That explains it." He looked at me. "Your dream didn't feel right. It was subtle, but not normal."

"You think the parasite's already in me?" I could hear my voice, and it had moved to squeak-of-terror level. Martini increased the massage pressure on my neck. It helped. A bit.

"No," Gower said reassuringly. "We know you're still you. Believe me."

"We couldn't touch you if you were infected," Martini added.

I thought about his and Christopher's reactions to touching Yates' image last night. "Why not?"

"Just something in our physical makeup," White answered. "We haven't been able to pin it down, though we do have a team working on it."

"Have them focus on what's different, really different, genetically between A-Cs and humans. Because when Mephistopheles picked me up, I didn't have any kind of reaction like the one you all did to just touching the image."

"What did you feel?" Mom asked quietly.

I tried to think back. "I wasn't scared," I said finally. "I was mad. Him picking me up made me madder. And I never got scared, even when I thought he was going to eat me."

"It's rage," Reader said immediately. "Humans have a greater capacity for rage than A-Cs do. Not that they can't get mad," he grinned at Paul, who laughed, "but they don't do it to our level."

"Yeah, but is rage really controlled at the genetic level?"

"It is in us," Martini said quietly. "Somewhat in you, too."

"I thought it was lame, too, what he said to me," I added. There was silence. I waited for the sound of crickets. "What?" I asked finally.

"You could understand what he was saying?" Christopher asked.

"Well, only two short sentences. I mean, it was obvious he was talking to you all in some alien language, and I couldn't understand a word of that. But he talked to me, when he had me near his head."

"How?" Gower asked flatly.

I shrugged. "His eyes changed. They went from that red, glowing, superbeing creep-out look to almost human. He said I was trouble," I added.

"He got that right," Christopher muttered.

I chose to ignore Christopher's little comment. "Then

when he was about to stick me in his mouth, he said I wouldn't be trouble much longer."

"They can't do that," White protested. "Human or super-being. No in-between."

"He did with me. Then I hit him with my hairspray, and he dropped me." I looked around. All the A-Cs looked, to a man, nervous. "Again, what?"

Gower broke their silence. "It wasn't a dream, Kitty. It's an implanted memory."

"It hasn't happened." I could hear the "yet" no one spoke aloud but I was pretty sure everyone was thinking. "I mean, what, do these parasite things work backward in time or something?"

"Not that we know of," White answered. "But you could be overlaying your own experiences onto the implanted memory."

"Maybe he's figured out how to make more super-beings." This wasn't a great thing to be suggesting, especially since I had a feeling I was supposed to be Test Subject Number 1.

"Maybe it's more that he's just remembering how," Christopher said quietly.

"From," Gower added, "touching you."

CHAPTER 25

"WE ONLY KNOW ABOUT THE PARASITES from our translations of the Ancients' texts," White explained as we all headed to the Research level. This was at my mother's insistence on knowing, fully, what the hell was going on.

Martini had his arm around my waist. He wasn't being possessive, he was keeping me up and moving. Hearing I was not only parasitic-alien bait but was also likely triggering some sort of alien Armageddon wasn't doing a lot for my ability to remain calm.

We arrived in what looked like the biggest library on Earth. I figured it probably was. The room was vast, bigger than the science level we'd been on last night. The stacks of books seemed to go on forever, like a huge maze of literature.

It was all computerized, though. A-C efficiency in action. Gower punched in what we needed on one of their free-moving light board screens, and then we went into a reading room to wait for our selection to arrive.

This room was big enough to hold fifty people comfortably, but it actually had walls. It also had a large screen in addition to another huge conference table and plenty of chairs. The translations of the Ancients' books were available in hard copy, but the originals were computer-created documents.

Everyone was arguing about what portion of the text

to look at first when Claudia and Lorraine came in. They grabbed me away from Martini and took me over to a corner of the room.

"We heard," Claudia whispered. "Are you okay?"

"I'm totally freaked out." I hoped they were talking about my dream and not my sexual escapades with Martini.

"Who wouldn't be?" Lorraine asked. "Mephistopheles has been in existence for twenty years, and we've never been able to kill him."

Twenty years? This was a little tidbit no one had shared with me yet. "How have you allowed him to do all he has as Ronald Yates?"

"We didn't make the Yates connection until a couple of years ago," Claudia admitted. "It's hard for a dead agent to tell us much."

This hit me in my stomach. I knew several agents personally now, one very personally. The reality of what they did for a living washed over me. Any one of them could be killed by these superbeings, just as a human could. For all I knew, one of their number had died at the courthouse—I hadn't asked, after all.

Martini came over. "Stop freaking her out; she's upset enough. None of us died yesterday." He put his hand on my neck and started massaging again. "No one can agree on what to look at first," he added with a sigh.

"I know what I want to look at." I did? "I want to read what the Ancients said about the parasites, how they came into being." Why did I want to read this?

"Okay." Martini gave me a funny look, but he relayed my request to Gower.

Claudia and Lorraine sat down with me while the text rolled up onto the screen. Gower handed me what looked like a superduper computer mouse. "You control the speed with this button," he pointed to a round knob on the top.

The text was choppy—you could tell it had been translated by people who had no idea of what the original language sounded like. Dad stood behind me, reading along. Mostly it sounded as though the Ancients were trying to explain who they were, so their warnings would carry weight.

"Can we see the original text?" Dad asked, his tone thoughtful.

"Why? It's in an alien language," White replied.

"It translated, didn't it?" Dad didn't sound huffy. He sounded as though he was getting excited. "I just want to see it."

A thought occurred. "Um, Dad? What is it that you do for a living? I mean really, not what you've told me all my life."

Mom was in front of me and to the left. I saw her give a small nod, and I assumed Dad had just asked permission to share the truth.

"I'm a cryptologist," he admitted. This was a far cry from college history professor, which was what I'd been told all my life. "But," he added hastily, "I do teach at the university."

"As your cover. Which agency do you work for?" Long silence. "Dad? I mean it, I want to know." I didn't turn to look at him. I had a feeling he wouldn't tell me if he had to look me in the eyes.

"NASA," he said finally.

"NASA. In their extraterrestrial division, right?" I'd never heard of this division, but after a day with the boys from A-C, I had a good idea it existed.

"Right." He sighed. "I don't see the kind of action your mother does. I don't see action at all, really. Cryptology isn't a field job. I didn't know we had ETs on the planet, though—that's on a need-to-know basis—"

"And you didn't need to know. Got it." Nice to see other people besides my mother were withholding information from my father. Of course, I'd spent my entire life believing he was a tenured history professor at Arizona State University, so clearly Dad was also into the need-to-know lifestyle. Chuckie and I had even taken his classes. Of course, most of his classes were taught by grad students. As I considered this, history professor seemed like a great cover.

"Right. My group works more with the transmissions we pick up from the other inhabited planets."

"Not just the Alpha Centauri planets, right?" I was taking this remarkably well. I wondered how long my calm would last.

"Right. This is the only alien text we've got. The rest are all audio only. It's why I want to see it." He was lying, I could tell—I'd lived with him the majority of my life, after all. The big lies, sure, both parents had done those well, but they'd had them in place before I showed up. But the little lies, not so much. Dad, in particular, had a lot of clues when he wasn't telling the truth. I knew there was more to why he wanted to see the text than curiosity. But I wanted to see it, too.

White shrugged and Gower left the room, presumably to go order up the actual volume. While we waited, I kept on scrolling through. I wasn't sure what I was looking for. I just had a feeling there was something no one was picking up.

I reached the part about a sun dying, and I slowed down. The description was sad, really. A well-inhabited planetary system had circled a star that went supernova with almost no warning. One day, everything was normal. The next, the star exploded. In a big bang.

I backed up. It literally said it—"big bang." There was text in parentheses after this saying "supernova."

"How do I mark something I want to come back to?" I asked Lorraine.

She reached over to the mouse and pushed something. The paragraph I was reading was now backlit in yellow.

"Nice, thanks. The words in parens, what are they?"

"Areas where the translation team wasn't sure of the accuracy," Claudia replied. "The information in the parentheses is the most likely guess."

"Okay." I kept on reading. The Ancients were describing what happened to the people on the planets.

They were stripped apart, and the portion that could live without the body (aka: parasite) was freed. These sailed through space, searching for their new home. But because of their innate being (best guess) they could not find it and so began to search for new hosts.

"Highlight this, please," I asked Lorraine. "Dad, I want you to find the passage that corresponds to this in the original."

"You got it, kitten." He sounded as if he knew where I

was headed. I hoped so, because I wasn't sure of my direction yet.

I kept scrolling. Many references to the big bang, to the portions that could live without the body—now only called parasites for ease of reading—searching for a place they couldn't find. Descriptions of horrors to come when the parasites found their new hosts. Details of why to avoid the parasites—death, destruction, horror—no details on how to live with them. Several references to the pain the parasites caused when they joined with a new host.

The book shifted, and now it was talking about the Ancients, how they had avoided the parasites, and how they wanted to ensure all the other planets would as well. They gave detailed instructions on how to keep the parasites away. Planetary protections were listed side by side with what sounded like the standard clean-living plan—be a good person, don't do bad things, don't get angry. Lots and lots of don't get angry and similar advice. Keep your cool, that was the Ancients' watchword for this section.

"Who did the translations? I know you said it took a supercomputer. Did any humans have involvement?"

"Some," White replied. "Most were our people, though humans created the computer program."

Gower and several women came in, including Beverly, the one with the boring speaking voice. The women were there, it was clear, to protect the original text, because they weren't allowing Gower to touch it. The situation and my request were explained.

Beverly appeared to be in charge, at least of the book. She moved it in front of me and Dad and reverently opened the pages. She turned carefully to the part I'd asked for. It was very near the start of the book.

Dad didn't try to touch it, he just leaned over my shoulder to stare. "It's all columns and rows, like a spreadsheet. Did you read it right to left, left to right, up to down or down to up?"

"We tried all of them," Beverly replied. She was still monotonal, and I was glad I felt reasonably rested.

"Which one worked?" Dad sounded as if he were vibrating behind me.

"None of them. It was an algorithm." Beverly sounded annoyed.

"Even or uneven?" Dad leaned on me now, trying to get as close to the text as he could.

"Uneven," Beverly admitted. "It was very odd. We had to run a huge number of variations through the computer to come up with anything coherent."

Dad stopped leaning on me. "Thought so." He bent down now. "If you're going where I think you are, chances are good you're right. You want to suggest it or shall I?" he whispered.

I thought about it. "Let me. If I'm wrong, you mop up," I whispered back.

He patted my shoulder. "I'm betting on genetics."

I cleared my throat and sat up straight. No time like the present to insult your hosts, after all. "I think your translation's wrong."

CHAPTER 26

BEDLAM'S AN INTERESTING WORD. I would have said the superbeing sprouting killer wings caused bedlam. But that was before I'd shared my hunch with the A-C crew in the room.

Every one of them, from White and Beverly all the way to Claudia and Lorraine, was talking, trying to speak over each other, countering my statement with a great deal of hyperbole.

Dad patted my shoulder. "That's my girl," he said in my ear.

I looked around, waiting for the crowd to calm down. Only two of them weren't freaking out—Martini and Christopher. They were both looking at me, and they both looked curious but not upset.

The room wasn't quieting, and I wondered if it was because no one actually wanted to hear my theory. It certainly wouldn't have been the first time.

Christopher looked around, and I saw his eyes narrow. "Everyone, shut up," he snarled. I wouldn't have thought they could hear him, but to a person the mouths snapped closed. Nasty seemed to have its benefits. He looked at me. "Please explain what you mean."

I waited until they were all looking at me. "It's not a textbook or a how to stop the invasion manual. It's a religious text."

"Oh, come on," Gower said with a laugh. "They came

to warn us, Kitty. It's a manual about the threat and how to protect ourselves from it."

I shook my head. "No. They came to convert us. They were missionaries. And that's their version of the Bible." I stood—it made me feel more like I could escape if they all jumped me. "It's an understandable mistake. Your religion doesn't think like theirs. But ours do."

I looked at Martini. "You don't believe in Hell, right?" He nodded. "And you also believe in evolution, not a creation story, right?" Another nod. I saw other heads in the room nodding as well. "And a computer is only as good as what gets programmed into it. I'm sure no one, A-C or human, thought to include the Bible in the computer's data banks for this. After all, this was a scientific threat, not a religious one."

I scrolled back to the first part of the text that had stopped me. "This talks about an explosion, a big bang. You interpreted it as a supernova—as the literal death of a star." I looked over to Dad. "But I interpret this as the Ancients' version of either the beginning of the universe or, more likely, the Garden of Eden."

He smiled at me. "An uneven algorithm creates challenges because you can get an algorithm that's close, but not perfect. Just as they did here." He pointed to the open book. "The problem with breaking a code is that you need to find the commonalities. Those are easier to identify the more text you have. But it's a common mistake to go with the first translation that finally makes sense. You did a good job," he added. "It's just not perfect."

"I'm sure you could perfect it," Beverly said, and her voice finally had a tone to it—deep sarcasm.

"Probably," Dad said with a shrug. "You've done the hard part. The next iterations would be the fine-tuning. That you didn't do."

"We double-checked," Beverly said hotly.

"I'm sure you did. But you checked only against your original idea of what the book was." Dad had his lecture mode on, I could tell. "In order to be completely accurate, you'd have to go in with no preconceived notions."

Mom must have picked up the likelihood of an impending lecture as well. "Sol, you want to let Kitty finish?"

"Oh, sure." Dad looked at me sheepishly. "Go ahead."

I scrolled to the text that had really stopped me. "I'm going to read this out loud, with some word substitutions. 'They were stripped apart, and the souls were freed. These sailed through space, searching for Eden. But because of their evilness they could not find it and so began to search for another place to live.' Sound familiar?"

"Adam and Eve being cast out of paradise," Reader said. "The fall of man."

"You could substitute Heaven for Eden, and Hell for another place to live. Same idea." I looked around. "Our world has flood stories in every culture, so Noah's Ark has a basis in reality. Almost all our Biblical stories are rooted in some fact. I'm guessing there really was a big bang, a supernova, if you will, that caused this story. The parasites are real, that's for sure. I think they're sentient, and they believe they're in Hell."

"Flying through space alone for millennia, no company, no warmth, nothing familiar. Yeah, that would be Hell," Martini said quietly.

"And your religion doesn't believe in a Hell, so your translators weren't thinking that way. You do believe in souls and that they can be redeemed, but you don't have the creation stories we do; you all believe in evolution."

"Our world's creation story is based on our double suns," Christopher interjected. "But the view is they created life together, not that they destroyed anything to bring it about. It's not scientifically logical, though, at least not in the way it's described. Which is part of why we don't agree with the theory."

"Alpha Centauri's is an affirmative story. Most of our Earth religions' creation stories are similar—a God-being created us, we showed up, fully evolved, from the get-go. None of our religions deal with evolution, and it's only science that gave us the big bang theory." I saw where this was headed, and it made my body feel ice cold. "We know the parasites are real. So the probability of the Ancients' religious text being accurate increases."

"Which means their suggestions for how to overcome the parasites are accurate as well," Beverly said, still sounding outraged.

"True. But no one's paid attention to the key thing. James has," I nodded toward Reader. "But you all ignore him because he's a human male who happens to be both handsome and not a rocket scientist."

Hit that one right, based on reactions around the room, from the women in particular. Reader cocked his head at me, though. "What do you mean, Kitty?"

"Rage. They talk over and over again about what to do to avoid the parasites. Put up defensive shields, yes, but most of those shields are based on being a good little girl or boy. That the A-C ozone shield actually worked against the parasites would reinforce their attention on physically preventing exposure. But you can have a moral shield, and anyone can do that."

I scrolled through again. "The first chapter in this book deals with the creation story, their Garden of Eden. The next one deals with the aftermath of this version of original sin, and details how to avoid becoming an outcast by ensuring one of these lost souls can't join with yours. And more than any other instruction, keeping your calm, not getting angry, is the one mentioned over and over again."

"I count twenty times just on this one page alone," Dad added.

"You all know they're attracted to rage; you've told me so yourselves. But you've been on this planet for decades, and you've never once mentioned that any A-C has been a target of a parasite."

"They aren't attracted to us," Gower said.

"Because James said you don't get as angry as humans do. You don't have the capacity for it, as a whole. I'm sure individuals can, but I've noticed you all really keep it under control, even when you're really angry with each other." I looked at Christopher. "You control it the least. Because you're not a scientist or an agent, you're an artist. And there are too many similarities between our races for me to doubt this one—artists tend to feel things more, and differently, from the average person."

I looked at Martini. "You're similar, but to stay sane you and the other empaths put up emotional and mental blocks. Meaning you can't get all that angry unless the blocks are down." I turned to Gower. "I'd also venture to guess that most of the A-C emotional activity happens here, or at Home Base, or somewhere else safe and secured and, above all, reinforced with whatever it is you brought with you that prevents most Earth governments from knowing you exist."

Gower nodded. "We have a variety of shields up, all of them based on the ozone shield or the invisibility cloaking."

"This is the second time it's been mentioned. You have an ozone shield?" I'd been wondering when Dad was going to go eco-friendly in the middle of this. Now was the time.

"Dad, yes, they do. Bigger issues than saving the whales right now, okay?" I sounded like Mom. I hoped this was a good thing.

"Oh, fine. Carry on." He looked mildly annoyed but not enough for me to worry about.

"Thanks. So the odds are in favor of no parasite ever catching an A-C with their emotions out of control, because most of that happens in the safety of your shielded fortresses. But we don't have an epidemic of superbeings. Why not?"

"The incidents are increasing, exponentially in the last twenty years," Beverly supplied.

The next connection waved merrily at me. "Twenty years. Exactly as long as Mephistopheles has been around, right?"

"Right. So?" Beverly was really taking this personally. I wondered how involved in the original translations she'd been and figured pretty close. Oh, well, she and Christopher could start the We Hate Kitty club.

"Think about it. He turns into a freaking devil."

"He's found his version of Hell and wants to populate it with his own kind," Reader said softly.

"Yes. I think he's calling them here. I don't know how, but it's at least a strong possibility." I took a deep breath. This was the part I was really dreading. "And he's figured out how to repopulate, because if we take this text to be an actual account, he probably helped create most of his race and was the reason they were cast out in the first place."

"How do you get that?" Gower asked.

"Missionaries tend to go out in waves."

"Mind explaining that?" White asked with a laugh.

"We have a lot of legends from Biblical times of angels coming to help us. I'm going to bet your planet does too. Every inhabited planet probably does. The Ancients were doing their best, after all. And if a missionary team didn't return home, well, they were going out to the boondocks of the galaxy, right? The next team was probably just told to find them if they were able or report back if they weren't."

"We told you, they couldn't survive on our worlds," Gower protested.

"Maybe they couldn't survive when they came in modern times because we've poisoned the air in both our worlds. You had to put up an ozone shield and we need one. Maybe our air or atmosphere was different several thousand years ago."

"Makes sense," Martini said slowly. "Pollution is something our races have had time to adapt to gradually. The Ancients might not have given it thought, could have been past it in their world, too, so it wouldn't occur to them."

"I'm back to how does this relate to Mephistopheles and Kitty's theory that he's the center of the Garden story?" Gower didn't sound angry, just confused.

"It's in our religious texts. Maybe it's in yours, too, maybe not. But the general Judeo-Christian opinion is that Lucifer fought with God for the throne and was cast out, along with his followers. Sent to Hell because of his hubris."

"So?" Beverly remained unimpressed, but I could see Martini's face, and I figured he was following my train of thought because his face had drained of color.

"One of the other names for Lucifer is the Morningstar. A star that was destroyed and sent away from Heaven, whether you consult the Earth Bible or the Ancients' text." I felt my throat go dry, but I pushed on. "Lucifer, now called Mephistopheles, considers that he has been sent here, to Hell—to rule over all its inhabitants in an eternity of torment and pain."

CHAPTER 27

NO BEDLAM THIS TIME, just silence. All the aliens were thinking. What a relief, someone else could take over that chore for a while.

I sank back into my chair, and Dad patted my shoulder again. Claudia and Lorraine each took a hand and squeezed. It was nice to know they didn't hate me.

Interestingly, it was a human who broke the silence. "Why are you the catalyst?" Reader asked.

"I have no idea." But it was a good question and bore consideration. Dang, I was going to have to start thinking again. No rest for the psychotic-alien bait, apparently.

"What do you mean, she's the catalyst?" Beverly asked.

Gower answered. "From what I saw in her mind, Mephistopheles implanted a memory into Kitty. A memory of how to create more superbeings. But I don't know why."

"Yates is an old man. James, you've said that more than once." I did my best to stay calm and not let this freak me out completely. "Yates must be dying. Mephistopheles wants to move to someone else before that happens."

"And Yates wants to complete his terrorism plan before he goes, which is why he's upping the game against your mother," Reader added. "It's why the plans are intersecting; he must be in the advanced stages of whatever's wrong."

Score two three-pointers for the humans. I could see A-C heads nodding around the room.

"It would be cancer," Mom offered. "Yates had it over

twenty years ago. He wasn't expected to live this long, but it went into remission."

"Because the parasite found him and turned him mostly invulnerable. It can't cure him, but it must have slowed the cancer down by quite a lot."

"Knowing this is great," Christopher said. "But what good does it do us?"

The words sounded as if they were being dragged out of him. "We finally have bait." Martini's jaw was clenched, and he had the stone-face on, just as when he'd told me about their being religious exiles this morning.

"What the hell are you talking about?" Christopher asked. He looked angry, but, then, so did my mother. I had a really good idea of what Martini meant.

"We use Kitty as bait." Martini's voice was starting to sound like Beverly's—monotonal.

"Are you out of your mind?" Dad grabbed me and pulled me toward him. This wasn't comfortable for either one of us, since I was sitting and the chair hit him in his gut, but I understood the reaction.

"I'm the head of Field Operations," Martini continued, voice still devoid of emotion. "We have someone who has been confirmed as a target by both Yates and Mephistoph-eles. We actually have a chance to do something about them, both of them." He looked at me, and though his face was still like rock, I saw his eyes. If I'd thought they'd been filled with pain before, it was nothing compared to right now. "But only if you agree."

"She does not!" Mom was furious. "She's not trained for anything like this operation will require. How dare you even suggest it?"

I looked at Reader. He noticed and cocked his head. I raised an eyebrow. He nodded.

"He's got the right, Mom, because he's the one in charge." I managed to disentangle from Dad's clutches and stand up again. I looked straight at Martini. "I pick who goes with me, I get some clothes I can move in, and I get fully briefed and equipped with all the standard field agent stuff." He nodded.

I looked at Gower. "I want James with me, Paul. But not you."

Gower looked as though I'd hit him in the gut. "Why?"

"He's not the one who needs to be angry. And I need someone who I can talk to, human-experience to human-experience." I looked at Christopher. "You, however, should plan on coming along."

He managed a grin. "I kind of figured. If that's all right with you," he added to Martini in a rather nasty tone.

"Fine." Martini's voice was still clipped. I didn't have to see him naked to tell his whole body was tensed.

I took another deep breath. "And I want some other female A-Cs with me."

This brought about pandemonium. From what I could make out through the shouting, the women were never allowed to do fieldwork. But I could also tell Lorraine and Claudia wanted to go with me.

"SHUT UP!" Martini bellowing was impressive—deep, angry and loud, with reverberations that continued for several seconds. So A-C's could indeed rage. Either that or all his empathic shields were down and he couldn't take it.

The room went deathly still. Martini seemed to calm instantly. "Thanks. Kitty, please explain why."

"Because I think part of the reason you can't catch these superbeings, Mephistopheles in particular, is that you're sending out the people who also can't actually reproduce."

Dead silence. Alien think time. But I decided to answer the questions that were going to come. "There are probably a lot of ways to change someone internally so it doesn't show externally, at least at first. However, there's only one way that's worked for all of recorded history."

"You impregnate them," Reader said with a grin.

I nodded. "In the case of this dream or implanted memory or whatever it is, I didn't die, remember? And neither did Mephistopheles. He put something inside me that made me change. But I changed only internally. Externally, no one could tell the difference." I took a deep breath and turned to White. "That's why I'm the catalyst. I'm the first female Mephistopheles has been close enough to to physically interact with."

"And you were angry," Reader added. "You weren't scared by him, you fought him. As an equal, not as a frightened animal."

"That's how he and the other parasites see us, I'm sure. As animals. We're not as evolved as they would be, we're so much younger in terms of planetary advancement, you've all told me this more than once."

"Wait a minute." Mom was still upset. Not that I could blame her. "Yates is around women all the time. This theory doesn't hold water."

"*Yates* is around them. But he's not going to turn super-being every five minutes. Is he?" I directed this to White.

"No. Mephistopheles only manifests a few times a year."

"Oh?" More information they hadn't shared with me. "I'd also like to get the full story, before I'm in life-threatening danger. Again." I directed this to Martini.

His eyes flashed. "Fine."

"And the female agents?"

"Who do you want?" Martini was angry as well as upset, I could hear it in his voice, despite his best efforts to keep his tone completely bland.

I shrugged. "Who's willing?"

"Me," Claudia and Lorraine said in unison.

"That'll do." I didn't want any of the other Dazzlers anyway. These two did the job I knew we'd need done with practiced skill.

"Anyone else?" Martini was barely moving his lips, let alone his jaw.

"You."

CHAPTER 28

I SAW MARTINI RELAX, just a tiny bit, but the anger was still there. At the same time Christopher's eyes narrowed. Good. I wanted them mad—at me, at each other, at the world. Frankly, I wanted everyone mad.

Well, everyone but Reader. Him I wanted calm.

However, that was later. Right now, I actually wanted the situation to diminish to something at least faking tranquillity.

My parents were still arguing about the latest wrinkle in what I was fast coming to accept as my new life. I decided to deal with the one in charge. "Mom, stop."

She closed her mouth but crossed her arms. Ready for combat. Ready to protect me with her life. Only, under these new circumstances, she'd endanger that life.

"Mom, as hard as this is to believe, I know what I'm doing."

"How? You've been living a secret life your father and I don't know about?"

"Hilarious. No, actually, I haven't been pretending to be anything I'm not all this time." Other than a virgin longer than in reality, but that wasn't important right now. "But I'm your daughter. Everyone says I'm just like you."

She shook her head. "I've had decades of training. You've had some Kung Fu and track and field. There's no comparison."

"Sure there is. You had to start somewhere. Well, this is

where I'm starting." I walked to her. "This is my Mossad. Understand?" I wanted her to, desperately.

She blinked. And I saw her look at me differently than she ever had before. "My baby's all grown up." Her voice caught, and I could see tears in her eyes. I did not want her crying right now, because I didn't need to start bawling again.

I hugged her. She hugged me back in that breath-removing bear hug way of hers I'd so recently started to experience. "I'll be okay, Mom," I whispered in her ear. "I think I know what I'm doing. And if I don't, I'll have people with me who will be able to bail me out. I promise. It's like you said—sometimes it's not about you and your family, sometimes it really is about saving the whole world."

"I hope you're right." She sighed. "I'll explain it to your father."

I pulled away and shook my head. "I bet you don't have to explain it to him." I turned around. "Does she, Dad?"

He gave me a small smile. "Like mother, like daughter. I wondered when it would show up in you. I don't like it, mind you," he added sternly. "But I also realize you're going to do what you think is best, no matter what I say." He looked innocent suddenly. "What about bringing in your Uncle Mort for this?"

"No," I said flatly. "I know what you're trying to do. I know Uncle Mort, remember? He'll take over, get me safely locked away, and have his leathernecks handle things."

Dad shrugged. "It's a decent plan from my viewpoint."

"Except that it'll fail," Martini said, voice still clipped. "Your military's had several chances at Mephistopheles. They've blown every one."

More information I didn't have. The debrief was going to take days. Days that what Martini called my female intuition said we didn't have.

"Not as if your boys have done all that well," Dad retorted.

"Better than you have," Christopher said. "We've managed to stop the majority of all forming superbeings while keeping your populace from total panic."

"By not allowing them to know what's really going on." Dad sounded huffy again.

"Oh, Dad, please. As if you're not the one who gave me all those 'herd mentality' lectures growing up. You know the herd would panic and stampede if they knew what was really going on."

"It's not as though Mort would recommend sharing this with the civilian public," Mom added.

"No, but I know he'd protect his niece with his life."

"Stop worrying. I'll take my hairspray with me." Crickets. Tough room.

Reader cleared his throat. "My parents have no idea what I do. They think I threw away a successful career to shack up with some black guy I barely knew who comes from an odd family. It's a lot easier that way." He winked.

Mom rolled her eyes. "Okay, fine. I give up. We'll stop acting as though we don't function in this kind of environment all the time. What do you need from us, Kitty?"

"Mostly for the two of you to stay here in the hollow mountain with the critters and leave me alone. About everything." I hoped they'd catch that this included my sex life and relationship with Martini, whatever that might be now.

Mom nodded. "Fine. Anything else?"

"Well, I would like all the information your two covert operations have on this."

"I had no idea we had ETs around, let alone on the planet," Mom said. "My knowledge is all Yates-based."

"Share it, he's got half the mind."

"This is considered highly confidential and requires a higher level of security than most people in this room are likely to have."

White cleared his throat. "I promise you, we have that clearance. Possibly higher."

"You didn't know about them, but they didn't seem shocked by you, Mom."

"Good point. I expect this to be treated as all classified information is, then." All heads in the room nodded. "The Al Dejahl terrorist organization is a worldwide group. Unlike most of the terrorist groups out there, they aren't religiously or racially based. They have as many members who claim no religion as they have who identify with all the popular religions. Their stated goal is overall chaos. However, it's clear that they expect to make a lot of money from that chaos."

"How is someone like Yates their head dude?"

"He's got the money, the means, and the drive. He comes up with wide-scale, intricate plans as easily as he does commando mission ideas, suicide bombers and the like, and small, targeted attacks. He recruits well, from all accounts, he's able to quickly identify what each potential recruit wants, what drives them, and exploit it."

"He personally recruits?" This seemed awfully hands-on for a guy with Yates' level of public profile.

"Not as much any more. He's taught his recruitment personnel how to imitate his techniques. But when he was first forming Al Dejahl, yes, he did the recruiting himself." Mom shrugged. "He has no scruples. He's got lots of attractive women available to offer the men, money and influence to offer to the few women who join, and the promise of world domination for all of them."

"How many do they number?"

Mom sighed. "We don't have an accurate count. They were in the tens of thousands, but we've made some real inroads in the last few years, and we honestly have them on the run. My team cleared out several terrorist cells recently, so we feel we have most of the foot soldiers in custody or in the ground."

"Well, that explains why Yates wants you dead." Nice to know my mother was efficient. Not so nice to know she was marked for death, but apparently that was running in the family, too.

"Yes, undoubtedly. If we can stop Yates, we have a chance of stamping out Al Dejahl for good. Due to the way they work, if we can get rid of the leader and his closest generals, the remainder of the organization should crumble."

"Kind of like the Nazis."

"Only the Al Dejahl organization wants to wipe all religion off the map, not just Jews," Reader offered. "They're open-minded that way."

"Wonderful. Dad, what about your need-to-know info that none of us knew but now actually do need to know?"

He cleared his throat. "I don't have as much exciting information as your mother does, kitten. However, it occurs to me that what the A-Cs do to hide the parasitic activity might be helping the Al Dejahl group."

"You accusing us of working with terrorists?" Christopher wasn't snarling, but he was glaring, and snarling looked imminent.

"No." Dad seemed unperturbed. "What I'm suggesting is that if you change a superbeing attack into a terrorist attack in the minds of the public, then you give the terrorist organization that takes the 'blame' more credit and airtime than they deserve. Just something to think about."

I'd mentioned this before myself, but right now it was bordering close to overload for me, and from the expressions on most of the A-Cs' faces, for them, too. "I think we'll tackle that one after we solve the itty-bitty Mephistopheles problem, Dad."

Mom chuckled and looked at Dad. "That's our cue to leave, hon. We'll be around to help if you need us, Kitty."

Dad sighed. "I liked this better when I thought it was just about Homeland Security."

I kissed Mom on her cheek, then gave Dad a hug and a peck. They nodded to everyone else and left the room. Whether this meant they were going to shadow me or actually leave me alone I had no guess.

"Now what?" White asked.

CHAPTER 29

"NOW, EVERYONE I DIDN'T NAME clears the hell out. You can take the book with you," I said to Beverly. "But I'd really suggest you ask my father to help you get the translations corrected. You might find something that'll help keep the rest of us alive."

Beverly pressed her lips together, snatched up the book, and then she and the rest of the Dazzlers on Book Duty stalked out of the room.

"No one talks to her like that," Lorraine said. She sounded impressed.

"I teach courses in how to win friends and influence people."

Reader laughed out loud. No one else cracked a smile, though I got the impression Martini wanted to.

"Miss Katt, I'd like to remind you that you're not in charge here." White was giving it a go. I was impressed. I'd just talked down my own parents over this issue, but he was going to try to pull rank. Fine.

"No, I'm not. But then, you're not, either. You're the front, the decoy."

Wow. I made alien jaws drop. It was turning out to be a cheerful morning.

"What do you mean?" Christopher asked, eyes narrowed into what I was coming to think of as Glare #3.

I snorted. I couldn't help it. "Please. The two people *arguing* about procedure and who's in charge of what are you and Martini. Your father never tells either one of you what to do, and he also almost never tells you two to shut up and play nicely, just like he almost never pulls rank. When he does, it's in front of someone who's not a part of the inner circle."

"He doesn't pull rank because he doesn't have to," Gower said. "We give him the respect he deserves without his demanding it."

"I'm sure you do. The head of any religious organization always gets a lot of respect."

Uncomfortable looks. It was great working with all these people who couldn't lie to save their lives. I'd spent the few years of my so-called career in marketing, a profession where everyone learns to lie to the entire world within their first week on the job. If Mephistopheles actually succeeded in his plan, I wouldn't have to kill them all—I could lie to them and make them do my bidding that way. A chilling thought, for a variety of reasons.

Reader was pointedly not looking at me. I figured he didn't want to get into a fight with Gower about him sharing trade secrets. Not that he had, but him confirming my suspicions would probably cause a domestic dispute.

"We don't have a lot of time, so I'll just say this and get it over with. You have two distinct agent divisions—field operations and image control. And as I've heard them tell each other more than once, Martini's in charge of the field and Christopher's in charge of image control. The two divisions have to work together, clearly, but they don't always agree about procedure. I realize there are distinct differences between A-Cs and Earthlings, but I've seen your bureaucracy in action, and it's just like ours. Layers—lots and lots of layers.

"Yet, who was at the scene when my personal flying nightmare showed up? Martini and Christopher. The heads of their divisions. Sort of overkill for a single superbeing, and before you try to say otherwise, there were other manifestations the same day, because agents were bringing in other boxes while we were at the storage facility. Agents who apparently could function without Christopher or Martini telling them what to do."

"So you lucked out," Martini said.

"No, you all just managed to avoid telling me something. It's about the only way you all successfully lie. You don't tell a falsehood, you just don't share the full details, unless you're asked a question point-blank. So, get ready. You all knew Ronald Yates was in Pueblo Caliente, didn't you? And that's why the heads of their divisions and, for want of an easier word, your Pope, were in attendance. Correct?"

Oh, easily correct. Not a one of them could meet my eye. Reader was looking up at the ceiling. He was grinning.

"I'll take the silence as confirmation. Oh, and all those SUVs full of agents who went with us to the crash site? They weren't along to protect me. They were along to protect *you*, Pope White."

"We use a different word," he said quietly. "Pope is really not appropriate."

"True, you get to marry and have kids. I could call you Rabbi Richard, but you could make it easier and just tell me what the title is." Silence. No problem—I knew how to get things out of these boys. "Bossa Nova? The Head Cheese? Mister Big? Papa Grande? The Head Honcho? Numero Uno? The Grand Poobah?"

Martini started to laugh. It was a relief in more ways than one. "I really like Bossa Nova," he said to White. "You should consider it."

"He's the Sovereign Pontifex," Christopher snapped. I'd figured he would end up the one to crack first. I was making fun of his father, after all. I decided not to point out the title would translate to Pope—they weren't stupid, and it's safer to try to blend in with the dominant religion of your new land.

"And he's the religious leader of your tribe. Which, I do realize, makes him your official leader. But like the Pope, he doesn't run the operations so much as he's the face of them. To the governments and to anyone who might want to talk to the head man. It's really impressive to the new recruits, too. Until we figure out that the Sovereign Pontifex here never actually calls any shots."

"Oh, I call a few," White said with what I realized was a smile. "I'm the one who passes judgment on whether or not an Earth recruit actually has what we require to join the team."

"Which is why you showed up at the courthouse with your adjunct," I nodded at Gower. "Or is he just called personal assistant?"

"He's called the Head of Recruitment," White said. "Officially, that is."

"When did I pass the test?"

White managed a chuckle. "In the warehouse."

"Thought so. You stopped ordering people around after that and never seemed fazed when Martini and Christopher were giving directions." I looked at Martini. "It was really obvious you were high up when we were in the dome at the crash site. Only the head honchos get to tell people whose entire job is guarding something to shove off, and get to do so with no arguments whatsoever."

He shrugged. "I told you, most people like me."

"So you claim. Now, I don't think we have a lot of time. I need to get a lot of information, and we need to form a plan for what to do and how to survive it. I really only want to discuss this with the people who'll be going on this little journey with me."

"Why don't you want any of the rest of us?" Gower asked. "We haven't been getting in your way all that much, and we might have some ideas that could help."

"I don't want you around, Paul, because you and the Pontifex here have to convince the various government agencies to clear out of a very large, secluded, and unpopulated desert area and not get involved, no matter what."

"Kitty, we need artillery to kill these things," Reader said, sounding worried.

"Apparently that doesn't work on Mephistopheles. So we're going with my plan."

"What, we'll all be armed with hairspray?" Martini asked, sounding as though he wasn't going to be surprised if I said yes.

"In a way, yes."

Dang. He looked surprised.

CHAPTER 30

AFTER A LITTLE MORE WRANGLING, whining, and use-less posturing, White and Gower left. Finally. Alone at last. Just me and the five other people I was going to put into mortal peril. I wondered if my mother felt like this every time she told her terrorism unit their next assign-ments. I had a horrible suspicion she did.

Claudia and Lorraine looked excited, Reader looked slightly worried, and Christopher and Martini still looked pissed off and suspicious.

"Now that it's just us, want to tell me what's going on?"

Martini shrugged. "You know most of it already."

"Oh? Let's see ... Mephistopheles manifests a few times a year. When, why, what's the pattern?"

"There is no pattern," Christopher said. "If there were, we'd have identified it."

"Really? Like you identified that the Ancients' manual was a religious text?" I decided that, as they went, Glare #5, which he was shooting at me right now, was probably his best. Eyes narrowed yet sending out laser beams of fury, face tensed, mouth poised to snarl something. Very impressive.

"Point taken," Martini said, defusing Christopher's snarl. "Feel free to tell us what you, having less than two days of this kind of experience, would like the rest of us to do. You know, those of us who have spent years," he nod-ded his head toward Reader, "or merely our entire lives in this line of work."

"Ooooh, that's put me in my place. Only . . . I don't have a place to be put into here. However, I know exactly where I fit in Mephistopheles' plan. And you don't."

"You're supposed to birth the babies," Reader said, managing to keep a straight face.

"Only sort of." Got their attention again with that one. Good. "See, there's a problem with implanting a memory in someone else."

"Uppity attitude?" Martini sounded as though he was headed back to normal. His body language was more relaxed—he was leaning his forearm against the wall, other hand on his hip—and his expression was amused.

"Limited control." I sat on the edge of the conference table. "Mephistopheles can't have had a lot of recent experience with this—I'm the first woman he's touched in twenty years."

"Lucky him," Christopher muttered.

"He'd like to get lucky," Reader said with a grin. Great, he'd appointed himself comic relief.

"Not so much. Look, let's make this clear—he doesn't want to have sex with me, nor does he want me to carry a zillion little Mephisties around. He wants to use me to get to all of you."

"To stop us," Lorraine said.

"No, I think Mephistopheles and all the other superbeings are here *because* of you, not in spite of you."

"What do you mean, because of us?" Martini's voice was low, but I recognized his expression—I'd seen it in the bathroom this morning. He'd also moved his back against the wall, crossed his arms over his chest, and one leg over the other at the ankle. It looked casual, but he was poised to move if he had to.

"You know what I mean, Jeff. Maybe the others haven't figured it out, but I really think you have." I looked at Christopher. He looked like Martini—face set like stone, eyes tortured. "You've figured it out, too. God, it must suck to be the two of you."

"Thanks, we're touched." Christopher had moved closer to Martini and was standing in a similar position. It wasn't a total surprise—when push was going to come to shove, it was going to be them against the world.

"It's not an insult. I can't imagine how the two of you have kept it together all this time. But it's the real reason Jeff didn't want to tell me about your religion. And, for the three of you who have no idea of what I'm talking about, this stays here, among the six of us, only."

Claudia and Lorraine nodded slowly. They looked confused. Reader gave me a long look. "I know. Paul doesn't, but I do."

"Because you figured it out a long time ago." He nodded. I looked at Martini and Christopher again. "See, it helps when you've dealt with prejudice all your life. It makes it easier to spot the lies that get told to cover up bigotry and the resulting actions that come from it."

"Lies?" Claudia asked, sounding scared. "What do you mean, Kitty?"

"You've all been told you were sent here to Earth because your religion made you outcasts on your home world and you wanted to help protect Earth, so your government sent you here as an easy fix."

I shook my head. I hoped I never had to tell my father about this. His righteous rage would go into overdrive. "But that sounds very familiar to me, as the granddaughter of people who were also part of what was, in some places, called a Final Solution."

"The Holocaust," Reader said quietly. "Over six million Jews, homosexuals, and others considered deviants murdered."

"Your planet did it more humanely. For them. But not for you or for us. They sent you all here as bait."

"No idea what you're talking about," Christopher said. He really couldn't swing the lying thing, since he was looking at his shoes when he shared this.

"Funny you should say that, since I've never heard a bigger line of bullshit than the one you tried to hand me about your transference system working one way but not the other. If you were talking time travel, I might buy it. But you're talking the laws of physics. I realize your planet's very different from ours. But not so different that an A-C man and a human woman couldn't have a functioning, normal child. Or is Paul some total freak by either race's standards?"

"He's as normal as the rest of us," Martini said. "For what that's worth."

"So if it works one way, it can work the other. If the door on the other end isn't locked, of course. Which it is. To you and to us."

"What makes you think any of this, Kitty?" Lorraine asked. "We've been told the full history of our world and why we came to yours."

"Have you? I doubt it. You're a new example of the immigrant experience that America had in the early nineteen hundreds. People fled their homelands, many times due to religious persecution, to come settle in the Land of Opportunity. It's what built this country. But what the immigrants told their children wasn't always the total truth."

"You've already said we can't lie," Christopher said. "Pick a side."

"You *can't* lie. But you all avoid giving out key information unless you're asked point-blank. But you know what was interesting about the whole scenario when I said your translations were wrong?"

"I'll play," Martini said as he leaned his head back against the wall. "What?"

"Your Sovereign Pontifex wasn't the one protesting against my charge. Oh, sure, he made a little show for the youngsters, but he wasn't the one defending the translations. He left that to Beverly."

"Because it's her job," Christopher snapped.

"No, because he can't lie any better than the rest of you, and he's started to pick up that I'm aware of it." I looked at Reader. "How long did it take you to figure it out?"

He shrugged. "A few months, but I wasn't kidding—we didn't have the same level of action when I joined up. You're right on schedule if I compress my first two months, and my first run-in with Mephistopheles into about a day and a half."

Reader looked at Martini and Christopher. "I haven't said anything because I couldn't come up with any idea of how to fix it, so why make it harder for you guys?"

"Said what?" Martini asked. It was clear he was asking to ensure we actually had guessed right.

I answered. "That your home world sent you to Earth not

to help us or give you someplace to go be useful but to use you all as bait to get the parasites distracted elsewhere."

Reader nodded. "And they don't want you back, any more than they want us to emigrate. We're on our own together."

"Why would they do that?" Claudia asked in a small voice. "We brought supplies to help. They still send us things."

"Now and then," Lorraine added.

"To ensure you don't die out here, would be my guess."

"Why would they need to?" Lorraine asked. "The ozone shield protects our home world."

"Yeah, but can it or will it forever? If we take the Heaven and Hell situations literally, Hell is hot, very hot. You all come from a planet with double suns. I'd have to guess it's pretty warm there, particularly since you all wear black in the desert in the summertime. And you don't sweat while doing it. None of you sweat, not even when you're running fifty miles in a second." Not even Martini through hours of vigorous, fantastic sex. I'd sweated, but he hadn't.

"If there was an entity searching for his new home and he came from someplace very hot, then why would he aim for, say, an ice planet or this little green and blue jewel in the middle of nowhere? He'd aim right for the planet with a lot of heat and burning suns, where his body would feel normal. The warehouse is boiling hot, yet none of you were uncomfortable there—and neither were the preserved bodies of the dead superbeings."

"The parasites would have come here no matter what. The Ancients warned everyone," Lorraine protested.

"I'm sure they did, or tried to. But plagues don't always hit everyone. Every dread disease leaves some alone for reasons only the disease would know. Vaccinations help, but not a hundred percent of the time."

"Thanks, Dr. Kitty," Christopher said, sarcasm dripping.

"Oh, stuff it. This is, essentially, a plague. The parasites don't hit everyone. They don't stabilize in most hosts. But in the ones they do, they create longer life, or Yates would already be dead."

"Diseases like to attack the weak," Reader offered. "But they also attack the strong. Polio, cancer, AIDS—they're indiscriminate, and sometimes they're more deadly in a healthy person."

Christopher opened his mouth, and I decided I didn't want to hear it. "You'd better have a snappier comeback than 'Dr. James' planned."

He shut his mouth. Glare #1 in full force. Nice to see he remained consistent.

"Anything else?" Martini asked.

"Yeah, actually. If I were a being looking for another host body, I'd seriously consider the benefits of two hearts, supersonic speed, hyper-reflexes, and incredible stamina over a single heart and vastly reduced abilities."

Martini shoved off the wall, flung himself into a chair, leaned back and put his legs up onto the desk, one ankle over the other. He looked straight at me. "The ozone shield wasn't going to hold up against continued parasitic attacks. It's another lie that the Ancients' arrival was an all-world wake-up call. Just like here, it was hidden from the general populace. Because we ran heavy on the scientific side of the house, we knew what was going on. Once we got the ozone shield up and it was determined to work as well for keeping the parasites out as the ozone in, we were considered expendable."

"You swore you'd never talk about this," Christopher said angrily.

Martini shrugged. "We've sworn a lot of things. But nothing's gotten better. The parasites arrived in our grandparents' time. When they wouldn't stop trying to get in, despite the shield, the same idea dawned on the world leaders as it did on you. They wanted A-Cs, possibly more than other races, maybe only. So, they decided to doom Earth. Originally they were going to send condemned criminals here."

"What a thoughtful bunch. How'd you all end up here?"

"Don't," Christopher growled at Martini. "Our entire race's safety depends on this."

"Our entire race's safety depends on us succeeding," Martini snarled right back. "Up until now, we've maintained, at best. Unless you have some brilliant idea you've been hiding all this time, stop getting in the way and break down and do something helpful."

He and Christopher stared at each other, Christopher used his perfected Glare #1, but Martini put his bland, genial, "it's all good" look back on. They looked as if they could do this for days.

"Guys, please. We have a world to save. The only one both of our races actually has left, right?"

Christopher spun and the glare was still going strong. "You have no right—"

"I have every right," I interrupted him. "Stop pretending, or the big bad fugly's going to win. And it'll be your fault."

"Actually," Martini said with false, hearty cheerfulness, "it'd be our grandfather's fault."

CHAPTER 31

STUNNED SILENCE FILLED THE ROOM. The girls looked shocked, but I didn't need to look at Reader or even Martini for confirmation—Christopher's expression was proof enough. Guilt radiated from him.

The full realization of what was going on hit me. "They did send criminals here, didn't they?"

"Just one," Martini said, his voice clipped. "As a test."

I wondered how to phrase this delicately and came up with no ideas. "What had your grandfather done?"

Christopher deflated. The anger just seemed to whoosh out of his body, leaving him looking sad and lost, like a little boy who'd never gotten to play with the other kids. "He was our religious leader. Only . . ." He stopped talking and closed his eyes.

"Only he wasn't peaceful like his son," Martini finished, voice still sharp. "He wanted to fight, to take what he considered our rightful place in the world."

"It's understandable. So why did they send the rest of you?"

Martini shrugged. "The shield was getting battered. They knew our grandfather had survived on Earth, so they could tell themselves they weren't killing us or dooming all of you by sending us here. They agreed to give us what we needed to keep the parasitic threat somewhat at bay."

"Everything but the materials to make an ozone shield here."

"Right." Martini looked exhausted. I wondered how long he'd been carrying this knowledge around. I checked out Christopher—at least as long as Mr. Surly had been, since he looked equally spent.

I decided to sneak up on the Horrible Truth. "You're susceptible to Earth diseases, aren't you? At least some of them?"

"Yes," Christopher said. "We don't get heart disease or anything related to it. But we're fair game for other illnesses."

"And, the real reason you have strict rules about inter-species marriages is, what?"

Martini looked as though I'd kicked him in the gut. Christopher didn't reply—he looked over at Martini and I didn't have to see his face to know he was glaring. It was clear he wanted me to hear this from Martini directly.

"The internal organs remain A-C dominant." The words sounded dragged out of him.

"I'll bet Paul's parents were allowed to marry as a test, weren't they? I'll meet some others, interspecies couples with the human side coming from, what, every country or just every race?"

"Country and race both." Martini's jaw was clenched again.

I nodded. "You're scientists, after all. Good testing theory." I didn't say that I figured all the tests had been run already. I'd save that for when I needed it. "So, how long before the parasites hit Earth did you arrive?"

"First waves came in the nineteen-sixties," Christopher answered.

"Right when the parasites really started littering the ozone shield," Martini added.

I shifted on the table, just in case I needed to jump out of reach. "Did your tribe reconnect with their exiled leader?"

Could have heard a pin drop. This time it was Martini who looked at Christopher with an expression that said it was time to return the Awkward Answer favor.

"We tried," Christopher said finally. "But . . ."

I decided to save him some pain and me a lot of time. "But he really wasn't like his son, and he'd discovered that he could get away with a lot more here on Earth than he had back home. Bitterness will do that to some people."

Martini nodded. "From what we know, he rebuffed Richard's attempts to reconnect."

And now, here it was. Time to unveil the Horrible Truth. I took a deep breath. "He was rich, powerful, and celebrating by creating chaos all over the world. Is that why you haven't killed him yet? Or is that just why the Mephistopheles parasite chose him?"

The girls looked sick. Claudia was obviously trying not to cry, and Lorraine was holding her stomach and rocking back and forth. Reader looked horrified. Martini and Christopher still looked exhausted, as if the weight of two worlds were on them.

Christopher managed to drag out an answer. "At first my father thought Yates could be redeemed. Then he decided we'd just ignore him. When we realized he was running a terrorist organization, we tried to stop him. But the parasites were coming, and that was more important."

"It's pretty odd on this world to have a terrorist group aimed at chaos only, not based on some religious belief. So what religious belief of yours is Yates actually working his terrorism for?"

"It's not a religious belief," Christopher said. "I don't know how to explain it to you."

"I do," Martini said. "Devil worship."

"Ah. He cracked and took the opposite side of the spectrum, religiously?"

Martini nodded. "Took every tenet of our religion and warped it."

"Not a surprise, all things considered. And Yates doesn't strike me as someone who controls his temper. But was it an intentional pairing?"

"We don't know," Martini answered. "It could have been, but I think you're closer in saying the parasite made the decision, not good old Granddad. We hate him, you realize."

"I can understand that."

"No, not really," Christopher said. "We're not supposed to."

"Religious rule?"

"Pretty much," Claudia said. She seemed back under a semblance of control. "Revere your elders, that sort of thing."

"We have that too. Some of us throw it out when said elders try to destroy entire populations."

"And some don't," Martini said.

I thought about it. "The older generation's split on this, at least."

"They don't know," Lorraine said.

"Sure they do. If they came here from A-C, they know. They're lying to all of *you*, but they know. And some of them feel they should turn the other cheek or just ignore Yates and he'll go away. From what I've seen, all the active agents are Earth-born, other than the Pontifex."

Martini took his legs off the table. "Yes. However, you're wrong in thinking all the older generation knows. Richard never told them what name and persona his father had adopted. He looks very different here than he did before exile, apparently. Ten years of hard living and disease warped him, externally as well as internally, and that was before the Mephistopheles parasite arrived, too. Most of our people don't know that Yates is our former religious leader let alone that he's Mephistopheles—they think he died right after we arrived here. Some figured it out, and of those, yes, the older ones are split about what to do."

"How long have you two known?"

"Since we were young," Martini said. "Richard isn't aware of how young. It wouldn't help him to know. He feels this is all his fault, his responsibility." He looked me straight in the eyes. "If killing Yates in human form would work to destroy the parasite, I'd do it myself, on national TV."

"But it doesn't work. And, now, let's all pull ourselves together. We know the truth, and it really and truly sucks. But it's going to suck a lot worse in a couple of minutes."

I had their undivided attention, and I saw Reader and the girls work to get themselves under control. I wasn't worried about Martini and Christopher—they'd been dealing with horrible news for a lot longer than I had.

"Mephistopheles knows all about you. He and Yates are still functioning as mostly separate entities, but he can pull up some of the A-C side when he needs to. Maybe he always could, maybe it's something he's learned. But he was talking to me, and I think that memory was implanted into me in case the Yates body died before the Mephistopheles side could enact his plan. And his plan is to use me to turn all of you into superbeings."

"How?" Reader asked. "Since you said he doesn't want you to birth those babies."

"I think he's figured out how to transfer his essence into someone else. He didn't have enough time to do it fully with me, just enough to send in some memories."

"Some?" Christopher was all over this. "I thought it was only one."

"I did, too. But Yates figured out what the Ancients were trying to do—he was your religious leader after all. I think he figured it out when he got to Earth and saw our variety of religions. He's known for a long time what the parasites really are. And, I'd guess he was setting himself up to attract the right one." I turned to Martini. "You said it's like a love connection."

He nodded. "All this makes sense. But why are you the person who's supposed to help spread the parasitic menace? I mean, you're not an A-C woman, and a smaller percentage of human women than of males remain in control when the parasite hits them."

"I don't know," I admitted. "Maybe we'll find out."

"Can't wait," Reader muttered.

"We won't have to wait long. He's going to come to us, and soon."

"How do you know?" Christopher asked.

I shrugged. "Like I know other things; it's just in there, in my consciousness. I think I picked it up from his breath. His awful, disgusting, stinky breath," I had to add.

"Air transferred?" Claudia suddenly looked normal. We were back into something she was comfortable with. "That seems odd."

"Maybe not." Lorraine was better, too. Good old science, the savior of Dazzlers everywhere. "The parasites travel through space, through the air, in order to find a host."

"But they're encased in the gelatinous substance that allows the safe space travel," Claudia argued. Gelatinous substance? I guessed that would apply to the jellyfish things, and it did sound more official.

"However, we know they alter when they join with an in-control superbeing," Lorraine countered. "For all we know, they do change enough to transfer via air."

"Wait a second. For all you know?" I managed not to ask them what, if anything, they *did* know.

"Every in-control superbeing's been killed using heavy artillery," Christopher explained. "There's nothing left for us to examine. Killing them's been more important."

"But Mephistopheles is immune to the big guns, right?"

"Right. Which is why you were going to unveil some great idea that involved your hairspray." I couldn't tell if Martini was making fun of me or not, but he was right—I hadn't actually told them what my plan was.

Possibly because I didn't think they were going to like it.

CHAPTER 32

"WE KNOW WHERE THE PARASITE IS. It's going to be close to impossible to hit unless someone's right up there in his maw." I wondered for a moment why I was doing this, but then the whole saving the world thing knocked on the door. "My hairspray worked—he dropped me screaming."

"I can't believe the properties in regular hairspray would cause the parasite to die," Lorraine said.

"It was extra-hold."

"Oh, that makes all the difference," Christopher said, as he rolled his eyes. Well, it wasn't a patented glare.

Claudia looked thoughtful. "It might . . ." She was lost in thought for a few moments. "Kitty, do you have the bottle?"

"In my purse. Which is in my room. Not that I think I can find my room from here."

"I'll get it," Martini said. He stood up and disappeared. Ten seconds later he was back, bottle in hand.

"What kept you?"

"That purse gets worse every time I look inside it." He handed the bottle to Claudia and then sat back down.

She examined it. "Lorraine, can you find some regular hairspray?"

"Sure." Lorraine disappeared, to come back about fifteen seconds later carrying several different bottles of hairspray. So the Dazzlers had to spray and tease to look perfect? I felt a little better.

They examined the ingredients while the rest of us sat there. I hoped my contribution as Impromptu Team Leader would mean I didn't have to come up with a brilliant scientific idea about what to do next.

"Well," Claudia said finally, "there's a lot of ingredients the same, but I think we can isolate one or two that might have been what affected him."

"The biggest difference between regular and extra-hold is alcohol—the extra-hold has a lot more in it," I offered helpfully. You can learn a lot in a beauty salon.

Reader stiffened. "Yates is a teetotaler."

"Is that a religious thing for you guys?" I asked Christopher.

"Not in the way you might mean. We didn't have drinking alcohol on our home world. We're not supposed to take impurities into our bodies, though—for a variety of health and religious reasons. So no one's ever had any alcohol here." He looked at Martini. "Other than you."

Martini rolled his eyes. "I tried it once, okay? Once. Made me sick as a dog, never touched it again."

"How did it make you sick? Did you throw up, pass out, have a headache the next day?" Not that I was asking from personal experience or anything.

"I wish," Martini said with a grimace. "I was in the hospital. They thought I was going to die."

"How much did you drink?" Good lord, had he imbibed an entire brewery?

"I had one shot of vodka. We'd taken out a superbeing in Russia, the nice people offered me a drink to thank me for saving them from the bear I'd made them think had attacked them, I took the drink."

"If I hadn't been there with him, he'd be dead," Christopher said flatly.

"Yeah, yeah, I owe you my life. We were twenty years old, cut me a damn break. You want me to start listing all the times I've saved *your* life, or can we get back to the situation at hand?"

Reader and I stared at each other. He spoke first. "Amazing, really."

"What?" Martini sounded exasperated. "No one on Earth's ever had a bad experience with vodka?"

"Not like that." I looked at him. "You're sure there wasn't anything in it? No poison, nothing like that?"

"No. For God's sake, they were grateful. They all drank it, too, poured from the same bottle. None of them got sick, so, no, not poisoned. One stinking drink, and some people will never let me live it down." He gave Christopher a disgusted look and slouched down in his chair.

"Some people never follow the rules," Christopher snapped.

I looked at the girls. Both Claudia and Lorraine looked at Martini and Christopher as if they were idiots.

"Who'd you tell?"

"Well, the whole hospital wing, for starters," Christopher said dryly. "He wasn't breathing, having convulsions, things like that. Made it kind of hard to pretend it wasn't a big deal."

"You couldn't wait to tell them I'd broken the rules," Martini growled.

"I did consider just letting you die, yeah," Christopher said. He actually sounded cheerful. This was a weird family.

"Boys? If we can get you to focus for just one moment, what we want to know is if anyone higher up in the organization, say your father, Christopher, made any connections?"

"My father was supremely disappointed that his nephew had used such poor judgment," Christopher replied. "And I got a lecture for allowing Jeff to be an idiot. As if anyone could stop him."

"You getting the picture for why we'd rather marry an Earth physicist?" Lorraine asked.

"Earth men are this dense, too." They needed to know the fantasy wasn't perfect, after all. "Jeff? Christopher? If we could get you two to stop squabbling and sort of focus here?" They both glared at me. Christopher really had the edge on glaring, though Martini was giving it a go, and, with some work, might give Christopher a run for the glare money.

"Focus on what?" Martini asked.

"On the fact that we need to get a lot of Everclear and put it into spray bottles."

Both of them looked blank. "What are you talking about?" Christopher asked. "Are you crazy?"

"No, I'm trying to destroy Mephistopheles and possibly Yates at the same time."

They both still looked blank. But they were both still gorgeous, so I could forgive them. I knew without asking that Claudia and Lorraine wouldn't.

"From Jeff's reaction, we're deathly allergic to alcohol if ingested," Claudia said, as if she were talking to the village idiots.

"From what Kitty said, the parasite is affected by it, too." Lorraine was also talking to idiots, but she wasn't trying to be kind at all. "If we manage to put this together, we realize alcohol might be the key to stopping Mephistopheles. At least, that's what the four of us have managed to grasp."

"And we're just sitting here in shock, realizing that the two people who know everything that's going on, who are also the heads of our agent operations, have also had the key to solving the entire Mephistopheles problem in their grasp for ten years," Claudia added. "And we are wondering if you can possibly be as dumb as you both appear right now."

"I'm just thinking I'm staying in charge of this team," I offered. "Apparently my two days is trumping your life's work."

Christopher looked as if he couldn't decide whether to yell, glare, or bang his head against the wall.

Martini slumped farther down in the chair and leaned his head on his hand. "I hate my life."

CHAPTER 33

I SENT CLAUDIA AND LORRAINE OFF to figure out what the best way to spray the alcohol would be. Portable and potent were going to be the most important factors. Reader went off to round up as much high-proof alcohol as possible, using as many agents as were available.

This left me, Christopher, and Martini with nothing to do. I considered sharing my first drinking experiences with them but decided against it. I cleared my throat.

"I don't want to hear it," Martini snapped.

"I wasn't going to say anything. Earthlings are used to making mistakes."

"Thanks, we both feel much better now," Christopher said. "Maybe you can point out what else we've been doing wrong all these years. Please wait for my father to be present, though."

I rolled my eyes. "Boys, you are both really dancing on my last nerve. You couldn't have figured it out before today, okay? Even if someone knew alcohol was poisonous to A-Cs, it wouldn't have meant it would affect Mephistopheles."

"Thanks," Martini muttered.

"Everyone was just shocked you didn't see the immediate connection when we identified alcohol as the key element and James reminded us that Yates is a teetotaler."

"You're not clear on the concept of stopping while you're ahead, are you?" Martini snapped.

"Not really. Not a lot of good examples of that kind of restraint around here."

"You want to tell us why you picked the team you did?" Christopher asked.

No, I didn't, because if I told them, then the rest of my plan wouldn't work. But I wasn't an A-C. "Sure. We're going to go out to whatever deserted desert area Paul gets cleared for us, and we're going to lure Mephistopheles there. I'm going to let him grab me, and we're all going to spray him with that alcohol, hopefully in the mouth, but it's worth a shot to try it everywhere."

"*That* is your plan?" Martini sounded incredulous. "Your entire plan? That's it?"

"It's insane, even for you," Christopher added.

This from the Density Twins? A lot of witty comebacks flashed through my head, but, again, I needed them saved for later. "I think it'll be best to brief the whole team at once."

"Don't let the power go to your head," Christopher muttered.

"I'll do my best." I thought about something I needed to ask them. "Is this the time when you tell the team to say good-bye to loved ones, just in case?"

"Daily," Martini said. He sounded subdued.

"Do Claudia and Lorraine know that?"

"In a way," Christopher said. "Probably not. We should have them do the ritual."

"Ritual?"

"Religious," Martini answered. "In case we die in the field." He looked over at Christopher. "I'm not doing it. You get the fun of handling this one."

Christopher gave him a dirty look. "It's more your line—they'll be functioning as field."

"And your father's the Sovereign Pontifex, and this is their first real mission," Martini countered "They also don't think you're quite as stupid as me, so it'll mean more coming from you."

"Fine. I'll take care of that now, so you two can be alone." Christopher sounded angry again.

"Don't start," Martini said, tiredly. "There's undoubtedly no reason anymore."

Christopher shot a piercing look at me. "We'll see." He stalked out, closing the door behind him.

Martini was still resting his head on his hand. His eyes were closed now. "Anything else you want to ask me?"

Yes, but it had to wait. "Not really."

"Yeah, I figured." He stood. "We normally regroup on a different level than you've been to. Just ask for the launch area, and someone can direct you." He headed toward the door.

"Jeff, why are you stomping off?"

He stopped at the door, hand on the knob. "It was a great day. One of the best I've ever had." He wasn't looking at me, just the door.

"What do you mean?"

He gave a bitter laugh. "I felt your reaction when I said we had to use you for bait. I can't blame you." He looked at me, and it was the shower all over again. "It's my job. I have to do what's best for the greatest number of people. Same with Christopher. We don't have a choice."

"There's always a choice."

"Yeah. And I made the one I had to. The one I always have to." He closed his eyes again. "Look, I just want to go, okay? I can't take it any more."

"Take what?"

He opened his eyes and looked at me as if I were taunting him. "Feeling you hate me."

I was prepared for a number of different responses, but not this one. "What? Jeff, what are you talking about? I don't hate you."

He gave another bitter laugh. "Empath, remember? I can feel it."

I shook my head. "No, Jeff. I don't know what you're feeling, but it's not coming from me. I don't hate you at all."

"Right. Look, there's no one else in the room, and I can feel the hatred just rolling off you. Please stop torturing me, Kitty."

I got a horrible feeling in the pit of my stomach. "Jeff, please don't leave. Don't leave the room, and don't leave me right now."

"Why not?" he asked, sounding so tired.

"Jeff, it's not me you're feeling. It's got to be him." I'd been pretty calm, all things considered. But this was beyond creepy.

Martini looked at me with his eyes narrowed. "You're human, you can lie well."

"I'm human, and I'm freaked out. You picking up any of that?"

I could see him concentrate. "Yeah . . . just vaguely." He was still vacillating, and I couldn't imagine what I'd do by myself right now. I couldn't feel Mephistopheles, but part of him was in me somewhere.

"Jeff, he's trying to take over. I don't know what to do, okay? I know what to do to kill him. But I need you. And he knows it and is trying to drive you away." I wondered what I was going to do to turn off Reader, Claudia, or Lorraine. Christopher was already barely tolerating me, so I didn't worry about him. "Why won't you believe me?"

"Because I can't feel it," he said sadly. He opened the door and walked out.

The tears came without my wanting them to. I was scared, and now I was alone. The one person I'd sort of thought I could rely on had bagged on me, and there was nothing I could do to bring him back. I still didn't know if I was in love with him or not, but I knew I didn't hate him.

I buried my face in my hands and sobbed quietly. I couldn't go to my parents because it would put them in danger. I couldn't tell anyone else—if they locked me up for study we were all going to be dead.

Someone's arms went around me, and I was up against a body. A rock hard, well-proportioned body. "It's okay," Martini said softly. "I'm sorry."

I couldn't keep from putting my arms around him. "What, I have to be hysterical for you to believe me?" He was going to have another wet shirt at the rate I was going.

He stroked my back. "In a way. You're right, there's an external emotional layer blocking yours. And what we've gone through this morning is grueling from an empathic standpoint. But I could feel it when you started to cry—it was just like last night at the airport and then after your nightmare." He kissed my head. "I'm sorry, baby. Please stop crying."

"You won't believe me if I stop!" I was losing it, and I couldn't get under control.

Martini shifted and slid his hands to the sides of my head. He moved me so I was looking into his eyes. "I'll believe you. This is going to be really hard. My empathic synapses are burned out, and all my normal blocks are shot. I need to regenerate, and the only way to do that is in an isolation chamber, and I need at least twelve hours of sleep in there, too. I know we don't have the time. I can feel the entity, but it's not connected to you like a parasite would be. It's got to be the implanted memories from Mephistopheles trying to take over. It seems like they're growing stronger over time."

"He wants me to kill you and Christopher. I know it. I know that's why I saw that in the dream. Everyone else will be taken care of—killed or turned into superbeings. But not you two. He wants the two of you dead."

"Do you know why?"

"No." I really didn't. I was sure I should be afraid of the answer, though. "I just know he's coming. And soon. You're right, we don't have time for you to regenerate."

A small smile crept across his mouth. "There are a couple of things that help." He bent and kissed me.

I could have cried with relief. Still felt great, still wiped out most of whatever was worrying me. One hand slid behind my head and the other down my back. My arms were already around him, and I tightened my hold, clutching at him.

It was a long kiss, but he finally pulled away a bit. "Is this room soundproof?" I asked as soon as I could form words again.

"It's a library, so, yeah, we followed Earth standards." He looked confused.

"Does the door lock?"

"Yeah. Why?"

"Well, I've always had this fantasy about being ravaged on a conference table." Odd but true. I hadn't shared this with anyone before, however.

His eyes were smoldering again, but he also looked a little frustrated. "I can't believe I have to say this, but that great idea's going to have to wait. This is one of those need-to-conserve energy times. And a good ravaging takes time and energy."

"I can wait." If I had to. Damned psychotic superbeings always messing up a great ravaging opportunity.

"Good. It'll give me something to live for." He kissed me again, then pulled me close. "I'm probably only going to pick up extreme emotions from you now, and they're likely to be really faint. So screaming for help out loud might be a good idea."

"I'll keep it in mind."

"Do. Now, you should do whatever ritual you have to say good-bye in case you're not coming back."

My arms tightened around him. "Can't we just pretend it's a given?"

"I wish. No, you need to see your parents. I'll take you there. Now." Martini lifted me off the table and stood me up.

"I thought I was in charge of this particular operation."

He grinned. "Only when everyone else is around."

CHAPTER 34

MARTINI KEPT HIS ARM AROUND MY SHOULDERS, and I kept mine around his waist as we left the library to head back to the transient section. I was still freaked that he might think I hated him, and besides, holding him felt good.

We didn't get too far, however, when one of the many A-Cs I couldn't place came racing up. The Armani fatigues and general hunkiness made them all look alike after a while. "Jeff, we have a situation."

"Unless it's Mephistopheles, it can probably wait." Martini didn't sound angry, annoyed, or uninterested—he sounded tired.

"We don't think it can," the agent said. "The teams involved called for direction."

Martini sighed. "Okay." We followed the agent out of the library, to the elevators, and back up to the level where we'd arrived, what I was pretty sure was the Bat Cave level. I wasn't positive—I could have been here before or never hit this floor at all. I felt like a small rat in a really large maze inside the Science Center.

We headed to a large room within the Bat Cave that was a lot like Batman's inner sanctum, only no one was in a rubber suit with a nifty cape. Lots of big screens, lots of computer terminals, lots of other things I couldn't identify. The décor screamed Command Center.

Martini and I unhooked just as Christopher ran in from

another door. "Glad they found you," he said to Martini. "It's more of a Field situation, from what little I've gotten."

Martini nodded, and they stood side by side in front of the main screens. Any animosity there had been between them in the library seemed gone. I had to figure this wasn't any ordinary problem.

"What *do* we have?" Martini asked as images came up on-screen.

A new A-C answered. "East Base reports clustered activity."

"Clustered activity?" I couldn't help it, I had to ask.

"Multiple parasites," Christopher answered. Without snarling or glaring. Either he'd taken a happy pill or this was a really scary thing. "We have the media under control—there was enough time for that—but not the actual manifestations."

"How many?" Martini asked. Just like at JFK, there was no indication of humor or lightheartedness.

The A-C who'd brought us here cleared his throat. "At least fifty." Images popped up on the big screens in front of us. This was a sports fanatic's dream TV set up—we had picture within picture, every game on side-by-side, and then some. All fifty manifestations were on-screen, which now meant we were watching horror movie tryouts.

Some of the hopefuls were really giving it their all to win America's Most Terrifying Monster. I wanted to figure out a way to tell them all they weren't going to make it to the finals, but considering what was in front of me, some of them had an excellent chance of making Mephistopheles really proud.

"Jeff, you're live to the Field," another one said quietly.

Martini started talking, with a lot of authority and very, very fast. As if he were the world's fastest auctioneer on some serious speed. So fast I realized I couldn't comprehend it; it was like a barrage of data. I caught snippets—he was deploying different teams from other regions, requesting some military support for some of the affected areas, ordering other teams to disengage, and so on.

I realized he was speaking at the standard A-C level, probably slowly, considering he seemed to be speaking clearly. It wasn't just that I couldn't understand it as a human—it was also making me feel dizzy.

I took a step back. Didn't get any better. My passing out right now wouldn't be helpful to anyone, but the dizzy didn't stop. The only saving grace was that I was pretty sure Martini wasn't going to be able to pick up that I was about to barf or pass out—one small benefit of his empathic whatevers being burned out.

Thankfully, for whatever reason, Christopher looked over his shoulder and backed up. Martini didn't notice, probably because he was completely engrossed in saving the entire East Coast from becoming superbeing sushi.

Christopher caught me before I went down. "I'm going to take Kitty to the Imageering side," he said quietly to the A-Cs near us. "Don't disturb him, but the moment he notices she's gone, make sure he knows where she is."

He moved me through the door he'd come in from. It had a lot of screens and crap in it, too. I was too close to barfing my guts out to really take it in. He put me into a chair in a far corner, then squatted down. "You going to be okay?"

I managed to nod, but I had to close my eyes. "That was almost as bad as the gates or hyperspeed."

"Yeah." Someone began massaging my temples. I assumed it was Christopher but didn't feel up to opening my eyes to find out.

I was still nauseated, but even through that the thought occurred that he was actually being nice. "You okay?"

"I'm an A-C. It's normal for us."

Not what I'd meant, but as my stomach started to settle, I had enough brainpower going to keep my mouth shut. This was probably the most pleasant Christopher had managed to be to me, and I didn't want a lecture from Mom about how he'd extended the olive branch and I'd burned it or something.

I finally felt well enough to open my eyes. Christopher gave me a small smile. "Better? Or do you need a wastebasket?"

I managed a chuckle. "I'm all for skipping lunch, but otherwise, I'm okay, I think."

"Good." He took his hands away slowly. "You sure you're up for what's coming?"

"As long as you all promise not to talk too fast for the humans, I think so."

He gave me a long look. "You realize the chances of our dying are exponential."

"I could drive my car down the highway and die, too. Well, I could if I freaking knew where you put it, that is."

Christopher actually didn't glare or snarl at this—he laughed. "It's safe. Not here, but safe. We stored it in Pueblo Caliente."

"Good to know. People die all the time. From all I've learned in the past day and a half, my mother's been living on the edge for most of her life, and she's still here."

"You're not afraid?"

I thought about it. "Yeah, I am. But I'm more afraid of Mephistopheles taking me over and enacting his version of the Master Race through me." I shrugged. "I guess I don't come from hide-under-the-bed stock."

He smiled. "Yeah, I've been picking that up."

Christopher smiling was something of a shock. Like all the A-Cs, he was gorgeous. But when he was busy scowling or glaring, it was hard to notice. Smiling, I realized, he was easily as handsome as Martini, albeit in his own way.

"Thanks for getting me out of there."

He shook his head. "Jeff shouldn't have brought you in."

"I don't think he realized what was happening. The guy who found us wasn't exactly forthcoming with the level of the badness. And Jeff's not feeling a hundred percent. He told me his empathic . . . thingies . . . are burned out."

"Synapses." He grinned. "Thingies can work, too, of course. Still . . ." His smile faded, and suddenly Christopher was looking at me with an intensity I wasn't prepared for. I felt my cheeks get hot for no reason I could name.

Someone came up behind him. "What's going on?" Martini didn't sound amused.

I jerked my head up. He didn't look amused, either. "I got sort of . . . sick."

Christopher stood up slowly, looking at me the whole time. Then he turned around. "I decided letting her collapse on the floor would be bad for morale. Problem with that?" Christopher was in profile to me, so it was easy to see that he was glaring. I was fairly sure it was the little-used but ever-impressive Glare #4, which was heavy on the slitted eyes while keeping the mouth ready for sarcasm.

"None at all." Martini's voice and expression said differently, though I didn't think his problem was with me not being in a heap at his feet. "Things are handled. You're sure your side has things under control?"

"Positive."

"I ask because you seemed a lot more interested in Kitty than in ensuring things are taken care of. We've had enough leaks these past few days."

"Oh? You're the only one allowed to focus on her instead of taking care of things? Interesting." He shifted gears from #4 to #1. I figured he'd learned to always go with the classics when things were tense.

"I told you not to push me on this," Martini growled in a low voice.

"And I told you to stop playing games," Christopher replied in kind. "She doesn't deserve that."

"I'll bet I know exactly what you think she deserves."

"More than you can offer her? Yeah, I do think she deserves that."

This was just like when we'd arrived from LaGuardia the night before, only Mom wasn't here to pull me away. I had a feeling they didn't remember I was sitting next to them, either, which was kind of awkward.

I cleared my throat. Both heads snapped toward me. Martini was glaring but put his bland "it's all good" face on. Christopher reduced Glare #1 down to what I could call sadly pensive.

"Um, can you two save this for when we engage Mephistopheles? I mean, all the testosterone's great, big cave men, girl impressed, and all that, but don't we have the fugly of fuglies to stop?"

Christopher closed his eyes. "Sorry. You're right." I had to find out what happy pills he'd taken—I wanted to be able to slip them into his drink whenever he was being normal.

Martini nodded. "Now that things are handled, maybe you should go take care of Claudia and Lorraine," he suggested.

Christopher's eyes opened. "Fine." He looked at me. "Be careful." He headed toward the door.

"I'll take care of her," Martini said.

Christopher looked over his shoulder. "Right. Because you're so good at that."

He stalked out, and I risked a glance at Martini. The "it's all good" look was nowhere to be found. He looked hurt and angry and a little bit scared. I didn't like this look. "Jeff? You okay?"

He managed a smile, which erased the other expressions so that now all he looked was tired. Martini took my hand and helped me up. "Yeah, baby. I'm fine." He kissed my forehead. "The world's safe for another few hours. So, let's go see your parents."

CHAPTER 35

WE GOT ABOUT TEN PACES outside of Command Center Central when Reader ran up. "Jeff, I just heard about the clusters. Are we secured?"

"Yeah." Martini managed to sound exhausted with only one syllable.

Reader's eyes narrowed. "You need to go into isolation."

Martini snorted. "Like we have the time."

"We can wait on this a day."

I cleared my throat. Both men looked at me. This throat clearing thing really worked around here. "No, we can't wait. I know Mephistopheles is coming, and this clustered stuff was proof."

"How do you mean?" Reader asked. "Clustering does happen."

"Yeah? Does it happen right after Mephistopheles or another in-control superbeing manifests?"

Uncomfortable looks between the two of them. Reader sighed. "Usually right before." Another fun fact no one shared with me. I wondered if they couldn't stop the fuglies because they didn't feel the need to trade information or do analysis. Then again, the person they weren't sharing with was me, so maybe it was just some sort of bizarre initiation rite—figure it all out without help, we teach you the secret handshake sort of thing. "But never as many as I heard. Thirty? Really?" he asked Martini.

"Over fifty." Martini sighed. "Kitty's right. We don't have the time. I'll manage. I've worked with less energy before."

Reader's expression said this wasn't a lie so much as scary business as usual. Didn't know whether to be relieved or freaked out. Went for both, to show my range.

Martini filled Reader in on what he'd done in the Command Center. It wasn't at hypertalk level, but after the first few "and then Team 27 was deployed to Sector WV1 while support was called up from AB12," lines, I stopped listening. It wasn't making me want to pass out from dizziness, just boredom.

Impromptu briefing of boredom completed, Martini and I headed for my parents' room. Again. Stopped by a variety of A-Cs along the way. Put my fingers in my ears and hummed Aerosmith's "Eat the Rich" to myself so Martini could do the hypertalk and we could keep moving.

I would have thought all this debriefing would have tired him out more—it certainly was making me feel tired—but by the time we reached the elevator banks, Martini seemed back to reasonably normal. We'd taken so long that I was pretty much over the nausea, too. We got into an elevator and spent the entire trip kissing. I was very disappointed and completely aroused when we got to the right floor.

He merely held my hand as we left the elevator, which was okay, since I had no idea if we'd come upon my parents suddenly and really didn't feel like explaining what was going on with me and Martini, since it was getting beyond complicated.

On the way down the hall Martini pointed out where my room actually was and where his room was in relation to it. I was on the elevator side, a few rooms down, he was on the opposite side of the hall, a few more down. Now that I was really looking around, it was like a combination hospital and hotel. Very austere, no decorations, but lots of rooms, and, once inside them, they were pretty darned nice.

My parents were near the end of the hall, much farther away from me than Martini. I wondered if he'd had anything to do with the room placement. As we neared the door, I could hear the sounds of four dogs barking. Ah, all was normal—as long as they could bark, our dogs were happy.

Martini knocked on the door, and the barking got much closer. "Hush!" Dad shouted as he opened the door. The tide of canines crashed into us. This time I steadied Martini as Dudley leaped up and put his paws on Martini's shoulders.

"Argh!" Dudley shared he really liked Martini by licking his face.

"Dad, any chance of calling off the hounds?" I grabbed Dotty and Duchess and wrestled them back into the room. Duke, however, followed Dudley's lead and jumped on Martini. I didn't think he was going to remain on his feet much longer.

"Down boys, down. Come on now, be good dogs, get down." Dad was not having the slightest effect.

"Dogs, SIT!" Mom called. Both male dogs' butts hit the floor.

"Thank you," Martini said weakly, as he wiped the slobber off. "Can I use your bathroom?"

"Sure, sure," Dad said, ushering us in while the dogs trotted over to Mom and pretended they were well-behaved. "You know where it is, Jeff?"

"Guh," Martini said, and walked through their living room. He closed the bathroom door, and I heard it lock.

"Nice digs. Your place is like triple the size of mine."

"Christopher took care of us," Mom said.

There was something about her voice that made me look around. "What are you doing here?"

Christopher was leaning against the far wall, standing behind a sofa, petting two of our cats. "I came by to visit your parents." He said it as if it were a totally normal thing. "Why is Jeff here?" he asked snidely. Ah, the Christopher I was used to was back.

"Because I can't find anything without an escort. Now, hope you enjoyed, sorry to see you go, catch you at the launch site." If Mister Pissy was here, I didn't want him around. I'd kind of liked him for a moment or two when he was being nice, but now I wondered if I should have instead taken the opportunity to throw up on him.

"Kitty, stop being rude." Mom gave Christopher a sympathetic look. "She gets cranky when she's tired."

"She's tired a lot," he replied with a grin. They shared

their chuckle. I tried to remind myself that I could just use this whole situation later to get my rage going.

"Did you take care of Claudia and Lorraine?"

"My father had already thought of it. They're both good."

"Then, again, nice to see you, clear out. I'd like some time alone with my parents."

"Alone with them, you, and Jeff?" Glare #1 was in full force.

Before I could answer this, Martini came out of the bathroom. He spotted Christopher, and his eyes narrowed. "Nice to see you. Why are you here?"

"I invited him," Mom said icily. "Unlike you, he wasn't suggesting using my child as bait for an alien monster."

Martini winced. "Look—"

"No, I think Angela's right to be upset," Dad interjected. "You were intimate with our daughter, and then the next morning you suggest she be tossed into the jaws of death."

Martini winced again, and Christopher was running through his full assortment of glares.

"Frankly," Mom said, "I really think we should ask you to leave, Jeff, not Christopher."

Martini had his eyes closed, and his expression headed from painful headache to total migraine. He looked awful and then started to look worse.

"Mom, Dad, shut up." I ran and got to Martini as he started to collapse. "I mean, it! All of you shut up and stop hating on him right now!"

I flung his arm around my shoulders and led him into their bedroom. I managed to get him onto the bed. His face was pale, and his skin felt clammy. I stroked his head, and he groaned. "Hang on, Jeff," I whispered as I kissed his forehead. It seemed to help him a little bit.

I went back out to the living room and spoke to my parents. "I need Jeff, and I need him functioning. He's an empath, and all his blocks are shot. This is grueling for him—he can't block out anything right now—and you hating him is making him sick. For all I know, it could kill him. He needs rest, and we don't have the time. And instead of helping me, you're sitting around with Mr. Wonderful here plotting against me and ripping Jeff."

"We're not plotting," Mom said. "We're upset, and, as your father said, I think we have a right to be."

"No, you don't. This isn't about whether you do or don't like a boyfriend of mine. This is about national freaking security. You of all people should be clear on that."

"We're clear, but we don't like it," Dad said.

"I don't care. What you do or don't like doesn't matter. You need to stop, to calm down, and if you can't calm down, to get the hell out of this room. Jeff can't take it, and he doesn't deserve it, either. If he hadn't been smart enough to suggest me as bait, I would have suggested it myself."

"Why?" Dad asked.

"Because it's the intelligent and right thing to do. That is, if we want to actually save the world. If we don't, then, by all means, please keep on raging and sending off emotions that Jeff can't deal with. Maybe you can kill him and save Mephistopheles some time and effort." I took a deep breath and tried to calm down. "I have to check on him." I went into the bedroom and saw an interesting sight.

Duchess, Dudley and Dotty were all on the bed with Martini. He was cuddled next to Duchess as if she were me, but I chose not to take it personally. Dudley was alongside his back, and Dotty had her head on his legs. Duke was on the floor at the foot of the bed, completely alert. All four dogs looked at me, but none of them barked or tried to get up.

Our cats were there, too, all three of them camped out around Martini's head. Sugarfoot was grooming Martini's hair and purring. Candy and Kane were curled up and appeared to be sleeping, but they both opened their eyes, and I got the same look from them as I had from the dogs. Martini wasn't reacting to anything—I got the feeling he was asleep, and I knew he needed to stay that way for a while.

I backed out of the room. "Mom, Dad, come here . . . silently." I felt them move up next to me. "You want to hate on Jeff anymore?"

They were both quiet for a few long moments. "No," Dad said softly. "I think it's clear we were in the wrong."

Mom closed the door as quietly as possible. "I think we'll meet you out in the hall."

We went back to the living room. Christopher still looked angry. I decided I wanted some of this handled before we went out to take on the big fugly, even if it meant I'd have him less angry out there.

"Mom, Dad, do you think you two can calm down so you could stay here and watch over Jeff?"

"Sure, kitten," Dad said. "We'll be fine."

"Good." I pointed to Christopher. "You, come with me."

CHAPTER 36

I HEADED OFF DOWN THE HALL. I considered going to my room but figured anywhere on this floor was too close to Martini to prevent his picking up the anger I was feeling toward Christopher. I wasn't sure if anywhere in the whole complex was going to be far enough away from Martini to be any kind of help, but at least I wasn't going to be screaming at Christopher right by his head.

Christopher didn't argue. He followed me out of the room and down the hall to the elevator banks. We got in—I wanted to hit the close button so the doors would slam on him but refrained. I was very proud of myself.

The moment the elevator doors closed, he was at me. "Why did you want me to leave?" He hit the button for Floor 15.

"Because you were trying to kill him."

He laughed. "Hardly."

"Right. Glaring and sending off all your nasty vibes wasn't going to affect Jeff, right? He's just an empath who's got no blocks left." I got right up into Christopher's face. "You, more than anyone else, should be ashamed of yourself. You know what happens to him if he's burned out, and he is, and you of all people would recognize the signs even if I hadn't told you. You went to my parents' room to get them riled up, so the moment they saw him, they'd be on his case."

His eyes were flashing. "I didn't go there with any evil

intent. I'm not the one who was intimate with you, after all."

I didn't do it consciously, but my handprint was on his face, so I had to figure I'd just slapped Christopher as hard as I possibly could. He stared at me, surprisingly not glaring in any way. "It's none of your goddamned business if I sleep with every man in the state of Arizona or every A-C on the planet. It's not my parents' business, either. It's mine. And we have a world of horror heading toward us, and all you can do is play games."

We were back to patented Glare #1. His eyes flashed, and I noted they were the sort of green that looked almost blue close up. "I'm not playing a game," he said through clenched teeth. He was leaning toward me. I resisted the urge to head-butt him.

"Then what do you call all the baiting, the insults, you being a nasty smart-ass every single time I'm near you except when I was ready to throw up in the Bat Cave? And what do you call your doing all of this while Jeff's basically in a state of collapse? Because I call it you being the biggest jerk on the planet."

We were almost to the 15th floor, but he hit the "stop elevator" button with his fist. I was prepared for alarms, but there weren't any. My fists clenched, and he must have thought I'd take another swing at him because he grabbed my upper arms. "Look, princess, you have no idea of what you're getting into."

"Awww, are you worried that Jeff's gonna break my heart?"

"Stop talking about him!" Christopher gave me a small shake. "This isn't about him—not everything is about him!" He was shaking, I could feel it. I wasn't sure if it was from anger or something else. I also didn't care.

I tried to pull away from him. "Well, then, who the hell is it about?" He didn't answer, and I tried to get away again, with no luck. "Let me go!"

He got a funny look on his face. Then he pulled me closer and kissed me.

I was so shocked I almost didn't register what was happening. But either great kissing ran in the family or I was just lucky, because it wasn't long before my body took over for my confused mind. All the things Reader and my mother had been saying, all the snarling between Christopher and Martini, suddenly made sense, and I realized my mother was right—I was really dense sometimes.

Christopher's lips were demanding, his tongue almost violent inside my mouth. But it was erotic—fury combined with passion. At first I tried to pull away, but he wouldn't let me, and after a few seconds I didn't want to pull away all that badly.

My body started to relax, and he slid his arms around me while mine went around his back. His kiss went deeper as he pulled me tightly up against him. One hand slid up my body to the back of my head; he controlled my movements, forcing our kiss even deeper.

Somewhere in the back of my mind I remembered we were all going to die soon if we didn't get moving. I tried to end the kiss, but Christopher wasn't having any of it. My attempts to move knocked us a little off-balance, and as he moved to keep us upright, we hit into the side of the elevator.

He was pressed against me, and our bodies started to move against each other. I tried to grasp at something to keep myself from just giving in to him, but I wasn't coming up with much. Then I thought about Martini and what his reactions to this were likely to be.

It took all my willpower and strength, but I managed to wrench my mouth away from his. "Christopher, let me go." I wasn't demanding, I was begging, my breath ragged.

"I keep trying to, but . . . I can't." He looked wild and completely out of control. "We can't really have you, can't keep you. But it's impossible not to want you." He bent and kissed me again.

It was the same—violent passion. And, let's face it, I already knew I'd won the Slut of the Month award. Plus, what if I died in a few hours and never found out if all A-Cs were sexually proficient? Maybe I owed it to scientific research and interspecies harmony.

A small part of me wondered if we were being affected by the implanted memories, but then Christopher moved his mouth to my neck, and I forgot to worry about anything.

He used his teeth as well as his tongue and lips—not enough to mark me but enough to arouse me to the point where he could do anything he wanted as long as he kept his mouth against my neck.

As his mouth ensured I wouldn't do anything other than gasp and moan, he ground against me and ripped my shirt open. The bra I'd been provided was a front-closer—he had it undone in about half a second.

All of a sudden my mind kicked in and suggested I pay attention to where this was going. It didn't matter if we were being affected by Mephistopheles or were just hot for each other. As arousing as being with Christopher like this was, I realized that what mattered to me was how this was going to affect Martini.

I shoved his head away. "Stop it, now!" I shifted my legs so my feet were against his hips and put my hands onto his shoulders, then pushed with all my might.

It rocked him, but he didn't really budge. "What's the matter, princess? You trying to tell me you don't like this?" He wrapped both arms around my back and pulled my breasts toward him. The thought that A-C men were as strong as they were fast flitted through my brain, but even a small woman can fight a strong man if she knows what she's doing.

Him calling me princess really helped, and I remembered I'd trained in kung fu for just this kind of situation. I wrapped my legs around his torso and started to squeeze. At the same time, I made an arrow point with my hand and shoved it into the base of his throat. I hooked my other arm around his shoulders to steady myself.

His head jerked back, and he dropped me, but I was still squeezing. As he backed up, I let go and swung my legs down, shoved against his throat again, hard, and landed on the elevator floor.

I backed away from him, but there wasn't anywhere to go. "Stay away from me." I wondered if there was an alarm on the elevator I could push.

Christopher was against the other side of the car, and he looked dazed. "What am I doing?" he asked under his breath as he stared at my chest and rubbed his throat. I closed my bra, pronto. He looked up at my face. "I'm sorry."

He looked almost like Martini had just before he passed out. He slid down the wall, ending up in a squat with his head in his hands.

It might have been a trick, but I was perfectly willing to ram my knee into his face, so I went to him and touched his shoulder. He jerked and looked up at me. "I don't know why I did that. I mean, I never intended to tell you, let alone . . ."

So he did like me. Then I had a good idea of why he'd gone all Kitty Does Roswell on me. I knelt down next to him. "It's the memories, or whatever they are. They affected Jeff, too." He winced at the mention of Martini's name. "Jeff thought I was hating him when I wasn't. It's probably something like that."

"I don't try to make love to someone I hate," Christopher snapped. Nice to see he was recovering quickly.

I chose to refrain from mentioning that what he'd been doing felt more like ravaging than making love. Not that I hadn't enjoyed it. I had. A lot. But that wasn't important now. "I don't know what was being sent toward you, Christopher. Maybe it was giving off lust pheromones to you the way it was giving off feelings of hatred to Jeff. I think the memories are trying to do things that will cause you and Jeff to be out of control. Mephistopheles wants the two of you dead, after all."

He nodded. "Makes sense." He rubbed his forehead. "Please don't tell my father."

"I should think you'd be more concerned about my telling Jeff."

Christopher stood up and pulled me to my feet. "Jeff's going to know the minute he's around either one of us. He'll just keep it between us, though; he's not big on telling the authorities what really happened."

Considering Martini and Christopher *were* the authorities, this was funny. But I knew what he meant. "No worries, you stopped. I don't see any reason to run to your father. Of course, you're the one who usually tells on Jeff." The last line slipped out, and I realized with horror that I wasn't the one saying it.

Christopher shot Glare #3 at me, but before he could say anything I put my hand on his mouth. "That wasn't me.

That was . . . him, I guess." My hand shook. "Please don't get mad, please don't get amorous. Please help me."

The glare left his face. He moved my hand down and pulled me to him, gently. "Okay." He stroked my back, and I leaned my head against his chest. "What does it feel like?"

"I don't know. I didn't know I was going to say that until it came out." The tears came, again without my being able to stop them. "It's something emotional, I don't cry all the time like I have been," I managed to tell him.

"I want to take you to the hospital section."

"No. We don't have time for me to get examined, and if someone wants to hold me for tests, we're all dead. He's coming. I think he's going to track based on me, and I'm here in the middle of your stronghold. And he has A-C blood, so that means he can see whatever you have cloaked." I could talk through these tears; this was getting freakier by the moment.

Christopher rocked me. "It's okay." He was quiet for a few moments while I made his shirt wet. Whoever did their laundry was not going to like me much. "We don't know for sure if an in-control superbeing can see through the cloaking or not. But the Dome is safe, so figure they can't. Right now, it's probably the least of our worries."

Something dawned on me, a question I hadn't asked. "What was Yates' power? I mean, when he was on your home world? Like Jeff's an empath and you're an imageer."

"We have a variety of talents aside from those two. But Yates was unusual, a combination of both empath and imageer. Very rare. It's one of the reasons he was made Sovereign Pontifex."

Things started to click together. "Can empaths make someone feel an emotion?"

"No. Not even Jeff. They feel them, but they can't manipulate them."

"But imageers manipulate images, right? Any image?" Thinking made the tears dry up. A double win.

"Sure." Christopher shifted me so we could look at each other. "Any image. We can create them, too. It's molecular movement, really." He looked wistful. "I used to think it was fun."

I considered how to phrase my next question. "Could you rearrange an image that wasn't on a surface?"

He gave me a look that said I was an odd girl. No argument there, especially after the last day and a half. "I don't know, you mean, like on the air?"

"Yeah, could you make a picture in the air? In here, for example?"

He shrugged. "I can try if it matters."

"It matters."

Christopher leaned me up against the side of the elevator and made some movements in the air. While he was engaged, I took the opportunity to button my shirt. All the buttons were still intact, which was nothing short of miraculous. As I tucked my shirt back into my skirt, I saw a shimmering in the air.

It took a while, but an image appeared. It was faint, but I could make out my sixteen-year-old face smiling at me, tiara in place.

Only it wasn't me. It was close, but I could see differences—wrong clothes, tiara not quite the same, nose a bit off, things like that. "Who is that?"

"My mother. From long ago."

Clearly, Christopher was attracted to me because I looked like his mother. I didn't know whether to be flattered or grossed out. I looked at his expression—he was staring at the picture he'd made in the air, his face a mask of sorrow. Okay, not the time to make a joke. Probably not the time to point out that she looked like me, either.

I decided to go for noncommittal. "She looks very happy."

"She was."

"She's not happy now?"

"She's been dead since I was ten." The picture disappeared, and he turned toward me. "So, yes, I can create a picture on the air. What's the point, though?"

I was happy to move off mother issues. I got the impression he didn't want me to say I was sorry for his loss, either. So I got right to it. "I'm wondering if someone who was an empath and an imageer could create memories and then manipulate them."

CHAPTER 37

CHRISTOPHER WAS DEFINITELY AN ALIEN. He didn't start talking, ranting, or running. He looked thoughtful, but he didn't say a word as he went to the elevator console and pushed a couple of buttons. We headed back up.

"You think he planted a memory in your mind and is manipulating it?"

We were back on the transient floor. At least, I thought we were. "Yes. Or something like it. Maybe that's how Yates gathers his followers. I mean, all your powers are intact here, so it stands to reason his are, too. And my mother said he recruits based on knowing what someone wants and exploiting it."

"They've been joined for twenty years. Might be long enough for the powers to bleed from one entity into the other."

We walked down the hall, but I realized it wasn't the transient floor—the living quarters all looked alike. "Where are we going?"

"Getting Lorraine and Claudia."

The girls were roommates, as it turned out, which was both convenient and a relief. I wasn't in the mood to deal with random Dazzlers right now.

They were sitting in their living area packing supplies. "James has all the alcohol and firearms taken care of," Claudia informed me without any ado after Lorraine had let us in. "We've got medical supplies, walkie-talkies, and water."

"How about your clothes?" They were still in the standard issue Armani fatigues.

"What do you think? Jeans?" Lorraine asked, as she rolled up some bandages. I got a sinking feeling that everyone expected to be hurt, if not to die.

"Jeans, sturdy shoes you can run in and are comfy, shirt, jacket, the usual." Of course, this was the usual to me. Maybe not to them.

"Okay, we'll be ready in a couple of minutes," Claudia said.

I looked at the medical supplies. "Jeff's not doing well. Anything you can give him that'll help him function? He's with my parents right now."

The girls passed a look between them. "Adrenaline," Lorraine said. Claudia nodded. "It'll help him a bit. I'll get more, you give him what we have now?"

"Yeah. You coming with me?" Claudia asked as she grabbed a hypodermic and a small vial and headed toward the door.

"No," Christopher answered before I could. "We still need to get ready. Can you get him to the launch site?"

"Sure." Claudia looked from me to Christopher, gave us a weak smile, then left. I looked at Lorraine out of the corner of my eye—she was giving the two of us a suspicious look, too. Great.

Christopher and I left the room, heading for the elevators again. "That was fun. Are they empathic?"

"No, most female A-Cs don't have those kinds of talent. Female talents run to science, medicine, mathematics. Almost all empaths, imageers, and troubadours are male. Dream reading is rare, and that goes pretty evenly to either sex." They weren't even empaths and they were onto the fact that something had happened between me and Christopher. Wonderful.

"Troubadours?" This was a new one. On the elevator, heading up again.

"Entertainers, really." He didn't sound impressed. "They function as politicians for us here."

"Your father?"

"No. Not everyone gets these talents. He's just a regular A-C."

I wanted to ask where he'd inherited the talent from, but something in his expression told me now wasn't the right time. We got off, and this time I was pretty sure we were on my floor. Sure enough, Christopher headed for my room.

"You have any idea where the launch site is?" he asked as he ushered me inside.

"None. You don't want either one of us around Jeff right now, do you?"

"You less than me. I've already guessed—you want to use anger to draw Mephistopheles. So, let's draw him where we want him, not here. The adrenaline will help him build back some of the burned out empathic synapses, at least for a little while. But the minute Jeff's around you, he's going to get angry."

"Can't wait. You going to change?"

"No. We're used to working in these clothes. But you're right to get Claudia and Lorraine into something different." He looked away from me. "Are you in love with him?"

"I don't know. I've known you all less than two days. Kind of fast to make that sort of declaration. At least for me."

He nodded and turned toward the door. "I'll wait for you in the hall."

I didn't argue. As soon as the door was shut, I went into the bedroom. The bed was made—this place *was* like a hotel. I didn't know if I was glad there was no evidence of everything Martini and I had engaged in or if I missed it. I tried to feel lucky that both Martini and Christopher wanted me, but I couldn't. Getting between friends was never a good idea, and getting between blood relatives was worse. And now that I knew what was going on, it was sort of hard to hate Christopher. It was a lot easier to imagine what letting him have his way with me in the elevator would have been like.

That line of thought aroused me far too much, and I forced my mind back to the problem at hand: Why did Mephistopheles want the two of them dead?

I pondered this as I searched for my clothes, which were neatly folded in one of the dresser drawers. I had no idea who handled the maid and laundry services around here, but I wanted to ask them to drop by my apartment once a week.

There had to be something more to why Mephistopheles wanted to get rid of the two of them, and I had to figure it out fast, or one or all of us was going to be dead. And why was I so important to all of this? I knew I was—the memories, or whatever was causing me to think of things I wouldn't normally, told me so.

Happily, my Aerosmith shirt was clean. I needed my boys more than ever. I dug through my purse, got my iPod out and tuned it to my best hard rock music mix, the one that had them, Motorhead, Metallica, and others. I even had a couple of Stones songs in there. Maybe Martini wouldn't hate me if he knew that.

I realized I was terrified of what he was going to do when he discovered Christopher had almost had me in the elevator. A normal man I could lie to, but I'd liked it, more than I figured I should have, and the likelihood of Martini picking that up was high, burned out empathic powers or not. I tried not to feel guilty, but I couldn't. I'd been a bad girl, and it was going to show.

I took a look in the bathroom mirror and could see why Claudia and Lorraine's suspicions had been raised. My hair looked as though I'd just gotten up or had been rolling around on a bed with someone. I brushed my hair and tied it back in a ponytail, did the face wash, avoided looking at the shower. I'd enjoyed my first shower here—I didn't want to think I might never take another one like it.

I made sure all the rest of my stuff was in my purse and left the room. Christopher was leaning on the wall outside, arms crossed over his chest, looking bored. "Took you long enough."

I didn't grace this with a reply. "Where are we going?"

"Top floor."

Another elevator ride. We stood on opposite sides. I thought about what being ravaged by Christopher had felt like. Okay, no elevator rides with Martini for a bit, that would probably be wise.

Between trying to avoid thinking about the bed, shower, and elevator, I was ready to have sex with the entire complex by the time we reached our destination level. I was overjoyed to see Reader waiting for us.

"We're pretty much ready," he said as we got out of the elevator. "I've got Jeff in my car. I think he'll be okay, but he's still kind of messed up."

"Your car?"

"We're taking two," Christopher said. "Standard procedure, just in case."

We walked through a lot of men in uniform, most of whom looked human. Human men, no longer tempting, maybe I'd just stay here a while. As we neared a large gate, I saw a crowd of people around two gray SUVs. "Everyone comes for these things?"

"To say good-bye, yeah," Reader said. He didn't have to add why.

My parents were there. Mom looked at me, then at Christopher, grabbed me, and dragged me aside. "What happened?"

"Not now, Mom, please."

"You two an item now?"

"No, we've just stopped trying to kill each other." Well that was true.

She sighed. "Kitty, you know you can't lie to me."

Damn, also true. Where was Dad? "Fine. I really don't want to have a fight with you or anyone else right now, okay? I'll tell you about it when we get back. It's all part of my secret plan," I added in a desperate attempt to get her off the scent.

She gave me the hairy eyeball. "We'll see." She grabbed me and gave me the bear hug. "I love you, kitten. Be careful."

"I will."

"Oh, almost forgot." She opened her purse and pulled out a gun. "It's a Glock Twenty-Three-C."

"It's a gun I can't shoot."

"Sure you can. Only point it at what you want to hit, never at anyone on your team unless they've gone bad, never at yourself. There's not a lot of recoil; a couple of shots and you'll be used to it. Safety on, safety off." Complete with live example. "It loads like this," she dropped the clip out and then put it back in, several times. Then she handed it to me with not one, not two, but ten additional clips. "These are fifteen-round magazines. Hope these'll hold you, but you'll probably run out."

"You couldn't have taught me this, say, last week when I'd have had time to practice?"

"No time like the present. Practice on the superbeings."

"Will do." I almost moved away but stopped. "Mom, how did you *know* Dad was the right one?"

She thought about it. "He knew all I could do but still tried to protect me. I think that was probably the deciding factor."

I kissed her cheek. "Thanks for picking him."

"Wouldn't have gotten you without him." She laughed. "He picked me, too, remember."

My brain waved urgently, but I couldn't tell why. "I want to say bye to Dad."

"Of course. Sol!"

Dad trotted over. "You all set, kitten?"

"Yep." Hugs and pecks all around.

"Dad, why did you pick Mom?"

He gave me an odd look. "Now? You want to know this now?"

"Yes."

He shrugged. "She was the only woman I'd ever met who had what I considered the entire package. When I realized I was willing to give up everything I was if that was the only way to get her, I knew I was in love with her. When I didn't have to give up the things that mattered to me to keep her, I knew she was the one."

I hugged him again. "Thanks, Dad."

"Not sure how that was a help, but any time, kitten."

I saw Gower give Reader a hug. No one reacted to this any differently than my hugging my parents. I liked these A-Cs, I really did. I liked them more than most of the humans I knew. I wanted to stay with them.

And just like that, I knew what was going on.

But I needed confirmation I wasn't going to get out of either Christopher or Martini. Reader wouldn't know, either. That left the girls. And White, who was hugging his son good-bye.

"Mr. White, could I have a word?"

Christopher looked panicked for a second, but he wasn't the only one who could do a withering glare. He seemed to get the idea and backed off. White gave me a long look, then nodded and came with me as I dragged him off to the side.

"How did your wife die?"

"I beg your pardon?" He didn't look happy.

"Sorry. Look, time's short. All sympathies, it was twenty years ago, though, right?"

"Yes. She became ill, quite suddenly."

"Was she here?"

"No," he answered slowly. "She was at our East Base location. She was one of our top diplomats, so she spent a great deal of time there. Why?"

"What did she die of? What killed her?"

"Disease. Fast-acting. Like a cancer, but we'd never seen anything like it, on our home world or this one. There was nothing we could do." He looked very old suddenly. "I hope you have a reason for asking me this, other than idle curiosity? The memories are still painful."

Not a time for me to panic. I wasn't an A-C. "The walkies we're bringing with us, will they allow us to reach someone here?"

"They should."

"Good. Keep one with you. I may have more questions."

"You're quite comfortable giving a lot of orders, aren't you?"

"Yep." I looked straight at him. "Just like your son and your nephew, both of whom I'm trying to keep alive. Got it?"

He nodded. "Thank you. Hope you're successful."

"Not as much as I do, trust me." I stuck out my hand. "Thanks for the help."

He looked at my hand. "We don't shake hands with people we care about." He reached out and hugged me. I managed not to be shocked and hugged him back. "Be careful," he whispered. "It can all go wrong very quickly when you're out there. But, for what it's worth to you, know that you go with my blessings."

I was touched. I'd never had the head of any religious organization give me a direct blessing since I was young. I wondered if this wiped out all the prior day and a half's sluttiness, particularly the part from the elevator, but I had to assume it didn't. My luck never ran *that* well.

Everyone having said good-bye, we headed to the cars. There was a male standing there I'd never seen before. He looked human, which was to say he didn't make me want to add in a third man to my romantic mix. "Who's the seventh wheel here?" I asked Reader.

"Tim, he'll be your driver."

Tim nodded solemnly. "Honored."

"And back to Triple A that fast, too, Tim. Give me the keys."

His mouth dropped. "But . . . but I'm the driver."

I looked at Reader. "You drive the boys, I'll drive the girls." Christopher and Tim both started to protest, but I didn't want to hear it. "Shocker alert—I'm a human, I know how to drive. And I don't want Tim here along, no offense to you, Tim."

"None taken." He was human, but it was clear he was lying.

"I think you'll be more useful as our man back at Base here, keeping tabs on everything, making sure if the capsule has trouble, the rest of the engineers can fix it, that sort of thing."

Tim looked at Christopher. "Why does Jeff like her?"

This was the wrong question to the right person, but it also proved to me, without a shadow of a doubt, that dumping Tim early was the right choice.

"Who knows?" Christopher snapped, while looking at the side-view mirror on the car. "Just do what she says. Give her the keys and take off."

Tim tossed me the keys and stalked away. Another friend made. Christopher went after him, presumably to tell him to stop whining.

"You want to see Jeff before we go?" Reader asked quietly.

"Um, yes but no."

He nodded. "Thought something was different between you and Christopher."

"God, is it printed on my forehead or something?"

"No, but I think we'll deal with it when we're at the war zone."

So that's what we were calling it. Well, it was going to be accurate. In more ways than one. "Okay, so, who's going first through the gate?"

"Me, you follow behind, they'll tell you when to go." He put his arm around my shoulders and gave me a squeeze. "It'll all work out."

"Oh, good. I was worried."

He grinned his awesome, cover-boy grin. "If I say it, it's so."

"Thank God you're coming along then."

CHAPTER 38

WE LOADED INTO THE CARS. Christopher got into the front with Reader; I assumed Martini was in the back. I hoped he was sleeping, but probably not with a bunch of adrenaline in him.

I got into the driver's seat of our car. This was a nice SUV. Like their clothing, the A-Cs went top-drawer in their vehicles. Lincoln Navigator, top of the line, with, as far as I could tell, a lot of alien extras added on. At least, I didn't think Navigators came with buttons for Invisibility Cloak or Laser Shield. I was amazed that the clock was normal and also amazed that it said it was only two in the afternoon. Plenty of daylight left for us to die in. Goody.

"Nice of you guys to buy American," I said as Lorraine took shotgun and Claudia climbed into the middle seat.

"Government contracts, you have to love 'em," Lorraine said with a grin. The doors slammed. "Okay, give. What happened between you and Christopher?"

"Nothing."

"And you said *we* couldn't lie." Claudia laughed. "You two were standing a lot closer; he's all upset but differently than before."

"Jeff's out of it for one minute and there's Christopher, right after his girl." Lorraine was finding this funny. I doubted Martini was going to share the mirth.

"I don't think it was like that." Well, it was like that, but different. "The implanted memories are affecting us. They made Jeff think I was hating him. I guess they made Christopher think I was interested."

"And you *being* interested probably helped," Lorraine said dryly. Reader's carload pulled up to the gate.

"I'm not. Well, I wasn't." Before he'd kissed me. Now there was a part of me that really wanted to know what it would have been like to make violent love the way it had seemed we were going to. The A-Cs standing at the gate motioned, and Reader's car started through. It was icky to watch—like a slow fade as the car moved. I chose to study the instrument panel.

"So, who's the better kisser?" Claudia asked.

I had to think about it. "They're both amazingly good. But edge to Jeff." Possibly more than just an edge. I'd only been kissed by Christopher in one way. But Martini had kissed me in ways I didn't think were possible. He'd done a lot of things I didn't think were possible. All of them great.

"Have you gone all the way with Christopher? I know you did with Jeff, don't try to lie." Claudia was giggling.

"Um, no. We stopped well short of that." Just barely, but still, we'd stopped.

"What's it like with Jeff?" Lorraine didn't sound as though she was asking scientifically.

I could lie, but why? "I've never been with anyone as great in bed. Ever."

"Mental connection too?" Claudia asked, sounding shocked.

"Um, no, not like you mean. I don't think humans connect the way you seem to, at least rarely. Besides, I don't have a lot of mental going on when it's good, other than please, God, do that again or don't stop what you're doing 'cause I'm gonna go over the edge." I wanted to be in bed with Martini right now more than anything.

They both cracked up. "I can't believe Jeff's that great. Who would've guessed?" Claudia was laughing so hard I thought she'd stop breathing.

"What was Christopher like?" Lorraine asked as she wound down. Reader's car was through, and we had A-Cs motioning us through just as if we were an airplane about to dock.

I tried to think about how to answer that. "Overpowering."

"Ooooh, sounds hot." Lorraine looked over her shoulder. "I told you he'd be like that. And I called Jeff right, too."

It was just like being with Amy and Sheila. "You don't seem all that upset about this."

"We're not. Like we'd want to marry either one of them?" Lorraine said with a snort of laughter.

"We might have to," Claudia added, in a voice of doom.

"Why?"

"Arranged marriage. We're still stuck with it. If they can make us." Lorraine sounded angry. I couldn't blame her.

"Which they can't," Claudia added vehemently. "That's why we aren't getting married. We know what we want, and if we can't get it, then we'll just be single, thanks so much."

"You want to marry humans, don't you?"

"Yes, we all do. Well, most of our generation does." Lorraine leaned on her hand. "Not that they'll let us."

"Jeff'll do it, no matter what they tell him," Claudia said quietly. "You watch."

My throat felt tight, but I had to ask. "Is that the only reason he likes me?"

"Oh, no, honey, not at all," Claudia said reassuringly.

"Why does he like me, then?" I knew why Christopher did, after all.

They were both quiet. We started through the gate, and I forced myself to keep my eyes open. It was horrid, so I looked at the steering wheel.

"He's an empath," Lorraine said finally. "He connects with people."

"But never as fast as with you, James told us."

"What's their relationship like? Jeff and Christopher, I mean." I didn't want to think about the possibility that Martini only liked me because I was a human and represented release from the arranged marriage trap or viewed me as an exotic event before marrying one of his own kind.

"Oh, they're real close," Claudia said. "But . . ."

"But?"

Lorraine shifted in her seat. "My mother told me most

of it, I was too young too remember. Jeff's a little older than Christopher, but they were born the same year. Christopher's an only child. Jeff's got a lot of sisters."

"That explains the ladies' man attitude."

"Not really," Claudia corrected. "Until they were ten, their personalities were totally different."

This was interesting. "How so?"

"I can just remember Christopher giving me a piggyback ride," Lorraine said. "And he was always calling 'C'mon, Jeff.'"

"Because Jeff was really shy. He was the youngest, but there's a big gap between him and his sisters. Christopher was always the one in the lead, dragging Jeff along. Christopher was a big joker, and Jeff was always the one saying they shouldn't do something."

This didn't sound like either one of them. "They were together a lot?"

"Oh, yeah," Claudia said. "Jeff's parents don't have any special talents. So getting an empath as a son was sort of hard to deal with."

"My mother said Christopher's mom sort of took Jeff under her wing. She was an empath, so she understood what he was going through. Until they're older, empaths have a hard time blocking anything. And Jeff's talent showed up so early, it was even harder than normal."

I thought about how Martini had been with me in the conference room and then with my parents. How miserable and hurt and ill all of our emotions made him. I could easily imagine what it would be like for a child—to know your parents really *were* mad at you, to know that someone truly didn't like you, to feel people in pain.

"So he spent a lot of time with his aunt and uncle?"

"With his aunt. Richard's been our Sovereign Pontifex since before we came to Earth, so well before all of us were born. His duties meant he was away a lot." Claudia sighed. We exited the gate into a big desert with some mountains all around, but at a great distance. "It was hard on all of them, from what I've heard and can remember. But Theresa was our head diplomat, so she was busy all the time, too."

"They used to live in East Base, and Jeff spent most

of his time there. We were there, too, until we were transferred." Lorraine pointed. "Follow James. I think he wants to get us away from the gate."

"Did they change after she died?"

"The next day, according to my mother." Lorraine squinted. "Is their car rocking?"

"Can't tell, could be the terrain, it's pretty bumpy." Trauma could certainly make someone's personality alter. "So Christopher withdrew and Jeff started taking care of him? Role reversal?"

"Yes. My mother said it was as though they exchanged personalities overnight while still being them. Christopher's never been the same since his mother died. Jeff sometimes gets quiet, like he did when he was little, but Christopher turned into . . ."

"His father," Claudia finished. "He was a lot more like his mother when we were all little. Now Jeff's more like she was."

"She was a horndog?"

Both girls laughed. "No," Claudia clarified. "But she was funny and outgoing and just someone you wanted to be around."

"Yeah, that sure doesn't describe Christopher." I thought about his expression when he'd drawn his mother's picture. He wasn't over her death twenty years later. Not that I could blame him. I didn't want to lose my mother right now, and the idea that she could have been killed when I was little because of her secret life made my skin cold.

"My mother said Jeff was like Theresa's second son. They were really close. She taught him everything about how to deal with his empathic abilities. It's probably one of the reasons he's in charge of Field and has been for so long, her training."

That seemed hard to believe—he'd been ten when she'd died. Sure, the basics, but full on super-empath skills? I didn't buy it. "Were they both always strong in their talents?"

"Yes, but they increased after Theresa died. Not that they wanted to do much for a while. It was hard on Richard, too. The boys lived with Jeff's parents for several months."

"My mother said he almost didn't recover from the

loss. He's never remarried. I don't think he's even considered it."

"So they've always been close, Jeff and Christopher?" We were really heading out into the middle of what could rightly be called nowhere. And Reader's car was definitely bouncing more than ours.

Dead silence. This was going to be juicy. I cleared my throat meaningfully.

"Until a few years ago, yes," Claudia said guardedly.

"Uh-huh. What happened?" Silence. "Let me guess. They both liked the same girl?"

"You're good," Lorraine said. I didn't agree—they were just obvious. She sighed. "Yeah, they both wanted to marry the same girl. Her name was Lissa."

"Was?"

"She was killed." Claudia sounded close to tears. "She was a really good friend of mine. They both adored her—she was about the only A-C they'd ever really been interested in marrying."

"How did she die?" I was proud of myself for not being jealous. I didn't think I had the right. I also was fast becoming aware that Reader wasn't kidding—the A-Cs truly were like an extended Italian family, complete with everyone knowing everything about each other.

"She was out with Jeff, and he was going to propose, but she was going to pick Christopher. So this was going to be the let-him-down-easy date." Claudia gulped. "They were attacked by a superbeing."

Attacked, not manifested. "That superbeing wouldn't have been Mephistopheles, would it?"

"No, actually," Lorraine said. "It was one we call Earwig." So much for that theory. "What's up with James?" she added.

Reader was flooring it and driving erratically. "He always drive that badly?"

"No. I wonder if something's wrong?" Claudia leaned forward. "You can call them on the box," she pointed to another button on the dash.

Lorraine hit it. ". . . show you why I'm upset!" It was Martini, and he was yelling.

"If you'd just listen to me—" Christopher, also yelling.

"I don't care what your damn excuse is!"

"Could you two just calm down?" Reader, sounding freaked out.

"Stop the damn car, James, so I can kill him, or I'll just use you as a bat!"

Lorraine hit the button again. We were all quiet.

"I think Jeff's figured out that you and Christopher, um, got friendly." Lorraine looked at me. "What now?"

Reader's car spun around and stopped. He jumped out of the driver's seat and ran toward us. I unlocked the doors.

"Now, we put my actual plan into action."

CHAPTER 39

I STOPPED THE CAR NEAR READER but still far away from the other SUV. He leaped in next to Claudia. "Lock the doors!"

"Jeff's a lot bigger than Christopher," I mentioned as Lorraine hit the lock button.

"Christopher's a lot meaner," she said reassuringly. I wasn't comforted.

"Girlfriend, you need to either shoot them or talk to them, but they're not going to listen to anyone else. Jesus, that was the most hellish ride of my life."

"How soon did Jeff start?"

"The second you were in your car. He didn't try to kill Christopher until we were through the gate, though."

Wonderful. I didn't want them dead. "Okay. I'm, uh, going in."

"Take a gun from the back," Reader suggested.

"Got my mom's Glock."

"Good. Aim for the thigh. It'll hurt but not maim." He was serious. Oh, this was going to suck.

"I'm hoping not to shoot either one of them." No sooner did I say this than they tumbled out of the car. It was hard to see because they were moving so fast, but I got the impression they were trying to beat the living crap out of each other. "Real fast, how did Christopher's mother die?" I wanted their version, not just White's.

"She went on a trip and got some disease. No one could

explain it. Killed her within a week." Claudia handed me a walkie. "You'll want this." I dropped it into my purse.

"Before or after Mephistopheles had first appeared?"

"Right after," Lorraine supplied. "How will we know to come and back you?"

"If I'm running toward you yelling, 'Start the car and open the door,' you'll know. Otherwise, I think I can stop them." This was a whopping lie, but I figured only Reader would guess that.

I steeled myself and got out of the car. Reader slipped into the driver's seat. "Try telling them you're actually in love with me. Might shock them into stopping."

"I'd be in love with you, but you're already married."

He grinned. "If I were straight, you'd be my girl."

"Something to contemplate. If this goes poorly, maybe you and Paul can consider the benefits of being bi. I'm open to sharing."

I put my purse over my neck and started off. They were still fighting. I could tell because Martini had thrown Christopher against the side of the SUV.

"Jeff, stop it!"

He turned to me. "I'll deal with *you* later."

That didn't sound good.

"Back off, Kitty, this doesn't concern you." Christopher swung a punch that landed, mostly because Martini had been looking at me. They were away from the car now, lunging for each other.

"I think it totally concerns me. Both of you, cut it out. If you kill each other, you let the big fugly win!"

"Don't care, thanks for asking," Martini shouted as he grabbed Christopher again and flung him around

"You always have to push it," Christopher snarled, leaping from the ground to tackle Martini at the knees. "It's always all or nothing with you."

"Like you're some saint and I've missed it all this time?" They were rolling around on the ground, again beating the crap out of each other.

They weren't going to stop. Okay. I had the Big Gun. I was prepared to use it. "Mephistopheles killed your mother and aunt."

I said it quietly, but they both heard it. I walked closer

to them. "She was a diplomat, and she was his daughter-in-law. She didn't know Yates was the parasitic host, right, because you all didn't make that connection until recently. But an in-control superbeing had created. I'll bet she went to Yates to ask him to help her, help all of you. He infected her, or turned into Mephistopheles and infected her. I'll bet he did to her what he wants to do to me, maybe what he's already done to me. But she was an A-C, and it killed her."

I reached my hands down to them. "Get up."

Christopher took my hand and let me pull him up. Martini ignored it and got to his feet. "Big boy, already a mess." But he wasn't smiling.

I leaned against the SUV. "She was an empath, and I've learned that's rare in your women. Jeff's the highest level empath you have. What about you?" I asked Christopher. "What level imageer are you?"

"He's the best," Martini spat out. "At everything, from what I've heard."

I ignored that one. "Mephistopheles wants to rule the Earth. And Yates wants to destroy it. And to do that, they both know one thing: They have to stop the two of you. Now, why would that be?"

"No idea." Martini brushed himself off. He looked like a big angry cat to me.

"Because if you procreate, the likelihood of your children being even more powerful is high. It's called genetics. And evolution."

Christopher's eyes narrowed. "So, why would he kill my mother?"

"Because she was so powerful. If he couldn't use her, and I'm sure he couldn't, he had to destroy her. Before she had any other powerful children or trained her powerful nephew any further. She was an empath—she must have felt the dichotomy when she was with Yates after he'd joined with the parasite."

"But she never told us," Martini said quietly. "We were with her the whole time she was dying. We were with her when she died."

"My father wasn't," Christopher added.

"Why not?" This sounded completely out of character.

"We don't know. He said he had to go on a matter of national security." Christopher's voice was bitter.

"He went to his father for help. I mean, who else? He couldn't know what had happened." I knew why White had looked so bad when I asked him about this. He'd figured out that his own father had had something to do with his wife's death. And he'd told no one, because who could he tell?

"Then why didn't she tell us, tell him, tell someone?" Christopher asked, the anger rolling off him.

"Maybe she didn't want you two to grow up knowing your grandfather was the most evil man on the planet. Maybe she didn't want her husband to carry any more burden than he already had over his father."

"That would be stupid, and my mother wasn't stupid."

"No," Martini said slowly. "I can see why she'd lie. She probably thought our agents would take care of Mephistopheles right away, and then no one would know. She thought like you." He looked right at me, and his eyes were cold. I knew he wasn't ever going to forgive me.

"Why are you the catalyst for all this?" Christopher still didn't sound as though he believed any of it.

I couldn't think of a polite way to put it. "You're both fighting over me. As flattering, and unusual, an event as that is, it's also why I'm the catalyst. Yates is an empath. He could feel how you two felt about me, couldn't he?"

"Yates, yes. Mephistopheles, we don't know." Martini wasn't looking at me now.

"Let's assume the talents have bled over. So he's coming here to make sure the two of you never procreate, and the only way to do that is to kill you."

"So does he want to kill you so we don't procreate with you?" Martini asked, still looking anywhere but at me. "And if so, why?"

"Probably and evolution. Paul's normal. You haven't said that he's the only normal hybrid. What if he's stronger or if the potential is there? What if your entire generation marries humans, spreads out, mixes in as the rest of our races have? You'll make humans stronger, not weaker, because the A-C internal organs are dominant."

"That would make us more appealing for Mephistopheles," Christopher countered.

"Maybe. Maybe it would mean we could fight him on a more even playing field. We don't know what would happen if a parasite attached to, say, Paul. Maybe he'd become stronger, or better, or both. Evolution's tricky, but this is what it's about—Yates and Mephistopheles both want to stop your evolution."

"I think she's right." Reader's voice came from behind me. "Sensors are showing that we have company coming." His voice sounded odd. I turned to look at him. He was pale. "Jeff, Christopher . . . there's a lot more than one heading for us."

CHAPTER 40

AT LEAST THEY KNEW HOW TO SWING into action when it mattered. "Get everyone armed," Martini snapped. "Aerosols may work on Mephistopheles, but we don't know about the others, so everyone should also take guns. You, too," he said as he moved past me toward the back of the SUV. Christopher and Reader both went to the other car.

I followed Martini to the back and grabbed a couple of spray cans. I could just barely get them into my purse. With everything in it, it weighed a ton. "Make sure none of this gets inhaled by any of you."

"I think we can manage to figure that out." Martini picked up what looked like a machine gun and handed it to me. "Here."

"I can't carry that."

"Take it."

"I can't even lift it, and I'm not going to try to lift it."

"Take it." He shoved it at me.

I shoved it right back. "Look, it happened, okay? We stopped it. Because of you. Get over it before we're all dead."

"Sorry to get in the way." He slammed the gun back into the car. "Hope you two will be very happy together."

"Why are you just assuming that I'm in love with Christopher?" Before he could answer the ground shook. "What was that?"

We both turned and saw what was coming toward us.

Mephistopheles was flying, horrible bat wings flapping lazily. Beneath him were five other monsters, all bigger than he was. It was clear he was herding them. The only aspects these things had in common were they were all awful to look at and their eyes were that horrible glowing red so popular with the superbeing set.

One had huge ears that draped down the side of its head and touched the ground. It was green and scaly and looked like a really bad cross between a dinosaur and a caveman. It had clawed hands and carried what looked like small trees in each one.

"Is that Earwig?" I pointed at this thing.

"Yes." Martini's voice was an angry growl.

"Then he killed Lissa under Mephistopheles' orders." Which made sense and confirmed my theory. How I hoped we'd live long enough for me to explain it to someone back at the Science Center.

"How do you know about that?"

"I have my sources." The next monster to capture my attention looked like that blind men with the elephant parable—as if someone who couldn't see and had never seen an animal had tried to create one. It lumbered on huge feet, six of them, and it was the reason the ground was shaking. Its body was pinkish purple and grotesquely rotund while its head was like an elephant's but with no trunk or tusks. Instead, it had fangs, and yet, somehow, a humanish face. "What's that one called?"

"The Pachyderm."

"Fitting. Sort of." I was trying not to be scared and failing utterly, no matter how many times I tried singing "Pink Elephants on Parade" to myself.

"You want to go be near Christopher?"

I spun around and looked up at him. "Stop it. You want to be mad at me? That's fine. Please give it a rest right now. I had a great plan. It's worked well. Mephistopheles is here, thanks for getting really angry. But I didn't know these others were going to show up, and I've got no guess as to what to do. Plus, before you go all righteous wrath on me, let's just discuss all those 'marry me's' you've been passing the last two days when you're actually forbidden *to* marry me. You're not exactly Mr. Clean here."

I spun back around to examine another superbeing and tried to stop caring about whether or not Martini was going to be nice to me, let alone kiss me, ever again. The giant black snake that moved out from behind the Pachyderm was certainly a good distraction. I was afraid of snakes, but this one was so big fear didn't begin to cover my reaction. And seeing a caricature of a human face shoved into the snake head was promising to give me nightmares for the rest of my life. If I got to have a rest.

"And that snake thing is?"

"The Serpent." He didn't say "duh," but I could feel him thinking it.

Our next contestant was almost normal, at least by comparison. It looked like a giant stick bug, with extra sticks. "What does that thing do?"

"It shoots poison from the end of every limb. We call it the Killer. Because no one's ever survived getting hit by it."

"Can we go home now?"

"I wish."

Last but not least was something that truly looked like a giant slug. "That called the Slug?"

"Yep."

A thought occurred. I was amazed I was able to form any. "You ever tried salting that thing?"

"What?"

I dug into my purse and managed to find the walkie-talkie. I hoped I was using it right. "Mr. White, please."

"Yes, Miss Katt?"

"I'd like a ton of salt, and I do mean a ton, to be airlifted to wherever the hell it is we actually are. Pronto would be the best. Please tell the human pilots that they'll be getting rid of a giant slug, only. I don't think they can help with the others." You only had to tell me twice that the existing in-control superbeings could withstand artillery.

Silence.

"Are you nuts?" Martini asked.

"Probably."

The walkie crackled. "Does the salt have to be dry or can it be, say, ocean water?"

I thought about it. "Ask my father. Tell him we need to get rid of a huge slug infestation."

More silence.

"You know, I meant it," Martini said.

"What? That I'm nuts?"

"That I wanted to marry you." Past tense. Why did that make my chest constrict? I'd known him about two days.

"Great. I want to have someone shower me with millions of dollars without any downside attached. I don't go around mentioning that to everyone I come across."

The walkie crackled again. "Mr. Katt says, in the case of this slug, ocean water will probably be fine, however, we're adding in dry salt as well."

"Great. How fast can that happen? Because these things seem to move slowly, but they can't move that slowly."

"They're on their way, should be there within fifteen minutes. We're calling in jets based out of San Diego and aircraft from Luke in support of those from Home Base."

Fifteen minutes might be too long. "Tell them that it's Top Gun time, okay?"

"Will do. Anything else?"

"I'm sure there will be. Please stay tuned." I dropped the walkie back into my purse. "Any giant mongoose around? 'Cause I'd love to see a humongous Riki-Tiki-Tavi right about now."

"We're fresh out."

"Do the cars protect from the Killer's poison?"

"They have shields, so they might."

I turned and trotted over to the others. "Jeff's really pissed," I mentioned to Christopher as I got to them.

"No, really? I hadn't noticed."

"James, you up for something scary?"

"Uh, girlfriend? This hasn't stopped being scary yet. Are you suggesting we're moving up to total terror?"

"Yes. Can you take one of the super-SUVs and use it to ram that stick bug thing? With shields on full."

He stared at me. "You want me to try to take out a superbeing with a car."

"It's a big SUV. Very sturdy."

"Not sturdy enough."

"You sure or just chicken?"

"Both."

I grabbed his walkie. "Mr. White?"

"Yes, Miss Katt. It's been so long."

"Truly. We need a really big, nasty Humvee, preferably military issue, and it needs all the A-C bells and whistles on it. Do we have such a beast?"

He sighed. "We do. It's on its way. May Tim drive it to you?"

"Only if he's keen on dying."

Silence.

"You're really good under pressure," Lorraine said.

"I'm really good at panicking with style."

White's voice came back through the walkie. "Tim shares that he's ecstatic about the opportunity to make it back to the majors. I have no idea what he's talking about, but I suspect you do."

"Baseball's the national sport. Perhaps you should watch it sometime."

"I prefer football."

"Good to know. Tell Tim to put the pedal to the metal and get his butt out here."

"I await your next orders with great joy."

I looked over at Christopher. "I see where your snarkiness comes from."

"I'm flattered by the comparison."

I turned around to see how far away the really big fuglies were. "Not that I'm complaining, but why do they move so slowly?"

"No idea," Christopher replied. "No one's ever complained about it. We have a hard enough time surviving them at this rate of speed."

"Girls? Any thoughts?"

"The atmosphere's too dense for them."

"Good one, Claudia. Lorraine?"

"They're in control, but they don't manifest often, so they aren't used to making these bodies function."

"I think we have two potential winners." I looked back at Christopher. "Perhaps a few more female agents would be a good idea for the future."

"I'll be happy to discuss integration if we survive. Though Jeff controls all active Field, including decisions like that one."

"Guess I'll just charm him into it."

"I'll watch from the next county."

"I see your dormant sense of humor comes out when facing death. Good to know." I already had a good guess as to what was going to stop Mephistopheles. But the Serpent, the Pachyderm, and Earwig were presenting problems. Martini was still by the other car, and Earwig appeared to be in the lead for the monsters. I didn't have to ask who his target was. After all, he'd missed killing Martini when he took out Lissa; I was sure he wanted to rectify that situation.

"I'll be back. I hope." I trotted back to Martini. He didn't take his eyes off Earwig. "Jeff, you need to get back with the rest of us."

"No, I'm planning to stay right here."

"She was going to choose Christopher."

"I know." He looked at me now. "She didn't have to tell me. Empath, remember?"

"Then why did you take her out to ask her?"

He shrugged. "Just in case she changed her mind." He looked back at the lumbering monsters. "I thought it would be worth the risk."

"It wasn't your fault."

"Maybe not. I couldn't save her. Earwig ripped her in half in front of me. Like she was a paper doll. I was glad Christopher never saw that."

What a great way to ensure someone wouldn't mate—rip apart the person they love in front of them. Mephistopheles had definitely gotten ideas from Yates and vice versa.

Earwig was a lot closer to us. "Jeff, we have to fall back."

"Why? Bullets don't work on that thing. They don't really work on any of these. The guns make you feel safer, but it's an illusion."

He really had his fatalism on. "Then why are we trying?"

"Nothing better to do."

"I can think of a few things."

"Can you? Any of them involve an elevator?"

I probably shouldn't have, but I kicked the back of his leg, between the calf and the knee. This was the nice way—I'd been trained to just take out the knee completely. Martini fell to his knees, and I hit him in the head with my purse. He went down and out. Oh, well, he hated me anyway.

Reader and Christopher raced over. "What the hell did you do to him?" Christopher shouted. Ah, that old thick blood thing.

"Get Mr. Custer's Last Stand into the car and keep him from just standing around being a target."

"What will you be doing?" Reader asked me as he and Christopher lifted Martini up.

I looked around and caught my reflection in one of the aerosol cans. I walked to the side of the car and looked at my chest in the side-view mirror. "Improvising."

CHAPTER 41

I WENT TO THE DRIVER'S SEAT and dug through my purse. iPod was still there, and, happy day, so was my car radio adapter. I plugged it in, turned the volume up to eleven, and hit play. Aerosmith's "Back in the Saddle" blared out, and I went around and opened all the car's doors, so the sound could travel. Then I turned around and watched.

They call him Screamin' Steven Tyler for a reason. And my hard rock music mix had a lot of Steven screaming, as well as many others. My parents had complained about my musical tastes for most of my life—I liked something in every genre, and I liked to play it all loud.

Reader was back with me. "We have a sound track?" he shouted. It was as if we were first row at a concert, only without my wanting to climb on stage and have my way with the singer and lead guitarist.

I pointed toward Earwig. "One that works."

The monster was writhing, and not to the beat. The ears weren't just lobes—the entire length of his body was ear canal. And he was being assaulted by the best rockers in the business.

The Humvee barreled up next to us, and Tim popped his head out. "Nice to be here," he yelled. "What's the plan, besides us all going deaf?"

I looked at Reader. "Who's the better driver?"

"None better than me, girlfriend. I know, I get to go ram that thing. You want Tim with me?"

"Is he better off with you or running the stereo?" The song changed to "Last Child." I noticed the beat was affecting both Earwig and the Serpent.

"If you don't want this car trampled, someone needs to drive it."

Reader had a point. The Pachyderm seemed unaffected, and it was heading for us. "Do the switch."

Reader pulled Tim out of the Humvee, rolled up the window, and then the car-tank shimmered. I took this to mean shields were engaged. Reader peeled out, heading for the Killer.

I flung Tim into the driver's seat. "Keep the music going, keep it loud, and keep from being trampled. Oh, and you have a ton of equipment in the back, try not to let it fall out."

Mephistopheles was hanging back. This didn't surprise me so much as piss me off. Typical evil overlord, sending his minions to do his dirty work. No worries, I'd just work my way through to him. Somehow.

Something very fast ran past me. Make that two somethings. I looked behind me, but Martini was still out and Christopher was with him. That meant the girls had gotten involved. I didn't have time to contemplate this because Tim drove off, seeing as Earwig was pretty much right on us.

On me, since I was now alone.

The good news was it had dropped the trees to hold its ears. The bad news was it was lurching and contorting right toward me. So I had to figure out where the parasite was on this thing and destroy it, without it killing me first. Good practice for the main event.

The sound track was getting louder. I wasn't sure how, but I decided not to argue. It was helping me and hurting at least one—and probably two—of the enemy, and that was good enough for right now.

It was possibly the grossest thing I'd ever done, but as I dodged Earwig's feet I managed to grab an earlobe and start climbing up. He was as disgusting as he looked, but not slimy, so not slippery. The scales actually helped me to climb, but I really wished I had no sense of smell, because it was like hanging onto a garbage scow.

Earwig felt me through his pain, and he grabbed me.

This was not my preferred plan. The thought that Christopher for sure and Martini very possibly were going to get to see me ripped apart wasn't at all comforting.

The music switched. We left Aerosmith and went right to Motorhead. I knew my mix, and this wasn't where the songs changed. Which meant Tim had used initiative and turned on the loudest rock and roll band in the world. Maybe he was going to end up a good pinch hitter after all.

As "Ace of Spades" and Lemmy's shrieking Cockney ripped through the airwaves, Earwig screamed and dropped me. I managed to grab ear again, or at least ear hairs. That a superbeing could have ear hair was ignorance I hadn't even known I cherished until this moment. But my track coach hadn't tortured us with rope drills for nothing—I could climb this.

I moved upward, so to speak, if you could count contortions that flung me around like a tetherball. As always, I was glad I'd hooked my purse over my neck, not that I could hope to get anything out of it right now.

During one exciting rope swing I ended up inside the ear canal. Repulsive in terms of location and odor, but enlightening in terms of what we were here to do. Because I caught a glimpse of a pulsing, shimmering blob. The parasite was in the ear.

I managed to swing back inside and brace myself on the sides of the canal. I had a clear view of the parasite, but I was nowhere near enough to have a hope of the aerosol reaching. Besides, I didn't know if alcohol would work on this thing anyway.

I considered letting go of the hairs and crawling into the canal, but the mere idea was enough to make me throw up, and I didn't want to be near enough to the parasite for it to get a chance at me anyway.

Mom's Glock was looking like my best option. If I could find it. With one hand. Hanging onto a big fugly's gross ear hairs. There had to be a better way to make a living.

I stayed braced in the ear and slowly took my right hand off the hairs. I didn't start falling, so I began the careful dig through my purse. This was complicated by Earwig's contortions. I had to grab with both hands far too often. But finally, on the fifth or sixth attempt, my hand closed around cold steel.

I pulled the gun out, and now came the really fun part. The safety was on, and it required two hands to release.

Telling myself I didn't mind this at all, I wrapped the hairs around my left upper arm, and let go. I was able to get the safety off, but then "Born to Raise Hell" came on, and Earwig went nuts.

The contortions were worse than ever, and I started to slip. Oh, well, no time like the present to find out what gun recoil felt like.

It wasn't all that bad, but my first couple of shots didn't hit. I managed to grab the hairs again with my left hand and did my best to steady my right. And then my stomach clenched, because the parasite was moving, right toward me.

Mom's words, aim for what you want to hit, seemed so logical right then. I took a deep breath, aimed and fired. I kept on firing until the clip was empty. My reward was the parasite being ripped apart. My punishment was Earwig going down.

He fell over onto his side, the side I was on. I was hooked in his ear hair and I couldn't get free. I held on as we went down, and then everything went black.

CHAPTER 42

I WAS LUCKY. I wasn't squished, and I wasn't unconscious. I was, however, in the ear canal and had parasite parts all over me. To say I started to freak out for real is an understatement.

My screams echoed in the ear chamber. I wasn't sure if Earwig was dead or not, but I wasn't trying to kill him, I was simply hysterical.

Somehow I still had the Glock in my hand. But the magazine was empty, so I couldn't shoot my way out. However, the thought that maybe I could got me somewhat under control, in that though I was still screaming, I was also digging through my purse for another clip. I dropped the empty on the ground and shoved the new one in, all by feel, since it was pitch black in the stinkhole that passed for an ear canal. Mom would have been proud. I hoped I'd get to tell her about it while still on the Earthly plane.

I was about to start wasting bullets when the body began to move. My arm was still caught in the ear hairs and I decided trying to shoot myself free was not going to be a smart idea. The one positive about being covered with dead jellyfish slime was that it made my arm slick. I had to really work at it, but I got my arm free as the body lifted off me.

I could see now, and what I saw were two pairs of black-clad legs from the knees down. A-Cs were strong. Thank

God. I dropped and crawled out. As soon as I was clear they dropped the body back to the ground with a thud.

Someone picked me up. "You're a mess. And thanks for the headache. I didn't feel bad enough."

"Jeff, I'm covered with dead parasite." I managed to get this out without screaming.

Christopher reached into my purse and pulled out an aerosol can. "Don't know why you have trouble, it's easy to find stuff in there." Martini glared. He was almost up to Christopher's standards. "Get back, Jeff. Kitty, stand still and close your eyes."

I did as he said and he sprayed me all over. I was wet but I felt the parasite bubbling away.

"Is any in your nose or mouth?" Martini asked.

"I don't think so." Christopher sprayed my face. "I said I don't think so!"

"Have to be sure." He sounded like he was laughing.

I opened my eyes. He was laughing. I was back to considering the benefits of just hating him. Martini, on the other hand, was staring at my chest. I looked down. My top was soaked and I was in the running for the A-C wet T-shirt contest. "How're we doing?"

"We're all still alive," Martini said, sounding somewhat surprised.

I looked around. Earwig was, thankfully, dead. His eyes were back to human. It made him look even more horrible than he had. Well, I'd avenged my sort of romantic rival's brutal murder. Maybe Martini would continue to speak to me if we survived.

We moved away from Earwig, and I could see that Reader was doing pretty well against the Killer. It had several limbs missing, and though the Humvee seemed to be covered with a nasty greenish-yellow ooze, it was still being driven, moving nimbly for something so ponderous. He was also keeping it away from the rest of us, which was one small blessing in a field of grossness.

The girls had somehow mounted the Pachyderm and were riding it like a bull at Gilly's. I was awed, and I found myself wishing I had a movie camera. "Girls Gone Wild" would have paid a fortune for this footage.

Motorhead was no longer on the audio menu. Tim had switched to the Beastie Boys and had the bass turned way up. He was dueling with the Serpent; the beat and their tonality seemed to be affecting it, and its strikes were off.

"Love your musical choices," Martini said to me.

"They're keeping us alive."

"Yeah. Rock and rap as the saviors of mankind?"

"Rock and roll will never die."

"We might," Christopher said, as the Pachyderm bucked and thundered nearby and the Slug inched toward us.

We backed away from the Slug, and then, over the sounds of "Fight for Your Right," our air support arrived.

The jets had a payload, and I knew we didn't want to be near their drop zone. "We have to get out of here."

Martini grabbed my hand, and we were moving at hyperspeed. We were far away from the action, which was good, and I was so far past grossed out and adrenalized to the max that I didn't get nauseous. I was worried about the girls, but the Pachyderm was frightened by the jets buzzing it, and it stampeded off, toward us, but away from the Slug.

The jets were amazing to watch, fast and expertly flown. They dropped their salt payloads with impressive accuracy while avoiding Mephistopheles, who was trying to knock them out of the air.

A larger plane arrived now, flanked by more fighters. This one I figured had the water. "How did it get here so fast?"

"We can create ocean water at the Science Center," Christopher informed me. "We need to be ready in case a parasite hits a whale." Wonderful news—they could get any mammal. I was glad our pets were safe.

The salt was working. The Slug wasn't moving, and even from this distance I could see it bubbling. The big plane was overhead and dumped its water load. "Wow." The slug disintegrated. "How do we know that killed the parasite?"

Martini grabbed my hand again, and we all raced back. There was a jellyfish in the midst of the muddy remains of the Slug. It was pulsing, but slowly. I could tell it was dying. But dying and dead weren't the same thing. I grabbed my other can of aerosol out of my purse and moved in.

The parasites could move when they had to. This one

gave it one last go and lunged toward me, as much as something with no limbs could lunge. But I was ready. This was a hairspray situation, and I was an expert. The parasite took a full blast of Ever-Hold and dissolved.

"I thought you said the superbeings were invulnerable as long as their parasite was alive," I mentioned to Martini as I slogged out of the mess.

"We've never tried hairspray, salt baths, rock and roll, or simply ramming them with our cars."

"You just lacked vision."

"Thanks," Christopher said. "We'll be sure to mention it when we're back."

The big plane took off, but the jets weren't leaving. Some of this was because of Mephistopheles. However, two of the jets were buzzing the Pachyderm. Tim and Reader seemed to be doing all right with their particular superbeings. I dug around in my purse and pulled out the walkie. "Mr. White, please."

"Here, Miss Katt. How goes the offensive?"

"We're still alive, so very well for the moment. The salt worked; however the jets aren't leaving as requested. They can't hurt Mephistopheles, and I have to assume they can't hurt the Pachyderm either, so they're causing more havoc than they're solving."

Silence. I watched the Pachyderm buck like a prized rodeo bull. The girls were still on it. Amazing.

"Miss Katt, apparently the pilots are concerned about leaving two young women on the back of, if I may quote, that butt-ugly bucking bronco. Could I inquire as to Claudia and Lorraine's whereabouts?"

"They're about to win the All-National Rodeo." It made sense. Pilots have great eyesight, and any normal man would want to save either girl, let alone both of them.

"I see. Perhaps the pilots have the right idea."

"What would that be?"

"They wish to get our girls off of their ride."

Worked for me. "Tell them good luck."

"Anything else?"

"Got a giant mongoose around?"

Silence.

"You're insane, you know that," Christopher offered.

"My crazy's working a lot better than your sanity."

"True," Martini sighed. "True."

The walkie buzzed again. "Sadly, no giant anything here or available, Miss Katt."

"Could you ask my father what kills snakes besides mongoose and bullets?"

"I live to serve." Short silence this time. "Strangulation. Chopping off the head. Crushing the head. And, oh, really? How interesting. Boiling water apparently works as well."

"We're gonna need a bigger plane, Mister White."

"We'll do our best."

I heard "Fight for Your Right" again. Tim had the song on continuous loop. That probably wasn't a good sign. "The faster the better."

I dropped the walkie back into my purse. "Okay, until the planes with boiling water somehow manage to appear, we need to try to stomp the Serpent's head."

"With *what*?" Christopher asked me.

I looked over my shoulder. The jet planes had what looked like cables hanging down. I hoped the girls would take the hint. "You boys spent a lot of time running around Mephistopheles at the airport. Why?"

"We try to herd them away from civilians."

"Oh, good. So you're all trained then." I gazed at both of them for a moment, the best looking rodeo clowns in the business. "The second the girls are off its back, herd the Pachyderm toward the Serpent. Use whatever you have to in order to keep it bucking and freaking out."

Martini stared at me for a moment, then shrugged. "Everything else has worked."

"Trust me."

He looked away. "Right." He took off, and I turned to watch him. I also didn't want Christopher to see that I had something in my eyes.

Christopher put his hand on my shoulder. "I'm sorry. I shouldn't have—"

"It wasn't all you. I didn't fight all that hard at the start." And, I had to ask, if Christopher had gotten to me first, would I still want Martini? I didn't like the answer I gave myself.

"Yeah." He squeezed my shoulder. "He'll come around, Kitty. I promise."

"What says I want him to?"

He leaned over, kissed my cheek, and wiped away a tear that had somehow gotten free from my eyelashes. "Your face." Then he was off after Martini. And I was standing there alone figuring I was going to stay that way, no matter what Christopher thought.

CHAPTER 43

I WONDERED IF MEPHISTOPHELES was going to engage me now, but he was still hanging back. As long as one of his minions was still functioning, I guessed he wasn't going to take any risks.

However, I was standing around out in the open, and while we had two superbeings down, we had four still functioning. Not good odds for me, seeing as I didn't have hyperspeed to help me out.

I decided getting into a vehicle would probably be a good idea. Conveniently, we had a spare that hadn't been hit, trampled, or washed away. I ran for it.

Behind the wheel was a nice place to be. I didn't unhook my purse, though, just in case. This made driving a bit awkward, but I figured awkward was better than losing my bag of tricks.

I took a look. Tim was having a lot more problems than Reader, and all his doors were open. I decided to go help out our team's rookie. I pointedly ignored that, in reality, I and the girls were the real rookies; we were doing pretty well so far, after all.

I hated driving without music, but Tim had my iPod. Even in this life and death situation, I wanted some tunes. "Fight for Your Right" was getting old.

I hit what I thought was the radio button as I headed toward Tim and the Serpent. I was very proud of myself for heading toward it, rather than away from it. But there was no one around to brag to. There was only static coming out of the speakers. I twisted the knobs and hooked into what I thought was talk radio.

"... not working any more." The voice sounded familiar.

"Might be time to close the doors and take off." That sounded like Gower.

"I do and we're all gonna die." Aha, this was Tim.

I looked around and found another button, pushed it, and gave it a try. "Hey, can anybody hear me?"

"Kitty?"

"Yes, Paul. If I live, can I have one of these cars?"

"Glad you can think of the future."

"James is doing better than Tim."

"I already told him that," Tim snapped.

I looked at the Serpent and another thought came to me. "Switch the music."

"To what?"

"Try something soothing, but with a beat."

"You have that?"

"I have everything." Well, almost everything. I didn't have Indian pipe music, which would have been my first choice. I thought about it. What song would lull a snake into submission? "John Mayer?"

"Over my dead body."

"Could be, Tim, could be." I thought some more. It needed a beat, and it needed to be soothing. And I needed to own it. This gave us a lot of choices. The Serpent had responded to the beats, but I wanted to soothe it. "Put on Tears for Fears. 'Cold.' On continuous."

"You have *got* to be kidding. I thought we were trying to kill the superbeing, not me."

"Tim? I'm in charge." Supposedly. "We'll know fast if it's not the right song."

"No Barry Manilow or John Tesh?" Reader was on the group radio.

"If you want. I have Rod Stewart, too."

"I'm ready to let the Serpent just kill me." Tim had switched the music. The Serpent started to sway.

"I point out that it's working, so stop complaining. Is there any way to make the music come out of my car, too?"

"Why?" This was Gower.

"Because then we could surround it with the sound."

"Turn on the radio."

"I thought I had."

"Under the buttons you used to turn on the intercom, girlfriend," Reader offered.

They marked where their invisibility shield button was, but the radio button was incognito. Aliens were weird.

I found the right button, and the music blared out. I rolled the windows down and drove around toward the back of the giant snake-thing. It saw me and expressed an interest, but its head was starting to bob, and its glowing eyes were drooping.

"We're boring it to death," Tim said. I was impressed I could hear him, but the intercom was pretty powerful.

"You know, I haven't passed judgment on your musical choices."

"Because you don't know them."

"Girlfriend, I was with you on all of the other stuff, but you're kidding me with this, right? You don't really have Manilow or Tesh, do you?" Reader snickered.

Well, I didn't actually have Tesh. "I think we have more pressing issues at hand."

We did. I could see the girls hanging off cables in the distance, and the Pachyderm was heading toward us. This meant Martini and Christopher were herding it. At least, I hoped so. But it also meant that Tim and I were going to be right in the path of the one-monster stampede.

"Tim, get ready to circle around this thing, and keep away from the Pachyderm."

"I knew you were going to suggest we stay close by."

"I did mention you had to be excited about dying to come along."

"Yeah, yeah, yeah. Can I close the doors at least?"

The Serpent was nodding and swaying. It really liked this song. "Sure, but be careful." I watched him get out and slam the doors and the hatch. The Serpent's head bobbed lower, and for a moment I thought it was going for Tim, but it was just relaxing.

He leaped back into the driver's seat. "Clockwise or counterclockwise?"

"No idea. Which works better to charm snakes?"

"Your father says counterclockwise," Gower offered.

My dad knew everything. No wonder Mom loved him. "Thanks, Dad!" Tim and I started off and circled the Serpent counterclockwise, keeping across from each other. I could see the Pachyderm, and it was coming fast.

"Girlfriend, are you singing along?" Reader was definitely snickering.

I was, and so what? Maybe I was adding resonance. This was the only time I'd had to sing along, after all. "Maybe."

"Good voice."

"Why, Tim, you're a suck-up. I like that in a team member." The ground was shaking, and it was harder to steer. "We're going to need to break off and try to help herd that thing onto the Serpent."

"That should be close to impossible."

"You can come over here and ram the Killer for a while if you're not enjoying yourself."

"Incoming!" I managed to floor it, and the Pachyderm just missed me. It trampled the Serpent's tail. This wasn't as helpful as one could hope, since it roused the snake out of its musically induced stupor. Tim managed to draw the snake's attention by driving erratically in front of it. Either its tail wasn't badly hurt or the music was really powerful, because it started nodding again.

The passenger door opened and then slammed shut. Martini was in the seat next to me. "Stop screaming."

"I always scream when someone gives me a heart attack. It's my clue." My heart was pounding. "How did you do that?"

"Hyperspeed. Really, try to keep up."

"Why are you in here and not herding out there?"

"I decided to live a little longer." He had a point. I floored it and went after the Pachyderm. "I think it's trying to run away from this music."

It might have been, but Mephistopheles was flying low in front of it, sending it back toward us. "Nice of him to help out."

"I doubt he cares how we all die, just that we do." Martini shifted in the seat. "You drive like crap."

"From someone who can't that's a real insult. Why are you in my car then?"

"I thought this was Tim's." That actually hurt, but I did my best not to let him know.

"Jeff, stop being such a massive jerk." At least Reader had my back, so to speak.

"The intercom's on?" Martini stabbed the button. "Why do you want everything broadcast?"

"I wanted to talk to someone because I was alone in this stupid supervehicle and trying to help kill monsters." I slammed on the brakes. "Get out."

"Drive the car." The Pachyderm was heading back toward us.

"Get out!"

"Kitty, drive the damn car."

"How about, get the hell out and let the door slam you in the butt?"

"KITTY!" He could really bellow. He was louder than the music.

"You're all Mr. Right To Die over there. What's the problem with getting trampled? Now, get out."

He made a sound of total exasperation, leaned over, grabbed my head and kissed me, hard. "Drive the car," he said quietly as he pulled away.

"Fine." I drove off, just in time. It was hard to keep the car under control because the ground was shaking so much. "So, was that supposed to make it all better?"

"No. It was supposed to shock you into action."

"Jerk."

"When can we change the song? I thought hearing that Beastie Boys one over and over again was bad."

"When the planes with boiling water show up or when the Pachyderm tramples the Serpent's head, whichever comes first."

"Never, then. Maybe I will get out. Death might be preferable."

I started singing along again. Loudly. It was a double win—helped relax me and drove Martini nuts. Good.

I got around behind the Pachyderm and tried to herd it from behind. "I think we should turn the intercom back on."

"Fine." Martini hit the button.

". . . please do something to get that song changed!" This was an unfamiliar voice, and it was crackling.

"I think it's a good song." That was Lorraine.

"Me too," Claudia chimed in.

"The girls are scared, let 'em listen to music they like." Another voice I didn't recognize. All four of them were crackling.

"Girls, are you in the jets?"

"Kitty! Yes, we are. With *pilots*." The way Lorraine said the word I got the impression these were smart pilots.

"They saved us," Claudia added. I waited to hear that they were dreamy, but perhaps she was playing hard to get.

"Fab. Can you and your new friends help us herd? We really need that snake trampled."

"Will do, little lady."

I looked over at Martini. "Did he just call me little lady? I mean, for real?"

"Army, Navy, Air Force, Marines. They all talk the same."

"You missed Coast Guard."

"They talk differently." He leaned toward the intercom. "Gentlemen, this is Commander Martini. Could we get a little more action and a lot less chatter?"

"Commander Martini?"

He shot me a dirty look. "Surprise."

"Commander White in the other SUV?"

"Yeah, I am. You want to cut the chatter? We have a high-priority situation."

"Pardon me. I missed the delusions of grandeur session back at Home Base." I looked over at Martini. "You're all freaking unreal."

"This from the girl playing Tears for Fears as a way of snake charming."

"It's working!"

"It's killing morale." This was from Tim.

"Oh, don't you start too."

The jets were buzzing the Pachyderm again, and they were doing a much better job of herding than we were in the cars. "Tim, break off, let's get out of the way."

"First suggestion of yours that's made any sense."

The jets were doing well with the Pachyderm, but they'd roused the Serpent. Oh, well, snake charming had at least stalled things a bit. "I think we can turn off the music."

"Thank God!" This was chorused by every male voice, including the one next to me.

Tim and I drove off, cars ready, just watching. Reader was doing some real damage to the Killer, and the jets that had been around Mephistopheles were helping him somewhat. The jets with the girls were herding and dodging the Serpent at the same time. "They're great fliers."

"Hopefully they won't get killed." He said it quietly. I turned the intercom off.

"You could call them off."

"I could. But they're providing the best distractions we have right now."

"How long before the planes carrying the water will get here?"

"No idea." He sighed. "Look, I'm sorry. It was just a shock, okay? I'll stop being upset; you two can relax."

"Why do you think I want to hook up with Christopher?"

Martini snorted. "It's really obvious."

It was? To whom? Not to me, and I would have thought I'd know. "Jeff, are you high?"

"We don't do drugs, remember?"

"Well, then, what the hell is wrong with you? Did I hit a tender part of your brain?"

"Not of my brain, no," he said under his breath. "Look, Kitty, I'm good with it, all right? I'm sure I'll manage just fine."

"Thanks a lot." My throat felt tight, but I refused to give him the satisfaction of seeing me cry again.

"Why can't you just be grateful that I'm stepping aside?" His voice was raising.

"Why can't you just understand that it was a mistake?"

"I know we were a mistake, okay? I got it. I'm clear."

I was having a little trouble seeing what was going on because my eyes were swimming with tears. "Fine." I managed to get the word out. Why did I care, right? Only known him for two days, not as if I'd really thought I'd marry him or something.

This might have gone on for hours or ended right then, but before either one of us could say anything else hurtful, Mephistopheles landed on the front of the car.

CHAPTER 44

THE FRONT OF THE SUV WAS CRUSHED. The car wasn't going anywhere but to the junkyard now. "Jeff? Get out."

"Good idea. Head for the back."

"No, just you. Get out and get away from here."

"What are you talking about?" He eased himself out of the seat and moved into the back. Mephistopheles' hooves were right in front of me. They were enormous. He'd been twelve feet tall at JFK, but he looked even bigger now.

I heard clanking, and then Martini shoved some aerosols at me and into my purse. "On three, we'll move out."

"Okay." I had no intention of moving, but I didn't think he'd want to hear that.

"One . . . two . . . three!" Martini was out of the car, the passenger's door behind me open.

Mephistopheles slammed his fist into the windshield, but on the passenger's side. I knew he didn't want to kill me, but I was glad the Navigator had shatterproof glass. His horrible hand was feeling around. I waited until it was almost on me, then I sprayed it.

He jerked his hand out, but then bent down, looked at me, gave me what I thought on his face might pass for a smile, and waved. With the hand I'd sprayed. It was unscathed.

I turned on the intercom. Amazingly, it was still working. ". . . get her out of the car!" Reader, sounding terrified.

"Where the hell is Jeff?" Christopher, sounding mad and freaked. "Why isn't their intercom on?"

"We were fighting. He's immune to the spray unless he takes it internally."

"You sprayed Jeff?" Christopher sounded horrified.

"Tempting idea, but no, Mephistopheles. You know, the big fugly waving at me right now?" I had to come up with a plan. Pity I didn't have one.

Mephistopheles made a fist, still grinning. He pulled his arm back and it was really clear he was aiming for me. I wanted to run, but I was frozen.

My door opened, someone grabbed me, and I was moving at hyperspeed. We stopped miles away—we were so far I couldn't see any of the superbeings, not even Mephistopheles. Which meant we likely had a few minutes before they found us. Which was good, as I fell to my knees and started retching.

Someone knelt down next to me and put his arm around my waist, keeping me from collapsing. "I told you to leave the car on three."

"He wants to kill *you*." I had nothing in my stomach, so all that was coming up was bile. This was gross. I wondered if I could safely drink the Ever-Hold.

"And what he wants to do to you is worse."

"Yeah, but you don't care anymore, remember?" I managed to stop retching but then started to cry. Not an improvement.

He pulled me gently into his arms. "Don't cry, baby." At this I started to sob for real. Martini rocked me and kissed the top of my head. "I'm sorry, Kitty. I just . . ."

"Don't want anything to do with me anymore. I got it, I'm clear."

His arms tightened around me. "I don't want you to think you have to stay with me when you're in love with someone else."

Well, that worked. I stopped being unhappy and got mad. I wrenched out of his arms. We were both on our knees, but that just meant I couldn't kick him. I could hit him, and I did, not well or accurately but wherever I could reach, which was mostly his chest. Repeatedly. While screaming at him. "I am so sick of your 'poor me' attitude! I make one mistake and you're ready to just walk away. Glad to know how much I meant to you. Hope you enjoyed your fling with a human before you marry some A-C girl like you're supposed to!"

"Whoa, whoa, stop. Stop!" He wasn't really trying to block my fists. I got the impression I wasn't hurting him nearly as much as I wanted to.

"Why? What would that change?" I was still hitting him as hard as I could, but I was getting tired, and I was so miserable that it almost didn't matter.

Martini grabbed my wrists. "I said stop it." I tried headbutting him, and he started to laugh.

"It's not funny!" I slammed my torso into his.

"Do that again."

I tried to wrench away from him. He let go of my wrists, and I started to fall backward. He leaned forward, caught me, wrapped his arms around my back, pulled me to him, one hand at the back of my head, and then he kissed me.

This wasn't like the kiss in the car. This was deep and passionate. I tried not to respond, but within moments my arms were around his neck. He slid his other hand down my back and pulled me closer into him.

We were like that for far too short a while when he slowly ended the kiss. His mouth moved to my cheeks, and he started kissing the tears away. "Don't cry any more, baby," he whispered. "Please."

"I keep saying I'm sorry, but you don't believe me."

His lips moved to my forehead as he kissed me softly. I sniffled, and his lips moved down the bridge to kiss the tip of my nose. "I believe you." He slid his hands to the sides of my face. "In the future, should we have one, if you decide you don't want to be with me, that's fine; you tell me, I'll deal with it. But you do something like this even once more, and I'll never speak to you or touch you again."

That seemed fair. I nodded. I was afraid to say anything.

Which was a good thing since my walkie crackled. "Jeff, Kitty, *move*!" Christopher sounded panicked. Apparently, our few minutes of breathing space were over. Oh, well, at least they'd been well spent.

Martini didn't hesitate; he grabbed me, and we rolled, fast. Which was good, because Mephistopheles' hoof landed where we'd been. We scrambled to our feet, Martini grabbed my hand, and we started off, but not at hyperspeed. It dawned on me that Martini was probably out of hyperjuice.

Thankfully, the remaining SUV was barreling toward us. It screeched to a halt, skidded and turned sideways. It stopped with its right side in front of us with about two inches to spare. Martini opened the passenger door, picked me up, tossed me in, and leaped in behind me. "Go!"

I was on the floor. "Um, a little help?"

Christopher put his hand down. Martini cleared his throat and Christopher's hand retracted. "I can handle it, thanks."

"There's nothing amorous about pulling someone off the floor," Christopher muttered.

"There is when I do it." Martini lifted me up and put me onto the seat. Somehow, he did manage to make this feel amorous. I decided not to question and just go with the fact he didn't hate me anymore.

"I want my iPod back."

"Now?" Christopher turned around. "You do know Mephistopheles is right behind us?"

I looked back to see the big red fugly running behind. "I want my iPod." I needed to hear music, or at least have the means with me. I was getting too nervous and frightened, and all the angst with Martini had made me tired.

Tim pulled the unit out and tossed it back to me. I dropped the car adapter into my purse and dug out my belt clip and earphones. "How does that thing hold all that's in it and not burst?" Martini asked as we sped back toward the main action.

"It's big and it's made out of cheap leather. It works for me." I hooked the iPod to my waist and put the earphones around my neck. There, ready for whatever was coming next. I looked behind us again—Mephistopheles was falling behind.

"You know, those things can tangle and strangle you," Christopher said as if he were passing comment about the weather.

"You sound like my mother. I think strangulation by earphones is the least of my worries right now."

"Good news," Reader's voice came through the intercom. "I think the planes with hot water are here."

We were close to the Serpent now, and it was fighting with the Pachyderm. "Tell them not to drop the water yet!"

"Why not?" This was Gower, and he sounded exasperated.

"Because the Serpent's pissed at the Pachyderm, and I think it's winning." As I said this, the giant snake wrapped itself around the Pachyderm's neck and torso. The jets were still buzzing around, and the big beast was freaking out. The Serpent sunk its fangs into the Pachyderm's neck, and some sort of fluid started jetting out.

"We're out of here!" This was from one of the jets.

"We need to help James," Lorraine protested.

"We can't hit that thing, it's too thin," the other pilot said.

"Don't be silly. It's a simple trajectory." Claudia sounded annoyed but in a fond way. "Here, let me calibrate."

"If I'd said that, she'd tell me I was a moron," Martini mentioned.

There was some arguing in the jets where the girls were occupants, but they were winning. I was proud, but I had to figure much of this was because they probably had their chests very close to the pilots' heads.

"She's right," the pilot with Claudia said. "I'll give you the info."

"No need, my girl's already done." My girl, huh? Oh, there was going to be some serious hell raised when we all got back to the Science Center or Home Base, but at least Lorraine and Claudia were having a good time now.

Christopher had his head in his hand. "I can't wait to explain this to my father."

"I'll do it, no worries."

"Oh, I feel so much better."

"Hey, my girl's handled things so far," Martini said with a grin.

"So glad you two worked that out," Christopher said snidely. "Of course, you almost died."

"And that makes today different from every other day how?"

"Good point."

"Okay, we're all set," Lorraine's pilot said. "Tell your boy on the ground to move out."

"I'm on the intercom too, flyboy."

"No need to get touchy, son," Claudia's pilot shared.

"I don't take orders from you, either, Top Gun. Girl-friend?"

"Move out, James. Meet us at the rendezvous point."

"You got it."

"Rendezvous point?" Martini asked quietly.

"Where we first parked. He'll know. Head there, too, Tim."

"Absolutely, your in-charge-ness."

"A trip back to Triple A could be in your future."

"The owner likes me. I think I'm safe."

"Don't count on it." I looked closely at the Pachyderm and Serpent. They were rolling around on the ground, but the big purpley thing seemed to be slowing down. "Can one of the extra jets do a flyby and tell me if the butt-ugly el-ephant-thing's eyes are still glowing red or not?"

"Will do, ma'am." This was a new voice. Apparently the whole team was patched in. It was chummy in a weird sort of way.

"He called me ma'am. I like that better than little lady."

"He thinks you're a superior officer," Martini shared. "Little lady will be back the moment he finds out you're a civilian."

"Humph."

"Ma'am? Butt-ugly elephant-thing's eyes are not glow-ing now. Repeat, not glowing now."

"I like him. And, um, boys in the big planes? I think we can dump the water now. If it's boiling."

"Yes, ma'am," a new voice crackled. "We've maintained appropriate temperature."

"Good, good. Carry on. Hit the huge black snake."

"Roger that."

"I feel all military and official."

"She's drunk with power again." Christopher looked

back at Martini. "I thought you said you could handle her."

"I think she's cute when she's giving orders." He reached over and stroked the back of my neck. It made me want to purr.

We pulled up by the semicrushed SUV. Reader was a few moments behind us. The Humvee was covered with goo. "Can James get out of there safely?"

"Ummm ... I'm not sure." Christopher sounded much less than not sure.

"Paul?"

"Yes, Kitty?"

"How much heat can a Humvee withstand?"

Silence.

"You're not going to suggest what I think you are, are you, girlfriend?"

"Yes, she is," Gower's voice came back. "It can withstand the water, but it'll be hot as hell in there, Jamie."

Jamie? It was a cute pet name. But it occurred to me that the danger we were in had to be higher than I thought, if Gower was using it over a wideband intercom system.

"Why me?" Reader asked. "I know, because the humans have to stick together." He barreled off toward the mass of superbeing flesh on the ground.

As he did so, the jets started firing at what was left of the Killer. I could see them hitting, and the thing started to disintegrate. "Bullets work on that."

"Wish we'd known that earlier," Reader said.

"It's only working because you weakened it so much, James. It's superstructure was damaged by the repeated—"

"Lorraine? Hon? I don't care right now as I'm heading for the boiling carwash."

Reader reached the mass of dying fugly just as the first plane dropped a load of boiling water onto the area. The Serpent writhed and screamed—a sound best not described, ever.

The second plane dropped its load. The Serpent bubbled, writhed, and screamed some more, and the Humvee seemed clean. But it wasn't leaving the area. A third plane dumped water and the Serpent exploded.

There were cheers from the various aircraft. But the Humvee wasn't moving.

A scary thought occurred to me. "At what heat level does rubber melt?"

CHAPTER 45

THE BEDLAM STARTED, with a lot of male voices talking over each other. I tried to make out what the girls might be adding, but I couldn't. The men in my car were suggesting their thoughts as well. What no one was doing was offering any kind of idea if Reader was stuck, trapped, alive, dead, or dying.

My mother had always told me that in a panic situation, the person who can stay calm and be prepared was the one most likely to live and help others live. I put my earphones on and tuned my iPod to the song I wanted to hear. In this case, I wasn't going with the tried and true—I was going with what I considered the best hard rock song ever made.

Martini was leaning forward, barking orders into the intercom, so he wasn't paying any attention to me. I slipped out of the car and started running toward the mass of exploded and melted superbeing parts, Metallica's "Enter Sandman" revving in my ears.

I had an aerosol in each hand, but it wasn't too much of a problem. It might be hot, but I'd run track in high school and college in Pueblo Caliente—running in the midafternoon in the middle of a huge desert with the sun burning down wasn't hot to me, it was normal. Sprinters had to run distance to build endurance, and my sadistic high school coach had made sure we learned to hold batons in either hand for relay training. My purse was an unhelpful addition, but I was more used to having it on than not.

There were fugly parts all over, and the ground was muddy. No worries. I'd had to run in the monsoon season, and I was a hurdler. I was one of those rarities with a perfect four-step, so I'd had to learn to hurdle with either leg leading.

I felt the ground pound and figured Mephistopheles was behind me. I didn't turn around. Runners who turn around lose their race. "Enter Sandman" was a great song to run to—excellent beat, lyrics discussing the scary thing trying to kill you. I hadn't realized it was based on real life before, but you learned something new every day.

The ground was slippery and gross, and the smell was unreal. I'd thought Earwig was bad, but this was worse, all decayed body and boiled meat. I wondered if this was what haggis smelled like and vowed never to find out.

The pounding was getting closer, but I was almost to the Humvee. It wasn't shimmering, and if the tires weren't melted, they were stuck in the sandy mud.

I might never cook willingly, but I knew how. Experience told me metal that had had tons of boiling hot water poured onto it would be boiling hot. I skidded up to the driver's door and sprayed the handle with the trusty Ever-Hold. I used the whole can, focusing on the door handle but also the lock.

I threw the can behind me and wrenched the door open. Reader fell out. I managed to get under him and keep him in the seat and off the ground. He was unconscious but breathing. I sprayed another can in his face.

"Ugh!" His eyes flickered and opened. "What the hell are you doing?"

The ground shook. "Trying to save the only person I can relate to."

He managed a weak grin. "I'm not joking—if I were straight, we'd just run off, get married, and forget we ever knew Alpha Centauri had populated planets."

"Stop making me long for the impossible. Can you move? The big fugly's coming, and we're targets numbers one and two."

He nodded, and I helped him out of the car and put his arm around my shoulders, keeping him on the side opposite my purse. "Here, take a weapon." I shoved an aerosol into his free hand.

"Oh, God."

I looked where Reader was staring. Sure enough, there was my favorite fugly, standing in front of us.

"Hey, Clifford the Big Red Monster! Get out of my way."

Mephistopheles leaned down, and his eyes changed. "You don't fear me. Why?"

Good question. I had no idea. "Because you're stupid?" I sprayed his face.

Reader reacted at the same time and also got Mephistopheles full in the kisser, to use that term loosely when applied in this case.

"Gaaaahhhh!" Mephistopheles staggered backward, clawing at his face.

"Time to move." I dragged Reader in the opposite direction.

"If we don't find and destroy the parasites, all this was for nothing."

I hated it, but he was right. "Okay, eyes peeled, spray cans at the ready." I tried not to think about how fast Mephistopheles was going to recover. I couldn't move quickly with Reader hanging on me, and it was clear he couldn't move without me.

Jets flew over our heads, bullets spraying. They ricocheted off Mephistopheles. "I think I can move faster," Reader said.

"Good, let's try trotting." We moved a little better, but there was a lot of Fugly Stew on the ground.

My walkie crackled. "Kitty, go to your right about fifty feet. The first parasite's been spotted there." Lorraine sounded tense. "It's still moving, so be ready. It'll try to connect with you or James."

"Oh, good." We moved the way Lorraine told us. Mephistopheles was being driven away from us by the jets. "I'm kind of glad they stuck around."

"Yeah. Pilots are short, you know."

"You sound jealous. I'm touched, and wondering if you're feeling okay."

Reader managed a laugh. "Just protecting Jeff's interests." He leaned his head against mine. "You two okay?"

"I think so. Hard to be positive, but he seems like himself again."

"Good." Reader stopped. "Look, do you see something moving?"

I stared where he was pointing. There was a curved carcass section in front of us forming what looked like a dead meat tent. I could see something shimmer in it, just for a moment. "Yeah, I think we have a target." I unhooked Reader from my shoulders. "You stay here. You're okay to stand?"

"Yeah." He reached into my purse and grabbed another aerosol. "I like to shoot two-handed."

"Me, too." I switched my music back to Aerosmith, "Toys in the Attic" album, and followed his example. "Okay, stay alert." Ahhh, nothing like my boys in my ears to make it all seem better.

I edged forward. I knew I didn't want to get too close, because these things could move. So I approached it as I would a snake—really slowly with my weapon held far out in front of me, ready to leap away and run at a moment's notice.

I reached aerosol range and started spraying as I moved forward about an inch at a time. I was at what now looked like a cave entrance, and I had the unenviable choice of dropping to my hands and knees to take a look inside or tossing the carcass part over. I wanted to do neither.

The ground shook, and I risked a look over my shoulder. Mephistopheles was heading for us, batting jets away. I decided touching the carcass was the lesser of two evils, and fear gave me that extra shot of adrenaline. I flipped it. It felt exactly as I imagined a boiled and burned giant rubber monster would feel. I managed to keep gagging to a minimum.

The parasite was there, still alive and moving. In fact, by the time I had the dead meat moved, it was on my foot. I didn't scream—I was too busy spraying with both hands. It didn't stop it, but it did release my foot.

One can was empty, and I tossed it aside as I leaped backward. I dug through my purse for the Glock. There it was, and I realized I'd never set the safety. I decided to consider this a great example of forethought rather than my being the stupidest gun handler on the planet.

Aimed, shot, scored. I was getting good with this thing. Either terror, genetics, or the combination were ensuring I could indeed hit what I wanted. I didn't have to empty the full clip this time. The parasite broke apart after six shots, and I sprayed the rest of it until it dissolved and bubbled away.

This didn't take too long, which was a good thing. "Ah, girlfriend? I think we're in trouble again."

I spun around to see Mephistopheles bat a jet out of the air as he moved toward us. The jet spun out of control and smashed into the ground about a mile away. I knew without asking that the pilot, and any passengers he might have had with him, didn't have a chance.

I hadn't seen any of them in person, didn't know their names, but they were my guys. And the chance that Lorraine or Claudia was in that jet was high, and they were my friends, even though I'd only known them a day. It was stupid, but I got mad, madder than I'd ever been before. And just like at JFK, I ran right toward Mephistopheles. I didn't shout or speak, I just ran, as if I were in the Olympics and he was the gold medal.

He saw me coming, this huge monster. I expected him to try to stomp me or catch me. But instead he spoke. "It's not over." And then he turned and ran.

I kept after him, but he built up speed and lifted off the ground, wings flapping. He could really book when he was flying, and he outdistanced the jets quickly. I stopped running, dropped the Glock back into my purse, ripped my headphones off, and pulled out the walkie. "I want everyone to disengage right now!"

"Yes, Miss Katt." It was White.

"Who died?" I was shaking, but I wasn't crying yet.

"One of the pilots. Both Lorraine and Claudia are safe; their pilots didn't engage because the girls were with them."

"Who was he?"

"Lieutenant William Cox," Gower answered.

"What do we do for his family?" Silence. "What do we do? Goddamn it, what the hell do we do for them?" I was screaming now.

Someone grabbed me and pulled me to him. "Shhh, baby, shhh." Martini shoved my face into his chest. "Everyone who works with us knows the risks. It'll be handled."

I pulled away from him. "How can you be so cavalier about it? He's dead!"

Martini put his hands on my shoulders and gave me a little shake. "Look at me. No, right at me, Kitty." He waited until our eyes were locked. "This is what we do. Every day of our lives. You want to know why we don't want our women out here? Now you know, in the harshest way possible. Old-fashioned? Yes. But we don't have an entire population to draw from. We lose one girl, we lose reproduction, and that heads us that much faster toward extinction. Every single one of us who works in the field knows the risks. Every one of your military personnel knows also. Maybe their families don't, maybe their families don't understand, but the fighting men and women who work with us do. No one comes to assist us who isn't trained for extraterrestrial situations, and no one comes who isn't prepared to die."

"No one's prepared to die. People pretend, but no one's ready for it."

"We'll argue that later. Right now, you have to get yourself under control. You're the leader, right? The leader has to keep it together, or everyone else falls apart. It sucks, but that's how it is."

I looked up at him. He'd been doing this his whole life, he and Christopher both. No wonder they were exhausted. "Who was he?"

Martini understood what I was asking. "He was the one you liked, the one who called you ma'am."

CHAPTER 46

WANTED TO CRY—my eyes were certainly filled with tears. But I didn't let them fall. Because Cox had thought I was his superior officer, and I knew Martini was right—Cox wouldn't have wanted his superior to break down while still engaged with the enemy. "Let's find the last two parasites."

Martini nodded. "That's my girl." He put his hand to my chin. "It's a war, baby. You have to remember that."

"But I don't have to like it."

"None of us like it." He gave me a small smile. "If we enjoyed it, we'd be like what we're fighting against."

I nodded. "Let's go."

I had two aerosols left, and I gave one to Martini and took the other for myself. I also got the Glock out again. We headed back toward Reader, both looking for anything that might be a parasite or parasite parts. But we didn't spot a thing.

Reader hugged me when we got back to him. "We'll talk about it when we get back, okay?" he said quietly.

"Sure." I leaned my head on his shoulder. It was a comfortable place to be.

Martini cleared his throat. "Still more than a little jealous over here."

Reader chuckled as I moved away from him. "You should be, Jeff. If I ever go straight or bi, I'm stealing her away from you."

"I'll keep it in mind." Martini pulled me next to him. "That's better."

I forced myself to focus. "How are we going to find the other two parasites?"

My walkie crackled again. Claudia's voice came on. At least, I was pretty sure it was her voice, filtered through tears. "We've found the next one. It's about half a mile from where you are, to your right. We're hovering over it."

More than anything else, this snapped me back. Cox flew with these guys, and they were still doing their jobs. So I had to do mine. "Thanks, Claudia. Talk us to it if we get off track."

"Will do."

The three of us headed toward the jet. "Are we heading toward the Killer's area?"

"Yeah, girlfriend, we are. Jeff, you sure you should be walking around here?"

"Well, I could let the two of you face it alone, but since I'm not an armchair commander, I think I'll come along."

"Can whatever the Killer sprayed out get to us through our shoes?" I didn't like the sound of this.

"We don't know," Martini answered.

I stopped walking. "Hang on." I pulled out the walkie. "Lorraine, I need a lift."

Someone sniffled. "Okay. We'll be right there." Well, all three of us were getting trained in what this was like. I wondered if we'd ever be the same again, and I knew the answer.

"Me, not you," Martini snapped.

"Ha. You, as has been proved, can catch me. I know I can't catch you. Plus, I had the most sadistic track coaches in the history of the sport. I can climb a rope."

"So can I." He sounded a tad defensive.

"Good to know. We can play Tarzan and Jane later, then."

"Have I mentioned lately that you're the perfect woman?"

"Not often enough these past few hours." The jet was above us, and it was hard to hear. Wet sand and fugly parts were starting to flip around. "See if you can spot number three," I shouted to them as I put my iPod and the aerosol back into my purse. I pulled out another clip and put it into the back pocket of my jeans. I considered putting the safety on, but I realized I couldn't get it off without two hands, so foolhardy was going to continue to be the watchword of the day. I stuck the Glock into the front of my pants and prayed it wouldn't slip out or go off.

Martini lifted me; I grabbed the end of the cable and moved up until I could hold on with my legs and feet as well. I could see Reader talking into his walkie, and then we flew off.

It was an interesting view. The parts were spread what I guessed was at least a mile in radius, maybe more. Added to this were the carcasses of Earwig and the remains of the Slug, looking gray and greasy. It was easily the most repulsive sight I'd ever seen. And even high up the place stank beyond belief.

My jet moved next to the one Claudia was in, and they sheared off. We were hovering, and I had to look closely. Finally I spotted it, moving like a big, fat worm. It was trying to get away. I would have felt pity, but there were lots of mammals in the desert, and the idea of some poor coyote getting turned into something like the Killer seemed like the height of cruelty to animals. In the fight between their world and mine, I was always going to pick mine.

I aimed the Glock and fired. I missed, but I did hit the ground right in front of the parasite. It stopped moving and turned around. It didn't have eyes, but I could feel it looking at me. I fired again, but I wasn't hitting it.

Someone must have told Lorraine I was having trouble, because the jet started to lower slowly. I had no idea how long the pilot could keep us hovering like this, but I had to guess not too long. I emptied the clip and managed to hit the parasite once. Not enough.

I dropped the clip out and watched as it fell right onto the parasite. The clip was engulfed and didn't show up again. I got the feeling this parasite was doing whatever its kind did when they wanted to indicate that their opponent was being invited to "bring it."

Now for the really tricky part. I shoved the Glock back into my pants and reached back for the clip. No matter how much I wanted to do it otherwise, I was going to have to use two hands to put the new clip in.

I considered my options. My legs were well wrapped around the cable. Way back when, I used to practice hanging upside down from the rope. Never when the coach was around, of course. But several of my boyfriends had thought it was the coolest thing in the world. Of course, I was pretty limber in school, and this particular skill hadn't been used for longer than I wanted to ponder. However, it would allow me to load the gun and possibly get a better shot at the same time.

I slid my purse over and down, so it was around my body, hooked just above my knees. Then I took the Glock out of my pants, effectively letting go of the cable, and leaned backward. I couldn't get my head to my heels any more, but it was close enough. I loaded the clip into the gun—it was weird but not impossible.

I had to focus to find the parasite. It had moved right under me. I had fifteen shots, it had a lot of malevolence. Evenly matched.

The jet wasn't steady, but I was getting used to the movement. I forced myself to relax, even though it looked as though the parasite was getting ready to leap. Why I thought that I couldn't say, but the feeling was strong, and I didn't argue with it.

I aimed and started firing. I hit it several times. It needed more shots than the one in Earwig had. I emptied the clip, and the thing was torn up but still alive. I shoved the Glock back into my pants and tucked my shirt in to keep it from moving. Then I felt around in my purse for the half-full aerosol can.

I pulled it out and started spraying. Nothing, too far away. I considered my options as I went back to upright. My stomach muscles complained, and I got a head-rush, but I got back up without slipping. Oh, well, nothing for it.

Holding on tightly to the cable, I shifted my legs and let my purse drop. Direct hit! The parasite splatted and burst apart as if it were a water balloon. Now my choice was to drop down or hang on. Conveniently, my arms shared that they were tired by having my hands release without my brain's consent.

I went down, but just as before, I didn't hit the ground. "I hate it when you do that," Martini said as his arms wrapped around me.

"I'll keep it in mind. Should you be standing on this stuff?"

"Probably not." He shifted me to one arm, and I wrapped my legs around his waist. He pulled my torso toward him and kissed me. "God, I love it when you do that."

"Focus. Spray the parts." I did my best not to grind against his hip, but escaping death was something of a turn-on.

He grinned but did what he'd been told to do. He sprayed my purse, too, then handed it to me and sprayed the bottom. "Guess that thing's wrecked."

"Hardly. It's cheap leather remember? It survives everything."

"Okay, all the parts are gone."

I looked down. "Jeff? Your shoes are starting to smoke."

He moved, and we were back to hyperspeed. He stopped the moment we were away from the Killer's remains. He let me down and then dropped to his knees. "I don't feel so good."

I grabbed an aerosol and sprayed the bottoms of his shoes. They stopped smoking. "It didn't get through the soles. I think you're okay." He was leaning, his hands on his thighs, head down, panting. "Jeff? Are you okay?"

"Overstrained."

"I'm not that heavy."

"No, you're not. I've just pushed it well past my normal limits today."

My walkie crackled again. "Kitty, James found the last parasite," Claudia informed me. "It was dead, but he sprayed it until it dissolved."

I dug the walkie out. Nothing inside was wet or even damp. I loved my purse. "Does that mean we can get out of here?"

"On our way to pick you up," Christopher replied. "Just stay where you are."

"No worries there," Martini said. I stroked his head, and he leaned into my stomach. "Ouch. Can you put your gun away?"

I tossed it into my purse and leaned his head back against me. He wrapped his arms around my waist. I rubbed the back of his neck. "He said it wasn't over."

"I know. But it's over for right now, and you learn to

take the break when you get it." He moved my shirt up and kissed my stomach.

"Jeff, they'll be here in a second." Not that I actually wanted him to stop, but I didn't think this was the place to get intimate.

"Mmmm, right." He ran his tongue around my navel and then slid my shirt back down. "Fine, I'll behave."

"Nah," I said as I moved his head and bent down to kiss him. "I like you just like you are."

The SUV pulled up next to us a few minutes later, and Christopher and Reader got out. "Jeff, is this really the right place?" Christopher sounded exasperated.

"He's exhausted."

"What she said," Martini added, head back to resting against my stomach.

Reader grinned, and Christopher rolled his eyes. They got on either side of Martini and hauled him into the front seat of the SUV. I crawled into the back, and they got in on either side of me. We started off. "What about the rest of the supplies?"

"Already moved them to our vehicle," Tim told me. "Took care of it while you were auditioning for Cirque de Soleil."

"She got my vote," Martini said, head leaned back. He sounded as though he was going to collapse.

Christopher spoke into his walkie. "We need medical ready for Jeff as soon as we get back. Standard procedures."

"Already waiting," Gower replied. "How's everybody else?" I could hear the fear lurking in his voice.

"No one bothered to let him know James was okay?"

"Been a bit busy," Christopher snapped.

Reader laughed. "I already talked to him." He spoke into his walkie. "Everyone's fine, Paul. I don't want to go into a sauna for a long time, though."

"Where are the girls?"

"They're being taken back to Home Base. All the jets are going with them." Christopher spoke into the walkie again. "We need massive cleanup out here. It's unreal. Parts of it are definitely toxic."

"Roger that, Commander," a voice I didn't recognize replied. "We have our top disposal teams en route. They'll be there before sunset, so plenty of time to set up. We'll get it cleared overnight."

"Good luck with that." Christopher shook his head. "If they can get it done before morning, it'll be a miracle."

"Does it matter if they don't?"

"Only if Mephistopheles comes back," he replied tersely.

I thought about it. "He won't. He's scared."

"Of what?"

"Of Kitty," Reader answered. "He ran away when she charged him."

"He's a superbeing, but he's not stupid." Martini sounded as though he was going to pass out.

"What's wrong with Jeff?" I tried to keep my voice calm, but I couldn't.

"He'll be fine," Christopher said only somewhat reassuringly. "He gets like this if he's gone too long without regeneration."

"How often does that happen?"

"Oh, once a month, month and a half," Martini said. "Old hat." I didn't believe him, mostly because Christopher's eyes were saying that they were both lying. I tried not to think about what Reader had told me in the limo, but it was hard not to—Martini was burned out, and that meant his condition was going to deteriorate fast.

We reached the gate, or at least where I thought the gate was. I couldn't see anything that looked like a doorway, but there was a shimmering in front of us, and it looked doorlike.

Tim stopped the car, hit the intercom and spoke. "You ready for us?"

"Need a couple more minutes; you've got something funny on the car." Gower sounded confused. Tim put the car into park.

I'd grown up hearing about guerilla fighting. I hadn't realized my parents had been speaking from experience, but they'd sure trained me for what to look for. "Everybody out of the car, *now*!" I shoved past Reader, opened his door and pushed him out. He'd been on the passenger side, and I scrambled after him. The other three were staring at me.

I reached in, grabbed Christopher, and pulled with all my might. He flew out. Reader was pulling Martini out. "Tim, move your ass!"

"Christopher, help me, *now*!" Reader had one of Martini's arms over his shoulders, but he couldn't move. Christopher stopped arguing and grabbed Martini's other arm. They ran for the gate.

Tim was getting out but too slowly. I ran around and grabbed him, dragging him toward the gate. "What the hell is wrong with you?" he asked, sounding a lot like Christopher.

"Yates is a terrorist, you moron!" Tim blanched, grabbed my hand, and we started to run as fast as we could. The others were in front of us, but too far from the gate. "We hit them and use the momentum."

"You got it, boss." Tim let go of my hand, and we barreled toward the others. We hit at the same time, and the three of them went flying through the gate. I broke the cardinal rule and looked behind me. The car exploded, and parts were flying straight toward me. Just before a section of the engine hit my face, someone grabbed my purse and pulled.

CHAPTER 47

I TUMBLED ONTO THE FLOOR, onto a heap of men. Tim's hand was connected to my purse, but I disentangled it. Under most circumstances, I wouldn't have minded being on top of the hunky mountain in the least. But I could tell Martini was on the bottom of the dog pile.

I scrambled to my feet, relieved I still had feet, let alone the rest of me. There were people all around us, most of them helping the menfolk up. There was a gurney, and Martini was loaded onto it. I got shoved away from him by a press of official-looking people I'd never laid eyes on before. Some were in suits, but not Armani suits, some were in uniform, and all of them looked deadly serious.

Reader was flung onto a gurney as well, despite his protests. I saw more gurneys coming and decided escape was the better part of valor. I wanted to be with Martini, but not if that meant being hooked up to an IV or sitting in some medical tube having brain X-rays taken.

I backed away right into two sets of ham-hands. "This one, too?" some man I'd never heard before asked.

"Let me go!" I started to kick. Which got me picked up by the waist. Martini did this a lot better.

"We need a sedative over here!" my other captor barked.

From my vantage point I saw Tim and Christopher both get the gurney treatment. Christopher in particular was arguing with this, but he was outnumbered. I couldn't believe this was normal.

"What in the Sam Hill is going on here?" The voice was loud, furious, and filled with authority. It was also a voice I'd heard all my life.

My mother strode into the room, flanked by White and Gower. "I asked a question, and I expect an answer." She was practically snarling, and she looked as though she was ready to take out every person within range—and she looked as though she could do it. She was wearing black pants, a shirt, and a shoulder holster, complete with gun. She was also wearing a black cap that had the letters P.T.C.U. on it.

"Who the hell are you, lady?" the man holding me asked.

Mom stalked up to him. "I happen to be the head of the Presidential Terrorism Control Unit, and unless you put this young lady down, you will be the head of janitorial services in Nome, Alaska, by tomorrow morning." She stuck her badge right up in his face. Her gun was somehow at his head, too. I was overwhelmingly impressed. I wondered if she'd teach me how to do this.

I was dropped to the ground, and I managed to land somewhat on my feet.

"You don't have authority here," the other man who'd grabbed me started to protest.

Mom smiled, and it was the most intimidating thing I'd ever seen. I studied it—a smile like this would come in handy. "You don't think I have the authority? No problem. Call the White House and ask about my authority. You'll need to speak directly to the President, of course. Let's see . . . think he'll take your call or mine?"

"We're C.I.A. We have authority here."

"Actually, this is NASA's jurisdiction," my father's voice came from behind us. "We have a joint agreement with the Centaurion Division, and you're in violation of every code we have. Additionally," he added pleasantly, "since your department answers to the P.T.C.U., not the other way around, you have no authority whatsoever in this situation." Dad moved up next to Mom and looked around. "And my, my, my . . . we certainly have a situation here. Oh, let the men who aren't hurt up, and, please, someone make sure our friends at the C.I.A. aren't taking Commander Martini off somewhere we wouldn't like him to be."

I'd seen where they'd shoved his gurney, and I took off running. To find Claudia, Lorraine, and two good-looking guys in uniform blocking the gurney from being taken out of the building.

I skidded to a stop. "P.T.C.U. has authority here. Get your goddamned hands off of him, or I'll break your necks."

The three people trying to kidnap Martini glared at me, but they backed away. I didn't have to turn around to know there were guns pointed at them.

"We're somewhat pacifistic," White said from behind me. "But we're getting quite angry, and it's amazing how anger clouds judgment."

Lorraine and Claudia moved to Martini now. "We need to get him to medical, stat," Lorraine said. She looked at their pilots. "Can you come with us for protection?"

"Absolutely," the one I assumed was her guy said with a smile. "You're our top priority, according to our orders." He looked over at the C.I.A. team. "And our orders over-rule yours, cowboys."

I wasn't sure if I should go with them or not. Martini grabbed my hand. "Stay here and sort it out. That's what the leader does."

I bit my lip. "Jeff, are you going to be okay?"

He managed a weak smile. "Sure. I told you, happens all the time."

I didn't even have to look at the girls to know he was lying. "Okay, I'll be down to see you as soon as I can."

He closed his eyes. "See you in about twelve hours, baby."

Claudia nodded. "We have to go, Kitty. Now."

"Okay, call on the walkie if anyone else tries to kidnap any of you."

They nodded and raced off. I could see the elevator banks off in the distance, but they didn't look like the ones at the Science Center. I turned around. Yep, there were a lot of guns being pointed. I decided getting behind them would be a really intelligent idea.

"We're at Home Base?" I asked White as I slid around him.

"Yes, we needed to call in too much military."

"Where did they take James and Christopher?"

"We have James back in our control; he's headed to the hospital wing. Christopher insists that he and Tim are fine, so they're still here."

Someone tapped my shoulder. "Need you back here," Christopher said as he pulled me away.

We got away from the crush of bodies. "Are they going back to the Science Center?"

"Yes, it's safer there, by a long shot. I sent Tim along to look after James, just in case." He looked at me intently. "How did you know? That the car was rigged, I mean?"

"Yates is a terrorist, and car bombs are to terrorists like groupies are to rock and roll—you rarely get one without the other."

"How'd he put it on?" Christopher looked worried. I didn't blame him.

"Someone planted it."

Christopher looked around and moved us into a more quiet area. "Okay, wasn't me, Jeff, or James. I know it wouldn't be Lorraine or Claudia. I have a really hard time believing it was you."

"The military personnel were never out of their planes. And Mephistopheles was only close enough to the car he smooshed. I think we'd have noticed if he'd been close to the other car."

"So it was Tim." Christopher looked upset and sick.

"Maybe." I thought about it. "He left the car last, and slowly. If he'd reacted before I did, or immediately, I'd have an easier time believing it. And he's the one who pulled me through the gate. Again, hard to believe he'd do that if he'd planted the bomb."

"Who, then?"

"Someone at the Science Center, maybe. If the bomb was distance activated, it might not have shown up on the sensors until we were coming back. After all, if the fuglies killed us, no need to blow us up." I thought about it some more. "Are all the A-Cs trustworthy?"

"Of course." He sounded offended.

"That's always a foolish assumption," Mom said from behind me. "Someone let the C.I.A. in, too. I was with Richard and Paul the whole time—believe me, they didn't call for this kind of support."

Christopher nodded. "We deal with the C.I.A. all the time, but Jeff and I do that, no one else, and we're the only ones authorized to call them in."

"Under normal circumstances, you mean. You know, when a traitor isn't mucking up the status quo. We're back to my question: Who doesn't want Mephistopheles destroyed?"

"Who would have a motive?" Christopher was upset, not that I could blame him. "We're here to stop the parasites, not help them."

"Where's Dad?"

"Kitty, your father is not the traitor."

"I know that. I need to ask Dad something."

Mom looked around. "Sol! Over here."

Dad trotted over. "What's going on? Have you figured out who the mole is?" The way he asked, it was clear my parents had discussed this and were both confident the operation had been infiltrated.

"No, Dad, I need to ask you something."

"Sure, kitten. Shoot."

"Christopher, I need to ask you things too." I could see it, forming in my mind. It wasn't pretty, but then again, in one sense it was.

"Waiting with bated breath." He could still snark under pressure. Nice to know.

"Dad, would you say it was common or unusual for a cryptologist not to triple-check their work before declaring it complete?"

He thought about it. "Rare, at least here. You have to prove you're right to too many different organizations not to do a variety of tests."

"But the A-Cs only have one organization to report to." I looked at Christopher. He was pale. "Was Beverly on the original translation project?" He nodded. "Is she considered your generation or your father's?"

"My father's." He swallowed. "And, before you ask, yes—she's one of the few who knows the truth about Yates."

"She's going to kill Jeff and probably James, maybe the others. We have to go, *now*. Mom, Dad, get rid of the C.I.A. and then figure out how to follow us."

Christopher grabbed my hand and we ran at hyperspeed to a gate. But the operators were fiddling with it. "What's wrong?" Christopher barked.

"We're blocked from the Science Center. Some kind of interference. It's affected all the gates."

"Did the teams with Martini and Reader make it back to the Science Center?" I asked.

"Yes, they did."

Christopher cursed. "We're too far for me to run us there."

I thought about it. "I know you can't actually fly a plane, but do you know how?"

"Yes, we all learned, just in case. I could tell someone how to fly, but I can't do it myself."

"Oh, good."

He stared at me. "You're not suggesting what I think you are, are you?"

"We don't, they die."

"You ever flown something before?"

I answered honestly. "I hold the highest score at A.S.U. for *Star Wars: Starfighter.*"

"I know, beyond a shadow of a doubt, that I'm going to regret this."

CHAPTER 48

WE ARGUED ABOUT ASKING for a human pilot as we ran to the jets. Since we were at Area 51, we actually had a lot of choices in terms of aircraft. Of course, since my pointing out that we couldn't trust anyone right now won the trained-human-pilot argument rather effectively, we needed an aircraft that Christopher technically knew how to fly, was fueled up, and could hold both of us.

We made do with one that he was familiar with, was fueled up, and could hold me on Christopher's lap. I tried not to consider Martini's reaction to this—I had to figure saving his life would outweigh unintentional snuggling with his cousin.

Christopher pulled some rank, and we climbed in. I could see why pilots weren't tall—there wasn't a lot of room in there.

"Do we have to have your purse in here with us?"

"It's more reliable than anything else." A thought occurred, and I dug out the walkie. "Lorraine, Claudia? You there?"

Silence. Nothing from Reader, either. I dropped the walkie back into my purse.

"Okay, let's do this," Christopher said briskly.

We put on a set of headphones each, he pointed out the buttons to hit to close the lid, start the engine, and so on. I did my best to focus on the instructions and not the thought that we could go splat at any second, as soon as I started trying to fly. The sound through the headphones was pretty good, but not as good as the intercom system in the cars had been.

"Okay, you're going to pull back on the stick. Remember, it works sort of opposite from what you'd expect."

"I've seen the movies."

"Well, don't I feel all confident now?"

"It's all down to the reflexes and your ability to teach."

"I wish we'd said good-bye to our parents."

"We'll be fine, Mr. Optimism."

"I want to be on record that this brings my tally for saving Jeff's butt even with his saving mine."

"I'll be sure to note it in my report."

Christopher wrapped an arm around my waist. I decided not to notice. "You ready?" He was trying to sound calm and confident. Key word was "trying."

Sort of. "Yes."

"Then let's go."

It was different. I'd seen scenes in the movies where someone who doesn't know how to fly, or hasn't flown in years, takes a jet and manages to get off the ground. I discovered these movies were documentaries.

We lifted up and then bobbed. "Back! Pull it back!"

"It's hard."

"The ground is harder!"

"Fine!" I pulled in the directions he shouted and grabbed or pushed the things he pointed frantically to, the ones he wasn't doing himself. Abbott and Costello had nothing on the two of us. As the jet started to bounce and spin around while somehow moving upward, I saw servicemen running away from us. I found that a rude comment on my skills.

We managed to get up above the other planes, then above the buildings. Once we were higher, it got easier, and Christopher's directions got calmer. "You ready?" he asked once we were up and facing the right direction. It had taken only a few turns to get there, and I was feeling pretty good.

"Sure."

"Okay, let's go."

I pushed the stick how he told me, and suddenly we were flying, really flying. I was shoved back against him in a way I knew Martini wouldn't appreciate. However, there was no way Christopher was enjoying it—his face was being squished.

This made it hard for him to give directions or me to hear them. On the other hand, time was of the essence. He'd made it clear that the nose of the jet shouldn't dip below some red line on the instrument panel, and I was doing very well. At least, I'd managed to avoid the buildings, other jets, and birds in the air. *Starfighter* was good training for this part.

"Just like a video game," I shouted to Christopher.

"Mmgh!" He managed to move his head. "I don't think video games can kill you."

"You don't go to movies much, do you?"

"Never. By the way, landing's the hard part."

Oh, good. "No chance you can do that, right?"

"Sure, if we want to die for certain, just give me the stick."

"Why so? I mean, really why?"

"It takes concentration or exhaustion for us to function at human levels. If we're tense, our reflexes take over, and we overstress the machinery. Believe me, they did a lot of tests when we first arrived here. We're trained from birth to slow down while walking, eating, talking, all those normal things. But flying isn't normal, it's a learned skill, and we haven't successfully learned to not overreact in terms of the machinery's ability to handle it."

"I'd guess you're too stressed to land the jet, right?"

"I'm too stressed to operate an espresso machine, let alone a jet. And I'm not tired enough. We have to be at near collapse, like Jeff was, to have a shot."

"Okay, no worries. Just checking." Sure, I was lying, but he didn't need to know that.

"We're almost there." He pointed to a very low-key complex in the middle of nowhere. It didn't look military, scientific, or even interesting. Without a doubt, this was the Science Center. "Okay, the nose needs to point down, so we have to go under the red line."

"You told me to never go under the red line."

"While we want to go up or fly, yes. Now we want to go down and land, so we go under the red line."

"You said under the red line was bad."

"Kitty!"

"Fine, fine." I eased off on the stick and, amazingly, we went under the red line, at least as far as the instrument panel was concerned.

"Pull up! Pull UP!"

I did. It was impossible not to with him screaming in my ears. "What's wrong now?"

"Under the red line means just a bit under, not nose-diving!"

The radio crackled. "Unidentified aircraft, you are not cleared to land."

"Who was that?"

"No one I recognize." Christopher pointed. "There's open desert. Let's land and then I'll run us back."

"You don't think I can land at the Center?"

"I think it's been taken over by hostiles."

"Oh, um, good point." On the plus side, there wasn't a lot of concrete in the area Christopher was directing us to. On the downside, if we crashed, it seemed unlikely anyone was going to come to rescue us. Ergo, I had to be sure we didn't crash.

A part of me wanted to do this with my eyes closed, but most of me wanted to survive, so I listened to his instructions and did my best to do exactly what he said. "Wheels down." I flipped the switch and we felt the machinery move. "Good. Now, the next part's the hardest, but people with less skill than you do it every day."

"You're not great with the idea of building confidence, are you?"

"I think you're the most amazing woman I've ever met," he said quietly. "And if Jeff ever hurts you, I'll kill him."

"Oh." I didn't know what to say. "I think you're totally hot and incredibly appealing even when you're being snarky, but I also think I'm falling in love with your cousin, and if I kiss you, he'll never speak to me again" probably wasn't destined to be the greatest line in the history of romantic entanglements.

He squeezed my waist. "It's okay. Let's get this jet safely on the ground and then go save everyone."

"Sounds like a workable plan." I took a deep breath. "Ready."

"We need to bank and come around, we've overshot." No problem, *Starfighter* training handled it. "Now, we're back to easing down. Good, Kitty, that's good. Even up a little . . . right . . . now down again . . . good."

It went on like this until we were close to the ground. "This is the hard part." I refrained from comment. "As we get down, you have to pull back up, just a bit, so only the tires hit the ground."

"Christopher? If we die, I just want to say that I really like you."

"Thanks, Kitty, I really like you, too." We sounded like junior high kids, but I just didn't want to die without saying something nice to the person who'd be dying with me. His arm tightened around me. "Okay, almost there."

The ground came up fast, and I did what he'd told me, started pulling up just a bit. The tires touched, and we bounced—high. The stick got hard to control, and we hit the ground again. I fought the stick, but it was winning. "Now what?"

He put his free hand over mine. "Now we find out if anyone up there likes us."

"Oh, great."

Christopher was trying to move the stick, and I wasn't sure I should let him. "That's good, fight it," he said, through clenched teeth. "You're slowing me down."

He pulled us up, and we were airborne again, going a bit too fast. I pushed against him harder, and we slowed down, banked, and then dived again. "I thought you said nose dives were bad!"

"You're not fighting hard enough."

I increased pressure again, and we pulled out of the nose dive a bit. Something was flashing on one of the monitors. "Um, Christopher? What's that screen?" I pointed at it with my nose.

"Oh, hell." He pulled the stick hard, and we went up, spinning. "Fight it, Kitty, those are missiles heading for us."

CHAPTER 49

AS IF THINGS DIDN'T SUCK QUITE ENOUGH. I wasn't sure what we were going to do, but avoiding the missiles sounded like the best idea. Christopher was yanking on the stick, and I realized he hadn't been kidding—he was causing the jet to do things I was pretty sure it wasn't supposed to.

It required a lot of strength, but I managed to counter him. I shifted a bit so he could see the monitor. He moved the stick hard, and we banked to the right. As I countered, a missile whizzed past us.

"This is a lot more fun to watch than to experience."

"How many unfriendlies do we have?" Christopher's tone was brisk. He had his Commander hat on. I decided not to argue.

"If the flashing red dots are any indication, we have four."

"Great."

We kept on managing to dodge, but we weren't lucking out like they did in the movies. We also hadn't put on parachutes. "Where's our miraculous backup coming from?"

Christopher managed to laugh. It was a bitter laugh, sure, but still, a laugh. "I don't think we have backup, Kitty, unless you count the missiles."

No sooner had he said this than the missile on our tail exploded. I looked back at the screen. "There are three green dots now." I looked around—Americans actually marked their radio buttons. I hit it, hoping it worked like the intercom had. "Hello?"

"Commander White, HQ requests you advise us the next time you and Miss Katt decide to take flight." That voice sounded familiar.

"Hey, were you just fighting the fuglies with us?"

"Yes. Is the Commander with you?"

"Yes," Christopher called. "Look, this is hard enough. Are you able to take out the rest of those missiles?"

The air shattered with explosions. We lost a bit of control, if you define a bit as a terrifying nose dive we just managed to pull out of. I looked at the monitor—no more flashing red dots. "We'll take that as a yes. Consider us droolingly grateful."

"Can either one of you actually fly?"

"Ummm . . . define fly."

I heard cursing over the radios. "How do you expect to land?"

"We're hoping for fairy dust. Got any on you?"

One of the voices chuckled. "Little lady, relax. It's like lickin' butter off a knife."

Christopher groaned. "She doesn't need the encouragement."

The relaxed voice spoke again. "I'm Jerry. What's your name, honey?"

I decided to not get offended. "Kitty."

"Miss Kitty, huh?" Who was this guy, Martini's human counterpart? "Where you from, Miss Kitty?"

"Pueblo Caliente. And, please, I've heard them all. What I haven't heard is someone telling me how to land without dying."

"That's okay," Jerry said. "That's why I'm talking to you."

"Where are *you* from, Jerry?"

"San Diego, at least presently."

"Navy?"

"Yes, ma'am." This meant he was from the Top Gun school. I tried to envision Maverick or Iceman, but I kept on coming up with Goose. The one who died.

"Jerry? Do you play volleyball shirtless?"

"Only with ladies."

"Works for me. What the hell do I do? We've tried landing a couple of times, and we're really good at bouncing."

Jerry chuckled again. He sounded very soothing. "No worries, little lady. I've taught a lot of boys and some girls how to fly. None of 'em crashed their first landings."

Oh, Jerry was an *instructor*. Suddenly this didn't seem so terrifying. "Okay, I'm ready."

Jerry talked to me about the same way Christopher had, gave the same or similar instructions, in the same order. But I wasn't worried. He did this all the time. Sure, his pilots came trained, but he'd probably trained a lot of beginners before he moved to Top Gun. I was in good hands.

"Now, I'm coming down right next to you, right by your side," Jerry said in his soothing drawl. "Sort of like we're holding hands."

"Holding wings?"

"Right."

"Don't touch his wing!" Christopher sounded both freaked and jealous.

"It was metaphorical."

"It was a come on."

Jerry chuckled again. "Commander, maybe you should try to relax. Miss Kitty's doing just fine." I started to like Jerry a lot. "Now, you know what we're going to do, right, honey?"

"Yes, I start pulling back a bit, and when the wheels hit, I pull back just enough so the nose stays up and the wheels stay down."

"You're a natural. And I'll be right next to you. You look over if you need to see if you're right. Now, here we go."

We were moving slowly, per Jerry's instructions. I checked a couple of times, but we were even with him. All the way down. The ground came up faster than I wanted, though. "That's okay," Jerry said, as I gasped. "You're all right. Pull back now, just a bit ... a bit more ... get ready, you'll hit the earth momentarily." We did and started to bounce. "No problem, just relax while you pull a bit back."

The rear wheels were down and seemed to be staying that way. "Just a tiny bit forward, like you're trying to put a doll onto the top of a house of cards."

Christopher was muttering behind me, but I ignored him

and did what Jerry said. The front wheel was down. "Now brakes, that's right, a little more but not too much, you're not making a pit stop at NASCAR."

The jet slowed gradually and came to a halt. Christopher pointed out which buttons to hit and switches to flip to turn everything off. We opened the hatch and climbed out.

One of the pilots was there to help me down. He looked pretty buff under his uniform, had a blond crew cut, seemed about twenty-two, and had captain's bars on his uniform. "Thanks." I looked around as Christopher climbed out. "Where's Jerry?"

The captain grinned. "Jerry Tucker. Pleased to meet you, Miss Kitty."

My jaw dropped. "How the hell are you an instructor at Top Gun?"

Jerry winked. "My daddy always says that the best thing you can do when someone's terrified is make 'em think you've taught plenty of others how to do whatever it is they have to do."

"So, how many people have you talked out of the air?" Christopher asked.

Jerry grinned again. "Counting Miss Kitty here?" We both nodded. "One."

Christopher started to laugh. In fact, he laughed so hard he almost fell down. "Captain Tucker," he managed to gasp out, "when you're done with your training, please let Centaurion Division know. Believe me when I say we can use a man like you on our team."

Jerry gave me another wink. "Happy to, Commander. Especially if there are more ladies like Miss Kitty in Centaurion Division."

I put my arm around Jerry's shoulders as the two other pilots came over. "Jerry, my love, trust me when I say that Centaurion Division is a single man's dream world."

"You'll show me around?" he asked with another chuckle as he put his arm around my waist.

"You're pawing Commander Martini's girl," one of the other pilots told him.

Jerry shrugged. "He's not here."

"However," Christopher snapped, back to business,

"he's about to be murdered, so, you know, maybe we could stop the flirting and get a move on."

Jerry shook his head. "Too much caffeine isn't good for a man, Commander."

"Can I keep him, Christopher? Can I?"

Patented Glare #3 made a surprise reappearance. "Sure. Discuss it with Jeff."

"He'll like him."

"Not if he keeps his arm around your waist, he won't."

"Spoilsport." I removed myself from Jerry's side. "Thanks again, but we have to get moving."

Jerry shrugged. "We're coming with you." He looked over at Christopher. "By order of Angela Katt." He looked back at me. "Your mother said to tell you she outranks everyone here, so do what you do best."

"Cause trouble?" Christopher said with a sigh. "She's great at that."

I managed to refrain from making any comment. Other than one. "My mom outranks your dad. Deal."

"He's not military," Christopher snapped as we started off toward the Science Center.

"Shouldn't we be running?"

"Not if we want the flyboys with us."

I thought about it. "I could hold your hand and Jerry's hand. Maybe the others can link up, too. You've all told me it's transferred through touch."

Christopher looked at Jerry, who was grinning. "Sounds like a great idea."

The pilots weren't thrilled about holding hands, but Christopher made it clear that this was an order, not a suggestion. The other pilots were introduced as Lieutenant Chip Walker and Captain Matt Hughes. They both looked around twenty-five. "Are you sure you guys want to do this?" I didn't want to lose another man. I could still see Cox's plane explode if I allowed myself to think about it for even a second.

Hughes nodded. "Whoever's taken over this facility helped murder Bill. Yeah, we're coming along."

"Glad to have you with us," I said softly.

He gave me a small smile. "We all saw you and heard

you, when Bill died. We've got your back for as long as you need us."

With that, Hughes, Walker, and Jerry grasped each other's wrists. More secure and also more manly looking. I took Jerry's hand in my left and Christopher's in my right, and we were off.

We came to a halt not at the Science Center but about half a mile away, in a wash in front of a large drainage pipe. It was hidden from the Center by a variety of cacti. The sun was starting to set. I hoped this was going to help us.

I was getting used to this mode of transportation, so my stomach was only flipping around, but the pilots were retching. Christopher glanced my way, looking smug. "You wanted to run."

I shrugged. "It passes."

"Like bad booze," Walker gasped out.

"Not that we'd know anything about that," Jerry added.

"Me either." I didn't want to wreck my reputation, whatever it was. "So, how do we get in?"

"We crawl."

CHAPTER 50

WE ALL HAD TO GO ON HANDS AND KNEES. There was a little water but not much. Just enough to make our lower legs and hands wet. I did my best not to focus on what was probably growing in the water.

Christopher went first, then me, Jerry, Walker, and Hughes, bringing up the rear. The pilots all had flashlights with them, so Christopher had Walker's, and Jerry and Hughes had theirs, all turned on. It was eerie but not all that scary in reality—I had four men surrounding me, so I was good. "Won't they know we're coming in this way?" I figured someone had to ask.

"No one knows about this other than me and Jeff."

"Wanna explain that?"

"No, but I'm sure you'll badger me until I do." Gee, he knew me well already. "We weren't based here when we were kids. We were ... with my mother at East Base. But we would come out for visits. There was nothing to do, and my parents were always in high security meetings."

Or they wanted to be alone, which would make sense. And who wants two young boys with you when you're finally seeing your spouse after weeks or months of separation?

"So we wandered the Science Center. We discovered this drainage pipe when we were seven." He chuckled. "Jeff didn't trust that the adults wouldn't try to stop us from playing in here, so we set up traps and a warning system to tell if anyone other than us came through here. No one ever did."

We continued on and hit a fork in the pipe. There was a baseball bat, mitt, and ball leaning against the right-hand fork. They were covered with dust and spiderwebs. "Warning system?"

"No, we weren't supposed to play ball in the Center. We smuggled these in here. We used to play in the wash." He touched the mitt. "I could throw the ball two hundred miles an hour, and Jeff could hit it. It went what seemed like miles. I haven't thought about this stuff in . . . years, really."

My heart ached for both of them. They hadn't really had childhoods, just stolen bits of one here and there. "Bring the bat and the ball."

"Why?" Christopher sounded confused.

"Weapons," Jerry answered for me.

"I'll take them," Hughes called. "Less likely for me to hit anyone with the bat in the back. Unless you want it, Commander."

"No, that's fine." Christopher handed the ball and bat back to me, but slowly, as if he didn't want to let anyone else touch them. "Mitt, too?"

"Only if it can block bullets."

He chuckled. "Don't think so."

We left the mitt and moved on. We came across various traps little boys would set—none of them dangerous and also none of them tripped. Christopher was right—no one had come down here since the last time he and Jeff had, which, from the dust, looked to have been twenty years easily.

"This doesn't really drain water?"

"It used to, before we arrived. Our engineers diverted the water runoff to recycle it, and this pipe wasn't part of that plan."

Poor pipe, discarded along with the their childhood. I was getting awfully sentimental about a long piece of metal, but it had been a trying couple of days.

We were crawling in silence when I heard something. "Hughes, you okay back there?"

"Fine, why?"

"I heard something. I thought you might have knocked the bat into the pipe."

"Nope. I didn't hear anything," Hughes added.

The others chimed in. Only I had heard something.

"You're just a little jumpy," Walker suggested. "It's natural."

I didn't feel any jumpier than I had for the past couple of days. But the sound wasn't repeated, and we had people to save, so I decided not to worry about it. There were plenty of other things to worry about. "Where does this pipe lead?"

"We'll come out on the bottom level," Christopher advised.

"Safe to assume the whole complex is taken?" Jerry asked.

"I think so. Christopher didn't recognize the voice telling us we couldn't land, and, let's face it, they shot missiles at us."

"Who do you think we're dealing with?" Walker asked.

I thought about it. "The Al Dejahl terrorist organization."

"You sure?" Christopher asked.

"Positive. It'd have to be more than one person to hold the entire Science Center hostage. From what my mother's indicated, Al Dejahl has enough people, and this matters to Yates in a big way."

"We're not armed well to stop terrorists," Jerry said.

"The element of surprise is on our side."

"Jeez, Kitty, did you buy a book of clichés while I wasn't looking?"

I resisted the impulse to hit Christopher in the butt, partially because he had a great butt and I didn't think grabbing it right now would be a good idea no matter how I looked at it.

We continued and finally hit a grate. Christopher moved it easily, but I figured it would have taken two human men.

"Why isn't it rusted?" I asked softly.

"Special alloy," Christopher whispered back. "Now, cut the chatter."

"Yes, sir, Commander."

"I'm going to ask Jeff to wash your mouth out."

I took that idea and ran with it, letting my mind wander through the gutter with it while we moved into the small utility room, clearly unused for decades. I really hoped Martini was going to be okay, because I wanted to jump his bones by the time Hughes was in the room with us.

"Okay, how do we tell the hostiles?" Walker asked.

"The people holding the weapons should be the hostiles." Why was I the one answering this question?

Christopher nodded. "If they've taken every floor, we're going to have to clear it and work our way to wherever they're holding Jeff and the others."

We moved out, staying in the same order as in the pipe. The floor was deserted. "Not a good sign," Christopher said once we'd determined it was empty.

"No, it means they've herded everyone to, I hope, one level."

"But we can't assume that," Hughes said.

"True. Are there stairs?"

"Of course." Christopher gave me a look that said that was an idiot question.

"I haven't seen them."

He rolled his eyes and led us to an unmarked doorway. Sure enough, it was the stairwell. I guessed the aliens didn't figure anyone would need to know where the stairs were. In case of emergency they'd just run out of the building at hyperspeed and be done with it.

We moved up through the A-C levels—no one anywhere, including in the transient wing. Well, no one human or A-C. Our dogs and cats were in my parents' room, but they were the only living things there.

"Should we bring the hounds?" Jerry asked as Duke licked his face.

"Only if we want to make a really loud entrance and give doggie kisses to the terrorists."

Duchess had jumped into Hughes' arms and was licking all over him. "I thought pit bulls were deadly killers," he said as he put her down.

"Only if they're trained to it. Otherwise, you're in greater danger of being licked to death."

"She was really protective when I visited," Christopher said.

I thought about it. She was the best trained of our dogs. "Okay, we'll bring her along, but believe me, leave the others here."

We hooked on Duchess' lead and then moved out. Hughes had her and the baseball bat. Christopher took the baseball back since Hughes had his hands full. I figured he was finding it comforting because he was spinning it in his palm.

It was the same thing on the next floors—all deserted. It was eerie now for real. But we made good time since Christopher, after the second deserted floor, just ran from room to room.

"Which floor is the launch one?"

"Top. That's probably where they are."

We hit Floor Two and finally found activity. This was human medical, but there were people here. Not too many, just several armed guards around one door.

"That's where they have Jeff and the others."

"How the hell can you tell that?" Christopher asked me.

"Genetics."

"Okay, so, we get them out."

I knew exactly how Martini had felt when he'd had to suggest me as bait for Mephistopheles. "No."

"No?" Christopher looked shocked and angry.

"Greatest number of people are in danger on the floor above us. Most of your population and, as a key point, almost all of your women. We have to save them, first, then come back down here." I tried to focus on the fact that this was what Martini would have told me to do. I didn't have to like it—the leader didn't get the luxury of liking all the choices he or she needed to make.

"She's right, Commander," Hughes said quietly. "We need to clear the last floor."

Christopher gave me a long look. "Jeff may be dead when we get back."

"I know what he'd pick if I gave him the choice of saving

him or saving your race. It's the choice you two have made every day for two-thirds of your lives."

Christopher nodded. "Let's go."

We moved up the stairwell to the top floor—away from all the people here who mattered to me. I knew now, without question, why war was hell.

CHAPTER 51

WE MOVED UP THE STAIRWELL. The biggest positive to the unmarked doors was, I had to guess, the Al Dejahl team wouldn't know what they were and therefore might have paid them no mind.

We reached the top floor and eased in. Hughes was doing a great job of keeping Duchess quiet. I couldn't even hear her toenails. I looked back to see him carrying her. Smart and an animal lover. And handsome for a human. That I could still manage to make hunkiness comparisons was good. That I was making allowances for humans to be less gorgeous than A-Cs was a reflection of how natural this all seemed by now.

Terrorists all seem to shop at the same stores. They were as regimented in their outfits as the A-Cs were, only theirs ran to fatigues, flak jackets, and a heavy assortment of guns. It was easy to spot the human and A-C males who weren't terrorists—they were all bound, most of them unconscious, all of them beaten up.

The women had been herded into an open part of the launch area. There were a lot of them here. Enough for Mephistopheles to do what I knew he wanted—make them all like him. He didn't want the males so much as he wanted the males out of the way.

I recognized two of the women near the front—Emily and Melanie, Claudia and Lorraine's respective mothers. "Where are our girls?" Melanie demanded.

One of the terrorists, who wore his love of Che Guevara pretty much all over walked to them. He stroked Melanie's cheek with the barrel of his rifle. "Maybe you and I will discuss that privately."

Emily shoved the gun. "Get away from her, you bastard."

He backhanded her. Melanie grabbed her before she hit the floor. "Why are you doing this to us?" she asked as she moved Emily back.

He laughed, and I decided that as far as targets went, he was number one. "Because we can."

I pulled the Glock out of my purse. As I did, my hand hit something I'd forgotten was in there—portable speakers. An idea formed. I put my mouth right next to Christopher's ear. "I'm going to create a distraction. How many of the guns can you get away in about ten seconds?"

He turned and did the same to me. It was far too erotic for the situation. "All of them."

I nodded, and dug out my iPod, took out the headphones and plugged in the speakers. What to choose, what to choose. Well, why not go with what we'd heard was working so well elsewhere?

Once the iPod was set up, we fanned out, staying low and quiet. I had no idea how Hughes could carry a baseball bat and Duchess while in a crouch, but he was the right man for the job.

The nasties were clearly waiting for someone or something. I didn't figure I was a genius to assume it was Yates. Who else, right?

We were as well situated as could be, guns out, except for Hughes, who was carrying the loaded pit bull. I saw Christopher scan the room; he did it several times, then looked over and nodded. Okay, he knew where the guns were.

I turned the volume up to eleven again, hit play and slid away as fast as I could. The Red Hot Chili Peppers' "Give it Away" blasted out.

The reactions were immediate—the terrorists, to a man, spun and started to fire toward my iPod. But they weren't quite fast enough. Christopher might have been tired, but you couldn't tell from how quickly the guns were flying through the air. The A-C women caught them—they might be scientists, but they sure looked as though they could handle an AK-47 if they had to.

The song was barely to the first chorus and we had the guns. Melanie pointed hers right at the head creep. "Give me another reason." He put his hands up.

The pilots and I stood up. "On your side."

Melanie nodded. "Nice to see you." She shot Christopher a worried look. "They have other hostages."

"We know," he answered. He sounded out of breath, and I knew without asking that he was finally out of hyperjuice.

The pilots started untying the bound men. Some of the women helped them and revived the ones who were out. I walked to the head creep; Duchess trotted over next to me. "When is Yates due to arrive?"

He sneered. It was clear he'd practiced a lot in the mirror. "Who?"

"Your fearless leader. You know, the one who always lets his minions do his dirty work? When's he due for the command performance?" I prayed he wasn't here yet. If he wasn't, Martini and the others were likely to still be alive.

"When he comes, he will crush you like the pitiful bugs that you are."

"Blah, blah, blah, heard it all before, not afraid of the creepy old man or his fugly alter ego."

"You should be," another one of the terrorists hissed. "He will remake the world in his own image."

"And you're okay with that? I realize that, as a group goes, you've all got real potential, if we clean you up and groom you, on a scale of one to ten, to end up somewhere around negative five, but that's still more attractive than anything Yates is offering."

"Laugh now while you have the weapons," the first one snarled as most of the Dazzlers giggled. "When our leader comes, you will pay."

"You laughed while you had the weapons. It seems only fair we do the same." I looked around. "Girls, we need to store the trash somewhere it can't get out or make noise. Any ideas? Me, I'm thinking there's this warehouse made of corrugated steel in the middle of the freaking desert."

Emily gave me a smile that should have caused several of the terrorists to wet themselves. "I love that plan."

"Do the gates work?"

"Yes, they only jammed them," Melanie said.

I took a deep breath. No better time for it than the present. "Where's Beverly?"

Emily's eyes narrowed. "You mean Beverly the traitor, that Beverly?"

"Yeah, her."

"She has our daughters, James, Tim, a couple of human pilots, and Jeff," Melanie answered. "If Jeff doesn't get medical attention soon he's going to die."

I'd known that already, but it still sucked hearing it. "That's the plan. Him and Christopher dead, the rest of you turned into parasitic spawners." The women nodded—beautiful but not dumb at all. "We need to get these slime-balls trussed up. Anyone have any duct tape?"

"Lots," one of the gals I didn't know said. "A lot of it on this level, too. It's amazing what you can do with that stuff."

"Good. Can you all handle them? We need to get them trussed up and out of sight before Yates shows up."

Ah, hyperspeed. All but the Che wanna-be were trussed up within seconds. He smirked. "You cannot touch me."

I looked down at Duchess. "Puppy girl? I don't like this mean man." Then I punched him in the face. And Duchess went for what I'd trained her to do when I was really serious about self-defense—his groin.

The screams were lovely.

"Marry me," Jerry said as he trotted over, my now-silent iPod in his hand.

"Taken, by the alien you were apparently separated from at birth." If he was still alive, of course. I dropped iPod and speakers back into my purse. I kept the Glock out.

Jerry sighed. "All the good ones are always taken."

I put my arm around his shoulders. "My love, take a look, a close look, at the mass of women before you, and then take heart. Most of the ones under thirty aren't married, and—here's your special bonus—they only want to marry human males."

He smiled. "I knew helping you land was the right thing to do."

CHAPTER 52

THE TERRORISTS WERE TRANSPORTED to the warehouse. The A-C males went there to guard them—it would be too hot for the humans we didn't actually want to roast, especially since the A-Cs planned to turn the thermostat up to broiling.

That left us a goodly complement of military personnel, but not as many as I'd hoped. Turned out most had gone to Home Base when White had realized they needed to move the base of Operation Fugly there.

Emily and Melanie wanted to come with us, but I wanted people I knew I could trust to pull the trigger up on this level. Their daughters were in danger— they'd shoot to kill without question.

"Who else is in on this with Beverly?"

Emily shook her head. "We don't know."

"I'm with you that she couldn't have pulled this off by herself," Melanie added. "But she hasn't indicated any accomplices."

"Figure out who's missing or might have been acting funny the last couple of days, last few hours in particular, but after you fix the gates. No one can get in here from Home Base. Just be sure that my mother and father are with whoever comes through. If they're not, then that side's been infiltrated, too."

"Got it. Kitty, please get them back safely." Melanie's voice broke.

"I'll do my best. Make sure Yates doesn't get away."

"He won't," Emily said.

I left Duchess with the Dazzlers. I didn't want her at risk, and, besides, she was getting so much attention and praise for her part in the chomping of the head terrorist that it seemed a shame to drag her off.

We went back, just our crew of five. All the guys had big guns now, though Hughes still had the baseball bat and Christopher still had the ball. I got the feeling they were both finding comfort in holding them, and who was I to argue? I wasn't going to give up my purse, either.

We slunk downstairs to see the same four terrorists guarding the doors. Thankfully, we hadn't made much noise upstairs, and the Che wanna-be's screams must not have traveled.

"How do we get them out of action and us inside that room?" Christopher whispered in my ear. "I can't move fast yet."

I thought about it. "Leave that to me." I dropped the Glock into my purse, crawled on the floor a little way, then stood up and sauntered over. "Hey, what's going on?"

Four big guns pointed at me. "Who the hell are you?"

"Gosh, I was going to ask you the same thing. I was napping. Where is everybody? Are we having some sort of a drill?" I did my best to look and sound as inane as possible.

The terrorists exchanged glances. "Why don't we take you inside?" one suggested.

"Sure, is that where we go for this drill?"

"Yeah, babe, that's right." He put his arm around my waist. I managed not to recoil or hit him, but it required a lot of self-control.

One of the others opened the door. It was a large medical bay, and there were several people in the room. As my personal escort shoved me through the doorway, I saw Lorraine and Claudia huddled next to their pilots. The men had been beaten up but were conscious, and they looked angry. Tim and Reader were near them, also looking worse for wear. There were six other terrorists in the room, four of them with guns trained on the six against the wall; two of them were flanking Beverly. But my eyes were drawn to the center of the room.

Martini was on his knees, hands tied behind his back. He looked worse than when I'd last seen him, and I could tell he'd been beaten up like the others. Beverly was standing over him, and her expression of triumph and viciousness made my blood cold.

She was doing something to Martini—his body was reacting as if she were kicking him, but she wasn't moving. He was trying not to make noise, but grunts of pain escaped. Even like this he was gorgeous. But I couldn't stand to see the pain etched into his face and body.

I looked back at her face, and I realized she was sending an emotional onslaught at him. The fear and anger from the others in the room would be bad enough, especially considering the state he'd been in when they'd kidnapped everyone, but she was adding on more. And it was killing him.

I'd thought I hated the terrorist who'd hit Emily. I knew I hated Yates for trying to kill my family and Mephistopheles for killing Cox. But I'd never, ever, known what it was to see someone and know, without a shadow of a doubt, that I'd do anything and everything I had to do in order to kill her or him for what they were doing to someone I loved.

"Well, well, if it's not our little Miss Katt." Beverly's eyes shot daggers at me. "Come to help make Jeff's last minutes truly horrific?"

"You seem to be all over it."

Martini looked over at me. "Baby, get out of here." It sounded like every syllable cost him.

"Oh, she can't do that," Beverly purred as she sent another emotional hit toward him. "She's required."

"Yeah, I know. Yates wants to meet me."

Beverly nodded. "He has something special planned for you."

As long as I could talk and keep her talking, we had time. This room had glass on the wall opposite the door, so I could see behind me. The terrorists hadn't closed the door, probably because they wanted to hear what was going on.

"Funny that he's more interested in me than in you.

And, you know, you'd think, since you've been his mistress all this time, that he'd want you."

"He has greater plans for me," Beverly snarled.

"Yeah, um, right." I nodded my head toward the girls. "I'm sure. 'Cause, you know, Yates is *known* for dating, ah, mature women. Not girls younger than Lorraine."

Her eyes narrowed. "What he chooses to amuse himself with doesn't matter to me."

"Really? Wow, are *you* understanding. Now, if it were me, and my so-called main man was shagging every hot young thing under the age of twenty-five, I'd be kind of pissed. So you're either gullible or stupid. Or both."

"You have no idea of what he plans," Beverly hissed.

"Oh, come on. It's so freaking obvious." I could see my guys moving up. They each had a cloth in their hands. I hoped they'd found some chloroform as opposed to just having allergy attacks. "Yates is dying, and Mephistopheles wants to make babies. But he doesn't exactly seem to have the right equipment. Believe me, I've been up close and personal, and there are no reproductive organs on any of Team Fugly. So they can only reproduce via parasitic infection."

"They represent our next level."

"Is that what he's telling you? Wow, and you believe him? You are one freaked-out piece of work, Bev."

"Beverly."

"Bev. You're acting like a human, babe, aren't you? Humans are the ones big on betrayal and lying, not A-Cs. I mean, that's why no one but Jeff uses a nickname. It's a human thing, and he's the only one who gets it."

"Gets what?" Beverly looked confused. So did the others. Martini just looked as though he was going to die.

"The right evolutionary choice is to mate with humankind. Make us stronger, spread out your genetics, combine the two races. But Mephistopheles knows what that would do."

"Destroy us!"

"Destroy him. And his kind. Either because we'd be able to reject the parasites or because they'd be able to join with us as they're supposed to."

"They create as they were intended."

"They create as *he* intends. Not as God intends."

I hit home with that. "There is no God." But she sounded unsure.

"Wanna bet?" There were no more terrorists at the door. "Girls? I'd like to mention that you're field operatives now." They didn't react. I hoped it was because they didn't want to give anything away, not because they had no idea of what I was talking about.

Beverly seemed to have an idea, though, because she grabbed a needle. "Now, now. I'm not going to kill Jeff."

"No? What are you going to do?"

She smiled, and it was a very evil smile. "I'm just going to make sure that he can't cause any more problems. He doesn't have to die. If I give him this shot, he'll be allowed to live. Christopher, too."

I knew without asking, but I had to ask anyway. "And what does that shot do?"

"Causes sterility."

Martini's eyes closed, and his face scrunched up. I could tell he was fighting to not react. *I want to get married and have a lot of kids.* He'd said it many more times than once. There was no way I was letting her do this to him. Plus, those were my potential babies she was trying to kill, too.

"Over my dead body."

"Gladly," she snarled.

"But, Bev, it'll be the A-Cs who die. And you'll go first. Or haven't you put it together yet and figured out what, exactly, killed Theresa White?"

CHAPTER 53

A MEMORY THAT WASN'T MINE came rushing over me, as if I were watching a scene from a movie.

A woman and two little boys were in a bedroom, all cuddled into bed together, the boys on either side of her, one lying down. The woman looked close to death, but I could see a resemblance to both me and my mother. The boy with the smaller build had his eyes closed; it was clear he'd cried himself to sleep. The other boy was awake, tears rolling down his face. He had light brown eyes and darker hair than the sleeping boy.

"Aunt Terry, you can't leave us," he sobbed. "No one else loves us."

"That's not true, Jeff. My . . . illness is affecting what you can feel. It'll all be okay." She pulled something out from under her pillow. "I've put everything you'll need in here. It's for you and Chris, only, no one else. It'll teach you what you need as you get older. Don't tell anyone you have it, not even your parents or Uncle Richard."

Jeff took what looked like a glowing cube from her and nodded his head.

"Now, I have to give you something, something only for you." She leaned forward and blew into his ear. Jeff's head rolled back, and Terry managed to hold him up. She rubbed his neck until he was conscious.

"What did you do? I don't feel any different."

"I gave you something to keep hidden. I hope you never

need it, but if . . . the bad monster isn't stopped, then I want you to give it to someone. Someone special."

"Who? Chris?"

"No, and you can't tell him, or anyone else, about this, Jeff. You have to promise me, a deathbed promise, that you'll never tell anyone else, ever."

"I promise, Aunt Terry." He sounded as though he was trying to be brave.

She nodded. "If things don't get better, then you find the human girl whose fear and hatred of evil give her courage. You're looking for a protector, Jeff. Someone who can put her own safety aside to protect people she doesn't even know."

"How will I find her?"

She shook her head. "You'll know when you do. That's all I can tell you." She hugged him and they lay down. She hugged both boys to her. Jeff went to sleep, too.

Terry looked right at me. "Save my boys. Please."

The memory washed away. No one had moved; it had only taken a second. "What are you talking about?" Beverly huffed, as the girls gasped and Martini's body sagged. I got the feeling he was trying not to cry.

I didn't know where Christopher was exactly, but I hoped he was close by and in control. "Theresa went to Yates right after Mephistopheles manifested. She went for help. I'm guessing that Yates transformed into Mephistopheles and did whatever gross thing they do in order to spread the parasite, but Theresa escaped. She knew what was going on, but this was her father-in-law, and her husband and son were already suffering enough for his sins."

I moved closer to Martini. "So she did what she had to do, the only thing she could, just in case things didn't work out and the A-C operatives weren't able to kill Mephistopheles."

Beverly grabbed Martini's collar and pulled him to her. "Don't come any closer."

"She implanted a memory into the only person she could, into the person whose talent was actually stronger than hers. A so-called memory that he'd be able to pass along to someone who'd interpret it correctly, when the time came. We're calling it a memory, but I know what it was—a prophecy, if all went wrong."

Martini opened his eyes and nodded. His eyes looked more tortured than I'd seen yet, which was saying a lot.

I looked over to Reader, but only so I could see the reflection. Christopher was moving in, as were the rest of my team. "Mephistopheles didn't implant that memory in me, James. Jeff did." Reader slowly closed and opened his eyes. Good. He'd seen them.

"That's absurd," Beverly said. "You've been affected by him. His implant is working."

"Not like he wanted it to. He hit me with some kind of emotional overlay he's been manipulating, that's true, but I could never actually feel it. Jeff could, and it made me say some things that I wasn't thinking to Christopher. But I have to believe Mephistopheles wanted me obeying him, and I couldn't even feel his influence. Because Terry's influence was already in me, protecting me so I could fight Yates and Mephistopheles both." I looked back to Martini. "You implanted it right when we met. That's why I fainted." He nodded again and looked even more ready to die.

Beverly laughed. "So you're saying Jeff knew all this time and did nothing?"

Martini shook his head, almost imperceptibly. But he didn't have to. I'd known the truth even before Terry showed me. "Jeff didn't know. Terry wasn't going to saddle a little boy with this knowledge." I looked into Beverly's eyes. "She programmed him to find me. And, by the way, girls? I'd say the time is now."

Claudia and Lorraine moved. Or I assumed they moved. Because things were a blur. But when the blur stopped, the terrorists were unarmed and on the ground, and my side had the guns.

Unfortunately, Beverly had Martini. She'd ripped his shirt open. Even in this situation I could look at his chest and get turned on. She held the needle right at the base of his neck. "You move and I'll ensure he never has a reason to care about proliferation of our race ever again."

There wasn't a lot of time. But we had all I needed in the room already. "Christopher, fastball!"

The needle flew out of Beverly's hand and shattered.

Being hit by a baseball traveling at least two hundred miles per hour will do that.

Beverly shoved away from Martini, but not before Walker slammed the door shut. She was in the room, but moving so fast I couldn't see her.

"She's going faster than we can see," Lorraine called to me.

Okay, no worries. "Hughes, batter up!"

He tossed the bat to me, high, and I caught it and stood in front of Martini. I knew she was going to try to get him again, even before Christopher, especially since my three pilots had him surrounded.

I swung the bat out and waited. She slammed into it, and the force spun me around. As we stopped—Beverly bent over the bat—I saw she had some nasty-looking implements in her hands as well as another needle.

I pulled the bat back and swung it, right at her head. "Get away from my man, you fugly-loving cunt."

I connected and she went flying. She hit the wall, and Jerry bent down. "She's dead."

"Good." I meant it. I dropped the bat and grabbed Martini as he slid to the floor. "Jeff, baby, hold on."

He leaned his head against me. "I had to—"

I kissed his forehead. "Hush. I know. You did the right thing." I reached behind him to try to get his wrists untied but I couldn't do it.

Christopher came over, knelt down and took care of it. "Jeff, why didn't you tell me?" He put his hand on Martini's upper arm.

"Couldn't ... promised ..."

"It's okay, Jeff. It's all right." I held him more tightly and tried not to be afraid.

"He's fading fast," Claudia said as she came over. "We have to give him some adrenaline." She had a needle in her hand.

Christopher grabbed her wrist as I shouted, "Nothing from this room!" Claudia looked confused. "Everything in here's suspect. Beverly wasn't kidding—Yates doesn't want Jeff or Christopher to reproduce. Jeff needs adrenaline when he's like this, so don't trust something that says adrenaline if it's in here."

Claudia shook her head. "We don't have any more time."

I couldn't let him die, couldn't lose him. But somehow, I knew what to do. I put my hands on both sides of his face, so he had to look at me. "Jeff, baby, it's okay. Just look at me, only at me. I know it hurts, all the emotions, all the feelings. They aren't trying to hurt you, baby. Come on, you can shut them out, I know you can."

"Can't . . . burned out . . ." His eyes closed.

"Jeffrey Stuart Martini, you open your eyes and look at me." He did, and he looked shocked. "You know how to block. I know you're tired, but it's not an option. Yates is still out there. If you die, he wins. You promised me you'd never let that happen."

"Mother?" Christopher whispered.

Lorraine came over and put her hand on his shoulder. "Hush."

I could see Martini trying and also see him failing. My mind kicked—I had to do something, too. Just as Beverly had, I needed to send emotions to him. But not the ones that caused pain.

I focused my thoughts onto how being around him made me feel—safe, happy, smart, funny, pretty. I concentrated on what making love to him had been like, how incredible and satisfying. And I thought about him and Christopher and what they meant to each other. "You can't leave us, Jeff," I whispered. "We both need you around too much."

It was helping, but it wasn't enough. "Take care of him for me," Martini managed to gasp out.

I had to hold onto him. There was only one thing I hadn't done, one emotion I hadn't allowed to surface. I admitted to myself that the emotion was real. I thought about what being without him would mean and how I'd realized somewhere in the last two days that I couldn't face it. There was a word for this feeling, but I'd been afraid to say it, because I wasn't sure if it was just lust.

But it wasn't.

His eyes opened, and he managed a half-smile. "Really?"

"Really."

He winced. "Guess I'd better . . . try to hang on, then."

"I'd appreciate it." I laid him down on the floor and wrapped myself around his head, stroking his hair and kissing his forehead. I could feel him getting a little stronger.

Footsteps, a lot of them. I could feel and hear them. "We've got company coming."

The girls flanked us, Christopher, Tim, and Reader moved in front of us, and the five pilots stayed spread around the room. Everyone had their guns cocked and aimed. We were ready, remembering the Alamo. Walker waited until everyone was set, then he flung the door open.

CHAPTER 54

"PUT THOSE GUNS DOWN," my mother snapped.

No one moved. "Um, guys? Meet my mother." No one moved. "Oh, and guns down." All the weapons lowered.

"That's my girl," Martini murmured.

Mom looked at the scene. She was next to me and Martini in a moment. "Jeff looks awful," she said as she pulled a hypodermic out of the pouch around her waist.

"It's been a crappy day," he croaked.

"Gee, thanks."

He managed to grab my hand. "Other than you."

I kissed his forehead. Mom handed me the hypodermic and a vial. "Excuse me?"

"He'll get like this more often than you'll be happy about. You want to learn how to save his life now or when you're alone?"

She had a point. I took the hypodermic. Mom talked me through how to fill it.

Claudia pointed to a spot on his chest. "He needs it right in his hearts when he's like this. You slam it in, then push the plunger down."

I was going to plunge a huge needle into Martini's chest. This didn't sound exactly like "good girlfriend" material. He squeezed my hand. "I'd like to live."

"Girlfriend, just pretend you're mad at him," Reader offered.

Actually, a good plan. I raised the needle and hit the magic spot on his chest. He bellowed, but I saw his body movements start to come back. I pulled the needle out once all the contents were inside him. Claudia disposed of it. I was too busy hanging onto Martini, who was thrashing.

"This is normal," Lorraine hollered as Melanie and Emily brought a gurney in. Christopher, Reader, and Tim helped us move Martini onto it.

"This is normal?" We were strapping him down. He was still bellowing.

"It's ugly, I know." Claudia said next to me. "But only when he's this close to dying. Otherwise, it's not too awful."

"Wonderful." A thought occurred. "How often is he close to dying?"

"Every month, month and a half," Reader answered.

Mom shrugged. "I told you to choose wisely."

Christopher grinned. "Thanks." He looked over at me. "He has to go into isolation. He'll need more than twelve hours, not sure how much. You can't go in there."

I kissed Martini's forehead. "Hang on, Jeff. I'll be waiting for you."

He moved his head and kissed my mouth. Even strapped to a gurney and at the edge of death the man was a great kisser. "Good." His head dropped back, and he stopped thrashing.

Christopher, the girls, and their pilots ran off, escorted by a few other Dazzlers, their mothers included.

"Where's Yates?" I asked Mom as we left the area.

"He didn't show." She sounded angry and frustrated. I could relate.

"We have what looks like all of Al Dejahl in custody."

"Yeah, I know." She smiled. "At least it'll slow him down for a while."

"Yeah, no more Fugly Army, no more terrorist scum. He'll have to start recruiting again."

"That's what worries me."

"How's Dad?"

"Fine. He's with the translation team. They're fixing up Beverly's misinformation."

"So, in his element."

"Pretty much. Duchess the Wonder Dog, as the other gals are calling her, is there, too." Mom was quiet. "You sure you want to pick Jeff?"

"Over Christopher?" She nodded. "Over anybody, even Christopher, so yes."

"Okay."

"But Christopher probably comes along with the Martini package, so you'll get to keep the son you always wanted."

She chuckled. "Nice work on Beverly."

"I killed her." I didn't feel remorseful at all.

Mom gave me a long look as we made the elevator banks and headed down to the transient floor. "I know."

"Who told you?"

Mom shrugged as we got off the elevator. "She was trying to kill the man you love. I didn't have to question what you'd do. Besides, who else but you would have used a baseball bat?"

"It's not like I spent my life hitting people with a Louisville Slugger."

"No, but trust me when I say I've seen you in action now, and using Beverly's head for batting practice is definitely your style." We got to my room and went in.

"Superfast beings shouldn't piss off the comics geek-girl."

"Glad all the money we spent on those things has paid off." Mom put her hands on my shoulders. "You don't feel remorse now, but you might later. Just remember—it's one thing to kill an innocent. That's hard, sometimes impossible, to get over. But many times evil needs to be killed in order to be stopped. And Beverly was evil."

"I know." I hugged her. "Thanks for backing me up, Mom."

She kissed my head as she hugged me back. "Thanks for letting me." She sighed. "I'm going to start identifying which A-Cs might have been involved in this with Beverly. It's possible she was acting alone, but unlikely."

"Emily and Melanie feel the same, but they have no idea who could be involved. Me, I suggest you start with the rest of Beverly's encryption team."

Mom gave me a "duh" look. "Thank God you're here." Her sarcasm knob was turned up to eleven.

"Hey, I've gotten used to dealing with people who trust everyone. What should I do?"

"Take a shower. You need one, and it'll help. You won't have Jeff to keep you occupied for at least a day, based on how he looked."

"Will do. Oh, and Mom? There's an abandoned drainage pipe on the fifteenth floor. It's how we got in, and I think we should put some security on it."

She smiled. "That's my girl. I'll take care of it."

She left, and I got undressed. My Aerosmith shirt was the worse for wear but still salvageable. Same with my jeans and even my Converse. I was about to step into the shower when there was a knock at the door.

I looked frantically for a bathrobe and found one hanging inside the bathroom door. This was definitely a five-star hotel. I wrapped it around me and answered the door.

Jerry was standing there. "Hey, I see you're about to shower, but I'm clear that Commander Martini has the prior claim. The guys and I just wanted to give you something."

"It couldn't wait?" I let him in.

"Nope. We have to head back for debriefing."

"Even the boys with Claudia and Lorraine?" My poor girls.

"Yes. However, Commander White's requested we be moved to Centaurion Division as soon as possible. Our superiors estimate the five of us'll be here within a month."

"I'm really glad."

"Me too. Especially since we're assigned to your team."

"Come again?"

He grinned. "You might want to talk to Commander White about it, but apparently you're in charge of a new active division, and he figured you'd want your regular team with you."

Christopher wasn't dumb at all. But this was sort of life-changing news. *If you join with us, you won't be going back there anyway.* Well, White had warned me.

"I'm proud to have you guys reporting to me."

"Yeah, our first orders are to teach you how to fly." Jerry grinned. "I volunteered."

"No one I'd rather learn from."

The smile left his face, and he reached into his shirt

pocket. "We wanted to give you something. So you'd remember all of us, just in case something happens between now and then." He handed me a photo. There were six young men in uniform in it. I recognized five of them. One I didn't. He was about Jerry's age, slender, with strawberry blond hair and a great smile.

I turned the picture over—they'd labeled who each of them were. The one I didn't know was Lt. Wm. Cox.

"He would have been proud to serve under you, too," Jerry said quietly. "We all loved him like a brother. Believe me when I say this, Kitty—we'll follow you to hell and back for how you reacted when he died. Not a lot of people would charge a monster, after all, and not too many more would worry about the family of someone they'd never met."

I nodded. I couldn't speak. He kissed the top of my head. "I'll let myself out. And see you in about a month, Commander Katt."

The door closed, but I didn't get up. I just stared at the picture. I finally forced myself to put it somewhere safe—into an inner pocket inside my purse. Then I went into the shower.

I stood under the warm water and finally let myself cry. I cried for what seemed like hours as the water washed my tears down the drain. Finally, though, the tears stopped. And I was left with one certainty: This wasn't over yet. I wasn't letting William Cox die for nothing.

CHAPTER 55

I SPENT MOST OF THE NEXT DAY and a half sleeping. I really wanted to see Martini, and during one period of actual consciousness I convinced a random A-C to take me to the isolation area.

It wasn't one or two chambers, as I'd been naively expecting. It was over a hundred isolation chambers covering a full half of one of the lower levels. The A-C explained that all empaths needed isolation from time to time, as blocks and empathic synapses wore out. Reader had told me this, of course, but somehow I'd still imagined something small and somewhat cozy.

The A-C went about his business, and I wandered through the chambers. There was nothing cozy here, and it was easy to see why Reader felt creeped out in this area. They reminded me of large tombs with medical beds and equipment in them and not much else. Each one had a large window in the door, so you could look in. The empath inside couldn't look out—the beds were turned so the occupant would be facing a blank wall.

Per my A-C guide, there were smaller home models for use with empathic children. There were a few of those down here, too. They looked like space-aged coffins. The mere idea of having to spend time in either kind of chamber was horrifying, but nothing compared to seeing Martini in an active one.

I reached his room. There were two A-C security guards

and some medical personnel outside, monitoring. I was allowed to peek in—and a quick look was enough. There were tubes and needles going into Martini all over his body. There were even some going into his head. I wanted to break down the door, rip everything out of him, and take him away, pronto.

"You need to leave," one of the doctors said quietly. She didn't sound as though she was trying to be nasty.

"Why?"

"The rooms are emotion-proofed, but Commander Martini is very powerful, and he can feel your distress." She showed me an electronic pad that was flashing red and orange.

I felt awful. "Sorry."

She smiled. "It's okay. Isolation is harder for nonempaths to watch than it is for the empaths themselves."

I found that hard to believe, but didn't argue. I headed back, but I got lost. This was like getting lost in some creepy Egyptian tomb or the Frankenstein burial ground. I wasn't a fan, and I got jumpy fast. I kept thinking someone was following me, but every time I turned around, no one was there. A few times, I was sure I'd just missed seeing whoever it was, but I was too chicken to go find out. By the time I finally found the elevators, I was an emotional wreck. I managed to find my room, crawled into bed, and hid under the covers until I fell asleep again.

For my next bout of consciousness I wanted to talk to Reader, but he and Paul were also sequestered, though only in their rooms, not in some horrible Chamber of Horrors. I couldn't blame them or resent it.

I spent the time instead sending a lot of text messages to a lot of people, in which I practiced lying in new and unusual ways. Work seemed to find my absence acceptable; I wasn't sure if this was a reflection on what they thought of my daily contributions or if White had cleared things for me already. I decided not to care.

To everyone else, I managed to make what was going on with me sound totally boring, to the point where no one other than Chuckie seemed worried or even interested. Chuckie refused to buy any line I tried to pass, mostly because I refused to let him call me. He was like my mother—

I couldn't lie to him because he never fell for it—and there was no way I could hope to fool him if he could actually hear my voice.

I finally told him that my parents were with me and they were okay with things, and he let it go. I rejoiced that I'd managed to lie to one of my best friends for exactly three seconds, congratulated myself for clearly hurting Chuckie's feelings for another three seconds, then wallowed in guilt over it for a nice long while. The guilt was exhausting, but the crying really tired me out, and I fell back asleep to dream about fighter planes somehow carrying everyone I knew and cared about crashing in the desert.

By the time I dragged out of bed in the late afternoon of the second day, I was lonely, and by the time I'd wandered the whole Science Center—avoiding the Tomb of Creepiness level, supposedly for Martini's health and well-being and not because it terrified me—I was getting pathological.

I was in full Dazzler uniform now, complete with rather sexy black Aerosole heels—at least they bought the comfortable designer shoes. My own clothes were still being cleaned, or burned, I wasn't sure which.

Talking to my parents would have been fine, but they were both busy. Mom was with White, discussing moving part of her antiterrorism unit over to base out of the Science Center, and Dad was so deeply engrossed in the translations that a food, drink, bathroom break, and bed rest team had to be assigned to him.

Tim, Claudia, and Lorraine were still debriefing the A-Cs and American military personnel on most of what had gone on. I would be asked to give a full report in a day or so, but since I was new to everything, I was given time off.

Our dogs had the run of the place, thanks to Duchess, who was still the heroine of the day. Pretty much every Dazzler wanted her own pit bull now, and I couldn't blame them.

The cats were still in my parent's room, and I went to visit them, to find Christopher in there, all three cats on the sofa with him, purring up a storm.

"Your parents told me I could come in any time."

I sat down on the sofa next to him. "That's fine. I don't think you're a total jerk any more."

He laughed. "Good to know." He looked down at Sugarfoot, who was in his lap. "Is my mother still in your mind?"

I'd been wondering the same thing myself. "I don't think it's her so much as her influence."

"What do you mean?" He still wasn't looking at me.

"She was dying, and she knew it. Either she willed it to happen, so she wouldn't give birth to a superbeing, or the impregnation, if we can even call it that, affected her system so badly it killed her. But she knew she was going to die."

He nodded. "She told us, me and Jeff, that she was."

My throat felt tight. They'd been ten years old. Too early to become men. "She couldn't put the memory, the feeling, into your mind—you'd create an image from it, and then you'd know . . ." I couldn't finish that sentence.

Christopher could. "I'd know my grandfather raped my mother, his son's wife." He looked back at me. "We can't tell my father."

"I think he knows, or at least suspects."

"I don't want to find out you're wrong."

"That's fair."

"Why Jeff?"

"Who else? He's the most powerful empath your race has—I'm sure your mother knew that. She was training him, after all." He nodded. I didn't mention the glowing cube I'd seen. I didn't want to let either one of them know what Terry had shown me. "So she did some empathic thing, I have no idea what—Jeff might not either—and programmed him. He knew she gave him something to pass along, but nothing more." Martini had been looking for me all his life. It made my heart ache to think about it.

Christopher closed his eyes. "You know, there were a few years when I hated him."

"After Lissa?"

"Yeah. They would have killed her no matter what, though. I know that now." He managed a weak smile. "At least they didn't get Jeff."

"He loves you very much."

"I know. He's more than my cousin, more than a brother."

"Yeah, she showed me. She knew that when it mattered, you two would always stand together."

"That almost fell apart these last couple of days," he said with a chuckle.

"No, actually, Jeff offered to step aside so we could be together. Right before Mephistopheles did his tap dance on our car."

"They won't let him marry you. I know you don't want to believe it, but it's true."

"We'll see. I've known all of you for less than a week. I think I can stand dating a bit before racing off to the chapel with Jeff."

"He'll suggest it the second he can walk again."

"It's part of his charm."

"Is that what you call it?"

"Yeah. What was your mother like?"

He leaned his head back. "Like I used to be. Like Jeff is now."

"You miss it? How you used to be, I mean."

"Sometimes." He grinned. "Jeff does it better than I ever did, though."

"What's that?"

"Being human. It's what all of us born on Earth want, to be human. Jeff passes without any issues. Not so easy for the rest of us."

"I'll start calling you Chris if that'll help."

"No. Don't take this the wrong way, but my mother called me Chris. And asked everyone to call her Terry, though only Jeff did." He gave a short laugh. "You'd have liked her, and she'd have loved you."

I felt a pang for her—so alone in this world, so clear on what her race needed to do to survive, and murdered by the person who should have helped her. I realized I had two people to avenge, not one.

"My mom really cares about you," I reminded him. "I think she'd be very open to, well, covering what you'd let her of the mother stuff."

"And here I thought she just wanted to marry me off to you."

"Oh, she did and probably still does."

"Your father prefers Jeff."

"Really? Sure didn't seem like it."

"Trust me."

We sat there in silence for a few minutes, petting the cats. It was relaxing. For a few minutes. Then the memory of the creepy Mortal Kombat Crypt Isolation Chambers inserted itself in my mind, chuckling evilly.

"Can we get out of here?"

"You want to tour the Science Center?"

"Been there, done that, still have no idea where I am at any given time. No, I mean get *out* of here."

He stretched. "You want to go to Pueblo Caliente?"

"Yeah, I do. Even if it's just to get another change of clothes."

"Okay. Not a surprise, by the way."

"Oh? I thought you weren't empathic."

"I'm not, but I remember what it was like for James, the first few days. He was overwhelmed and burned out and just wanted to go home and remember what it was like to be a regular human who didn't know aliens walked the Earth."

"We safe to go?"

"Sure, I have the highest security clearance. You do too, now."

"I meant from a safety perspective."

He grinned. "I think I can catch you if you fall out of a plane."

"I'd rather take a gate."

"I call that personal growth. But I'm not carrying you through it—that's Jeff's jurisdiction."

"That's fine. Just promise me we'll run slowly and land in a clean men's bathroom."

"Boy, are you picky."

CHAPTER 56

WE WENT TO MY ROOM so I could grab my purse, then strolled to the elevator banks. Still stood on opposite sides of the car from each other. No need to put ourselves into another awkward situation.

We got to a gate, calibrations were made, and then we whooshed off to the men's room at Saguaro International. It felt like years since I'd been here, not days. We were between flights, and the bathroom didn't require me to act like an idiot, which was a relief, although I was a little let down. I'd prepared a great routine.

We strolled out. "You want to take a cab?" Christopher asked me.

"Do you guys do that? I mean, no gray car, no hyperspeed?"

"Sometimes."

It was a human thing to do, and he wanted to be human. I might not be allowed to call him Chris, but I could help drag him along. "Sure. You have money?"

He grinned. "Always."

We walked to the curb, and he held the door for me, but this time he climbed in next to me. I gave my address, as well as the fastest way to get there at this time of day, and we drove off.

"You folks got no luggage?" the driver asked.

"We're having an affair. My husband thinks I'm out

with the girls, his wife thinks he's in Omaha." Christopher looked at me as if I were insane.

The cabbie nodded. "Makes sense. You live close?"

"I live here, he lives in Vegas."

"Ah, Sin City. Guess you can't meet up there, though, huh?"

"Nope, but this works out. I use my friend's apartment."

"Nice friend."

"She owes me." I leaned back in the seat and patted Christopher's leg. "Relax, honey, we finally get a few hours alone."

The cabbie chuckled. "Your boyfriend's probably worried your husband'll drive by and spot the two of you together."

"Yeah," Christopher muttered.

"I could put my head in your lap."

"No, not in the cab," Christopher said quickly. He looked panicked.

The cabbie chuckled again. "No cameras in this cab, honey. You feel free to have a good time if you want to."

"Thanks, but I guess we'll wait."

We reached my apartment, and Christopher paid up. I made him give the cabbie a generous tip. "Good luck to you two. Hope I get your fare next time." He drove off, still chuckling.

"Why did you do that?" Christopher demanded as we went upstairs. "Are you crazy, is that your problem?"

I laughed. "You need to relax. It was fun. And your expressions were priceless."

"Jeff wouldn't find it funny."

"No, he'd find it hilarious. And if he'd been in the cab with me, he'd have let me 'hide.' "

"I'm not Jeff."

I patted his cheek. "I know. But I like you anyway."

We got inside, and I took a look around. "Someone's been in here."

"How can you tell? It was a mess when I was here before, it's a mess now."

"It's my mess, and it's been moved." Only a bit, but everything was moved a bit. I took his hand. "In case we have to leave quickly," I explained as he gave me a panicked look.

We walked through. All my fish were dead. "Overfeeding?"

"Maybe. Maybe they think I love my fish."

"Who could love fish?"

"Someone, I'm sure, just not me." I moved us through the apartment, opening everything carefully. We got into the bedroom. No one there. I pulled out a suitcase, shook it out, and then started to toss clothes into it. I moved all my pictures into another bag. There wasn't that much more I needed, though I grabbed my spare hairspray and put it in my purse.

Christopher checked under the bed. "Nothing. You sure stuff's been moved?"

"Yeah. You sure you didn't see anything foreign on anything I packed?"

"No, all your concert T-shirts are devoid of suspicious powders."

"I packed other things."

"But nothing else carefully."

I looked at my bed. "Christopher? I think there's something in my bed."

"Bomb?"

"Could be." No sooner had I said that than whatever it was moved under the covers. I managed not to scream.

Christopher looked at it closely. "Are you afraid of snakes?"

"Pathologically."

"That popular knowledge?"

"I'm a girl, the bet is always good for snake fear."

"It's a snake, then."

"Rattler?"

"Most likely."

I was taking this extremely well. "We have to kill it. By we, of course, I mean you. I'll stand here and scream."

"No screaming. Screaming tells the people watching your apartment you've found their gift."

"Oh, great."

"I don't want to let go of you. You're right, we're going

to have to move fast. But I need something to use to cut the snake's head off."

"You think you can do that?"

"Um, yeah. Hyperspeed and all."

Duh. "Right. I have knives in the kitchen."

"No, needs to be in this room. I think if we go back into the kitchen, we'll be dead."

"Why?"

"I can hear ticking."

The Nareemas were not only the landlords but the owners of the entire building. Since they'd come from that very war-torn country and were total paranoids, they were well trained in hasty exits. They routinely made the tenants practice emergency escapes—a small price to pay for great apartments in a great location at a very reasonable rate.

In addition to the drills, all the apartments had an emergency alarm installed, always in the kitchen and bedroom areas, high enough up that most kiddies couldn't reach the pull levers but most adults could.

The emergency alarm sounded vastly different from the fire alarm, and the Nareemas literally made each tenant sign a contract that if they heard the emergency alarm, they would grab all living creatures, only, and run like hell out of the building. They kept a roster of all the living things. I hadn't included my fish on the list, but if you considered a cockroach a pet, the Nareemas had it marked on your lease.

If the building was going to go, I was going to clear out my neighbors if at all possible, and the snake could fend for itself.

I looked around quickly. Anything else I had to have before it blew to smithereens? I grabbed my laptop bag after a quick examination that showed no bombs or slitheries. Because I traveled a lot for work, it contained my passport and all my personal information, and it was also where I stored checkbooks and other important things. I cleared out some more clothes and shoes, filling my five-piece luggage set to the brim.

"How do you expect us to carry all this?" Christopher asked as I continued to pack like mad one-handed.

"You sling this one over your neck," I put my garment

bag over him, "and you hold the really big rolling one." I slung my purse over my neck to one side and the laptop bag over my neck to the other. Cosmetics bag that actually contained my personal care items hooked through the smaller bag that hooked to the medium rolling bag. "There, all set."

"We look ridiculous."

"Maybe so, but I just want to get my stuff out."

"How can you even stand?"

"Practice."

"You don't want us to save the Coca-Cola and frozen dinners, too?"

"Yes, but you said we couldn't go back into the kitchen." I thought fondly of my stereo equipment and TV, but I had my iPod and all its paraphernalia with me, so my music was safe. "You ready?"

"I was ready fifteen minutes ago."

"Fine." I hit the alarm. "Let's go."

We moved at a sluggish version of hyperspeed. It was enough to get us out of the building without being seen, at least as far as I could tell, since no one seemed to know we were there. We stopped in the park and watched. The folks in my building were pouring out. Good.

Everyone was out, pets and children in tow, over at the park where Mr. Nareema was counting noses and Mrs. Nareema and their children were counting pets. Mr. Nareema announced all humans but me accounted for, and the rest of the clan shared that all the pets were present, too, when the bomb went off. It was impressive. But if the Nareemas hadn't been totally paranoid, at least some of these people would have been killed. Innocent people.

"I want to hunt Yates down, okay?"

"Works for me. I don't think I can get us back to the airport with all this stuff, though."

"Can you get us back to wherever you stashed my car?"

"That I can do."

"Okay, give me a minute." I took the bags off and ran over to our clutch of tenants before the Nareemas could call my parents to tell them I was dead.

I shared my living status, feigned ignorance about all the

whys and wherefores, and, joyous reunion over, headed back to Christopher. No one mentioned him or my luggage.

"Did you do something to their minds?"

He shrugged. "Just made them see me with your dogs, not your luggage. It'll make it easier all the way around."

"Do you need to manipulate any images before we go?"

"No. This wasn't caused by a superbeing."

"In that sense."

"Good point." Christopher looked around. "Nice area."

"Yeah."

"You can't come back here to live, you know."

"Picking that up. I'm sure I have options." My parents' house, for one. "Can I rent a room in the Science Center?"

Christopher chuckled. "Sure. Most agents don't pay rent."

"Oh, bonus." This A-C gig did have its advantages.

"Let's get out of here before someone else tries to blow you up."

"I thought this was all in a day's work for you."

"Superbeings, yes. The additional action you drag along? Not so much."

"I'm special."

Christopher smiled. "True."

CHAPTER 57

I PUT THE LUGGAGE BACK ON, he took my hand, and we moved at slow hyperspeed, which should have been an oxymoron but wasn't. We were still moving too fast to be seen clearly, but I wasn't nauseated at all. We reached a part of the desert preserve and moved toward an abandoned dam.

"We're at another alien crash site, aren't we?" I asked as we slowed to human speed.

"Yeah, how did you know about that?"

"One of my best friends was into this stuff." He still was, but why share that? I might need a source they weren't mind manipulating. "The rumor is that this dam was actually built to hide an alien burial ground or something."

"Actually, it was built so we could have a safe location here. A lot of activity goes on in Arizona, so we needed a small base."

"Makes sense." We moved into what looked like a cave. "You sure this is safe and hasn't been infiltrated?"

"Hands up." This wasn't a familiar voice.

We put our hands up. Christopher kept hold of mine, though. "What's your rank?" he asked, sounding very calm.

"Amateur."

I felt Christopher relax. "It's me."

A guy who was far too handsome to be human stepped

out of the darkness. "Sorry, Commander, but you know the rules."

"Just get someone to take this luggage," Christopher said as he dumped my garment bag on the ground. "It weighs a ton."

The guard spoke into a com attached to his shoulder, and within seconds more A-Cs appeared. They took my luggage, and then we wandered in.

"Welcome to Caliente Base," Christopher said as we got fully inside, and I saw a mini version of the first floor I'd ever seen at the Science Center.

"You all were here when my superbeing created, weren't you?"

"Yep. Monitoring Yates."

"So Jeff didn't run to a gate to get to the airport to get to me."

"No, he ran from here. It's farther, actually."

"Awww, I'm touched, and I wasn't mad, just clarifying."

"I need to check a couple of things," Christopher said, as he let go of my hand.

"Do I get to watch?"

"Sure. I'll warn you if I have to talk at regular A-C speeds." We went to a set of consoles and monitors that sat in front of some huge screens, similar to the conference table from the debriefing session, only these screens were on the walls. As there had been in the Field command center room back at the Science Center, there were images from all over the world. Unlike the Field stuff I'd seen, these all seemed random—I didn't spot any superbeings in any of the shots. Some were news feeds, some were streaming video, some seemed to be from cell phones. A variety of the images would show up on the consoles, where some A-Cs were sitting, looking intent.

"How do you get all of this?"

"We created your satellite and cell phone technology," Christopher replied absently. "We have a constant wiretap going."

"I feel so Watergate."

"We're really only looking for parasites and superbeing activity."

"Where's Yates?"

"Reports place him in Saudi Arabia, visiting a Saudi prince," one of the A-Cs nearest us replied. At least Yates wasn't nearby this time when his goons tried to kill me. One small favor.

"Who's the lead empath on duty?" Christopher asked.

An A-C who looked about twenty-two came over. "I am, Commander. I have some areas identified. However, the emotional signals are weak."

He and Christopher stood next to each other, with a monitor each. The empathic A-C had a stream of images scroll through on the large screens. "Stop." Christopher pointed to a screen that showed bombed out squalor. "There. Send that to me."

"Commander?" one of the other A-Cs asked. "There's nothing living there." However, the image of nothing there showed up on the monitor in front of Christopher. He put his hands on the monitor. "Hot spot. Send a team, now."

The lead empath put his hand over Christopher's. "Confirmed."

"How can you tell?" It still looked like nothing to me.

"There's a parasite here," Christopher answered. "You've seen them; they're hard to spot."

"I thought the parasites aimed for a mammal of some kind."

"It has." He pointed. An ancient Jeep rolled into view, one passenger.

"He doesn't look angry."

Christopher put his hand on the man in the Jeep, and the empath did the go team move as well. "He's leading a terrorist cell. Not part of Al Dejahl, just one of many random factions out there."

"And he's joyously happy while filled with rage at the same time," the empath added.

"Why didn't the parasite aim for him?"

Christopher shrugged. "It was probably aiming for someone in this village." He looked at me. "They were all killed about an hour ago."

"I don't want to know."

"Good, because I'm sure it's classified."

I saw two A-Cs appear out of nowhere on the screen. "How did they get there?"

"We have floater gates, remember? Allows us to arrive anywhere."

"How do they work? And why don't you use them all the time instead of the stationary gates?"

He looked at me out of the corner of his eye. "You want the full scientific explanation?"

"Not so much, no." I looked back at the monitor. The A-Cs were clearly searching for the parasite. One of them jerked and pulled the other out of the way of the man in the Jeep, who started shooting at them. "How did he know to do that?"

"All field teams are empath and imageer units. We try to never send an agent out alone."

The agents weren't shooting back. "I know you guys are pacifistic, but why aren't they trying to protect themselves?"

"We're here to protect humanity, not kill it."

"Even when it tries to kill you?" The Jeep stopped, and the man got out. He was carrying a machine gun. The agents were trying to stay out of his range while still searching for the parasite. "You know, wearing black Armani suits and white shirts, complete with tie and dress shoes, while fighting parasites in far-flung, foreign locales, seems sort of . . . stupid."

"We wear what we wear. If he lives, he won't remember what happened."

"But he's intimately involved."

Christopher sighed. "There are ways. I need to concentrate."

"Why?" His hands hadn't left the monitor.

"Because while you're seeing the real thing here, I'm manipulating it for mass consumption. This is being filmed live."

I looked up at the larger screens. It looked similar to the monitor, but there were no A-Cs visible. The guy from the Jeep was just firing at nothing. "You know, if it's being filmed, that means someone's working the camera, right?"

"Right. As far as I can tell, anyway. The camera operator isn't in the picture, so I can't touch or feel his image."

The empath closed his eyes. "Commander, I think we have a problem."

No sooner said than the camera jerked wildly and fell to the ground. "Um, Christopher? I think the parasite wants to explore its more artistic side." The camera was still aimed toward the guy with the machine gun, who looked beyond terrified and also seemed to be screaming like a little girl. Something horrible and extremely nonhuman clawed at him. He was reduced to shreds in a matter of moments.

Christopher cursed. "Send another team, *now*!"

There were a few tense minutes while we watched the superbeing stomping around. The A-Cs on site were moving too fast to be seen. The main screen showed a regular citizen fighting the bad guys. Nice to see someone got to look like a hero. Finally, the action stopped, and there was nothing, just the Jeep sitting there idling. A disembodied voice came through over a speaker system. "All secured, Commander White. Footage in the camera altered."

"Good work. Clean up, box it, bring it home. Fast. That area's not safe." Christopher rubbed his temples. "Anything else?" he asked the lead empath.

"Not right now, Commander. Not as far as we can tell."

"Good work. Okay," he said to me. "Let's get you back to the Science Center."

"You sure? This was kind of interesting." And it was a refreshing change to merely watch the action. Plus, since it had been one incident and not fifty, there hadn't been too much for me to take in.

"You can watch from the Science Center, too, on even more screens, remember? I realize you were sick to your stomach when we were handling the clustered manifestations, but it's a larger version of this."

I remembered, my stomach in particular. "Wow, my own multiplex of horror. It's almost too good to be true."

We reached the motor pool area. "Your luggage is in your trunk, the car's gassed up, and we made a few modifications," the A-C who handed me my keys advised. "I think you'll be pleased with the performance."

"It's still painted black, right?"

"Right."

"Then it's all good." Went to my car; it looked fine. We got in, and I examined the instrument panel. "Oh, yeah. Lexus does not an invisibility shield make." It looked as though they'd installed all the alien bells and whistles. Fine with me. I never argued about a free upgrade.

"What are you doing driving a Lexus anyway?" Christopher asked as he buckled up. "These things cost a fortune."

"This is their sporty, entry-level model, and I saved up for three years and took the bus or rode my bike instead of buying something I didn't want, and I love this car, far more than any fish. It handles like a dream, gets good gas mileage, and is a stick shift, meaning that it's for *real* drivers." I meant it, I loved my car.

"You and James can drool over it together. To me, it's just a metal box that goes slower than I can."

"Philistine."

"Jeff'll love it, don't worry."

We drove to a gate, it was calibrated for the Science Center, and then we drove through. It was no better in my own car than it had been in the Navigator. "Do they install hyperspeed in the cars?"

"No, get used to the gates."

"If I must."

We got to the Science Center without incident, which seemed like a first to me. My car was added into the motor pool there with instructions that it was mine, not for general use. Tim met us there. "Christopher, we had a report that a bomb went off in Pueblo Caliente."

"Yeah, it was at my apartment. Can I get my stuff to my room before we go into the next big briefing session?"

Christopher nodded and called over some A-Cs I didn't know but had seen around. "Run everything in these bags, computer especially, for bugs, bombs, toxins, and anything else you can think of."

"Snakes," I added.

"Do it fast, get anything uncontaminated to her room right away." They took my stuff and trotted off.

"Okay, I want to go back to my room, just for a minute. Particularly since it is, for the moment at least, my home." Boy, saying that made it feel final and scary.

"Can you get there on your own?" Christopher asked.

"Sure." Hopefully. "Where are we meeting?"

"Fifteenth level."

"Okay, see you there in a few."

"Make it snappy, we're back into a situation."

I rolled my eyes. "Got it, Commander."

CHAPTER 58

I WALKED TO THE ELEVATOR BANKS and managed to get to the eighth floor all by myself. Found my room. Nothing I'd packed was in it yet, but I had to assume a thorough check took longer than five minutes, even using hyperspeed.

I eyed the bed, but it was made, and there were no unusual bumps in it. Good. Still safe to lie down here. I plopped my purse onto the bed. I had to figure I wasn't going to need it for a while.

Brushed my hair but opted for no ponytail this time. Washed my face. Ready for anything.

I went back to the elevators. I was sort of ready to roll into action again, but I was also tired and still worried about Martini.

The elevator doors opened, and my jaw dropped. He was in there, leaning against the side wall, full Armani ensemble in place, looking drop-dead gorgeous and as though nothing had happened to him. "Get in." He didn't sound happy, and he wasn't smiling.

I got into the elevator and felt immediately guilty. "How are you feeling?"

He hit the button for the fifteenth floor. "Fine."

Okay, he was mad at me. No idea why, but I had a feeling I was going to find out. "What's wrong?"

He gave me a long look. "What were you doing at your apartment with Christopher?"

"Getting my stuff out before we got snake-bit or blown up. Jeff, are you seriously accusing me or Christopher of doing something, anything, while you were out of it?" This time, I had to add in my mind for honesty's sake.

"Maybe."

I felt hurt and found myself wondering if the ordeal he'd been through had damaged him in some kind of lasting way. "Well, we didn't." I looked down, mostly because I didn't want to cry again. I felt cried out and wanted to stay that way. "Do we have to talk about this right before a meeting?"

He hit the "stop elevator" button. "Meeting's canceled."

"What? Then why—"

He grabbed my upper arms. "Prove it."

"Prove what? Jeff, I—"

"Prove who you belong to." His eyes flashed as he pulled me to him and kissed me.

He'd never kissed me like this before. It was violent, more violent than Christopher's kiss had been, almost bruising in its intensity. His tongue was beating mine, forcing my mouth to submit to his.

Martini moved his hands, one to the small of my back, the other to the back of my head. He twined his fingers in my hair and controlled my head. I couldn't move my head or body, he had such a tight hold on me.

His kiss grew deeper and more demanding, and I realized my arms were around him, my fingers clawing at his back. Martini slammed us into the side of the car, though his hand prevented my head from being hurt.

He was pressed against me, his body grinding against mine. Then he pulled away, and, still with one hand wrapped in my hair, ripped my shirt open and flicked my bra undone at the same time. It dawned on me that he knew exactly what Christopher and I had done in here.

He slid my body up against the wall so I was off the floor and being held up by his pelvis. I wanted to say something, tell him I was sorry again, that he didn't have to do this, but I didn't—because I liked it. Instead, I wrapped my legs around him, and he ground against me. As my eyes rolled back, he stroked and squeezed my breasts, and then he let go of my hair, grabbed my waist, pushed me a bit higher up, and let his mouth have its way with my breasts.

The thought that I had an important briefing meeting to attend with a large number of people waiting for me flitted through my brain. But Martini *had* said it was canceled, and besides, his teeth found my nipples, and all coherent thought was being asked to leave and not let the door hit it on the way out.

However, coherency did make a last-ditch attempt before it left the building. I grabbed his head and managed to wrench him away from my chest. He looked up at me, let go of my waist, and then caught me as I slid right back where I'd been before—pelvis locked against his, mouth being ravaged by his tongue.

Coherency gave up and went for a latte.

The slide down the elevator wall had scrunched my skirt up past my hips. Martini helped that along so the skirt was bunched around my waist. Then he slid his hand beneath my underwear, and the real howling began.

His fingers danced over and inside me, moving fast and expertly, centered on the spots guaranteed to make me helpless to do anything but beg for more. Just like everything else he was doing to me, my climax was violent— sharp, fast, and strong. Again I found myself praying for soundproofing.

Martini moved and let my legs drop, though he still held me off the ground. He stripped my underwear and shoes off with one motion, then he flipped my legs back around his waist. His mouth assaulted me again, and while his tongue controlled mine I felt him undo his pants.

I probably should have said no, or stop, or any number of things to establish myself as an independent woman who didn't need a man to make her complete. Instead, I just moaned into his mouth and shoved my pelvis closer to his.

He didn't wait for a wordy invitation, just slammed inside me, causing another orgasm. I had hopes this one might not be heard by the entire complex, mostly because I was screaming into his mouth.

Martini pulled his head away as my scream subsided. One hand was back to my head, his fingers wrapped in my hair, controlling my head's movements. The other he slid under my thigh, which caused him to go deeper inside me. I gave a strangled cry.

"Does it hurt?" he growled at me, his eyes burning.

"A . . . little, but . . . oh God . . . ." He stopped thrusting. "Don't stop . . . please don't stop, Jeff, please."

He smiled slowly. "You like this, baby?" he asked as he thrust back into me. My wailing must have been correctly taken for a yes, because he kept driving into me, hard and fast and deep. I wrapped my limbs around him and held on.

Martini moved my head again, so he could spend some time on both sides of my neck. This combined with what the rest of him was doing brought on another climax. This one triggered him, and he bit down where my neck met my shoulder. I almost fainted, but I managed to hang on as my orgasm spiked and I felt him throb inside me.

Then it was over, and my whole body went weak. Martini was still inside but no longer controlling me. He held and kissed me softly, first where he'd bitten me, then up my neck to my ear, the line of my jaw, and then my mouth. This kiss was tender, not violent.

He let me slide down his body until my feet were on the floor. Then he leaned me back against the wall.

I couldn't do much more than stand there, whimpering and trembling, but he seemed to know this. He zipped his pants and then rehooked my bra, stroking my breasts as he did so. He buttoned my shirt, and I was amazed again that all the buttons were still on it. Armani was clearly worth the money. He slid his hands over my hips and down my legs as he knelt to pick up my underwear.

As he slipped it over one foot and then the other, he took a moment to run his tongue over an area of my body that was again hovering on the brink. His hands stroked the skin on my legs as his tongue stroked what was in between them. This orgasm was intense, almost painful it was so strong, and I grabbed his head, half to keep him down there and half to drag him back up.

He captured my wrists in one hand. It didn't hurt, but I couldn't get out of his grip. He finished making me sob with erotic exhaustion and then pulled my underwear on with his free hand.

He stood up and pushed my wrists over my head and held them there as he smoothed my skirt down. Then he looked right at me, and his eyes were burning again. "Are you mine?"

I didn't answer. I didn't want to say it.

"Kiss me."

I tried to resist this, but I couldn't. I moaned as I tried to move to him, but his hold on my wrists kept me locked against the wall.

He moved his face closer to mine. "Kiss me." It was an order, and I tried to obey it, but he was still too far away.

His mouth was right by mine now. "Kiss me," he growled.

I could finally reach him and as our mouths met he released my wrists and used both hands to pull me against him. I wrapped my arms around his neck, and he held me as though he was never going to let go, while his tongue ravaged mine again, and I submitted to his will.

He ended the kiss slowly. "Are you mine?" he asked, looking right into my eyes. "Do you love me?"

I couldn't avoid saying it aloud any more. "Yes, Jeff. I'm yours, only, and, oh, God, I love you so much."

Martini gave me another slow smile. "Good. I'd hate to be madly in love by myself."

CHAPTER 59

MARTINI PICKED ME UP and cradled me in his arms while I buried my face in his neck. "I thought you hated me again."

He kissed my head. "I just didn't want to have to feel your guilt anymore. Seemed like a good way to solve your issue of being in an elevator with me." He had that right.

"Your blocks aren't back?" I looked up from his neck, worry crashing over me.

"No blocks from you."

"But—"

He kissed me, deeply, but not violently. "I don't want to explain it now, but it has to do with being in love with you."

"Oh. That's okay then."

My body finally stopped trembling. He put me down, though he kept one arm around me. Then he hit the button and the elevator started moving again. "Jeff, I can't go to a meeting looking like this."

"You're not. I wasn't kidding—the meeting was canceled. I was coming to tell you it was moved to tomorrow so we could get the rest of our team assembled."

"Then why are we going down?" I had no argument about how he'd chosen to share this news. I was ready to stay in the elevator and stop it on the way up, too. The elevator doors opened, and he pulled me out.

"Because I want to be alone with you, and there are only a few places where we can do that right now."

"One of our rooms wasn't an option? Or staying in the elevator?"

"No." He led me into a room that didn't look as though it saw a lot of visitors. It was the most normal room I'd seen at any of the A-C locations. It looked like a typical family living room—couch and love seat, a couple of easy chairs, large television set placed, as almost all humans with TVs do, as the room's centerpiece. There was a wall unit with stereo equipment, VCR and DVD players, and a variety of books and magazines, the usual coffee table set, some throw pillows, and an afghan.

There was also a small refrigerator. Martini went to it. "Regular Coke or Cherry Coke?"

"Um ... Cherry." I stopped worrying about how they got this stuff and rejoiced that my soda habit wouldn't suffer.

He opened the fridge and handed me a can and a straw. He took one as well and settled himself on the couch. I curled up next to him. He lifted a remote off the end table and turned on the TV.

"Really, 'Fantasy Island' reruns?"

"I like them. 'Love Boat' comes on later. Besides, there are no baseball games being televised today."

"How do you know?"

"I checked the cable guide earlier."

I thought about this as Mr. Rourke and Tattoo waved to de plane. "Who designed this room?"

"Aunt Terry." A commercial came on and he changed the channel. Now we were watching "Scooby-Doo."

"Oh, this is the one where the ghost is actually the handyman."

"That's every one."

"Then why didn't you just stay on Fantasy Island'?"

He grinned. "I'm male."

He was that. I leaned my head on his chest while he hugged me close to him and flipped through all the channels. I do mean all. They had top of the line cable here, and we had over 200 choices. Springsteen was right, though—nothing much was on.

"Is it hurting you to hold me like this?" I remembered what he'd looked like the other day.

"We heal fast, too. I'm still a little sore, but no bruises left."

"Not even on your chest?" I'd slammed that needle in pretty hard.

"Maybe there."

I unbuttoned his shirt. Everything looked normal other than right above his hearts. There was a small bruise still obvious. I couldn't help myself—I started kissing his chest.

"Mmmmm, God, that feels good." He stroked the back of my neck while I ran my hands, lips, and tongue over his bare skin.

I was getting aroused, not that this took a lot of effort when I was around him. I moved up his neck, and he shifted me into his lap, on my knees facing him. He unbuttoned my shirt and undid my bra, slowly and sensuously this time.

I kissed his mouth as we ground against each other, the bare skin of our torsos creating erotic friction. His hands slid up my back, under my shirt. He pressed me down against him while his fingers massaged my flesh, making me moan with desire.

He flipped us so I was lying down and he was on top of me, and within a few moments we were making love again. It was fast but not rushed, like doing it in your parents' house when they could come home at any minute—the urgency made it better, hotter, and our simultaneous climax was intense.

Our bodies finally stilled, and we redressed. Making love mostly clothed was becoming something I wanted to do a lot more of. Every few minutes, if I could get away with it.

I snuggled next to him again, and he put his arm around me. "Fantasy Island" was almost over.

"Jeff? Does anyone come here besides you?"

"No, not really." There was a significant pause. "Christopher used to, when Aunt Terry was alive. And Lissa did." I decided not to react. He kissed my head. "She was going to choose Christopher, remember?"

Oh, right. Empath with no blocks against me. "I know."

"But it's kind of flattering that you feel a little jealous. I swear, I don't have a wife hidden somewhere." He slid a finger along my jaw and moved my head so I was looking at him. "I want to marry *you*."

"Christopher and everyone else says we won't be allowed to get married. Ever."

He shrugged. "I don't have to stay here, you know. I could leave."

"How? I mean, really, Jeff, how? I can easily imagine you needing the same medical care as the other day and then what? You die? You're imprisoned for Earth doctors to torture and dissect?" I could see these things happening, and I had to bury my face in his chest.

"Oh, baby, it won't be like that." He stroked my head and my back.

"No," I forced my head back up. "It will be just like that. I love you, Jeff. I can't ask you to leave your people just to be with me."

He stroked my face. "I don't want to live without you."

My turn to shrug. "I'm a modern girl."

"What do you mean?"

"No one's told you not to be with me, not to sleep with me, right?"

"Right."

"Well, it's not like babies show up only if you have a marriage license."

I saw the realization of what I was saying dawn on him. "But . . . I can't ask you to do that."

"Human couples do it all the time. Would I rather be married, walk down the aisle, go under the canopy, visit a justice of the peace, get married by an Elvis impersonator in Las Vegas? Sure, it'd make my family happy. But . . . I'd rather be with you, without pain and angst, without you becoming ostracized or worse by your family."

"But you'll be ostracized by yours."

I thought about it. "No, I won't be. Mom and Dad understand all that's going on. If they say they're good with it, no one else will fight too hard." I had to laugh. "They did something similar to this, too, when they met."

"Your parents don't like me all that much."

"Christopher says my dad likes you a lot. Frankly, he got all happy the moment you said you wanted to marry me and have a lot of kids. I think he's good with it."

"What about your mother?"

"I think she wanted me to be with someone who wasn't going to be at risk of death all the time." I leaned up and kissed his cheek. "But she's fine with it. She likes you more than you think she does."

"True. I don't pick up hatred from her. Just worry."

"Because she's sane. I worry about you, too."

He grinned. "No idea why."

"Because," a male voice I'd never heard before said, "you're going to die."

CHAPTER 60

MARTINI MOVED US OFF THE COUCH at hyperspeed. We couldn't get out of the room, though, because there was a man standing in the doorway.

I recognized him. "Ronald Yates, what a total displeasure." So much for those rumors of him being in some Saudi Arabian palace.

He looked point-blank awful. "Yes, for you in particular, my dear."

"I'm not your dear."

"No, you're Jeffrey's." His smile was quite evil, making Beverly's look merely tame.

"How the hell did you get in here?" Martini shoved me behind himself.

I looked down at Yates' pant legs. "He came in through the pipe." I looked up at his face. "You flew off, changed, and snuck back." Yates smiled. "But I told my mother to get security on that pipe." Yates smirked and I examined his pants again. They were grossed out, but they were also dry. "Oh. I wasn't imagining that noise behind us, was I?"

"No. You're far more observant than Jeffrey or Christopher."

"Only when it comes to fuglies. So you've been here for days? Why didn't you do something the other day, when everyone was trapped?" Or when Martini was out of it and helpless. I decided not to ask that. Why give the evil overlord more ideas?

"As my late Beverly told me, you're aware I've been ill. I needed to . . . regenerate my strength."

So, the creepy was explained. "You were hiding in the isolation chamber wing."

He shrugged. "It's amazing how few want to spend any time down there." I found myself overwhelmingly thankful that they had security and medical guarding Martini when he was in isolation.

"Yeah." I managed not to mention that most normal people didn't want to hang out on the Creepshow Level. Martini had to spend a lot of time there, after all. Why point out that I thought it was a horrible place to spend five minutes? "So, you were the thing I felt following me when I went down there."

"Of course. I was hoping you'd investigate."

I thanked God for being freaked out. Because if I hadn't been, I probably would have investigated. Another thought occurred. "Was it you making me feel . . . afraid down there?"

"Naturally. It's difficult to move too quickly in my present state. Easier to make you come to me."

He clearly wasn't firing on all cylinders. Either that or he thought all fear made me mad and caused me to charge. It usually did, but he hadn't taken emotional exhaustion into consideration. Good. He wasn't infallible. "So you're out of hyperjuice?" It was worth hoping for.

He was next to us in less than a second. "Hardly. Unlike Jeffrey, I conserve it for when it's necessary." Martini moved and got us near the door, but Yates beat him. He chuckled. "You were always an impetuous boy."

I knew this was patently untrue. I squeezed Martini's hand, hoping that he was picking up my emotions. "So what? What's wrong with impetuous?" I hoped I sounded cavalier, but I doubted I was managing it well.

Yates laughed. "Nothing. In the right situations. But this isn't the right one." He walked over and sat on the love seat. "Please, sit. We have much to discuss."

"Why should we?" Martini asked.

Someone grabbed me and moved me, wrenching my hand out of Martini's. I was on the floor by the love seat on my knees, head forced down, with Yates' hand on the back of my neck. "Because I'll break her neck if you don't."

Martini moved to the couch. I could hear him and just see his feet. "Let her go." His voice was strained.

"I'm not sure." Yates shoved me down until my forehead was on the floor, at his feet. "I think I want her to acknowledge her leader."

"Richard White."

This earned me a knock against the floor. Martini growled. "Jeffrey, refrain from posturing or I snap her neck. Now, again, young lady. Acknowledge your leader."

"Angela Maria Fiore Katt."

Big knock, but I'd slid one hand under my forehead so it wasn't too bad.

"Try again."

"Solomon David Katt." Bang. "Christopher White." Bang. "Jeff Martini." Bang.

"Stop it." I could tell Martini's teeth were clenched. "What do you want?"

"Obedience or death."

"I'll take death, please, Alex, for five hundred." Bang. My fingers hurt.

"You get one more chance."

"Terry White."

He flung me across the room. I just missed the wall unit. "How dare you say her name to me?"

Interesting. "Why not? She married your son."

"That impure bitch was never my son's wife." The rage was rolling off him. I shot a glance at Martini. He looked confused.

"They were married."

"Not in our way."

The light dawned. "She wasn't one of your religion, your people."

"No, she was not. And I forbade Richard to marry her."

"Guess you shouldn't have become Public Enemy Number One then. The minute you got sent to Earth, he married his girl, didn't he?"

"And had a son. Born on this planet of fools." He spat, literally, on the floor.

"What's wrong with Christopher?" I, personally, would have done a lot to see him in the doorway at this point.

"His blood is unclean."

I looked at Jeff. "Your father, was he—"

"Also impure," Yates snarled.

"It's what made the two of you stronger. Not Mister Crypt Keeper here's blood, but you added blood from outside your families, and that's what did it." I looked at Martini. I didn't know how to send an emotional message to keep this guy monologing.

Martini nodded. "I suppose."

"Is that why you don't want to convert Jeff and Christopher to the fugly lifestyle?"

Yates gave me a withering look. Apparently glaring ran strong in this family. "I want them dead because they are not worthy to carry on our race."

Oh, I'd heard this one before. Everyone alive on Earth had, after all. "Racial purity. It's never been a great idea, Yatesey, and it's still stupid from both a genetics and evolutionary standpoint. Not to mention God probably knows what He's doing—if you can mate true and create something the same or better than you were, then said mating's in God's overall plan."

"There is no God!"

"Oh, sure there is. Your little alter ego's proof of that. I mean, I know he believes. What do you believe, Yatesey?"

"Stop calling me that! My name is Mr. Yates!"

"Yeah, yeah, they call me MIZ Tibbs. Not impressing anyone over here; we've seen the movie, too, Yatesey."

He was turning a nasty shade of purple. The A-C gang really had a thing about formality in their naming conventions. Paul's mother must have had to fight hard to get a single-syllable name assigned to her child.

Martini moved, and he was in front of me again. "Stay away from her."

"Yeah, bring back the Supreme Fugly. I like him better than you. He just stinks. You smell like old person, and I mean that in the worst way possible."

Yates was snarling. It was interesting to watch, but I would have preferred to be doing so from a much larger distance than about ten feet. "I will not grace you with eternity."

"Can't grace yourself with it, why should I feel like I'm missing out? Fugly International can't claim eternity, either. In case you've forgotten, we took out all your buddies the other day."

Martini had hold of my hand, and he was tensed to move, but we had nowhere to go. Yates was fast enough to stop us, and we didn't want him loose in the complex anyway. I found myself wishing Christopher were empathic. A thought occurred. Two, actually. But both could be dealt with at the same time. "Yatesey, you seem like the skills aren't working up to standard."

His eyes narrowed. Direct hit. "Everything I need is functioning perfectly."

"Really? Jeff, baby, please put up a block." I focused all the hatred I had, all the anger, right at Yates.

He grinned. "Thank you."

Aha, he could feel them, the negative emotions. And he liked them, which wasn't a surprise considering how twisted this man was. But what did the positive ones do to him? "You can take the block down."

"Make up your mind," Martini muttered.

I focused again on how much I loved him. And not just him—everyone in the complex who I knew and at least liked. I concentrated on the feelings of love, friendship, loyalty.

Yates glared at me. "It doesn't affect me. Nice try."

"It should have," Martini said slowly. "I could feel it through my blocks, both kinds," he added to me. "You're losing your empathic abilities."

"Hardly," Yates said dismissively. "Your inamorata just has no idea of how to send an effective emotional attack." His eyes narrowed, and I could tell he was attacking Martini.

I wrapped my arms around his waist. "Hang on, Jeff."

Martini started to laugh. "Not a problem, baby." He moved me to his side, keeping his arm around my shoulders. "He's got nothing left. Beverly was hell on Earth, but Granddad here's shooting blanks."

"You have no right to claim me as your blood," Yates hissed.

Martini snorted. "Like we want to? Come on, Gramps, we hate your guts."

"Why is Mephistopheles allowing you this little grandstand?"

"He is not in control!"

"Um, yeah, actually, I think he *is*. He's not the one dying." I actually knew why the grandstand was taking place. It seemed both cruel and showing my hand to say why, however. Especially since my purse was up in my room.

I knew Mephistopheles was going to manifest soon. I also didn't want this room destroyed—it meant too much to Martini. And I liked it here, too. After all, we'd made love on the couch and had the most normal hour of our admittedly short lives together here. It was ours, ours and Terry's, and I didn't want it to be ruined.

"Tell you what, Ronny. We're just gonna walk out, and you can follow us. I mean, that's what you want, isn't it? Run of the place? Lording your might over everyone else?"

Yates glared again. I really thought I could see Christopher's Glare #4 in this one. Eerie how genetics worked. "You think I'll allow that?

I shrugged. "You might not like it, but I think Master Fugly wants a tour. Don't you, Mephistopheles?"

Yates' eyes glowed red. "You intrigue me. Lead on, little one." The words had more resonance, as if they were coming out of a much larger body.

"Yeah, I have that affect on scary monster-men."

CHAPTER 61

WE STROLLED OUT OF THE ROOM, and Yates followed.
"Thanks a lot," Martini said under his breath.

"Didn't mean you were a monster. Other than in bed."

"Uh-huh. What are we going to do?"

"Trust me."

"I'm beginning to hate it when you say that."

"You okay with the elevator?" I asked Yates. "I mean,
are you okay with waiting to manifest until we're all out of
it? These suckers are really expensive to fix."

Yates' eyes were still glowing. "Yes," he said slowly. "You
have accepted the transfer?"

"Um, sure, possibly, maybe. Let's discuss it somewhere
else."

Martini's arm tightened around me. "No."

"Not your choice, Jeff." I tried to send an emotional clue
but I wasn't sure if he got it. From an emotional standpoint,
I was vamping like a two-dollar hooker in Old Downtown
Caliente, but I wasn't sure if Martini was getting or understanding it. I just hoped somebody else was. And I hoped I
was sending the right signals, because if they didn't do what
I needed, we were all probably dead.

"It would be preferable to do it now," Yates said in Mephistopheles' voice.

"Oh, come on, big guy. You're telling me that you want
to miss the big reveal? You know, where you manifest in
front of all the chosen people and declare yourself their

god? And then you choose your next human vessel and go all soul-transference and mysterious? You really want to pass that one up? With a freaking captive audience in attendance?"

"The one you cling to must be destroyed, you know."

I snorted. "Hardly. You're saying I don't get to pick who I bang when I'm your vessel? Yates got his pick of the kiddies. I want this one. And his cousin, too. And a few of the others, as well."

I really prayed Martini was picking up where I was going with this, because if he wasn't, it was going to get scary ugly fast.

"Perhaps. If they do not try to interfere."

"Oh, they won't. Right, Jeff? No interference, you let me go mano-a-mano with Master Fugly?"

Martini looked at me. "Sure. If that's what you want." He looked freaked out but not panicked. Hopefully this was a good sign.

"I do. Now, be a good boy and get the elevator down here."

Martini pushed the button, and we all waited, as if we were in an office building and going up for a meeting. Elevator doors opened, no one inside. Good.

The three of us got in and Martini looked at me. "What level?"

"Top." I hoped. It had the most open space I'd seen.

He pushed the button, and we went up. Just like every other elevator ride, no one looked at each other. Nice to know the big fugly had that bit of humanity still in him. Yates wasn't really human, but if they could breed with us, the spark was there. At least, this was what I told myself. Because I was counting on it.

We reached the top and exited. No one around. This was a really good sign.

"Where are the masses?" Yates asked in Mephistopheles' voice.

"I'm sure they're coming. It was sort of an off day today." I moved us into the biggest open area. "We'll wait here for them."

"There is not much more time," Yates said. "I grow tired of waiting."

"Well, while we pass the time until the others get here, why me?"

He looked at Martini. "Leave us and bring the others. My words are for my next vessel only."

Martini clutched me to him. "Jeff, it'll be okay."

He kissed me, not too long, but with a lot of meaning put into it. "Be careful, baby. Please." He let go of me and moved away. Yates let him go, and I relaxed a tiny bit.

Now it was just the two of us. Alone at last. Me and the ickiest man in the world. I was actually looking forward to the fugly of my nightmares making a return appearance.

"So, Yatesey, you have about, what, an hour to live?"

"Possibly less." The eyes were still red, so it was Mephistopheles.

"Okay, we're alone. Why me?"

"You are . . . different. You don't fear me. I anger you, but you turn that into courage. You, more than any of the others, are the protector, the right one to take up the mantle."

"And yet somehow you picked Yates last time? Not exactly a protector."

"He was, once. I searched for one like him for so very long, a charismatic leader without fear. I almost had him many decades ago, but he was sent away."

"From Alpha Centauri? You went there first?"

He nodded. "It was a more appropriate world for us, much more than this one." He smiled. It was official—Yates and Mephistopheles both were scarier smiling than when they tried to look threatening. "Soon, we will own this world fully, and I will remake it as it should be. We will have enough power then to claim a better home world, to expand our influence as is our right."

"Fab plan. So, Yates was actually heroic at one time?" No time that anyone who knew him could come up with, of course, but maybe Mephistopheles had a different perspective. Some people liked Hitler, after all.

"He was willing to do what was necessary to lead his people. That they and others did not appreciate his sacrifices does not diminish them."

"He was a megalomaniac with a serious racial purity issue. And while money and power is a big deal on our world, we still respect courage and decency more."

Mephistopheles shrugged. "He corrupted, as you will corrupt, as all leaders and protectors corrupt."

"I can think of a few who didn't."

"Absolute power corrupts absolutely. He chose this path without my help. You will come to see why as well. The more you lead, the more you will learn the truth." He shifted impatiently. "Where are the masses?"

Distraction time again. "So, Lucifer? Can I call you Lucifer? Lucifer, why do you manifest so damned ugly? I mean, biblically, you should be the hottie of hotties, yet Yates is not the snazziest A-C on the planet, and your manifestation is, let's be honest, butt-freaking ugly."

He didn't answer. No problem. As long as one of us was talking, we were all still alive. Of course, to kill him, I had to get Mephistopheles to appear. This superbeing extermination gig really wasn't anything close to glamorous or fun. Pity I seemed so good at it.

"See, to me, you should look like Jeff or Christopher. They're totally hot. All the A-Cs are. And we have human hotties, too, like James, for instance. Any one of them could get any woman or gay man hooked into you instantly. And as for the straight men and lesbians? Jeez, man, pick a chick here and go for it, right? So, again, why?"

Silence, but I thought I saw a little steam coming out of his ears.

"Oh, by the way, did you know that Yates tried to blow me up this morning? I really doubt you wanted him to do that."

This did it. Yates shimmered, bubbled, and boiled. It was truly gross, like all the werewolf transformations the movie special effects guys love to do, only far more disgusting. In the movies, you don't get the full smell-a-rama that I was privy to. Yates had carried the odor of walking death, but the transformation smelled like every kind of dung boiled up together and then stir-fried. I managed not to gag, but only because I was revved up more than before a race or sex with Martini.

Mephistopheles burst through Yates' so-called skin and grew. It was like a Harryhausen film on steroids. He ended up at his twelve-foot range. Nice of him not to try to break through the roof, all things considered.

"Minion, you will accept me!" he thundered. Interestingly enough, Martini was able to bellow a whole lot louder. I allowed myself a moment of possessive pride. I hoped he was keeping his cool wherever he was. I knew what I was doing . . . I hoped.

"Nah, don't think so."

He looked at me in shock. "But . . . you have been prepared. Trial by fire. Death of loved ones. Murder. You are ready."

"Dude, did it really work like that on your original world?" I shook my head. "Trial by fire? C'mon, Mephs. You have nothing on my track coaches. Those people *knew* from torture. Stair drills when it's a hundred and twenty-five in the shade. Hill charges during a monsoon. Twenty-mile runs in the desert when you're a freaking sprinter. You think a couple of fuglies are a match for that?"

Now that the Head Fugly was fully here, I sauntered around. I didn't want to be in one place too long, just in case. And I was looking for something. Something I hoped someone had placed strategically for me. I didn't see it yet, but it was, after all, a big room. Mephistopheles trailed after me. I resisted making another Clifford the Big Red Monster comment.

"Murder? Maybe. I don't count killing your fugly buddies as murder. No one on Earth would. Alien monsters don't count as having souls to us. They might, but we don't care. Show us a fugly monster, and we want to kill it. Hell, half of us don't like spiders or snakes, and at least they're from around here. No one's going to say I murdered anything, including me."

"Beverly was killed by your hand."

"Yeah, and you should take a note. She threatened my man. I get really testy about that. Do you know how hard it is to find a man who's fab in bed, wants to settle down and have kids, and is drop-dead gorgeous, who also happens to be straight? Harder than killing a fugly, let me tell you." I really hoped Martini was nowhere within view of Mephistopheles.

"Things you loved died."

"You killed my *fish*. I don't know how to break it to you, but I name all the fish the same thing. The Siamese fighter is Carradine, and the guppies are Mickey and Minnie. I've had at least twenty Mickeys, about thirty Minnies, and more Carradines than I can count. I don't love fish, they're just living décor that requires my attention."

"They were not the only things killed."

"Oh, good point." I was there. Someone had gotten my message. God love them, whoever they were. "Yeah, I'm still pretty pissed about Cox. He represented everything you're trying to destroy—goodness, decency, bravery, duty—and I'll never forgive you for killing him. Or Terry."

"You didn't know her."

I looked at him. "Actually, I know her really well."

He lowered his face to look more directly in my eyes. "How could that be?"

"She's in my head. And she, like me, really thinks you're a moron."

I grabbed the aerosol canisters that were on a table and hidden by a couple of well-placed boxes and sprayed, two handed.

There are those who would question how I grabbed and sprayed correctly without looking away from Mephistopheles, but these would be people who hadn't used hairspray every day of their lives. I knew the feel of a spray button against my index finger better than the back of my hand.

He grabbed me, screaming, as I sprayed his face. I focused on his eyes, nose and mouth. I was going to run out of aerosol, but I was hitting what I needed to.

"Kitty!" I turned toward the sound to see another can flying through the air. Christopher had a great arm. I wondered if he'd consider a career in professional baseball when this was over. Our team could use him.

I dropped the empty cans and caught the one in the air. He threw another, and I caught that too. I went back to spraying.

I could see the parasite. It was moving toward me, slowly, but with a lot of determination. I knew it was going to do the parasitic lunge soon. It was waiting, though, until I was out or had to catch something.

It was on the back of his tongue, definitely within lunging range. And I was almost out of Ever-Hold.

CHAPTER 62

I HEARD THE BAYING OF HOUNDS. I risked a look to see my dogs barreling toward Mephistopheles' feet. They were leading the charge, with my parents and most of the other people I knew well right there with them.

It looked like the entire A-C population in the Science Center and a goodly number of the related human personnel were heading toward us. Everyone but the dogs was equipped with aerosols and heavy sticks. Better than guns—there were too many of us to risk the bullets.

The dogs slammed into his feet, causing him to lose his balance. I didn't want to look down and see someone get squished. I looked back at Mephistopheles. The parasite was quivering. Ready to lunge. "Your people are coming. You might want to stop and say hello." And, I hoped, good-bye.

Mephistopheles looked at me, the parasite still quivering on his tongue but not moving. "They come to save you. Why?" He didn't know, I could see it. He was confused by me, by the situation, by all of them.

I felt sorry for him, all of a sudden. "I don't think I can explain it to you. It involves love and sacrifice and caring. And you've never understood those things, have you?"

"There is only survival. And making the world in your image. Nothing else."

"I wish, I truly wish, I could explain it so you'd understand. So you'd change. People can change, A-Cs and humans alike. But maybe you can't. Maybe you never could or you've forgotten how. And for that lack or loss, you have my sympathy. And my pity."

"I don't need your pity." He was angry again, and the parasite started to move toward me. I was out of spray, and I let the cans drop.

"No, maybe you don't. You need my soul. But you can't have it."

"KITTY!" Ah, that was what a bellow should sound like.

I wasn't sure what part of Terry had been transferred to me, if it was her or just my own feminine intuition, but as I turned my head, I ducked.

To see Christopher pitching a fastball to Martini. Martini had the bat, and he connected with the ball. It sailed toward us, possibly the best hit I'd ever seen, home run all the way. I ducked lower.

Mephistopheles turned to look as well, his mouth still open. He made an excellent catch, denying the hitter a trot around the bases. I covered my head with my arms.

The explosion was immediate, and I was lucky—Mephistopheles let go. I dropped straight down. And landed in Martini's arms, just like always. He ran. Everyone was running the other way now, dogs included. "We have to kill him," I shouted in his ear.

"Stop yelling, I'm not deaf! And, trust me, he's going to die."

I looked back. Mephistopheles' head was exploding, and the explosions were moving down his body. "What did you send into him?"

"High-powered, self-contained nuke."

"Jeff, that means we're all going to die."

"No," he said as he slowed down. "We won't."

"It's got a lot of Everclear in it, along with our technology. No spread, no afterlife, perfectly safe." Christopher was next to us. "Did you get the parasite?"

"Sort of."

"Sort of?" He was shouting. I chose to believe it was because of the explosions. "How the hell are we supposed to be sure it's destroyed?"

I thought about it and looked up at the ceiling above

where Mephistopheles' head had been. "We have to get up there." I pointed to the spot where the parasite was clinging. "Or make it come to us. Jeff, put me down."

He did, unwillingly. "What are you going to do now that's going to give me a heart attack?"

"You don't get heart disease, Christopher already told me."

"I think I'm going to be the first."

I looked around. "Lorraine, Claudia! Over here!" They came over. "Girls, it's going to be up to us. I need more Ever-Hold."

Someone dumped a case at my feet. "Ask and ye shall receive, girlfriend."

"Thanks, James. Nice to see you."

Reader grinned. "Nice to be seen. Quite the rave you're throwing. By the way, all the empaths wanted me to tell you that they got your messages, loud and clear, the first time you emotionally screamed them out, and you didn't need to keep shouting at them."

"Oh, duly noted. Next time the world's in danger, I'll be sure to whisper my emotions."

"I wasn't complaining," Martini said. "I was too busy wondering if I was in love with a crazy girl or a girl who was crazy like a fox. I picked fox," he added with a grin.

"Not a lot of time," Christopher said meaningfully.

I tossed two cans to each girl and took two for myself. "Mom! Need you and a gun, now!"

My mother shoved her way through the crowd. She had her shoulder holster on. "What are you doing?"

"I'm really hoping you're a sharpshooter." With that, I ran back to stand under the parasite. Lorraine and Claudia came with me. "Get ready. It's going to drop, most likely on me. It can't connect immediately, it needs a few seconds."

"We're ready," Lorraine said, as the parasite dropped down, right toward me.

I wanted to duck or run, but I sprayed instead. So did the girls. But we didn't have to. Mom shot it fifteen times before it hit the ground. My mother, the Annie Oakley of Antiterrorism. Maybe one day I'd be as good as her, but at least the last few days had been a decent start.

The girls and I sprayed all the parasite parts until they

dissolved. Reader had to bring over reinforcement cans, but finally it was all gone, the last bits of the devil incarnate destroyed by things most would say he'd invented himself.

Ironic justice. I could dig it. And it would make a great title for a monthly comic, too.

CHAPTER 63

THE NEXT FEW DAYS WERE A BLUR. Christopher and the top imageers had to spend inordinate amounts of time altering footage, including showing Ronald Yates' plane crashing in the Nevada desert. There was a lot of mourning for his passing around the world that, strangely enough, wasn't shared by anyone connected with our group.

My appointment as the head of the Airborne Division was confirmed. I couldn't tell who was trying harder not to laugh—Reader, my parents, Christopher, or Martini— but I decided not to care. I'd been given the rank of Commander, and that made me equal to the heads of Field and Imageer Divisions. They could snicker all they wanted to—they'd had to work years for it, and it had taken me less than a week. I decided to save that tidbit for when I was angry with them. It would be more satisfying that way.

I brought my resignation in to work, and Reader went with me to clear out my office. We caused quite a stir, to the point where people I'd never met from the neighboring office buildings came by to say good-bye to me, just to get a look at him.

He made sure to let drop that he'd left male modeling because of me and was thrilled I'd finally consented to stop working and run off with him to the Mediterranean so we could make love on the beach every day. Reader was right—if he'd been straight, Martini would've really had something to worry about.

My parents offered to let me move back home, at least

until I could find a new apartment. But I didn't want to for a variety of reasons, all of them related to Martini.

I had my pick of rooms at the Science Center, and while moving next to Claudia and Lorraine sounded kind of fun, I still didn't have a lot of faith in the soundproofing.

"I need to figure out where I'm sleeping," I said to Martini as we left the dining room on the first quiet night since we'd taken out Mephistopheles a week prior.

"What's wrong with where you've been sleeping?"

"Nothing, other than the damned morning alarm system. And the fact that I really think everyone can hear me, more so from your room than the one I was in before."

"Awww, you're shy. Who knew?"

"Not my personal empath, apparently. Besides, that's the transient floor, and pretty soon someone's going to suggest you go back to your own place." I didn't want to dwell on that.

"So? Come back to my own place with me."

I took his hand. "Jeff, I love you, but I need time to love you before I live with you. Do you understand?"

He stopped walking and pulled me into his arms. "Yeah. I'm not wild about it, but I understand it." He kissed me, and I stopped thinking about anything else for as long as that lasted.

Martini had a funny look on his face as he pulled away from me.

"What?"

"You know . . . I have an idea." He took my hand again and led me to the elevators.

"Love this idea."

He laughed. "Not right now."

I felt his forehead. "Who are you and what have you done with Jeff?"

He swung me up into his arms as the elevator doors opened. He hit a button and we went down. Sadly, only in the literal, in-an-elevator sense. My disappointment was somewhat appeased by him kissing me the whole way.

We got off on the fifteenth floor. Martini put me down and led me into his human lair. But we didn't stop at the couch. Instead, he walked us through the room to something I hadn't noticed before—a door.

He opened it, and we walked into a full bedroom suite. But it was a real, human bedroom, not a hotel room. "This was where she stayed when we were here. Christopher and I were usually with other kids, but we stayed here sometimes, too."

I looked around. "I love it."

"No alarm down here. She hated that too." He pointed to the clock on the nightstand. "The lighting, though, has to function here like everywhere else, or you'd be wandering around in the pitch black."

"Lighting I can ignore with a pillow over my head."

"I'll be sure to get you up in a timely manner."

I leaned against him. "It's a king-sized bed."

"Yeah. Comfy, too, as I recall."

We tested it out. Yep, it was very comfy.

"I'll have your things brought down here," he said as we were lying together in the happy afterglow.

"Bring some of your things down here, too. You trotting back to your room when we were on the same floor was one thing. This is another."

He kissed my forehead. "Yes, ma'am, some of my things will be brought down as well, ma'am."

"Oooh, I feel all military and official."

"I think you're cute when the power goes to your head."

"I like it when the power goes to your head, now that you mention it."

He grinned and pulled me on top of him, just as a woman's voice spoke in the room. "Commanders Martini and Katt, Pontifex White requests your presence at a briefing tomorrow at oh-nine-hundred. Can you confirm attendance?"

I looked at Martini. "You didn't mention the intercom system."

He sighed. "Confirming attendance for both Martini and Katt, oh-nine-hundred tomorrow. Good night, Gladys."

"Good night Commanders. Those of us who are light sleepers thank you both profusely for moving to the fifteenth floor." Gladys signed off.

"God, I need a vacation."

"I know how to fix that." Martini got out of bed, pulled

out a dresser drawer and put on the standard issue night-clothes. He tossed me a pair as well. My size. His fit perfectly, too.

"How do these get into the rooms, no matter where you go?" I asked him as I put on the nighttime fatigues. "And the Cokes, how do they show up, frosty cold and just when you want them and in the variety you want?"

"Tell you later. Have to keep some secrets from you. I've heard that a little mystery is the key to keeping a relationship fresh." He took my hand, led me to the couch, and turned on the TV.

"They actually show reruns of 'Lifestyles of the Rich and Famous'? And you watch them?"

He shrugged as he pulled me onto his lap. "I like them, and the other shows, too. They're nothing like my life's ever been."

I thought about it. "Mine either."

CHAPTER 64

"YOU NEED MORE SUNSCREEN?"

"You'd be a better judge of that than me."

"Roll over and take your bikini top off. I'll let you know."

I rolled. We were in a private cabaña, after all. I lowered my top slowly.

Martini gave me a lazy grin. "I think I'd better protect those. I don't want them injured, and I don't think we have enough sunscreen to cover them."

"Flatterer. I have other areas that need protecting, too."

He bent and kissed me deeply. "I'm on it, baby." He rolled on top of me.

"I love Cabo."

"Not me?"

I laughed. "I adore you. And you know it."

"Yeah. Glad you finally came around." He kissed me, for a long time. "Hawaii next?"

I thought about it. Well, I thought about it after we made love for the next several hours. "Nah."

"Nah?"

"I don't want to go to Hawaii just yet."

"Where, then? I'll take you wherever you want to go. As long as you're there, I'm good with it."

"Even if it's around the world?"

He grinned his killer grin. "Especially if it's around the world."

I reached up and ran my fingers through his hair and along the line of his jaw. "I want to go back to the Science Center. Fifteenth floor."

He raised his eyebrow. "Oh? Why?"

"'Fantasy Island' and 'Love Boat' marathons start next week."

"You really are the perfect woman, on this or any other world."

"That's why you love me."

Martini smiled, and I saw my future. It was the future of a superbeing exterminator from Pueblo Caliente in love with an empath from Alpha Centauri who had two hearts, hyperspeed, and a killer smile. Maybe life got better than this, but I was in no hurry to find out. The journey itself was the reward, after all. Especially if you didn't have to take that journey alone.

"You want to swim before we go in for dinner?"

"And wash off all this sunscreen? Sure. Race you to the water."

Martini pulled me to my feet and kept hold of my hand. "No. Like everything else, I'd rather go there with you." We ran off into the sunset. It was perfect.

Laura Resnick

Doppelgangster

"Resnick introduces a colorful cast of gangsters and their associates as she spins a witty, fast-paced mystery around her convincingly self-absorbed chorus-girl heroine. Sexy interludes raise the tension as she juggles magical assailants, her perennially distracted agent, her meddling mother, and wiseguys both friendly and threatening in a well-crafted, rollicking mystery."—*Publishers Weekly*

"Esther Diamond is the Stephanie Plum of urban fantasy! Unplug the phone and settle down for a fast and funny read!"—Mary Jo Putney

"*Doppelgangster* is a joy from start to finish, with a sexy hero, a smart heroine, a fascinating plot, and a troop of supporting characters both lovable and otherwise. It's a wonderful blend of comedy and surprising suspense. If you haven't met Esther Diamond yet, then you're missing out on a lot of fun."
—Linda Howard

978-0-7564-0595-3

To Order Call: 1-800-788-6262
www.dawbooks.com

DAW 145

Seanan McGuire

The *October Daye* Novels

"...will surely appeal to readers who enjoy my books, or those of Patrica Briggs." —*Charlaine Harris*

"Well researched, sharply told, highly atmospheric and as brutal as any pulp detective tale, this promising start to a new urban fantasy series is sure to appeal to fans of Jim Butcher or Kim Harrison."—*Publishers Weekly*

ROSEMARY AND RUE
978-0-7564-0571-7
A LOCAL HABITATION
978-0-7564-0596-0
AN ARTIFICIAL NIGHT
978-0-7564-0626-4

(Available September 2010)

To Order Call: 1-800-788-6262
www.dawbooks.com

DAW 142

There is an old story...

...you might have heard it—about a young mermaid, the daughter of a king, who saved the life of a human prince and fell in love.

So innocent was her love, so pure her devotion, that she would pay any price for the chance to be with her prince. She gave up her voice, her family, and the sea, and became human. But the prince had fallen in love with another woman.

The tales say the little mermaid sacrificed her own life so that her beloved prince could find happiness with his bride.

The tales lie.

Danielle, Talia, and Snow from
The Stepsister Scheme return in

The Mermaid's Madness
by Jim C. Hines
978-0-7564-0583-0

"Do we look like we need to be rescued?"

DAW 109